SHUTTER

SHUTTER

Melissa Larsen

BERKLEY
NEW YORK

BERKLEY
An imprint of Penguin Random House LLC
penguinrandomhouse.com

Library of Congress Cataloging-in-Publication Data

Names: Larsen, Melissa, author.
Title: Shutter / Melissa Larsen.
Description: New York : Berkley, [2021]
Identifiers: LCCN 2020052594 (print) | LCCN 2020052595 (ebook) |
ISBN 9780593101391 (trade paperback) | ISBN 9780593101407 (ebook)
Subjects: LCSH: Psychological fiction. | GSAFD: Suspense fiction.
Classification: LCC PS3612.A7728 S58 2021 (print) |
LCC PS3612.A7728 (ebook) | DDC 813/.6—dc23
LC record available at https://lccn.loc.gov/2020052594
LC ebook record available at https://lccn.loc.gov/2020052595

First Edition: June 2021

Printed in the United States of America
1st Printing

Book design by Alison Cnockaert

For my uncle Tony

SHUTTER

1

Since landing in New York and crashing on the small, lumpy sofa in Ben and Sofia's apartment, I've heard Anthony Marino's name a thousand times. Apparently, there isn't much this guy can't do. Or at least that's how Ben sees it. *If Anthony was here.* That's a refrain I've heard so often I've begun to wonder how a person can even exist without him. But that's all he's been to me, a name. Anthony Marino. The star of a million unlikely stories. A mythical hero. Sofia has promised me that Ben can secure me an audition with him. But after a month, I still haven't met him. And I'm starting to lose faith. I'm starting to think it's a mistake to count on this meeting, to believe that somehow the great Anthony Marino can help me.

Ever since my father died, I've been drowning. Or close to it. Like that moment when you're in the pool, underwater, holding your breath, and you cross that invisible threshold and suddenly your heart is racing and you realize your chest is about to explode.

You don't stop to reflect, you don't have time. You simply break for the surface. Except I haven't been able to reach it, no matter how hard I kick. Nothing has helped. Not breaking up with Tucker, not escaping to New York. Nothing. And it's hard to feel like yourself when you can't breathe. It's hard to think when you're desperate.

Then, without warning, at a dive bar in Greenpoint, where Ben has dragged Sofia and me to watch his musician friends perform for what feels like no one but us three, there he is. Anthony Marino. He appears over Ben's shoulder, looks at me, and asks, "What are you doing with these two clowns?" And like that, the name becomes a man.

Whether he knew to expect him or not, Ben seems just as unprepared as I am. I get the feeling he never imagined Anthony would accept his invitation. Ben claps him on the back and says something I can't quite hear over the music, while fighting to catch my eye at the same time, unable to suppress a burst of pride. Sofia gives the tall man an awkward shove that somehow feels rehearsed. "Don't be such an asshole," she tells him, barking out a forced laugh. Turning to me, she explains, "We told him all about you. So now he's too shy to introduce himself. Anthony Marino," she says, "meet Elizabeth Roux."

That's how it starts.

And then we're outside, alone together, and I lose track of time.

Not just because of this man's presence. Because I can't focus on anything except the air. It stinks like rotten milk and warm metal. Sofia tells me this is the real smell of New York, only unveiled at the height of summer, like the fumes everyone's been choking on the rest of the year have been as fragrant as perfume. But I'm taking deep, dizzying lungfuls of it anyway. Anthony Marino hasn't done anything except ask me two inconsequential questions since introducing himself—"So, you're Elizabeth, then?" and "Join me outside?"—but already it's starting to feel like somehow this will work. Like somehow I might be able to breathe again.

I told Ben and Sofia the reason I left home was to become an actress, and they accepted this explanation without question. Sofia knows the real reason why I'm here, though. She's just too polite to mention it. She and I were best friends in high school. She knows my family. She knows what happened. Instead of saying the obvious—*Your father killed himself and you ran. You ran as far away as possible, without looking back. You found me in a brief moment of clarity, and now you're clinging to me like a lifeline*—she let me lie.

And then she told me about Anthony Marino, as though I had never heard of him before. The director, writer, and star of *Reverence*, who happens to be Ben's personal savior. They knew each other at NYU. And Ben worked sound on *Reverence*, Anthony's first and so far only film, and this apparently changed Ben's whole life. He didn't earn much from it, except a reputation, but it's been three years and he still doesn't need a day job. Now Anthony's set to start filming something else, his second—the next big thing, I guess—and Ben can't contain his excitement. From what I gather, this one is going to be even better than the first. If that's even possible.

What Sofia told me next still doesn't feel quite real. I know objectively that this all has happened, but it's too perfect for it to be happening to me. *He's looking for an actress,* she said.

He could have anyone, Ben told me with a groan. *Anyone. But he's so picky, and we can't start filming until he chooses someone.*

What's he looking for? I asked. *I mean, who does he want?*

Hopefully, Sofia said, *you.*

So maybe I'm light-headed because this is a dream. Maybe the stink of the city doesn't have that much to do with it. Maybe it's because I'm standing out here with this man who can turn my lie into a truth. Like water into wine. And there is something compelling about him. Something mesmerizing. How relaxed he is. As I followed him through the dark bar, out onto the street, I couldn't help but watch how he moved. The slow, loose gait. Ben and Sofia suddenly seem like mannequins compared to him. They act like they've figured out something no one else our age has yet—blissful, comfortable love—but they're uncertain. Their smiles are bolted on. They worry about everything, like it might all be taken away from them, everything they have, at any moment. And I'm no different. I've stopped glancing into shopwindows. I've caught my reflection too many times and had the disconcerting jolt of not instantly recognizing myself. Anthony, though, is languid. He seems entirely at ease, not just with the world around him, but with himself.

But he doesn't seem to know much about me, despite Sofia's reassurances, or maybe he just doesn't care. When I say, "I hate Elizabeth. Call me Betty," all he says is "Oh." His eyes glitter blue and yellow in the glare of the streetlights, and I wait, unsure of what pose to strike.

4

"Let's get out of here," he says, stuffing his hands into his pockets. The gesture emphasizes his height, the square breadth of his shoulders. I'm tall, but he towers over me.

"What?" I raise my voice above the shrill siren of a passing ambulance, not because I didn't hear him but because I'm not sure what he wants from me. I imagined we were going outside to talk for a few minutes, or whatever, and now suddenly we're about to abandon Ben and Sofia.

"Yeah," he says, as though that answers my question. "Are you hungry?"

I shrug helplessly. Sofia swore she and Ben would secure me an audition, but it feels like I'm agreeing to go on a date with him instead.

Not that I mind, exactly. Maybe it's better this way, how informal this is. Let him get to know me. I've never been good at first impressions. And to be honest, I'm actually more relieved than upset with this turn of events, because now that this is happening, I realize how unprepared I am. I haven't practiced anything. Not enough anyway. I don't know a complete monologue yet. That's what I've heard you're supposed to do in an audition, deliver a monologue you've memorized, but not like something you're reading, something you're just saying. I had decided to use the final lines of the film *Brooklyn*, something about being lost in a foreign city full of strangers, wondering what brought you there, what you thought you were looking for, then one day waking up, opening your eyes, and realizing this strange place has become your home. That passage always makes me cry. But it wouldn't be anything impressive if I had to try to recite it now.

With a satisfied nod, Anthony steps around me. "I'll just dip inside to say our goodbyes," he tells me over his shoulder. He disappears before I can object, though I don't know what I would say. Maybe something like *Don't speak for me*. But he's gone.

Our goodbyes. I turn the words over in my mind, smoothing them like a stone in my palm. We don't know each other, and he's already co-opted the night from me. Well, Betty, what does it matter? I'd like to see where this goes.

And I would like to act in his film, even if it does feel like a fantasy when I say it. I haven't exactly tried acting before—I don't count the sixth-grade production of *Macbeth* because I only had one scene and about three lines, which I screwed up completely when the time came—but I know I can do it, because I'm always doing it. Acting is pretending. I pretend.

Left alone, though, I don't know what to do with myself. I won't look at my phone to pass the time—any messages will only be from my mother. *Where are you? What are you doing? Are you okay?* So instead I lean against the window of the bar, casually glancing over my shoulder to peer inside. I realize, with a wave of embarrassment, that I've left without paying for my drinks. Yet another debt owed to Ben and Sofia. Maybe Anthony will cover my tab this time. They've told me how rich his family is. But if he does pay, that's another, more nebulous debt to stress about. What will he expect from me in return?

Through the window, it's easy to find him. He's a head taller than everyone else. His hands bracket Ben's shoulders. In this light, he's Nosferatu perched behind his next victim. The three of them—Anthony, Ben, and Sofia—seem to be embroiled in conversation, something deep, leaning in close to one another, though maybe this is just because it's so loud in there. When someone I don't recognize—teetering off-balance like he's been given a gentle shove, flashing a glance backward at his pack of friends—approaches Anthony with a tentative touch to his elbow, Anthony takes a few beats, then finally acknowledges him with a nod of his head. After a brief exchange, he poses for a selfie with the stranger, who returns to his friends with a goofy grin while Anthony turns back to Ben and Sofia. He must say something funny to them, because in unison their heads snap back like they're laughing. For a second, I'm breathless, and I don't know why.

And then it hits me, with a bit of a shock. This is anger. I'm feeling angry, though I'm not immediately certain why. It's burning in the back of my throat, my anger. I'm gagging on it, swallowing it down like a sudden scalding rush of vomit I can't spit out.

I'm a stranger. Maybe that's what it is. They're probably laughing at me, too. At the pathetic girl who sleeps on their couch and eats their food and offers them nothing in return. But I have nowhere else to go. Nothing else to do. I haven't even thought of auditioning anywhere else, and clearly I'm not prepared for an audition now. I've been telling myself I'm still getting my bearings here—I'm sleeping on a sofa, after all—but that's another lie, isn't it? I didn't look for anything because none of this has felt real. The truth is, at the bottom of it all, I haven't tried to find anything permanent because *I'm* not permanent.

I take a deep breath and let it out slowly. I can't afford to feel this way. The last time I allowed myself to be angry—to be truly, unabashedly angry—I broke up with Tuck and woke up here. I turn away from the bar, in case one of the three looks out the window and sees my face pressed against it like I've been locked outside, forgotten. I have to recover my balance.

For a moment, I struggle to assimilate where I am. Then I tell myself to slow down. Appreciate this. I've come pretty far. I'm in New York City. The streets in Greenpoint are somehow wide and narrow at the same time, and the effect is surprisingly cozy, despite the rat infestation, not to mention the constant screech of sirens. I need to hold on to this moment. I'm actually here, with Anthony Marino. This man has a cult following, that's what they've said. He's only released the one film, *Reverence*, but he's already a celebrity. I've never been with anyone a stranger would want to take a selfie with before.

When Anthony possessively slips an arm around my waist, I flinch. He asks if I'm ready and, without waiting for an answer, starts down the street, his fingers sliding off my hip. When I catch up to him, he doesn't touch me again. It feels like he's making a point of keeping some space between us. It's better this way, I tell myself. Keep it professional. This isn't a date. But still, I find I miss the warmth of his hand, the span of his fingers unconsciously—or consciously—measuring my waist. They had fit.

With a couple of quick turns, I lose my bearings. I've never been down these streets before. "Where are we going?" I ask, aware of the knee-jerk alarm in my voice, but it's too late to do anything about it now.

Anthony gestures to a restaurant at the end of the block. "Food," he says, drawing the word out, like I'm a hayseed. What did I think? That he was kidnapping me? Then, stopping to look at me under a streetlight, he asks, his voice surprisingly sympathetic, "Is this your first audition?"

So it *is* an audition. "No," I lie, my cheeks burning. "They've just never been this"—I search for the word, turning away from him—"informal."

"Well, then," he says, like he knows I'm lying but is too kind to call me out, "so you know there's nothing to be afraid of." He curls a hand around my elbow and guides me across the street, barely looking both ways before stepping off the curb onto the asphalt. At the sound of a car accelerating toward us, I pivot, but Anthony only laughs. He doesn't so much as glance at it. "You *are* new," he says, giving my elbow a reassuring squeeze. We pause outside the doors to the restaurant, and he holds up a small camera. It looks like every other digital camera I've seen, but he's obviously proud of it, so I pretend to admire it. "Like I said, there's nothing to be nervous about. We talk. I push your buttons a bit. And then I take your picture. Okay?"

As I nod, a shout echoes down the empty road. "Hey, man! Your bitch has a nice ass!"

I pinpoint the source of this comment. Anthony, meanwhile, doesn't react at all. About ten feet away, hidden in greasy shadows, a guy gives me the thumbs-up. I smile back before I can catch myself, at first because I don't want to be rude, and then out of confusion, by my own reaction. What the hell is wrong with me? The click of Anthony's camera gives me a little pause, almost like a tiny shock, like the buzz a battery gives you on your tongue, and it takes me a few seconds to understand why. Digital cameras don't have shutters, do they? He has deliberately chosen to add the sound effect. This isn't pretentious—it's surprisingly garish. He wants to draw attention to himself, as a celebrity filmmaker. He slips the device back into his pocket as he pulls me into the restaurant.

As soon as we step inside, we're hit with a blast of air-conditioning and a steamy wave of garlic-laced fumes from the open kitchen. The hostess asks if we want a table or the bar, but Anthony is already headed to a spot in the back corner by the time he answers, "Table." The hostess and I follow, nearly colliding when he stops. He takes a step back, considers me, the table, then me again, then tells me to take a seat with my back to the wall. It's a choreography that only he knows. He snatches the menus out of the hostess's hands with an acknowledgment thrown midsentence into his explanation: "That way my pictures are (*thanks*) concentrated on you." We haven't been seated more than a few seconds before he grabs me by the wrist and splays my fingers. "No nail polish?"

I tell him, "No." But that doesn't feel like enough of an answer, so I find myself explaining, stupidly, "Color makes my hands look stubby." Looking down at them myself, I'm horrified. I've been biting my nails again. I forgot, somehow, that other people can see me, that they will notice my obviously ragged fingernails. Dried blood is caked on the cuticles. No doubt Anthony has already clocked this. But maybe this is better, because he'll focus on the torn nails and not the white scars crisscrossing the fingers of my right hand. They aren't noticeable unless you're looking for them. In this light, they're close to invisible. Sofia has seen them. I've caught her staring. I know what she's thinking. *Like father, like daughter.* I haven't corrected her, not because I want her to think this but because the truth sounds too much like a lie. *I was angry, and there was a lamp. There was a lamp, and there was a wall. I don't remember the rest.*

Anthony holds up his palm, indicating for me to mirror him. When I do, his bottom lip sticks out slightly. His face is gaunt, but full. He's all cavernous cheeks and plush lips. He interrupts his appraisal with a declaration. "But your fingers *are* stubby."

I look at my hands. I'm still hot from the walk, so my veins are bulging, but otherwise my fingers are nice. I tell him this. "I said color only makes them look stubby," I say. Nevertheless, I ball my fists on my lap, to hide them below the table.

"I didn't say they weren't nice," he says with a shrug. "They're your hands, right? Who cares if they're stubby?"

I clench my ugly fingers until the broken nails dig into my palms. I can feel my right cheek twitch, which I mask with another confused smile. I blink, and there's that camera again. The electric shutter clears its throat. I try to relax my face, but no one has ever spoken to me quite this way before. I feel insulted and somehow accepted, simultaneously. I try to change the subject, or at least speak more freely. "For this project—I mean, that's what this is about, right? Your movie? Would I need to paint my nails?"

He waves a hand at me. His fingers, I notice, are elegant, like the stark branches of a tree in winter. "That's not something—" He seems to lose his train of thought, but hasn't. "Maybe it will help, I don't know. You don't have a problem with something like that, do you? Making yourself up?"

Before I can answer—*No, I don't have a problem with that*—a waiter approaches. Anthony asks for a gin and tonic, no lime,

Sapphire gin, while I reach into my purse to silence my buzzing phone. And to see if I have a message from Sofia. She might have sent me some tips on how to get on Anthony's good side. But it's only another call from Mom. That's three so far, in the past hour. No voice mail. We have an unspoken rule about this. After my father's death, as much as we seek to reassure each other, voice mail hurts too much. It feels like a cruel trick, a reminder that the other person isn't there with you.

The waiter turns to me expectantly. I order a tequila soda with lime juice. I don't care what brand of tequila.

The camera clicks again.

"Why do you keep doing that?" I ask Anthony, when the waiter's gone.

"Right then? You looked like you were going to cry," Anthony says, "but somewhere the impulse turned into a smile." When I don't respond, he leans forward, setting his elbows on the table, letting the camera sit between us. "Relax," he tells me. "You're doing great."

I unclench my fists in the dark shadow beneath the table and take a deep breath. Does this mean that the audition has already started? "I guess I got homesick," I say. "They call tequila soda, with a splash of lime, the 'poor man's margarita,' or, more specifically, the 'NorCal margarita.' It reminds me of home."

"Ben said you were from . . ." His voice trails off. He's forgotten and doesn't care enough to connect the dots. But he doesn't blush or show any sign of embarrassment. So maybe he's pretending not to know, to remind me how many me's there are compared to the one of him. Regardless, he doesn't try to finish the thought or turn it into a question, but just watches me for a reaction.

"Humboldt County," I tell him, whether he cares or not. "I came out here a month ago. Got on the bus and didn't look back."

"A *bus*? How long did that take?"

I shake my head. Of course he took that literally. Why does this have to be so difficult? "I flew," I tell him.

I had boarded the flight without knowing anyone here in New York but Sofia, and she and I hadn't spoken since high school. I had kept up with her, at least on Facebook. I'd watched her life unfold on the computer, one enormous milestone conquered after another—NYU on scholarship, graduating with multiple job offers, a loving live-in boyfriend. She and Ben had graciously invited me out for drinks and pizza when I called, which I did barely a day after I arrived and realized how lost I was. She had taken me by the arm and Ben had gamely grabbed the other, and together, we'd walked to the Hudson, her leaning in close to tell me which neighborhoods we were crossing on our way to the water. All I can remember from that night is a blur of lights and her breath on my ear, a staccato of "This is, this is, this is, Chinatown, SoHo, Nolita, NoHo." Like she was casting a magic spell. Afterward, they had escorted me back to my dirty hotel room and pronounced it too depressing to waste money on. So now I'm staying in the tiny one bedroom Sofia shares with Ben, with nothing but a thin wall and a flimsy door separating us. It's not an ideal situation, but at least I'm not alone anymore.

Anthony's eyes narrow, like he's seeing me for the first time.

"My bad," he says. "I mistook you for a stereotype." At my confused look: "Beautiful, naive girl steps off the bus into the big city."

The drinks arrive while I try to decide if I've been complimented, insulted, or, worst of all, neither. We touch our glasses together. Anthony's throat works like a pelican's as he downs half his drink. He gestures to the menu, indicating I should order, but I don't look down. I'm trying to figure out a way to say, *Who cares?* Who cares how naive I am? Who cares if I'm new to the city? I'm not some starry-eyed twenty-four-year-old girl who got drawn like a moth to New York City with a dream of becoming an actress. Am I? No. But it's not any business of his if I am. He has no right to judge me. I left everything behind to come here. Not that my life in Humboldt was so full. Whatever, I'm doing this alone, with no safety net to break my fall.

And yet, next to Anthony, I don't feel brave. I feel ordinary. *Beautiful, naive girl steps off the bus.*

The waiter materializes again, and Anthony asks where the salmon is from, seems satisfied that it's been flown in from the opposite coast, orders it, medium, no potatoes, and another Sapphire and tonic. He turns to me, rolling his eyes, and says, "It's always the details. It's one thing to say, 'Let's get dinner!' But then suddenly here you are, and you have to dive through all this crap just to fucking eat."

"You would think a director would appreciate the details," I say, more dismissively than I had intended. Turning to the waiter, I ask for the chicken. The camera doesn't make another appearance as I order. I'm pretty sure I'm giving him a terrible first impression.

When the waiter is gone, Anthony shrugs. "I guess I was just trying to be charming."

"Personally," I say, pausing to take another sip of my drink, "I like the details." His eyebrows rise a little, but that's all I get. "I'm embarrassed to admit this," I continue into the silence, "but it took me years to realize people think differently from me. I always figured I was exactly like everyone else, or maybe everyone else was exactly like me. And I'm still learning that lesson. How not everyone is the same, I mean. So, for instance, when I hear that you want a gin and tonic, say, and with a specific type of gin, like you can taste the difference, as opposed to what I'm drinking, it's a surprise. Fireworks."

Take my picture. Take my picture now, damn it. I know I look good. I can feel it. And I can see it. He's leaning in, even farther, over the table, hanging on to my words.

But he doesn't touch the camera. Instead, he's nodding at me, eyes bright. "You know what?" he says. "I think I actually know what you're saying. It's liberating, isn't it? It's like stumbling onto your own personal superpower."

"Realizing you're different?" I ask. "I don't know. Sometimes you can feel like a freak."

"Realizing that you are your own person," he corrects me. "That you are your whole universe. And at the same time, realizing that everyone else is experiencing their own universe." He waits, as though I'm going to chime in. When it's clear I'm not going to, he continues. "I mean—it's empowering. Do you realize how little people think about anyone else?"

It takes me a moment to realize he's actually asking me. I shake my head no.

"Well," he begins, turning the word into two syllables, "even now, are you thinking about me? About how I came to such a conclusion? Where was I? How old was I? What does it mean to me, personally, and how does it affect how I engage with the world? Or are you thinking about you? How do you feel as I speak? Are you reacting well to me? What must I think of you? Even when I'm the one inspiring them, these thoughts, they're really about you." He fiddles with the camera, and I can feel him watching me through the eye of that lens. I swipe at the sweat beading on my upper lip, certain that I'm failing this test. "All of this is to say," he tells me, "you're free. It's a cliché, but it's true: You are the main character in your own story. You can do whatever the hell you want—within reason. Because—wait for it—no one else cares."

I clear my throat, searching for something to say in return. "I only meant," I start, heat prickling my scalp, "I think I'm boring. I don't care what brand of alcohol I drink. I don't even care what type. And I'm every bit as selfish as you are, I guess. Because that's what it is to think about yourself first, before you think of anyone else, right? Selfish."

He surprises me with a laugh. "I'm not calling you selfish," he tells me. "Or maybe I am. But then no more than everyone else. What I'm trying to say—tact has never been my strong suit—is you can stop trying to impress me, Betty. I'm impressed."

My stomach flips. I try to look out the window to the street, anywhere but into his bright blue eyes, but the storefront has become a mirror, and through the crowd I catch a glimpse of a girl fresh off the bus, nervously trying to impress an insanely handsome, charismatic man. At another table, a woman with big, fuzzy hair throws back her head and laughs. Her face is striking, like she's sitting in a spotlight. For a moment, I wish I were her. I hear the shutter's electronic click, and the sound comes as a relief. I watch goose bumps prick my forearms while I wait for him to tell me what he's captured of me this time.

Instead he clinks the remains of his Sapphire and tonic against my glass. "So, how much has Ben told you?"

"About what?" I know what he means, of course, but what does he expect me to say? What response can I give that would satisfy him? That I know everything about him, or just enough? Or the truth—I know his name, like everyone else, I know how big he is, but I've never bothered to dig any deeper than that.

He starts to speak, but he's interrupted by the waiter bringing him a fresh drink. He nods his thanks, then seems to remember something. He calls the retreating waiter back with a simple "Hey!" and digs into his pocket. His trendy hipster jeans are so tight, he has to be strategic with how he shifts in his seat to reach the thin case, but then he's produced a black credit card. The waiter accepts the payment without comment. Me, I have to clamp down on my inner cheek and force a neutral expression onto my face, like I'm posing for a picture, to keep from betraying my surprise. He already thinks I'm a rube. No need to give him more ammo. But I've never seen anyone pay for a meal before analyzing the check like the restaurant was trying to cheat them into paying more, let alone before eating. He wants me to know how rich he is, as though that's who he is. As though that's who he thinks I want him to be. I realize I should be a bit offended, because it probably doesn't even occur to him what the implication is, that the dinner is on him. But the sad truth is, I'm grateful. Or to put it more precisely, I would be grateful if this isn't what I'd already presumed. Maybe he's guessed right—maybe I do want him to be rich.

If he can read my reaction, though, he doesn't acknowledge it. He just presses on. "So what did they tell you about me? Ben and Sofia?"

The waiter returns with our food while I decide how to answer. Anthony eats his salmon methodically, apparently unconcerned by my hesitation. Across the table, I'm a mess. I keep cutting the chicken into pieces that are too big or too small, and it's impossible to negotiate the steamed spinach. The silence is almost unbearable, and I become aware, too late, that I'm already talking. Not answering. Deflecting. "I could ask the same of you." I hate myself right now. What would be so wrong with leveling with him? *I don't care what this film is going to be about. I just want to be in it.*

He places his fork and knife at a precise angle on his plate, knitting his brow in obvious confusion. "What?" The question seems genuine, like he's actually forgotten what we were talking about. For a moment, I think I understand what people mean when they say they want the floor to open up and swallow them whole. I've been having a conversation with myself while he's just been savoring his expensive fish. But then I catch sight of his fingers, drumming the edge of his camera, and I think maybe he's only playing dumb. He doesn't want to answer the question, either.

"What Ben and Sofia have told you about me, I mean," I say, forcing the point. I realize I'm looking him square in the eye, hard, and I make an effort to soften my expression. I'd like to hear his response. Have they told him about my father? I don't think I could talk to him about it. I don't want to become the sad girl to him, too, where all he can see when he looks at me is my grief.

"They said you've never seen *Reverence*," he says at last. "Or even heard of it. Is that true?"

His first movie. Released almost three years ago, and he hasn't filmed anything since, at least that I have been able to find. *Reverence*. It hit me like a wrecking ball when I first saw it, just like it had everyone else. "Yes," I say, though automatically, because that's my story. That I haven't seen it. That I don't even know the name Anthony Marino. I'm trying to summon the courage to ask him, *Why would I lie about that?* But in the end, all I do is apologize. "I didn't know I'd be meeting you—I mean, I don't normally watch movies like that."

I wonder how much he can read in my face, what he's even looking for. I imagine he's going to ask me, *Movies like what?* But instead he says, "Good," clearly, like he's shutting a door. "Don't."

Here's the truth: I have watched it. Many times. I didn't just rent *Reverence*. It is actually one of the few movies I've bought. It's true that it isn't something I would normally watch. At the time, I watched only love stories. The more heart-wrenching, the better. Before *Reverence*, I was quietly obsessing over *Ghost*. The first time I watched Patrick Swayze say goodbye to Demi Moore, I cried so hard, I got the hiccups. I never would have watched an art house movie if it weren't for Sofia. It was her last year of college, in New York City, and she had her glamorous life and her perfect boyfriend, Ben, who had worked on a movie that was going to be the next big thing. I was the one who had stayed at home, who had halfheartedly applied to community college and then dropped out after my first semester. Sofia posted a link to the trailer, and I clicked on it out of spiteful curiosity. The truth is, my obsession with *Reverence* has as much to do with Sofia as the movie itself.

I don't know why I decided to lie about this, not just now, to Anthony Marino, but to Ben and Sofia as well. When it became apparent that I might one day be sitting in a chair like this one, asking to be taken seriously, maybe I understood somehow that it would be better not to look like just another fan begging for a selfie.

If I'm going to be honest, though, there's another aspect to my lie. When Anthony asked the question, he hadn't been able to disguise his own disbelief. Everyone has seen his movie. At least everyone *he* meets. Something inside me resists giving him the satisfaction of hearing how much of an impact he has made on my life, too. I am my own person. This girl fresh off the bus is not who he wants her to be. Is she? No, she's who she is. I mean, *I* am. I am who I want to be.

I had had this fantasy of meeting Anthony Marino ever since I'd watched the film, when I hadn't just watched it. I'd fallen in love. Not with the movie. With its star. With the man who made it. With Anthony Marino. Or maybe not with him. With his character. Whatever, I couldn't look away from him, not once, during the short eighty-minute film. I memorized every beat, every swell of music, every inflection of his voice, every expression on his face, every shadow in his eyes, in that movie. So much so that it's surreal to be sitting here with him now. I'm not sure if he's bigger or smaller than I'd expected him to be. Maybe both. Bigger because he's more than the man in front of me trying to impress me with his black card. And smaller because that in fact is who he is when I take the time to unwrap him from the shroud I've dressed him in and watch him overpay for a pretty ordinary meal with a desperate girl from Humboldt.

Why don't I just tell him how much I admire him? Or how meaningful his movie is to me? Or that the way he says "Please," right before his character dies, resonates so deeply within my consciousness because I still don't know what he's asking for—*Please don't kill me*, or, what I think it really is, *Please do it*—and I never want to know the answer. Suddenly, I'm full of regrets. My decision to tell this lie is a mistake. I should flatter him, the way everyone else does. After all, he deserves it, whoever he actually is, because he did make that film, he did touch me. And then I should dazzle him with an impeccable, gut-wrenching, well-rehearsed performance of my monologue. He would be sensitive. He's an artist. He wants to know who I am. I should be able to tell him about my father. My old life. My new life. He would understand.

But I can't. I simply can't.

Maybe this is why I'm making such a terrible first impression. Because I can't just speak the truth, even when I know I should. But I keep expecting him to be different. I know the lines of his face, the subtleties of his expressions. I have stared into those eyes on the screen and shared something with him that I could never adequately put into words. But he isn't a character. He's a man. Someone who eats salmon and drinks Sapphire gin and burps when he drinks too quickly, and I realize, all in the space of a breath, that this is what he was saying, how little we think of other people. He has his own thoughts, his own experiences and expectations. He's a living, breathing person, not just my fantasy.

And here's the real truth, and it comes as a shock even to me: I like this disappointing version of him better. He isn't reading from a script. He can surprise me. Most important, he can see me, too. He's not staring into some impersonal camera, into some anonymous audience. He's looking at me. Trying to figure out who I am. And here I am, screwing this whole thing up. Turning him into the very celebrity I'm so determined to pretend he isn't.

You can stop trying to impress me, Betty, he said. *I'm impressed.* He saw me, after all. I was the one who hadn't seen him.

We sit in silence while the waiter replaces our plates with dessert menus. Anthony ignores his, so I follow suit, tracing b's into the condensation on my glass. "Since you're obviously not going to tell me what Ben and Sofia have told you," he says finally, "even though I'm sure you must know something about me, or you wouldn't be here, why don't you tell me what brought you here instead? To New York. Why did you hop on that bus?" My face must reflect some of my embarrassment, because he adds, not unkindly, "Don't worry. Almost no one was actually born here. Something calls to them, and they come running."

He waits while I consider my next words. I could close the

door on myself, the same way he closed the door on our discussion of *Reverence*. It's a new beginning, being here in New York, and it would be easy enough to gloss over all the sad realities of my previous existence. *I'm a wannabe actress, just like you said. I hopped on a bus full of wannabe actresses exactly like me and came running to find you. That's all there is to know about me.* But there's something in the earnest tilt of his head that propels me to speak. This is all so formal suddenly. He's talking to me like I'm a stranger to him and there's a structure to all this. The interview, before the audition. I'm determined not to give him anything just because he wants it. I'm actually here at this table with him. That's who he needs to see. Me.

"Grief," I say simply, as though that should be obvious. "That's what brought me here. Grief."

He raises his eyebrows a little, surprised.

"I wasn't chasing anything," I tell him. "I was leaving something behind."

I brace myself for the pity. For the mask people put on when you mention death. The stilted, empty way they apologize for your loss.

Instead, he teases, "And here I thought you were going to wax poetic about your dreams."

I find myself laughing, even though I have nothing to laugh about. Maybe it's just relief. I brought a corpse to the table and he doesn't seem to mind. He leans over the table, so close I can count two nearly invisible freckles in between his eyebrows.

"Finally," he says. "A genuine smile."

Out of nowhere, I reach out to cup his jaw, brushing my thumb

23

down the ridge of his cheek. I can't help myself. He's warm, despite the chill from the air-conditioning.

He play-bites at the air, grins, then lets his own smile drop. "This isn't a date," he reminds me, his voice soft but—thankfully—matter-of-fact. "Much as I'd like it to be." Nonetheless, I pull my hand back, mortified.

"Sorry."

Waving away my apology, he swivels the camera around on the table to show me the digital screen, clicking through the pictures of my face at various angles. "What do you think?" he asks. When I don't answer fast enough—*Much as I'd like it to be*, that's what he said—he keeps scrolling, stopping at a video back at the beginning, from inside the bar, when I was sitting alone on my barstool. I don't know how he took it. I don't remember being alone there. It seemed like I hadn't been able to escape the sweat and the noise of people scream-talking all around me over the music. But the proof is right there in front of me, even if I can barely recognize myself. He presses PLAY, and the girl on the screen smiles. Not a big smile, but one for myself, like I'm satisfied with something. Anthony's voice cuts through my thoughts. "A person could get lost," he says.

I let out a shaky breath I hadn't realized I'd been holding. When he doesn't continue, I ask, "What do you mean?"

"Looking at you," he says, replaying the short clip. "It's like wandering into a labyrinth."

"Thank you," I say, though it sounds more like a question. I tear my eyes away from the camera, back up to his face.

All at once, the reality of this night hits me. I'm sitting in a restaurant in Brooklyn, talking to Anthony Marino. No, *auditioning* for Anthony Marino. And he thinks I'm beautiful. *Like wandering into a labyrinth.* I don't know how I got here. But this is real, isn't it? This is happening.

Without lifting his gaze from the screen, Anthony tells my video self, "This would be a commitment. This isn't your usual film. It's not a big-budget sort of thing. It's going to be an intimate shoot. We'll live in my family's cabin up north, for about a month. Maybe more, maybe less. And that's where we'll be filming, in the cabin. On the water. It's just a small group of us—you, me, Ben, and Mads, the other actor. Mads Byrne. Well, you won't have heard of him since you haven't seen *Reverence*. Sofia's taking some days off work to join us for a bit, too. But this film is low-key. No extra crew, just me and Ben working the set. Are you comfortable with that?"

I sit back, considering him. This is so fast. We haven't done anything close to an audition. And I could believe, maybe, that he doesn't care whether I tell him yes or no, because he's been so casual about everything. He hasn't asked for anything from me yet, no references, no monologue, nothing. But he's looking at me too intently—his knuckles turning white around the camera—for this to be a spontaneous offer. Didn't Ben say that Anthony was too picky? He could have anyone, that's what he said. He's delayed filming to search for just the right actress.

It seems he's found one. *Me.*

I find myself saying yes before I can properly catch my breath. It doesn't even sound like a word, *yes*, just an emotion jettisoned into the air.

"It's a demanding project," he tells me. "Most of it is pretty intuitive. But you'd have to be comfortable with some things. Nudity, for instance. Some violence."

"Violence?" I feel another smile climb my cheeks, this one an imperfect reflection of my unease. How can there be violence when the film consists of just Mads Byrne and me? "What kind of violence? Like in a horror movie?"

He laughs. "Nothing like that. Arguments, shouting, you know, that kind of stuff."

"Does it pay?"

"Of course."

"How much?"

"Twenty thousand dollars."

I try to stifle my gasp. What happened to the small budget?

"That's upon 'signing.'" He crooks a finger in halfhearted air quotes. "And then another twenty thousand after we finish filming. Sound fair?"

Maybe there's more to this than I understand. Forty thousand dollars? That's a lot of money. A person will do a lot for that. A person will be expected to do a lot. And I know this should make me nervous. Everything about tonight should make me nervous. Suddenly, I wish I were older. Maybe then I would know how to handle this situation. I would know the right thing to say, the right thing to ask about this project, and why he's so convinced I'm the one he wants, after such a short time together. I would know how to look at this man, and how to be looked at by him in turn. I wouldn't be so overwhelmed.

But I'm not older. I'm just me. And no matter how much I

know I should be, I'm not worried. This is like a dream come true, and I'm not going to question my impossibly good luck. I told people I wanted to be an actress in New York, and I meant it, even if it felt like a flimsy way of saying I wanted to figure out who I was, after Dad, as far away as possible from anything that reminded me of him. Here is the opportunity to do exactly that. With Anthony Marino.

I suck out the dregs of my NorCal margarita through a pink straw. I don't know why this drink is so region specific. Nothing of the tequila or lime reminds me of the wispy fog rolling off the cliffs, the soft, moist bark of redwood trees, the dusty roads. But the name is enough to transform it into home. I close my eyes on the last swallow. When I open them again, my mother's voice and the images of my father hiking through the brush, out to the dazzling expanse of the Pacific, are replaced by Anthony's eyes.

I nod—*Yes, yes, I am comfortable with all that*—but I can't seem to find my voice yet.

He reaches for my wrist. "Are you sure?" he asks. "I'm not going to lie, I think you're perfect for it. There's something about you." He motions to the camera between us. "Like I said, it's impossible to look away from you. But a location shoot and the lead role are a lot to ask of an inexperienced actress. Do you have the energy for it?"

I nod again, once.

"I need to hear you say it," he says, releasing my wrist. "Are you in, one hundred percent?"

I take his hand. He thinks for a second that I'm holding it, but I turn the gesture into a businessman's handshake. His bones, as rigid as they look, bend a little in my grip. "Yes," I hear myself say. "Of course."

This is my new beginning. This is what I want. This is what I need.

Anthony pushes his plate farther into the center of the table, to rest his elbows in its place. Fiddling with the camera, he winks at me and asks, "So who died, anyway?"

The camera clicks with a shudder.

2

A hollow slam wakes me up early the next morning. Apparently, the bathroom door jams in its frame in the summer. Ben mentioned something about heat and swollen wood. He said to push down on the handle before drawing it toward you. Somehow, though, Sofia still hasn't figured out the trick, because she struggles with the door during every early-morning bathroom run. She's the smartest of us three. She works for some big firm as a metadata analyst, whatever that means. But the simple mechanics of her own bathroom door elude her. I check my phone: five thirty. I close my eyes and try to fall back to sleep, but it doesn't come.

These days, all my dreams are about my father. They aren't memories, necessarily. Only images. Before Sofia woke me up, I was somewhere familiar. In the passenger seat of our old Ford SUV, next to Dad as he drove us up into Washington, only vaguely aware that my mother was in the backseat behind us. I was transfixed by my father's steady breathing—loud, short exhales that seemed to propel the car forward—and by these white foamy dots that peppered the asphalt in front of us, which the wheels were kicking up with muffled pops against the underside of the car. I asked my father what they were. In my dream, he considers the question. Finally, he points a finger over the wheel, just as we strike another one, and says, *Toads*.

Normally, my dreams about Dad give me a sense of safety. A feeling that there's someone in control. But this morning all I can focus on is his clipped breathing. Like he had been running, and his pursuer was closing in on him fast. After his death, when the police asked Mom and me to accompany them to the station, we had both approached the Ford on the passenger side. Neither one of us had ever had to drive before, not when Dad was there with us.

The toilet gurgles and Sofia yanks the door open. Through the haze of her curly hair, her eyes widen in surprise. "Sorry for waking you up," she whispers. I lift my arms in a *What can you do?* gesture. She perches on my legs and groans. "God, it's like sitting on kindling. Scoot."

Nauseous from last night's tequila and the humidity choking the air, I shift farther into the ratty sofa cushions, allowing her enough space to lie down next to me. She curls herself into a ball, nestling her back against my side, and I find I'm taking deep breaths like my father, like I've been sprinting, too. She smells like a damp forest.

"I think he liked me," I tell her.

She flips herself clumsily over on the couch to face me. "I knew he would," she says at full volume, the words practically echoing in the tiny apartment. "I'll ask Ben." She waves a tired hand in the air, as though to say, *Later, when he wakes up.* Lowering her voice, she says, "I love it when I'm right." She closes her eyes with a satisfied sigh.

The rush of air tickling my cheek brings back a memory from last night, and it makes me flinch. At the end of the night, when Anthony walked me back to the apartment, I had stood up on my toes to give his cheek a quick peck, and he had brought his lips to mine. We had both drunk more than we should have. I was so exhausted, I was bleary-eyed. But for more than a couple of beats, longer than it should have, our goodbye turned into a kiss. Had this really happened?

I start to confess everything to Sofia—though maybe I won't tell her *everything*, not the solid pressure of his hands low on my waist, or the groan that seemed to have emanated from his throat rather than his mouth—but stop when I realize she's falling back to sleep. One hand, tightened into a fist like a sleeping infant's, lands on my chest. My heart aches at the intimacy of this touch. I don't really have friends. Or I don't make them easily. Back home, even though I've lived in our small town my entire life and I went to school with the same thirty faces since kindergarten, I hadn't really spent time with anyone except Tucker. Tucker and my father. They were the only ones I knew how to talk to. I'm not sure what it is with me. Since I was little, I only had one friend at a time. Maybe that's all I wanted, or maybe that's all I could handle. I went from best friend to best friend. Sofia was the last one, in my junior year of high school. Eventually, after a couple of years, they all outgrew me. It would begin with us not seeing each other as much. They'd tell me stories about what they did with other people. They'd invite me to spend time with those friends, but not all the time, so the gulf between us kept growing. In eighth grade, I summoned all my courage and asked Susie April Yamamoto, who had outgrown me that summer, what her secret was to making so many friends. Just the way she'd looked at me had been the answer—*Don't ask that question, that's a start*—but then she'd considered it, and said, "Most people think you're nice. But that's all they know about you." Susie and I didn't hang out much after that.

I must have fallen back asleep, too, because the next thing I know, a hand is jostling my shoulder. I open crusty eyes to find Ben's face looming over mine. Sofia mutters and buries her head in my chest. Ben pulls her up to sitting like a rag doll. "Seven forty, babe," he tells her. "Time to get up and bring home the bacon."

They share a wet kiss—it's too early for that, isn't it?—and then Sofia staggers back to the bathroom like a drunken sailor. Ben turns to me. His voice is cheerful. It's too early for that, too. "Good morning! Do I need to pull you out of bed, too?"

"No, don't," I tell him, repeating myself a few more times for good measure. Satisfied that I'm awake, he disappears into the tiny kitchen, while I rub the sleep from my eyes and check my phone. The dog-walker app, Walking Miss Daisy, has a few hits already. If you have nothing to do during the day, don't have to pay for housing, and can stomach picking up after a team of dogs, it pays well enough.

I'm really checking to see if I've gotten any texts from Anthony. We exchanged numbers, just before that unfortunate kiss, in the shadows inside Ben and Sofia's lobby. I tell myself not to expect anything. He won't be awake yet. Nevertheless, I'm disappointed. I had hoped he'd send something quick, maybe in the middle of the night. Some proof that he hadn't been able to stop thinking about me. Rather than moping around, though, I force myself to be the brave one and send him something now myself. In the end, all I come up with is Thanks for last night. By the way, what's my character's name? It feels almost like I'm trying to trick him into hiring me. I hate how drinking does that. How the next morning everything feels like a gigantic mistake. I hesitate, but I press SEND anyway. He did say I was perfect. Nevertheless, I drop the phone on top of my blanket like it's a bomb.

Ben and Sofia and I have refined our morning routine into a well-oiled machine, out of necessity. I can't be in the apartment during the day, because Ben's either writing or recording music in here. So while Sofia performs a mysterious ritual in the bathroom—every day it sounds completely different and yet she always emerges looking exactly the same—Ben prepares breakfast, and I schedule my dog-walking shifts. Then Sofia disappears to the office and I make myself scarce until evening.

On my first morning here, I hadn't known what to do. Ben offered me a cup of coffee and a bowl of oatmeal while Sofia asked what I had planned for my day. My answer was stuttering and inane. *Look for an audition? Apply for a day job?* The next day, Sofia told me, "Don't worry about those auditions. We'll introduce you to Anthony."

Ben clarified, "Anthony Marino," with as much gravitas as Sean Connery saying "Bond. James Bond." And they both stared at me expectantly.

This was the beginning of my lie. It was better this way, for them to think that I didn't know who Anthony Marino was, that I had never even heard of *Reverence*, or that they were close friends with him. They were so happy to tell me all about him. To brag about working with him. It was easy enough to play along.

"He's brilliant," Ben told me. "He hid cameras all over his family's house. Microphones everywhere. I would hide in closets sometimes with my sound mixer, you know. It was—"

Sofia interrupted him with a concise summary: "It's one of those really artsy films. I can barely understand it." She flashed Ben an embarrassed smile. "But it is beautiful."

"It's like reality TV," Ben explained. "It's scripted to some extent, but it's real. There's a theme, but no one knows how it's going to end. Anthony's a master at creating a construct, then turning it into drama."

"Sounds interesting," I said.

"Not just interesting," Ben corrected me. "Compelling. You get to know the actors. Everyone wants more."

It was self-preservation, I think, that caused me to lie. Introducing me to Anthony Marino so I could be one of his subjects became a gift they could bestow upon me, as opposed to a favor I had demanded from them. Not that it had started out this way. When I left for New York, my only thought had been to get out of California. Reconnecting with Sofia hadn't occurred to me until I got here. She offered me a point of safety. And then, like she was reading my mind, she offered me a new purpose. Something to run toward, as opposed to what I was running away from. I'm glad I lied. More than glad—I'm grateful.

Now Sofia hurries from the bathroom to the kitchen, racing through her breakfast. She and Ben stand side by side at the kitchen counter to eat, both riveted to their phones. They seem impossibly simple. As though it's entirely natural they found each other and decided to love each other. I wonder how they did it. But I've never asked. You don't question why a tree has decided to grow in one specific spot.

Usually I hurry to time my exit with Sofia's. Today, though, I linger. I take my time in the shower. I idle at the mirror. I perfect my makeup in slow, deliberate strokes. Trying to spend as much time as possible away from my phone. I'm sure Anthony hasn't answered yet, but there's a chance he has, and I don't want to spoil the magic by confirming otherwise. And even though he apparently hasn't yet, maybe he'll contact Ben before me. By the time I'm done in the bathroom, Sofia's rushing into the bedroom to accessorize her work outfit. I nibble at the cool, congealed oatmeal next to Ben at the kitchen counter, while he politely waits for me to finish before cleaning up.

In a few short strides, Sofia crosses the apartment, asking if I'm ready to go. I hold up my cup—now filled with unappetizing lukewarm coffee—and beg off. Unconcerned, she bestows Ben with another kiss. Turning to me, she wobbles on her tiptoes to kiss my cheek with a *smack*, and tells me she'll see me tonight. I find myself wondering whether she's happy or not I showed back up in her life after she thought she'd moved on from me. Sometimes old friends feel like mistakes, the same way you feel when you've had too much to drink. She creates a racket at the door, searching for the right pair of shoes underneath a pile of handbags and cleaning supplies, dropping her keys no fewer than three times in the process, then straightens up with a loud "Oh!" Sending an apologetic grimace to me, she asks Ben, "What have you heard from Anthony? About Betty?"

Ben dips his head, hesitating. And my heart drops. Anthony texted him already. He's decided, in the light of day, he wants an actress with actual experience. He wants someone who's more confident. Charming. That's why Ben looks so awkward. Because he has to be the one to break the news to me. I didn't get the part. I was right after all—last night was too good to be true. Maybe it had all been a lie. A cruel joke. And to complete my humiliation, Sofia—successful, smart Sofia—is here watching.

I'm opening my mouth to tell Ben not to say anything, it's okay, I understand, when he finally speaks. "No decision yet," he says. Giving my shoulder a kind squeeze, he adds, "But I'm sure there'll be reason to celebrate tonight."

"I'll pick up something on my way home," Sofia says, winking at Ben as she unlocks the door. "A bottle of champagne maybe?"

Distantly, I can hear Ben's reply—something about champagne hangovers—but I'm not really listening. My relief is too overwhelming. I'm being melodramatic. Insecure. Anthony offered me the role last night, didn't he? Why can't I just relax?

"The great Anthony Marino," Sofia intones, pulling me back to the present. She rolls her eyes, as though she isn't completely starstruck by him, however long she's known him. To me, she says, "I wasn't even sure I was going to be a part of this, until a week ago. I'm lucky I could get the time off from work."

"Anthony mentioned you were going to be up at the cabin," I

say, trying to keep my insecurity from sounding like an accusation. "But he didn't say what you were going to be doing. Are you acting in the movie, too?"

She steps out into the hallway, shaking her head. "Don't worry," she tells me. "I'm not going to steal your spotlight. I'm like a glorified extra." Before I can react, she disappears out the door.

"Don't quit your day job!" Ben shouts after her. I imagine I hear a muffled laugh through the door, but it could be someone shouting outside on the street. With a sigh, Ben turns to me, his beard glistening with Sofia's saliva, and says, "You might as well get going. It'll be hours before he's up. And Sofia's right. It might be weeks before he makes up his mind." He returns to the sink, watching me out of the corner of his eye while he finishes with the dishes. "Those puppies must be ready to piss by now."

I'm taking a last gulp of cold coffee when my phone vibrates on the table—only about five feet away—and even though my heart skips a beat, I don't want to jump to get it.

"Don't worry," Ben says. "I'm sure he liked you. He would have sent you home after fifteen minutes if he hadn't." He sounds defeated. I want to tell him about the kiss, but I'm not sure if it's to reassure him or to preen myself, like a peacock. Ben reaches for my abandoned bowl and cleans it meticulously. "You are just his type," he mutters. "Tall, thin, and lost."

"Thanks," I say, trying to sound appropriately casual. But I'm actually seething. *Tall, thin, and lost.* What a kind assessment. "He's not the kind of guy to give a girl a part because he likes her, is he? That's not what you're suggesting, right?"

"What are you asking?" Ben says, even though he knows exactly what I'm asking. And it occurs to me how hypocritical my anger is anyway, because that's what my supposed audition devolved into in the end, right? A date. A kind of awkward first date. And I hadn't exactly bridled at the turn of events. It's pretty much what I'd ended up wanting, too, as confusing as my emotions were. "This is a serious film," Ben tells me. "Anthony's a respected director. He's not going to fuck it up for a lay."

"What does he want from me, then?" I ask.

Ben's posture stiffens, but he doesn't respond. I hand him my coffee cup, and he runs it under the tap, automatically.

"As an actress," I persist. "What's this film about?" I had asked Anthony the same question last night, and he'd deflected. He'd said this wasn't something I should worry about. *You're perfect for this role,* he'd told me. Which was a nice thing to hear—I hadn't known how to respond to such a declaration, so that was the end of that discussion—but I have no idea really what might be expected of me here. I could use a little hint from Ben. The only solid bit of information Anthony shared with me was its location. His family's summer cabin, though he didn't even tell me where it is. A real remote place, he'd said, on the water. Made for this story, though I still have no idea what it is. "I should probably know what I'm signing up for," I say, "don't you think?"

Over by the couch, my phone vibrates again, and then another two times in quick succession. Only this time, my heart doesn't leap into my throat and I don't have visions of hearing from Anthony. Texts coming in this fast can have only one source. I haven't returned my mother's calls from last night. Even though we spoke two days ago—a conversation that had quickly devolved into an interrogation about my living situation: She and Sofia's mother are part of the same yoga group, she'd warned me, so I should be sure to be a good guest—she's probably furious.

Not worried. Mom is a mother who's exasperated by her own maternal instinct. Even if I went legitimately missing, I doubt she'd file a missing-person report. She'd be the one suffering the injustice, because of the stress I was causing her. When I was nine, in the emergency room with a cast set on the elbow I'd dislocated on a neighbor's trampoline—I had leapt onto it from their second-story balcony—Mom had kept hissing at me to stop announcing how I'd gotten hurt, because I was making her sound like a terrible mother. No, she's not worried for me. She simply doesn't like to be ignored, especially by her ungrateful daughter.

Ben's hairy hands turn pink under the hot water. His gut grazes the edge of the sink, so the front of his T-shirt is now damp with casualty suds and spray. He's surprisingly delicate for his size. He's stocky and wide, but it took a while to see it, because of the way he moves. I've only watched him mess around with his guitar a couple of times, but he plays with his entire body, not just his fingers. Sofia said he'd make a lot more money sound mixing—whatever that means—full-time, but he refuses to give up on his own musical aspirations. He dries the dishes and replaces them so lightly, they hardly click.

"Ben?" I say. "You don't think I should know something about this film? It doesn't even feel like I'm being *cast* for it, you know what I mean? It feels like I'm being—I don't know—judged. Like a beauty contest."

He wanders into the living room and gathers my blankets and

sheets from the couch. "It's nothing like that," he says. "Anthony will tell you what you need to know. When you need to know it." He waves me away when I offer to take the sheets from him. "He has his own way of doing things." It takes him only a few seconds to pile all of my worldly possessions—an overnight bag filled with clothes and one book—on top of my musty sheets in the far corner of the room. "Your phone," he says, when it starts buzzing again.

I glance at the screen—Mom—then shove the phone into my pocket and put my shoes on. Grabbing my small purse out of Sofia's mess, I pause at the door. I'm still thinking about the film. Does Ben have a script I can look at? He must have something. This isn't just Anthony's decision. I've got to make up my mind, too, whether or not I actually want to do this. Finally, I ask Ben, "What's it called? The movie, I mean."

Ben's phone lights up, and he is momentarily distracted, reading a text. His thumbs fly across the smudged screen. *"Fear."*

I open the door. The coffee and oatmeal have turned into lava in my stomach. *Fear?* I thought Anthony said this wasn't going to be a horror movie.

I'm halfway out the door when Ben stops me with a gruff bark. "Betty?" He scratches his thick beard, and he looks uncharacteristically uncomfortable. "I didn't mean to shut you down. It's just Anthony, you know? He isn't very traditional, but he's brilliant. He knows what he wants from all of us. If he didn't give you any details yet himself, I'm sure that isn't an accident. You know what I mean?"

"It's okay," I say. I smooth my T-shirt down my stomach, leaving a trail of sweat where it touches my skin. It's so much hotter here in New York than I ever imagined. "I understand." But I don't. Ben clearly knows what Anthony's got planned, so why can't he tell me anything? He sounds so nervous. Like he's worried about what he might let slip. I'm starting to feel used. In a way, at least. Like Anthony has some less-than-honorable reason for wanting to cast me, and Ben is on his side, helping him. At least I've got Sofia. I'll talk to her. She'll tell me the truth. So long as she knows anything.

Without another word, I let the door close behind me. As I round down the seemingly endless staircase to the lobby, already late for my first puppy pickup, my phone buzzes again. I glance at the screen, furious with my mother for being so goddamn persistent. I ran away from home. All the way to New York. As far away as I could possibly get. And still I can't escape her. If not now, I never will. This time, though—miraculously—it's a text from Anthony.

Are you free this afternoon? 5pm?

And then, beneath it, answering my previous text, echoing Ben's words from just seconds ago:

Don't worry. I'll tell you what you need to know when you need to know it.

3

By the time I reach Anthony's building, I'm covered in a thin layer of sweat. I haven't been able to return to Ben and Sofia's apartment to freshen up after walking dogs for the past six or seven hours, in the parks, on the crowded summer streets, with sunshine reflecting off every shiny surface in Manhattan. My cheeks sting with sunburn. I wish I wasn't such a mess. Even though I've already been offered the part, somehow in the pit of my stomach this feels like it might be a continuation of the audition.

Taking my time on the front steps, I wipe my forehead, blot my upper lip on the neck of my T-shirt, straighten my hair. My hand shakes as I reach for the intercom. Almost immediately, there's a loud *thunk* as the door unlocks. It's made of steel and glass and weighs a ton, and I push it open into a marble lobby that, however elegant it might be, reminds me of a crypt. A tinny but cheery "Come on up!" follows me inside from the intercom.

As I climb the stairs—shocked each time by the single doorway on every landing, whereas Ben and Sofia's building has about eight units per floor—I try to keep my breathing measured. But the stairs are steep, the air stifling hot, and after a few floors, I'm winded. Anthony is already on the landing, waiting for me.

"You have something against elevators?" he asks me, then signals for me to hurry inside with an exaggerated complaint: "You'll let the cold air out."

I obey, stammering out a nervous excuse on the way. "Ben and Sofia's building doesn't have an elevator."

Inside, it's chilly enough for Anthony to be wearing a long-sleeve shirt and sweatpants. Goose bumps prickle my exposed legs, and my shirt clings to me like a wet towel. "Is this place really all yours?" I hear myself ask. It's a stupid question, but I forgive myself. I knew to expect grand, but I hadn't expected *this*.

Anthony doesn't stop moving to savor my small-town awe. By the time the door has closed behind me, he has retreated into the kitchen to dig through the cabinets. I take the opportunity to catalogue the rest of his apartment, which is relatively easy to do. As big as it is, the entire space is on display. I guess this is what they mean by a New York loft. He has gutted whatever was here before, down to the brick walls and oak beams, and he lives now in its shell. The huge space is organized into informal quadrants—kitchen, living room, bedroom, office—but except for the bathroom and closets, all it is is a giant box, furnished in an eclectic mix of sleek modern furniture and heavy antiques.

In *Reverence*, he had still been living at home with his parents. Their apartment is one of those old-school New York co-ops, hovering somewhere on the Upper East Side, full of nooks and crannies and elaborate furniture that looks too delicate or uncomfortable to use. His room had been on the far end, tucked away from the living spaces, behind an old washroom. He'd never said it outright, in the movie, but it always felt like his parents wanted him hidden, out of the way.

Here he's chosen the exact opposite for himself. A place where he will be on display wherever he is. I like it.

Humming to himself, Anthony sets two glasses of water on the coffee table. Then, as though he's noticing me for the first time, he gives me an abbreviated wave. "Do you want to come in?"

"Oh, sorry," I say. For all of my visual snooping, I'm still standing at the front door. I drop my purse to the ground and join him in the living room quadrant, dodging a pile of precariously stacked books.

"Thanks for coming all the way out here," he says with a laugh, and I'm not sure whether he means Williamsburg or his living room. "You've got to be curious about the project."

I nod, not bothering to hide my eagerness, but not exactly trusting my voice. Again, I find myself wishing I were just a bit older and more experienced. I would know how to act around Anthony. I wouldn't stand, frozen in place, in his doorway, nervous and quiet. Maybe I would walk around, admire the artwork he's installed on the walls, make a joke about my day. But I can't think of anything to say. Instead, all I can do is wonder what he expects from me, and what he is thinking of me.

"Have a seat," he says, gesturing to the couch.

I half comply, sitting in the crook of its arm, while Anthony strides across the room to a camera atop a spindly-looking tripod. I don't know how I missed it. It's next to the TV. I was right after all. This is still the audition. I run a hand nervously through my hair, trying to fluff it up. I should have brought a brush. Most of the time, the length of my hair hides the tangles. I'm sure Anthony is going to notice. To him, the mess will signify an unprofessional lack of preparedness.

He fiddles with the camera. The red light—nearly hidden in the glare sliding across the glossy lens—blinks on, and my face appears on the TV screen. I release a breathy "Oh," and the camera catches it in real time. I tell myself to slow down a bit. Relax, Betty. This entire experience is a lesson. I hadn't realized how much of a hayseed I actually am, but now that I'm here, in Anthony Marino's apartment, I should try to enjoy myself.

I watch my lips curl in an embarrassed attempt at a self-conscious smile, then tuck a lock of hair behind my ear and settle back into the couch cushions, trying but failing to back myself out of the camera's line of sight. For a moment, I forget what it is we're doing. I'm transfixed by my own reflection. Not because of how I look but because this girl seems so separate from me. It feels like she's the one initiating my small movements, the nervous tics. I think it's because of the camera's angle. She's looking away, while I'm looking directly into her eyes.

Anthony's voice brings me back into the moment. "Pretty amazing resolution, right?"

I tear my focus away from this girl. "This is crazy," I say. "I mean, it makes me feel crazy. I don't know where to look."

"Don't overthink it," he tells me. "Look wherever you want to."

He zooms in slightly, and the movement draws my gaze back to the screen. "We won't do this long. I just wanted to see how you translate in higher definition. And to show you what I saw last night. You didn't believe me."

I wait for him to finish the thought, but he doesn't. "Didn't believe you about what?"

"Who you are," he says. "On camera. It's not about the way you look. Well, it's that, too. But there's something about you that a person wants to—I don't know." He searches for the right word, then hesitates before he voices it. "Touch." This reminds me of our aborted kiss, and I wish he hadn't said it. Maybe the same thought occurs to him, too, because his face flushes and he looks frustrated. His eyes narrow as he focuses again on the screen. "Take a look at your image, how accessible it is. You're not doing anything specific, but it's like you're confessing your every thought to the camera. It's simply part of who you are. Do you see it?"

I stare back at my second self, who in turn stares off to the left side of the room, and I wait, watching the blush creep up my cheeks to match his—though at least mine could just be my sunburn. "I guess," I say, unconvinced, but flattered nonetheless.

"Ben said you modeled back home?"

"A little," I say. A few professional shoots, but those were rare. The reality is much less glamorous, but he wouldn't understand. He lives on the top floor of a converted warehouse in the heart of Williamsburg. He went to film school at NYU. His first film won multiple awards in festivals. To him, modeling means walking a runway in some over-the-top costume in front of a room full of celebrities. He doesn't know what it means to don polyester tops for snapshots for local small-town sporting goods stores, to be paid a flat rate that barely covers the gas it took to drive there.

But no, that isn't me anymore. That's the past. That's why I'm here. I'm starting over. I'm doing things differently now. I don't articulate these thoughts. On-screen, though, I can see their contours pass over my expression.

"Not proud of it?" Anthony asks, reading my face correctly. "I know the feeling."

"Do you?" I ask. I'm surprised. The camera catches this, too. "Ben said you were some kind of prodigy." I realize how this sounds, so I try to soften it, though I think I only make it worse. "I mean, from the outside looking in, it doesn't seem like you've got anything to be ashamed of."

"I guess it isn't a matter of pride or shame," he says, scratching the back of his neck. "Even if it feels that way sometimes. It's more that—" He struggles to gather his thoughts. "I liked the process better than the product. Being in the moment, filming. With *Reverence*, if that's what you're still talking about. Watching it again, it lacks something. Soul, maybe. It's more self-conscious than I wanted it to be. All I see is the choreography, the rehearsed lines, the structure I imposed on the story. I think that's why I haven't done anything since. I've been nervous it won't be the same, or maybe that it'll be exactly the same. It's hard to look back."

"But you're—" I fumble with the words. *You're Anthony Marino.* "Ben said it's a great movie. Brilliant, even. You don't like it?"

"Ben's a prince," Anthony says with a shrug. "He'd say that about anything I did. It's a good enough movie, I guess. Entertaining. And it made money. But it's ordinary. Bland."

"Do you think you feel that way about it because you made it?" I persist, offended on the movie's behalf. And on my own, too. How can he be so critical of something so beautiful? "Maybe you know it too well? Or when you say it's too self-conscious, maybe you mean you're just too conscious of it yourself."

"I'm not going to let myself off the hook that easily," he says. "Look, I know I shouldn't criticize something that's affected my life so positively. People—well, *some* people—love the movie so much, they seek me out. They thank me for making it. So I know it served its purpose, and I'm grateful. But when we started filming, I was fresh out of school. The story was so overwritten, it became sterile. I was so concerned with the mechanics of the shoot. We had producers, gaffers, a script supervisor. The more I tried to structure it, the emptier it got. This next one, it's going to be different. I want it to be real. I want it to surprise me."

He tilts the camera's monitor and watches me for my reaction there, through the camera. I have to fight the impulse to laugh. Because this situation is so strange. Here I am, on TV in Anthony Marino's apartment. And he's telling me he isn't proud of *Reverence*. The movie I loved so much is apparently empty, according to its creator. Sterile, even. But then the laughter dies in my throat. Because this is important to him. He has to do this through his camera. It's a bit pathetic, or at least that's how it feels, as much as it's relatable, too. It's like talking on the phone. That's how I told Tucker I loved him, the first time. Even though we saw each other every day, I'd waited until he called me on his drive to the grocery store to speak the actual words. *I love you, Tuck. Don't forget the oranges.*

Back in Williamsburg, Anthony asks, "Who was your last boyfriend?"

I get the feeling he can read my mind, and I can't hide my shock, but Anthony bats my reaction away, as though it's something hanging in the air. "Don't be bashful," he says. "Everything's fair game here. That's the way this is going to work." And then, after a beat: "Sorry for being presumptuous. You're not seeing someone now, are you?"

And what if I am? I wonder. But I shake my head. "Tucker," I say. "He was really nice." I cringe at the bland description, but I'm not sure what else I should say. What else does he want to know? Why does he want to know about Tucker, anyway?

"How long were you two together?"

"Years. Three, I guess, but we've been off and on since high school."

"When did you break up?"

"A little over a month ago," I say. Will he do the math? It's an easy equation, but he doesn't give anything away. Or maybe he doesn't remember how long I've been here in New York.

"Who broke up with whom?"

This makes me smile. *Whom*. Who says that? "I did. Broke up with him, I mean."

"Why?"

I close my eyes and try not to squeeze them shut so I don't look like I'm avoiding the question. The problem is, I know the answer. *Because my father killed himself and I couldn't stand to be there anymore. Because, if I'm being honest, I hated Tucker the instant he said he was sorry for my loss. The very instant he tried to hug me and pretend he could make it all better.* But how do I tell this to a virtual stranger?

Anthony graciously offers, "You broke up with him because you weren't the same person you were when you thought you fell in love with him for the rest of your life. Close enough?"

I open my eyes, grateful for the generic assessment. "I definitely didn't want to see him anymore."

"I know the story," he says with a laugh. "Ben-and-Sofia relationships are the exception, not the rule. They don't know how lucky they are. Or maybe they do. Whatever. Sofia wasn't much help explaining your situation to me." He turns away, squatting in front of a pile of books by the TV stand, while I digest this pronouncement. I know she's said she and Ben have told him all about me, but I had hoped—I had convinced myself—that they were telling him only the good stuff. That they were talking me up. Selling me to the famous director. Anthony had seemed not to know about my father. But maybe this was just a ruse to hear how I would present myself to him. After all, he just asked me if I'm single, when he knows full well I am. I know I shouldn't be upset. He wants to hear everything from me for himself. My truth. And this is all information I would have willingly offered him—maybe not my embarrassing high school years, the awkward attempts at friendship—and maybe it's a gift, somehow, that I don't have to confess to all of my personality, my shortcomings. But it doesn't feel like a gift. It feels like yet another reminder that I'm the odd man out, an outsider in this group of friends. That Sofia's loyalty is to Anthony, not me.

I'm jolted out of my self-pity when a book lands on my lap. "Do you want to hear about this project?" Anthony asks me. In answer, I turn the slim electric blue paperback in my hands. The pages are so old, they're starting to disintegrate, and when I open it up, the smell of must wafts to my nose. *The Executioners.* "Have you ever read it?" he asks me. "Seen the movie?"

I shake my head, and flip through the pages of the novel, searching for some kind of hint.

"The movie was called *Cape Fear*," he says.

"That sounds familiar," I tell him, finally finding my voice. "I think. But I haven't seen it."

"The original was released in nineteen sixty-two. It was re-made by Scorsese in nineteen ninety-one. Maybe that's the version you're familiar with. I saw the original when I was fifteen. I was home alone one day. Pretending to be sick. This was before cable on demand. I switched on the TV, and that's what was playing. Afternoon cinema on our huge old RCA color TV. The movie scared the hell out of me."

I flip through the pages of the novel, stopping to read a paragraph out loud that catches my eye. *"Such a precious and precarious age. Half child and half woman. And when she was all woman, she was going to be extraordinarily lovely. And that would create its own special set of problems."* I shut the book. "Is this me?" I ask.

Anthony doesn't answer. Instead, he says, "The story is pretty simple, but scary. This violent criminal, Robert Mitchum, fresh out of prison, holds a grudge against the lawyer, Gregory Peck, who was responsible for his conviction. He wants revenge. So he stalks the lawyer's family to their houseboat—which is moored in this place called Cape Fear—and he terrorizes them. The film pretends to be about fathers and daughters. The lawyer has a young daughter, Lori Martin—that's the girl you just read about—and the criminal fixates on her. He tells the father he's going to hurt her. Rape her, is what he means. So the father becomes more and more vicious, protecting his daughter." Anthony pitches his voice low, for dramatic effect. "Revenge," he intones. "That's what the film was really about. Revenge. Gregory Peck is clearly the hero. He's Gregory Peck, you know? At the end of the film, though, he isn't just trying to protect his family from Robert Mitchum. He's exacting his own sense of justice." With a shake of his head, Anthony stops himself. "Maybe instead of me telling you all this, we should watch it. What do you think? Do you have time?"

"Why not?" I say. On the one hand, I'm delighted. I still can't believe I'm here. That this is happening. That Anthony Marino is analyzing *revenge* with me in his apartment, like it matters if I understand the concept. It's the difference between exacting justice and pain, I guess. On the other hand, though, the longer I stay here, the greater risk he sees how inadequate I am. I don't want him to realize his mistake and change his mind. "If you think it's important," I add. I check my phone for any texts from Sofia, but there's nothing except another missed call from my mother. She has never been this insistent before. I wonder what she wants. But I brush the thought aside. I don't need another lecture on how ungrateful I am, or what a terrible houseguest I must be. She can wait.

"And don't worry," Anthony tells me, turning the TV back on with a few complicated clicks of the remote. "I have your check. Don't let me forget to give it to you before you leave." The screen goes black for a few beats, then lights up again, bathing half his face in its glow. The other half remains shrouded in shadow.

He looks so casual. Apparently $20,000 doesn't mean anything more to him than the salmon dinner did. I wonder if I should say thank you. But he hasn't left that kind of an opening. It sounds like a chore to him, a reminder to take out the trash or call the dentist. And I guess this makes sense. In his mind, he isn't doing me a favor, giving me this money. I'm going to earn it. He hasn't realized yet I would have done this for free.

A thought occurs to me. "You said there's a family in this story that's being terrorized, right? So if I'm the helpless daughter, who's going to be the father who saves me? You?"

Anthony looks shocked. Then he blushes. "No." His eyes dart sideways to meet mine, but only for a second. "Not me. This isn't a remake of the movie. Not literally. We're responding to it, in a way. I've always wanted to make a scary movie—to scare an audience the way this movie riveted me—but not just for the thrill of it. The film has to mean something more. Anyway," he says, changing the subject before I can ask what he means, "you're not going to be anyone's daughter. You're going to be paired up with your boyfriend. Up at my family's summer cabin, like I told you."

"Your own Cape Fear," I say.

"Exactly," Anthony says. "No houseboat, though. But close enough. The cabin's on its own little island off the coast of Maine."

"So who is the boyfriend, then? You?"

Anthony offers me a casual shrug, though there's something practiced about it. I get the feeling he's nervous. "There's this actor I've worked with before, from *Reverence*. You're going to like him."

For a second he pauses, as if to consider what he's said, and it might just be my imagination, but I think his expression darkens. He can't hide it from me. I'm sure of it. He's not just possessive. I think he's already a little jealous, in anticipation. "Mads," he says. "Mads Byrne."

Now it's my turn to try to conceal an unflattering emotion. Not jealousy in my case, but eagerness. Mads Byrne. This guy is just about every girl's dream. He's a jock, but he's smart. And he's sensitive, too. In *Reverence*, he's the one who finally shoves the knife into Anthony's torso, and afterward his tears are so genuine, I believed that Anthony might well have been killed in real life. Since then, he's been in some other indie movies. Nothing as good as *Reverence*, though. But I haven't seen *Reverence*, right? So all I can do is fake a shrug to hide my thrill. I'm going to meet Mads Byrne. Not only that, I'm going to play his girlfriend. And then something else occurs to me. "So who's going to play the criminal, then? You?"

But Anthony cuts me off. "Listen," he says, "we really aren't remaking the movie. We're capturing its essence. Its fear. This"—he gestures to the TV—"is for you to have something to hold on to. Think of it like a mood board. It's something you can refer back to as we proceed, because—I don't know if Ben or Sofia have told you—we aren't filming off a script. Not even a treatment. Nothing."

Talk to Anthony is what Ben had basically told me when I'd asked him for a script. *He has his own way of doing things.* I had assumed he meant that Anthony would decide when to give me the script. Not *this*.

"Nothing at all?" I ask. My stomach flips. I've never acted before. Am I going to have to improvise? Opposite Mads Byrne?

"Think of it like reality TV," Anthony says, which is what Ben had told me, too—as though that explains anything. "You're going to play a character, one that's really close to who you are, in real life, but certain things are, for the sake of storytelling, emphasized." In the glare of the TV, Anthony's teeth are almost blue. "It sounds more complicated than it is. It's like a game. You don't understand the rules until you start playing, right?"

"Sure, but—"

"Trust me, Betty," he says. "You're a perfect fit for this. It will come naturally to you once we start. You just have to trust me. Or yourself. You have to have faith in yourself. And look at it this way. You don't have to memorize someone else's words and try to act them out until they feel like yours. Anyone can do that. I want you in the movie. *You*."

Before I can even try to respond—again, I'm stunned by the force of his conviction—he turns his attention to the TV. It takes him a moment to start the film. While the colors on-screen flatten into gray scale and the room fills with the reverberations of a deep, ominous fanfare, he settles in, draping a long arm down the back of the cushions. "Relax, Betty," he tells me. "Just watch the film. You have nothing to worry about."

4

The next morning, my head is still buzzing. It feels like a hangover, even though we didn't drink. All we did was watch the movie. Evening had begun to fall by the closing credits, and Anthony had shuttled me out like one of the stepsisters whose feet were too large for the glass slipper. Maybe my headache is just from the stress. I only half slept. All night long, scenes from the movie continued to pummel my thoughts. Gregory Peck reminded me of my father, how morally correct he was, how protective he was of his daughter. Watching him compromise those morals and become a savage to rescue his daughter had grabbed me. More than that, it had triggered something deep within my psyche. He would rather have died than allow his daughter to suffer. It hasn't been that long since I lost Dad. And I couldn't help but see the two of us, in nearly every frame. Even the quaint, conventional ways Gregory Peck and his on-screen daughter spoke to each other—*Daddy*, the girl called him, in her high-pitched saccharine voice—had been almost unbearable to watch.

Still, though, there had been something disappointing about the movie, at least by today's standards. Not just tame, but predictable. The daughter is as innocent as a fawn. The evil the film wants to depict never actually seems to touch her. In the end, what it's really about is the men, Gregory Peck and Robert Mitchum, who are at war with each other. The daughter is just a pawn. What she feels—her terror, even—doesn't matter, except as an element of that conflict.

As I race into the city to start my dog-walking shift, with Ben's oatmeal churning in my stomach, I find myself wondering again what Anthony has planned. We aren't filming a remake of *Cape Fear*, he'd insisted. But the movie that's inspiring our shoot is about a brutal fight—almost to the death—using an innocent girl as a weapon. Its tension derives from the threat to this girl. If what Anthony intends to do is take this threat out of the safe confines of an old-fashioned staged drama and make it real, what does that mean for this poor girl? I mean, for me. *Think of it like reality TV*, he'd said. But how can he make this real? What is he expecting of me? And how will he contain this violence, if it's real—if it's as raw as he seems determined for it to be? Will I even be safe?

I try to put these thoughts out of my mind. Of course I'll be safe. Sofia wouldn't have arranged for me to audition for Anthony's movie if the danger were real. And she wouldn't put herself in danger, either. What am I worrying about? This is Anthony Marino making this film. He knows what he's doing. He's done this before. And who knows? Maybe he'll even play the criminal himself. He had been reluctant to tell me what part he'd play in this whole drama. I'm overreacting for nothing.

Besides, I've already said yes. There's no turning back now. I'd be forever disappointed with myself if I chickened out. Someone else would play the girl, and I'd have to watch her on the screen with Mads Byrne and Anthony Marino. No way, Betty. This prize belongs to me.

For the next hour, anyway, I'm in charge of two dogs. That's my life this morning, and I have nothing else to worry about. The Pomeranian is my favorite. Her name is Peaches, and she walks with obvious pride. The other dog is a mutt, one of those old-man dogs with a beard and weird smile. His name is Forsythe, which suits him. The three of us are hustling through SoHo to Washington Square Park, where the dogs can mingle. I'm avoiding eye contact with passersby, a technique I've developed to keep the people on crowded sidewalks from careening into me. The dogs swarm one of the stands that sells bracelets on Prince Street while I pretend to read a text, when in fact I'm double-checking Google Maps. The park is only five blocks from the apartment where I picked up Forsythe, but somehow I'm lost. This city is a grid. I should know it after a month. I want to feel as if I'm home here. But I'm still not sure which street will lead me to the park. On the way back, it'll be easier. I can retrace my steps.

My phone rings when we finally hit Houston and West Broadway and I can see the canopy of the trees surrounding the park. I pull Peaches out of the gutter and check the screen: Mom. I can't keep avoiding her. I take a deep breath and answer the phone.

My mother's voice blares like a car's horn. "Elizabeth! Where are you?"

"I'm fine," I say at the same time, answering the wrong question. The light changes and I walk, tugging the dogs along behind me. "I've had a busy couple of days. Sorry."

She repeats herself, her words coming out in a rush of impatience. "Where are you?"

I answer, "New York City," with a confused twist of my lips. Then just, "Here and there," figuring what she means is, where have I been? I catch a stranger's eye as I speak and for a moment the woman looks startled, as though she had thought she was invisible. When we reach the other side of Houston, Forsythe stands on his back legs, yoked by the chain, to challenge a passing Chihuahua. I can hear my mother's heavy sigh between barks. I yank him backward. Just a few more minutes and he can roam untethered in the tiny dog park.

My mother's sigh transforms into a question. "But where in the city?"

That's not what she's really asking, is it? She means, why haven't I been accepting her calls? I'd rather not tell her, so I answer literally, "Washington Square Park." I can hear rustling on her end, then a thump. I continue, breathless as we race across the final street to the park. "And I'm almost there, so I should probably get going."

"Stay put," she commands. "I'll be right there."

I pause at the gate. "What?" Peaches and Forsythe gaze up at me in polite silence, as though they're as stunned as I am. I can feel myself grinning. "What do you mean?"

"I'm here. Surprise!"

I look wildly around, convinced she's actually here, but am met with only the indifferent yet intrusive stares of strangers. Mom tells me she's staying at a hotel in Greenwich Village, and she can be here in a few minutes. I don't know how to assimilate the information. I tell her I'm with the dogs and hang up as quickly as I can, the world gone fuzzy with shock and fury. We had spoken only a few days ago and she hadn't mentioned anything about coming out here. She had been the same dreamy, pushy mother who wanted to know that I wasn't walking alone at night and was still checking my horoscope to plan my days. It's impossible, apparently, for her to talk to me about anything real.

I hunch on a bench at the far end of the dog corral and watch Peaches and Forsythe play. I consider leaving. I can disappear into the chaos of the city. I can turn off my phone, drop the dogs off, and park myself in a library for the rest of the day or week, however long she is here. But underneath my indignation, something else is welling up. Until this moment, I hadn't realized how homesick I was. So I wait obediently right where I am and try to calm myself down. Mom's sudden arrival here doesn't change anything. I'm still going up north with Anthony. She didn't tell me she was coming, so she can't be upset that I have other plans. Especially when they involve Sofia. She's always liked her.

I could have told Mom, I guess, about my audition with Anthony. I could have warned her I would be leaving the city to make a movie. All of this is happening so fast, though, I hadn't thought of telling her. But that's a lie, isn't it? She's called me a dozen times in the past couple days. I could have told her at any point. Maybe I didn't want to jinx it, by telling her. Maybe the magic would have been ruined if I'd said it all aloud.

Or maybe I just hadn't wanted to tell her. She isn't the parent I would have called about my good news. I would have called Dad. And then he would have been the one to tell her.

Something brushes my ankle. I expect Peaches or Forsythe, but look down to find an even tinier dog, barely larger than a rat. Its buggy eyes meet mine, then stare off stoically into the middle distance. It has a vest tied around its body labeled SERVICE DOG. Evidently, the creature has intuited that I'm in distress. This thought makes me laugh, but I stop myself with a cough. Mom's in the city. She's here. It comes over me slowly. I'm actually glad. I lean forward and drop a hand on the creature's soft fur.

||||||||||||||||||

Not so long ago, I walked in a place where you could hear the stars. I stopped to listen, and I stood still until my toes ached. The Northern Lights glowed and fizzled, then spread like pale green fireworks. Dad sidled up next to me. I caught his eye. He laughed wildly in the darkness—as if there was no other way to express everything he was feeling—and reached for my gloved hand.

I have never been colder. I have never been happier.

I try not to return to this particular moment often. I don't want the memory to lose its sharp edges. But it comes back to me anyway with my mother's first hug—a dizzyingly tight embrace that infuses her French perfume into my clothes. She hadn't gone with us because she said she was too afraid of the weather. She didn't even like the name of the place. Iceland. She told us we were crazy to go, and right up until the very end, at the airport, she was convinced we would change our minds and stay. It was all one big joke we were playing on her.

My mother takes a seat on the bench with a mulish expression on her face. "This?" she says. She gestures to the dogs and sweeps a hand across the rest of the park. "This?" My father's grip had been so strong. Even through the many layers of our gloves, I had felt the contours of his palms.

As incoherent as Mom's question is, I know what she is asking me. *This* is what I've chosen to do? Have I really abandoned my life in Humboldt to care for dogs richer than me? But I ignore her as Peaches approaches our bench, circles it a couple of times, then hesitantly releases a stream of pee that barely misses my feet. Reflexively, I squeal, "Good job, Peaches! That's a good girl!" I can hear how shrill I sound through my mother's ears. My cheeks burn as I try to explain. "They told me to cheer her on so she doesn't pee at home."

My mother dismisses me by rearranging her hair into an effortlessly elegant bun. I haven't inherited her Dutch coloring, no blue eyes or silver-blond hair, though people do say I look like her. I think they're just being kind.

She crosses her legs and gestures again to the dogs. "You must be joking."

"This is my *life*," I snap. "Not a joke."

Her expression softens, and she reaches for my hand. "You're

SHUTTER

an Aquarius, a wanderer. An old soul. But this"—she uses our
joined hands to gesture at the air—"the dogs? You came to New
York for this?"

I resist the urge to pull my hand away. I tell myself it's because
I don't want to hurt her feelings, but the truth is, I like the touch
of her fingers. "No," I tell her. "I'm going to be an actress. This is
to keep me fed." My phone vibrates in my pocket, giving me an
excuse to look away. The Walking Miss Daisy app issues me a
warning that I'm reaching the time limit for having Peaches and
Forsythe out. Apparently, some walkers kidnap the dogs. "And I
need to go," I say, showing her the screen to demonstrate I'm not
lying.

"'We're set to leave tomorrow. Smiley face,'" my mother reads
with a frown. "What's this about, Elizabeth? Who's Anthony?"

I whip the phone around to see for myself what she's talking
about. My breath catches when I read the text, and I can't stop the
smile from cracking my cheeks. "It's a role," I say. "A big one." To
her bemused expression, I repeat: "Mom, I'm going to be in a
movie."

"Where are you going?" she asks, without acknowledging the
significance of my accomplishment.

I tell her it's a location shoot—words Anthony had used—
somewhere in Maine. She doesn't react except to pull her hand
from mine. I recover from the sting by standing. My knees are
shaking. I turn my back on her and text Anthony a quick reply.
My misgivings are all gone. Suddenly. Maybe because Mom is
here. Because I feel safe with her next to me, and eager once again
to make my escape. Great! Can't wait! I deliberate over the emoti-

cons, but finally decide against inserting one. Let Anthony be the demonstrative texter.

"Where in Maine?" Mom asks me.

I realize, with a pang of shame, that I don't know, but since I don't want to admit this, I pretend not to have heard and instead tell my mother that it really is time to go, and I walk into the fray of dogs.

Once Peaches and Forsythe are back on their leashes, we hustle back to the bench. Mom hasn't moved except to rearrange her purse on her lap. Her silk pants billow in the breeze. Every person passing through the park stares at her, as though they know she's famous but can't quite place her.

They can't because, as beautiful as she is, she is no one. She should be more, but she isn't. She is my mother, that's it. A woman who spends her days writing poetry in dazed spells, like Muhammad receiving divine dictations, only to forget them in piles in the wastebaskets. I'm used to these second and third glances from strangers. She has always possessed this same presence.

"So you're an actress now," she says. "You never mentioned wanting to be an actress before."

"Well," I stutter, "I'm fine. See?" The dogs tangle themselves around my legs. "That's what you came here to find out, right?" But that wasn't it, was it? And we both know it. It was to verify that I'd fallen on my face, and then to scoop me up and take me home. My father's laughter had exploded in my ears like shots fired from a gun, somehow echoing in the cold. We were in the middle of nowhere in Iceland, but I had felt so safe. So sure of who I was. He would be gone just a week later, vanished from our lives with barely a trace to prove that he'd ever actually been there. But this laughter was genuine. I know it was. He was happy. In that moment with me, he had been. I close my eyes and picture instead the glossy lens of Anthony's camera. My reflection on his TV screen, Anthony's soft voice telling me, *I want you to see how you look on camera*. This is it, I remind myself. This is my chance. Opening my eyes, I tell my mother, trying to keep the tremor out of my voice, "It was nice of you to come here. But I don't need your help."

"You can't be serious," she says, pushing herself up from the bench. She's wearing wedge espadrilles, so when she straightens, we're eye to eye. "I flew overnight."

I tighten my grip on the leashes. The dogs strain to escape, but I won't let them. "Without asking or telling me." Maybe I'm only trying to convince myself.

Her eyes fasten on mine. Where my father would shout when we'd argue, my mother simply watches, waiting for me to buckle. I lock my knees and focus on my diaphragm, forcing myself to breathe. The dogs tug at the leash. Before I moved here, I would have fallen to pieces beneath that gaze. But not anymore. I stare right back at her and think about the promise Anthony is making me with this film. I can be more—I *will* be more—with him.

Mom hitches her purse higher on her shoulder, her mouth turned upside down in thought. I pull the dogs in closer to me, then make up my mind to speak these next words, which have never come easily: "I love you, Mom."

"I'm here," she answers quickly, as if she is returning the same expression.

"I know," I say.

She frowns. Maybe she wants to elaborate. Maybe she wants to tell me I've already stayed here too long and I'm not ready yet to make my own decisions. But her lips only twitch, and I feel myself crumble inside. My mother gave me secret presents, once or twice, out of the blue. A flower she had pressed that her grandmother had given her, a poem she had cut out of a magazine, an orange pouch she had found at the flea market that she might have wanted as a young girl. I said thank you, but that was never the right thing. There was an absence I could never fill, and I could always see the exact moment I had disappointed her. I watch it happen again, in real time, in this wretched, loud dog park in the middle of nowhere important.

"It's time to come home," she says, finally admitting why she is here. Her face is wooden, her eyes blank. There's a note of finality in her voice, but she speaks in a monotone, as if she's reading off cue cards. "You're all I've got." What she means, though, is that I have nothing else but her. I'm the one in need of rescue, and she's ready to make the sacrifice.

I close my eyes, and for just a second, I'm in Humboldt again with Dad. I had left home to move in with Tucker. This was only a few months ago now, but it feels like years. I was homesick. I called Dad every single day, and sometimes he would even drive me to work. One morning, I received a call from him. His voice sounded unusually frenzied, and he practically begged me to stop by the house as soon as I could. I found him sitting on the floor in the living room, surrounded by travel magazines. Neither of us had ever traveled outside the country, but he'd buy those magazines at the supermarket sometimes to indulge his fantasies. "This is it," he'd told me, pointing to a photo of green ribbons of light in the sky. "This is the place for us. Here—read. They eat sharks there. From the *ground*, Betty. They take sharks from the sea and bury them in hot soil, then dig them back up and eat them. Everything is opposite. They have glaciers and volcanoes in the same valleys. Sunbeams that light up the night sky. It's so upside down it can't be real. And look at this: We can just get on a plane and fly there. In twelve hours."

But even though the memory is so real it feels as if I've been transported there and I can even smell our living room, the dust and my father and a faint whiff of rosemary, I try not to think of home. Instead, I think of Anthony. I think of that walk from the restaurant. How he placed his hand on my hip. He told me about the first night he'd spent at summer camp as a kid. The camp was only a thirty-minute drive from his family's cabin, but he said it had felt like an alternate universe. At night, he had listened to the frogs whistling in the woods, and that was the only time, he said, he had ever truly believed in vampires. He had called his mother on the phone in the office and told her he wanted to come home. In the background, he heard his father barking words like "toughen up" and "c'mon," but his mother drove out to the camp in the middle of that very night, as if she wouldn't have survived until the morning without him, not the other way around. The next day, his father drove him right back again, and he didn't so much as hug him when he kicked him out of the Mercedes. He didn't stop long enough to turn off the engine. "I understand, you know," Anthony told me quietly as we walked through the glow of the city's lights. "What?" I asked him, lost in thought but assuming he'd continue the story. "What it's like," he said, "to be—" He cut himself off, shaking his head. Finally, he said, "I mean, I think you have to be almost destroyed by the people who are supposed to love you the most in order to become your own person."

I look at my mother, dressed in her billowy silk clothes, her thinning silver hair unraveling from its bun, staring back at me as if I've just thanked her, yet one more time, for a gift that I was simply supposed to accept. I tell her again that I love her. But I know she cannot hear me.

5

The next day, Sofia wakes me up late, not with a loud trip to the bathroom but with an insistent shake of my shoulder. "Time to hit the road," she tells me. "Anthony's on his way."

I had packed my one pathetic bag the night before, but I assumed we would be leaving later in the day. When I mention this blearily to her, she collapses on the couch beside me and says, "Anthony wants to leave now. Ben's grabbing us some coffee." She stifles a yawn. "At least we got to sleep in a bit. You should hurry, though. We only have a few minutes."

Heart pounding, I speed through my morning routine, stumbling over rugs and bumping into furniture. Now that the time has come to leave, I can't believe I'm actually doing this. This is nothing, I tell myself. Nothing compared to leaving home for New York, without having any idea of what I was going to do and nobody to count on. This time, at least, there's Sofia. And Anthony Marino. There's a real purpose.

But still, when the front door opens and Ben announces, "He's here!" I don't know whether to laugh or vomit.

There's no time, though, to hesitate. Ben hoists our bags into his arms, then disappears down the staircase. Sofia gestures for me to exit in front of her so she can lock up. She grins at me, the traces of her earlier fatigue vanishing in the wake of her excitement. "Let's go," she says, prodding me again. I'm not moving fast enough. "I haven't been out of the city in months. I need some *air.*"

As I descend the many flights of stairs to the street, I swallow an unexpected burst of tears. Everything feels so permanent. As though every decision carries a repercussion. When I rebuffed Mom's offer to return home, I rejected the opportunity to be a little kid again. To go back to the known. And now leaving this apartment feels like I'm abandoning another buoy. I wish I were different. Even just a little bit. An ounce more outspoken. Confident. I could stop in the lobby, hold Sofia back, and whisper to her that I'm nervous. That I don't know what I'm walking into and I'm overwhelmed with anxiety. I know Sofia. She wouldn't be able to conceal her surprise. This is just a fun vacation for her, with her group of friends. She hasn't thought about this from my perspective, as the outsider, and I would sound like a wet blanket. But she's a good person. After a minute, she'd soften up and understand. She'd circle her arm around my waist and squeeze me and tell me to breathe. *We're only going for a short trip,* she'd say. *There's nothing to worry about.* And maybe, if I were this other version of myself, I would be comforted by this.

But I'm not that person. I don't want to burden Sofia with my insecurities. And I don't want to be burdened by them myself, either. If I talk about my anxiety, it becomes something real. She'd watch me the entire trip, and I'd feel obligated, somehow, to stick to this story. Once I did overcome my panic, I would still be tethered to it, because of her. So as I cross the threshold of Sofia's building, into the morning air, which is already tinged with the weight of summer humidity, I steel myself. I can do this.

Instantly, my eyes find Anthony. He's standing beside a dilapidated white van, holding a Starbucks coffee and talking to Ben, who has apparently had time to load the bags into the back. When Anthony spots me, his face breaks out into a smile. I make my way toward him, relieved by his easy confidence. There's no sign he's regretting his decision. He's still happy he's chosen me.

"Driving this," Anthony says to me, gesturing to the van with a laugh, "makes me feel like a serial killer."

"It's—," I begin, accepting a coffee from Ben. *It's pretty beaten up* is what I have to stop myself from saying. Instead, I ask politely, "Is it big enough for all of us?"

"See for yourself," Anthony says.

Ben slides open the back door. The backseat looks comfortable enough for two people. I'm glad I'll be in the front. And the rest of the space, behind the uncomfortable vinyl seat, has been cleared out for cargo, down to the van's steel frame.

"Do we really need all that equipment?" Sofia asks Anthony,

eyeing the carefully packed crates stuffed into the back, which loom precariously over the seat.

"You're just lucky there's room for you," Anthony tells her. She frowns when he nudges her toward the backseat, where she joins Ben with a groan. "This one's riding shotgun," he says, pointing at me.

Once I'm in my seat, my nerves start to dissipate. I don't know what it is. As we pass through the neighborhood I've circled endlessly on foot over the past month, everything feels new. I don't recognize the deli on the corner. I'm staring at it like it's a still life in a fancy, hushed museum. The rumble of the van's engine vibrates through the seats, like a hum in my skeleton, and I feel myself relax. You can just pick up your life and change it all, in a second. I had forgotten this feeling, sometime in these past four weeks. You can get used to anything, and quickly. I had let myself settle into Greenpoint. But what am I attached to, really? Can I even trust my own emotions, if only a few minutes can change my mind so radically?

I carry this newfound resolve—like I've swallowed a beam of sunlight—with me, quietly, as Sofia chats excitedly with Ben, and Anthony negotiates the traffic, until finally we escape the city, and then my confidence is quickly replaced by another, less existential concern, that this old grease bucket might splinter apart if Anthony keeps pushing it so hard.

Despite how large the van appears on the outside, Anthony's limbs are too long for these seats. While I'm able to at least tuck my feet into a cross-legged position, Anthony is all angles, like a praying mantis behind the wheel. He fiddles with his phone, searching for the right playlist, while I turn back to check on Sofia and Ben. Sofia, earphones in, gives me the thumbs-up. Ben is already asleep, head resting on her shoulder. I return Sofia's gesture and force myself to face forward again. I'm actually doing this. And what's more, I'm actually having fun.

As we race down the highway, Anthony sings softly along to the music, a strange, twisty song that's a mix of rap and maudlin pop. I don't like the tune at first, but then it ends too soon. I ask him to play it again, and suddenly I'm singing along, too. I discover in the choruses that Anthony can't sing, either, but his quavering falsetto lifts me anyway. His confidence is contagious. He smiles at me, sideways, holding on to a note at the end of the song. It's a meaningless gesture, but I can't help it. I know I'm going to remember this music for the rest of my life. It will always bring me back to this moment, instantly and magically. Every time I hear it, I'll think of Anthony's face—that inconsequential spontaneous smile—but what I'll remember most of all is how happy I am, because in this instant I know I've made the right decision. Not just to trust Anthony, but to leave home. To try to become someone new. And maybe, I think, holding this same note with Anthony as best as my own singing voice will let me, I already have.

About four hours later, halfway through the fifth round of his playlist, with New York City a distant memory behind us, surrounded now by the rocky, overgrown wilds of New England, Anthony finally takes his foot off the pedal and maneuvers us off the highway, down an old stretch of road. We aren't following any maps—Anthony seems to know the way perfectly, from memory, despite the many turns we've made, onto smaller and smaller roads as we've crossed state lines and meandered into what feels like the uninhabited reaches of a forest. As we slow down, the car fills with fumes from the overheating engine. I hadn't realized how hot it is out here, or how quiet. The sun beats down on the roof, and the air is muggy and thick and still. For a moment, as we navigate the narrow road through the woods, it feels as if I can't breathe. I remember my thoughts from this morning, how quickly things can change, though in reverse this time, and I tell myself not to lose my grip on the euphoria I'd just been feeling. It's like sailing, Dad had often said to me. When you hit a rough patch, you have to keep your eyes on the horizon.

"Anthony," Sofia calls. She has to shout over the music and the buzz of the van's frame rattling over the many potholes. "Where the hell are you taking us?"

Anthony gives his phone a few taps, silencing the music. Without it, the engine gets louder still, but I'm somehow aware at the same time of the stifling silence all around us. It shrouds us like a thick blanket. Just a few hours out of the city, and suddenly we are in the middle of nowhere. It feels like we're alone, just the four of us. As if there's no one else for miles and miles around. And we're not even there yet.

"We're picking up Mads," Anthony says. "Betty needs her boyfriend."

Sofia mumbles something about not killing us on the way there, but I can't focus on what she's saying. Anthony's driving is making me nauseous, and it's too hot in this van, even with the

AC blasting. I jolt at a sudden warmth on my knee, and locate Anthony's hand there. He squeezes, clamping his fingers around the soft, ticklish spot where my knee and thigh meet. I don't intend to, and I don't expect it, but with an unanticipated yet welcome sense of relief, I find myself smiling again.

6

A few miles down this road, Anthony makes an unexpected turn and pulls the van into the parking lot
of a train station, which materializes like magic out
of the thick tangle of trees strangling the asphalt. Mads's train
should arrive in no time, Anthony tells us. The station is hardly
more than a shed next to the tracks. We are deep in the country.
The buzz of cicadas punctuates the stillness as soon as Anthony
cuts the engine, and waves of yellow pollen drift lazily by, coating
the windshield after only a few minutes. This is the closest train
station to the cabin, and apparently there is still an hour's drive in
front of us.

When Sofia asks Anthony for the address so she can look at
our journey online, he tells her, "You won't be able to find it. We're
officially registered in the county's books as the Mission San Juan
Bautista." When I raise my eyebrows, he shrugs. "My parents are
Hitchcock fans." I'm not sure which film he's referring to, but I

nod anyway as if I do. I don't know why I always feel so inadequate, as if the knowledge I do possess isn't enough.

"While we're waiting," I ask him, "could we talk about the movie?"

Out here, away from the glamour and chaos of the city, Anthony looks smaller somehow. His wiry arms, so fashionably thin in the city, are rangy against the backdrop of the open country. The relentless burn of the sun adds a green tinge to his blue eyes. He glances back at Sofia and Ben, cuddled together in the backseat. They don't seem particularly interested to hear what he has to say. They must have had these conversations already. Of course.

"We're just a group of friends on vacation," Anthony tells me. "That's it."

Sweat trickles down my lower back. "What does that mean, though?"

"There's nothing more to it than that," he says with a shrug, as though everything's explained and I'm being petulant. "There's no plot. No script. It's just us. You're you. On vacation, with your boyfriend and his friends. Understand?"

"Not really," I admit.

"The whole cabin will be its own soundstage," Anthony tells me. "We won't have to set up shots or film rehearsed scenes. We're just having a party. I've invited the DP from *Reverence*, Ben, who's brought his charming girlfriend."

"That would be me," Sofia chimes in.

"Director of photography," Ben says, helpfully, at the same time. "When I wasn't sound mixing and taking care of everything else."

"And," Anthony continues, "I've invited Mads Byrne, also from *Reverence*, who's invited his current acolyte. You."

"Acolyte?" I ask, before I realize I'm the only one in the van who hasn't heard the word before.

"Follower," Sofia says.

"Girlfriend," Ben says.

"Conquest," Anthony says. All of them reply at the same time.

"Okay," I say, "so technically I shouldn't be in the van yet. I'm on the train with Mads Byrne."

"Exactly," Anthony says.

"Are you going to film us getting off the train together?"

"No. We won't start shooting until we're up at the cabin."

"You're picking us up, and we're joining you for some kind of extended party, and the whole thing is going to be filmed on cameras we're not supposed to see."

"Good girl," Anthony says, like I'm a child. "You've got it."

I shake my head. "Not really," I say.

Anthony spreads his hands. He looks flustered. I'm not just a child. I'm slow.

"I don't get how this is supposed to be interesting. This is a movie, right? Isn't it supposed to have a story line? Isn't it supposed to be fun to watch?"

"Editing," Anthony says. "After we're done, I can pick and choose what goes into the film. Even the order. The actual chronology doesn't matter. I can even splice together different conversations. Like you said, this is a film. It's real but it isn't." He stops talking to assess my reaction. "You're still not happy," he says.

My cheeks begin to burn. Ben and Sofia, too, are looking at me like I'm an idiot. And then it hits me. The crux of what's still bothering me. "So what about *Cape Fear*?" I ask Anthony. "That's what you're aiming for, right? A scary movie. A girl who's being terrorized. So where does this fear come from?"

Anthony doesn't answer. In fact, he turns away from me, to stare instead out the window, down the tracks.

"Anthony? What is it I'm supposed to be so afraid of?"

In the silence that follows, I feel the weight of everyone's gaze on me. The more I think about it, though, the more confused I feel. Where is the tension in a party among a few good friends? And what bugs me the most is that it feels as though Anthony's keeping whatever danger is supposedly lurking out here in the woods from me. Is Mads going to attack me or something? Is Anthony? Is there a monster out here in this forest? Another actor I don't know about? Why am I the only one who doesn't know what's going on? These three are all in on the secret. Mads Byrne, too, I'm sure, or he wouldn't have agreed to this. They take their friendship for granted. They're all three—four—together. I'm the only one left out in the cold.

The blare of a distant horn draws everyone's attention to the train tracks. "Saved by the bell," Ben jokes.

"We'll take this up later," Anthony says, giving his door a shove with his shoulder. He climbs out of the van with a languid stretch. "Come on. All of you. We're the welcome committee."

As Ben lumbers out of the van, Sofia stops me with a hand on my elbow. "You okay?" she asks.

"Fine," I lie. "Don't I look okay?"

"You look stressed," she tells me. Then she laughs. "Don't get upset. We're on vacation, like Anthony said. Just trust him, okay? And now you get your own mail-order hunky boyfriend. He's an upgrade from Tuck, you'll see."

I force a laugh. "You're right," I say. "I'm sure it will all make sense."

"Soon," Sofia says. "And in the meantime, just enjoy yourself. Have a little fun. Smile."

Together, we join Anthony and Ben at the depot. Ben drapes his heavy arms over Sofia's and my shoulders. I resist the impulse to shake off his arms. Sofia is right. I need to relax. Why have I always had so much trouble fitting in to a group?

"Prepare yourself," Anthony tells me. "You're about to meet the last member of the *Fear* family." He eyes me significantly, like he's joking, but I can sense something more under his gaze. "Your new man."

The train arrives in a dazzling rush of movement. The windows glitter in the sunshine, almost too bright to look at. When it finally pulls to a stop, only one person stumbles out, carrying some kind of duffel bag, immediately recognizable though I can't see him clearly. Anthony breaks away from us to hug the shadowy figure, grabbing him by the shoulders and holding him at arm's length, as though to get a better look at him. Ben, meanwhile, tightens his hold on me for a strange half hug, telling me in so many words to buck up, then releases me with an excited shout for this charismatic new arrival. They slap each other's backs in a practiced motion and ask each other how they've been, dude. Sofia ducks into the fray, giggling at everything he says.

I can't move. *Mads Byrne.* This is really Mads Byrne. Mads from *Reverence*—he'd kept his own name in that film, just like Anthony had. It feels like I'm still watching that movie. These people are so separate from me, they might as well be on-screen. In person, though, Mads is *huge.* Much bigger than I'd expected, though I'm not sure if I'm measuring him or his presence.

He's big all right, but he's not quite Anthony's height. He's just much larger, and not by a little bit. A lot broader, like an athlete. He looms over Ben and Sofia. He looks like a teen-movie heart-throb, with the colored khakis and polo shirt to match. He has filled out since *Reverence*, I think. In the movie, I had the impression he was lankier, like Anthony. It looks like he's spent hours in the gym every day since. The smile, though. His eyes. They're exactly what I remember. Only infinitely more dazzling in person.

When he finally turns his attention on me, all the apprehension I'd been feeling just a few minutes ago seems to melt away. There's no way I'm going to feel threatened by this man. I don't know what it is, but instinctively I feel better now that he's here. Safer. Not just that he'll protect me. Not that at all, in fact. More like nothing bad can happen to any of us while he's around. Because nothing bad will happen to him. He doesn't exist in the world like the rest of us do. The world exists for him.

Looking at me, his curiosity apparent, he unleashes this slow, blushing grin, like he's picking me up for prom, and I've just descended the stairs in my best dress. Then he drops his leather duffel bag and brushes past Ben to saunter toward me. "You must be Lola," he says with a slight drawl. His voice is like caramel. "I'm Mads Byrne. Bring it in."

I return his hug automatically, and find myself wrapped up in his arms. He's built like a bull. I'm so overwhelmed, it takes me a moment to process what he's said. "Lola?" I ask, when he's let me go and I'm no longer swimming in his embrace. But I'm not looking at him. I'm looking at Anthony. I know already this isn't a mistake. Mads hasn't gotten my name wrong. This is another secret that I'm not part of. Another element of the shoot I've been excluded from.

"We'll talk about it later," Anthony says.

"Why?" I insist. "I'd rather talk about it now, if that's okay."

In front of me, I'm aware of Mads's face dropping. I'm making him uncomfortable. Maybe I'm ruining this introduction completely. But I can't seem to stop myself.

"If I'm just being me for this movie," I continue, "why do I need a new name?" All of a sudden, I'm angry. More blindsided than I should be. But I can't help it. I feel singled out. No one else has a new name.

"Would you just relax?" Anthony retorts. "Trust me." Then, his expression softening, he adds, "Listen. It's to help you while we're filming. To free you up, so you don't feel confined to doing what Betty would do. Don't look at it like a restriction. It's a license. You're whoever you want Lola to be. You're everything—every single thing—you wish you could be."

Our eyes connect, and for a split second, I recognize how important this whole thing is to him. Up to this point, this film has felt haphazard. Slapped together. As though every decision had been made impulsively. Who's acting in it, when we're leaving, what we'll be doing when we get there. Now it hits me how controlled this impulsivity is, if that makes sense. Anthony knows what he's doing. It's clear he has a vision. He has seen something in me that resonates, and he knows how to coax it out of me.

"I'm sorry," Mads mumbles, "if I said something I wasn't supposed to."

Anthony waves him off. "I was going to tell you when we got there," he says, speaking to me still, not Mads. "You're going to know everything, Betty. Really. In the meantime, though, I just want you to learn to trust me."

"I do," I tell him. Our eyes connect again, and then I let myself glance at Mads, who's looking sheepish. When he smiles, I realize, in the split second of an epiphany, that he likes me, too. More than that. This man—this huge, larger-than-life man—is attracted to me. Maybe I'm having the same effect on him that he's having on me. I feel goose bumps prickle my arms. It feels like sunshine, breaking out from behind the shadow of a cloud.

An instant later, though, the moment is ripped from me. Ben's voice slices through the air, bringing us all back into the parking lot beside the train tracks. "How much farther, dude? My butt is sore."

Shaking his head, Anthony leads us back into the van. Mads waits for Ben and Sofia to climb into the back, then wedges himself between them, his impossibly broad shoulders cleaving them apart like an ax splitting a log—politely allowing me to resume my place in the front seat next to Anthony. "You guys would have been lost without me," he says facetiously, though he's echoing my thoughts aloud, as Anthony starts the engine and, only yards away from us, the rusty train finally disembarks from the station in a plume of diesel smoke. "Now let's get this show on the road, or we'll all suffocate in here. We're off to see the wizard, right?"

"Follow the yellow brick road," Ben croons, making Sofia laugh.

"We're not in Kansas anymore," Anthony mutters.

Mads leans forward and grabs my shoulder. Surprisingly gentle. "Your turn," he says.

I shrug, though it feels like my body is tingling. Not just because of the unexpected caress. Because he's included me. "There's no place like home?" I hazard, and this makes him laugh. Everyone does, probably because they didn't expect me to join in. Everyone but Anthony. He's become sullen, as he guides the van down an uneven, barely paved road that narrows as it leads into the woods.

His mood seems to infect the van, and we all fall silent. After a few miles, the asphalt disappears completely, and we're on a bumpy one-lane path that alternates between packed clay and gravel. Just when I'm ready to vomit, the road smooths back into asphalt. When Anthony does finally choose to speak again, however, his voice sounds as steady as it always does. Cheerful, even. "Now it's a straight shot to the end of the line," he tells us, revving the van back up to a reasonable speed. "The hardest part is behind us. If you haven't thrown up yet, you should be okay the rest of the way."

Mads seems to take a cue from this. He leans forward and places his hand on my shoulder again. "You in school?" he asks me. When I finally comprehend the question, for the first time I catch a glimpse of this man, not the slick movie character. I have this sudden vision of him holding one of those red Solo cups and chanting *Chug chug chug* on some front lawn at a frat party. I wonder how old he thinks I am. Or if he has somehow misjudged me as a kindred spirit, a sorority girl shrieking at his antics on that same front lawn.

"No," I say. I don't add *I never went to college,* but I imagine he can see that written on my face, and maybe hear it in the dull tone of my voice. "Are you?"

"Yale," he says, too proud of himself to hide it. "MFA." At my blank look, he explains, "Grad school. I decided to get a real education."

I hate myself for this, but I'm feeling suddenly inadequate again. I can barely keep up with Sofia's and Anthony's references, so what will I ever have to talk about with someone getting a master's degree at an Ivy League university? But then I see the color draining from his tan cheeks, the unfocused way he's staring past me, out the windshield. He could be carsick, like me, but maybe he's just as unsure as I am. Maybe he's simply making conversation because he's nervous. He wants to get to know his new costar. His new pretend girlfriend. So rather than shutting him out, I hear myself asking how long the train ride was, and I smile encouragingly while he answers, though the truth is, I don't really hear what he's saying.

Watching him speak, as he tousles his hair from side to side with his fingers, making invisible adjustments until he's pleased with the result in the rearview mirror, I realize if I had met him a few days ago, I would probably have fallen madly in love with him. I wouldn't have begrudged his easy, sheepish charm—not for long, anyway. I would have been powerless against it. I could have nestled my body into his and slept for the rest of my life in that embrace, buoyed and protected by his ability to connect with the outside world. Even now I can't help but love him a little. But not in that way. That feeling belongs to a different reality. One where there isn't Anthony seated right next to me, his eyes fastened on the road in front of us like he's determined not to hear a word we're saying, his face lit softly by the sunshine filtering through the trees.

To tell the truth, as attractive as Mads is, I actually feel a little resentful of him, though I don't know why. If I had to guess, it's because he's been thrust upon me so forcefully as my boyfriend. I didn't pick him. And now I have to pretend to be in love with him. Day and night. This feels unnatural. More forced than if we were acting in a film, scene by scene, because at least there would be boundaries. Most of the time, we wouldn't be on camera, required to be infatuated with each other. From what I've gathered, we won't have any of those breaks at Anthony's cabin.

"We're going to make a pit stop at the market," Anthony tells us, breaking into my thoughts. I turn my attention to the road again, and see that we're meandering into a small town, or at least a cluster of ramshackle buildings planted on the side of the narrow highway. "Snacks, extra bug spray, milk. I packed a lot of staples already, but—" He shrugs. Then he tosses me a quick, unreadable look. "When we get there, you're Lola. Okay?"

Ben pipes up, "And I'm Keyser Söze, right?" I get the feeling everyone else understands the reference, though I don't, but when no one responds, he adds, "*The Usual Suspects*." And then, "Get it?"

Mads gives Ben a shove that crushes him against the side of the van. "Too soon, dude," he says.

"Think of it as a trial run," Anthony tells me. "You're test driving your new identity. Which reminds me—" He tugs at a stray lock of my hair. "We need to do something about that."

"About what?" I ask.

"We need a couple of spray bottles. Don't let me forget."

"For what?"

"Your hair," Anthony answers. "I mentioned making a few changes in your appearance, didn't I? You said you'd be comfortable."

"Painting my nails," I say.

"Lola has bleached hair," he tells me. As quiet as he has spoken them, the words seem to reverberate off the windshield.

I don't know why I'm so surprised, but I am. What happened to me being in charge of who Lola is? What happened to Lola being me? Or at least an exaggerated version of me? I have never touched my hair, beyond a few cuts for maintenance. Now that I think about it, I can't even remember the last time I got it trimmed. I can feel Anthony waiting for a response. I stumble on the first few words. "But—I, uh, you—I don't even know how to go about doing that."

I risk a glance at the backseat, to gauge the others' reactions.

Mads, hands laced behind his head, has his eyes closed, like he isn't even here. Ben gives me a noncommittal shrug. Sofia, meanwhile, is lost again on her phone. Even from this distance, I can hear the tinny music blaring into her ears.

When I face the front once more, I'm shocked all over again. We seem to have driven into a cloud. The sun had been shining just five seconds ago, but now we're entrenched in mist. As we enter the village, the trees that had seemed so beautiful, so lithe and defined, only milliseconds before, have turned into a cage of sinewy arms and legs, which encroach on the scattered buildings like a hungry jungle. This forest isn't enchanted. It's haunted. Anthony nonchalantly flicks on the lights, and then, a moment later, the heater, to defrost the windshield. The sun that had been baking us is gone, and to my surprise it's cold here. New York had been stifling. It's the middle of summer. But here in Maine, if that's where we are, there's a real chill in the air. It's so dank I can feel it in my bones. I wish someone had told me to bring a jacket.

"Stop stressing," Anthony tells me, reading my mood. His hand drops from the steering wheel to my leg again, this time my thigh.

I know there are others here. I know that we're all five of us cooped up together in the cramped confines of this dilapidated van. But as Anthony's hand squeezes my leg, in an attempt to reassure me, I suddenly understand something. It's just me and him now. Alone. His touch is different from Mads's. More urgent, somehow. Electrifying. As comforting as Mads's hand had felt on my shoulder, as warm, the feeling was diffused. Anthony's simple clasp, however, travels through my body like a shock. I know I'm supposed to be Mads's girlfriend, but it feels like Anthony has claimed me as his. And I don't think he intends to let me go.

The thought sends a jolt through me as my leg jerks reflexively under Anthony's grip. As nervous as I am—I don't know—maybe I'm also a little bit pleased.

7

As we slow to a crawl in the center of the small village, Anthony casually informs us that the Mission San Juan Bautista is not just the Marino family's cabin but a tiny island a quarter mile off the coast, not too far from here. Hence the fog. Even though it doesn't feel like it, we're on the coast. This happens to be the closest town, so everyone here knows them. There are other private islands in Maine, but none so close, so most of the inhabitants here have a sort of mixed-up relationship with the Marinos, the überwealthy, out-of-touch foreigners. On the one hand, they hold the family in a kind of awe. Like their lords of the manor. "On the other hand," Anthony tells us, "they resent us. You'll pick up on it pretty quickly, with whoever we happen to talk to. They love us, but really, they hate us." I get the impression that Anthony isn't bothered by their enmity. In fact, it looks like he enjoys this strange relationship.

"Wait a minute," I say. "Your own private island?" I remember him saying something about an island in Maine, but I hadn't realized we would have the entire island to ourselves. I seem to be the only one surprised by this piece of information, though, or if anyone does share my surprise, they don't comment on it. Sofia looks embarrassed for me. Likewise, Ben goes to pains to demonstrate how clued in he already is.

"You said there's a trail around the island, right?" he asks Anthony.

And Mads, too: "The pictures make it look like *Lord of the Rings*," he tells me.

Technically, Anthony continues—I think I'm the only one still listening to him—the Mission is considered part of the small unincorporated village we're pulling into. While this gathering of shops and homes has no official name, Anthony says, the locals refer to it as the Strip. My first impression is that it's not much more than a branch off the highway. You take a couple of seemingly wrong turns down some narrow, winding roads and, after an hour and a half without passing another car or another soul, around the camouflage of a bend, the road is suddenly dotted for a mile or so with old pastel-covered Victorian houses, decaying and molding as they're swallowed back into the forest. Anthony cranes his neck to indicate which of the houses we should be admiring. One has a man-made pond in the front, the water a brackish color, with an inflatable puffin floating in the center. Another, right next door, is decorated with what appears at first to be strands of a spiderweb, but which I realize belatedly are ropes of old Christmas lights.

Even with all this land around them, the structures are pressed right up to the road, with no real lawns, just yellowing porches, the paint peeling in swaths from the salt in the air—or a lack of care. Some of them have been converted into stores or salons or offices, probably because they wouldn't make comfortable homes any longer. Even as commercial establishments, though, they don't seem to be doing well. One building that looks as if it might tip over—if it doesn't disintegrate first—has a message scrawled in white letters across its darkened windows reading EVERYTHING MUST GO. MAKE AN OFFER. It looks, though, as if there's nothing left to buy.

My hometown is not particularly big or fancy. It's an unassuming spot outside of Eureka, right on the California coast, where the sea breeze and dust from the valley meet in quaint neighborhoods. I'm used to forgotten remote villages. But this place is different. There's something dark about it. Something ominous. It's not just forgotten—it's unloved. And it's so far off the beaten track, I doubt many outsiders stray through, and even though we haven't seen anyone yet, it doesn't seem as if we are particularly welcome. The village itself doesn't want us here. I can't suppress a shiver, especially when I notice, suddenly, that there are actually any number of faces, half hidden in shadows behind various windows, watching us as we cruise past. They must recognize Anthony in the driver seat, but not one person waves. No one even smiles. One man's face catches my attention. His cheeks are gaunt and dirty with stubble. His eyes are hollow. When I meet his stare, they narrow into an unfriendly squint, like he's measuring me.

Anthony pulls up behind what he tells us is the general store.

It's the last structure on this stretch of the road, and the only building that isn't a narrow Victorian, but rather a dilapidated old warehouse, its loading bay converted into a storefront with a set of rusting stairs.

"You're Lola," Anthony reminds me as he shuts the engine off. "Mads's girlfriend. Okay?"

I meet Mads's eye, and he shoots me a wink. Somehow, this doesn't comfort me. We're supposed to be a couple, like Ben and Sofia. But they've been together so long, it seems that they are two halves of the same person. They know how to talk to each other. How can I emulate that with this stranger?

"How long have we been together?" I ask Anthony. Then, when all he does in answer is raise his eyebrow, I realize my mistake. I turn to Mads and repeat my question. "Sorry," I add, unable to stop myself.

Mads runs a hand through his hair, once more tousling it to movie star perfection. "Let's just keep it as close to the truth as we can," he says, as though that should have been obvious. And maybe it is. He and Anthony have most likely already discussed this without me. "We met recently. You were a fan. I had been invited here already. I asked you to come with me. It's casual. Nothing too serious. That way, everything's new and fun and we're still getting to know each other, in case we slip up. Right?" He turns to Anthony, who nods in confirmation.

I say, "Okay, I can do that," more for my own benefit than theirs. They clearly don't need my input.

"Let's go," Sofia says, giving Mads a hard shove. "You're blocking the door."

Anthony climbs out of the van and leads us to the shop. The iron stairs vibrate as we climb them, and our footsteps echo hollowly down the empty road. A sign taped to the glass front door, its letters chipped with age, tells us WE HAVE WHAT YOU NEED. Below that, there's another scrawl: TAROT CARDS/PSYCHIC READINGS. THE FIRST ONE IS ON ME.

Sofia stops us with a question. "Is there a bathroom? I can't think, I have to pee so bad."

Anthony indicates a blue Porta Potty just beyond the shop, its plastic faded by the sun and sea air. Sofia makes a face, but nevertheless skips back down the stairs and hustles over, slamming the door behind her. I pause for a beat, then follow at a quick clip, giving Anthony an apologetic shrug. I do have to use the bathroom. But it's not urgent. I just want to take a second alone to gather myself, before I have to do whatever he's asking of me. To be Mads Byrne's girlfriend. Behind me, Anthony holds Mads and Ben back from entering the store. I guess we all have to go in together.

When it's my turn in the Porta Potty—maybe because I'm suddenly by myself in a stinky plastic box in the middle of nowhere—it hits me how real this is. This isn't some adventure I'm thinking of taking. I have already left. I'm actually here. Wherever *here* is.

I survey the little plastic booth, taking shallow breaths to try to stifle the smell. It feels like I've encased myself in a tomb. Purple liquid bubbles just underneath the open hole of the toilet seat, like one of the sulfur springs Dad and I visited in Iceland. As I carefully squat down, I have to turn away from the sink—or maybe it's a urinal, I don't want to examine it too closely—because it's covered in what looks like yellow slime. On the door, facing me at eye level, is a message scratched painstakingly in the plastic: *Ash Bode is a whore with big tits.* It's an unusual name, but I knew a girl in school named Leslie Bode. By the time she hit puberty, the boys would call her "the Body." I doubt there's any relation, but I can't help but stare. Even when you're on what feels like the edge of the universe, you can't escape yourself. You can't escape home.

But I have to push these thoughts from my mind. It won't help to scare myself. I have to let go of my stress. I have to let go of my memories. I have to let go of Betty.

I'm shivering by the time I rejoin the group, huddled by the store. I'm only wearing a thin T-shirt, and I don't think I brought anything much heavier for the shoot. Why the hell didn't anyone tell me how cold it is up here? Everyone else is wearing a sweater. Anthony waits until I've joined them, then leads us into the shop. Mads holds the door for me, then trails in behind Sofia and Ben. I know my clothes have already absorbed the pungent perfume of incense that greets us, even before I take my first lungful of it. But I'm grateful for the warmth in here, however clammy the air is.

As the door closes with a rattle and a clang, a voice calls out from the back, "There's a special on milk and blackberries, picked wild by the Kaine boys."

I drift away from the voice, toward the small shelf of produce, suddenly aware of how empty my stomach is. Isn't anyone else hungry? But then I catch the end of Ben's complaint to Sofia—*"starving"*—and feel reassured. Before I can grab an apple, though, I'm stopped by a hand on my arm. It's Anthony pulling me in tight.

He lowers his voice to a whisper. "Do you think you can charm her?" he asks, but it feels more like a command than a question, and I don't have time to ask him what he expects of me because we're already walking in lockstep to the checkout counter. I'm going to disappoint him. Charming people has never been my strong suit. I'm not Mads. Speaking of Mads, though, where is my new doting boyfriend? Why can't he join me? But he's in the back, in the refrigerated aisle, calling out to Anthony if he brought any beer.

"Grab some more," Anthony shouts back. Then he addresses the woman at the register, even before we've navigated through the aisles. "Mrs. O! How are you? How's business?" The tone of his voice suggests he knows her well enough that he doesn't have to remind her who he is.

The woman is smiling as she comes into view, but her expression changes into something I can't quite read as soon as she catches sight of Anthony. It isn't necessarily displeasure, but it's definitely more charged than mere recognition.

She isn't sitting on a chair, but rather is perched on the edge of a couple of tall boxes like an owl. She seems to be leaning her entire body weight onto one flattened hand on the cardboard. The other holds a novel, a bodice ripper, the same chunky, brick-shaped book with an embossed glossy cover you find in every convenience store, in a wire rack next to the greeting cards. She looks comfortable enough, ensconced in a collage of strange objects. This is where she must do her tarot readings, right up at the register, because there are mildewed card boxes and kitschy scarves draped over every conceivable surface, along with candles and bottles of incense, as well as a few tiny troughs filled with brass trinkets that remind me of the flea markets that come into town sometimes, back home. The warmth that hits us as we approach is explained by a small space heater, glowing orange beside her.

I wonder how long it's been since she and Anthony have seen each other. The old woman—who's reached that nebulous age where you could tell me she was sixty or eighty and neither would surprise me—blinks a few times before she feels ready to speak. "Anthony Marino," she says. She sets her book down to lift both hands and shake them in his direction. "You didn't warn me you were coming."

"Is that something I'm supposed to do?" he asks, scratching the back of his neck. "Warn you?"

"Well," she says, with a slightly uneasy smile, "I don't know if that was the right word. It wouldn't hurt, though, to give us a call first so we could prepare a welcome for your arrival. It's something we look forward to all the rest of the year, seeing your handsome face. And you are handsome, aren't you? Why, you're turning more and more into your father with every passing minute, it looks like." She winks at me. "Handsome runs deep in the Marino family. Don't you think so?"

It feels rude not to agree, even if Anthony and I are practically strangers. But I don't really have to. My blush has already given me away.

"Now, who are you?" she asks me. "Another of Anthony's young girls?"

My reaction is to tell her I'm an *acolyte*, but Anthony steps in to save me from this embarrassment. "Not mine," he says. "She belongs to one of my friends, back there, getting the beer."

My face flushes again, this time because I don't know how I feel about this description of me. Actually, I do. I hate it. He makes it sound like Mads *owns* me. I can feel myself bristling at the implication, but I stop myself from correcting him. Anthony told me he wants me to be charming. It won't help to get angry.

"So tell me, then, what can I do for you?" Mrs. O asks as she slides off her perch, dropping gracefully to her feet and stepping behind the counter. She's much smaller than I had thought, at least in height. The waxy tips of her closely cropped curls barely reach my chest. Her shoulders, though, are broad. "I thought you weren't coming in for another few weeks. Or did I get that wrong?"

"No," Anthony says. "You had it right. Mom and Dad are coming at the end of August. I decided to come up now myself. A little vacation with some friends." He nudges me forward as he slips his hand from my arm. I can't help but feel like I'm being shoved between the two of them.

Mrs. O examines me again for a long moment. I can read her expression. She's waiting for me to speak. She's wondering why I'm so shy. But I'm doing my best. I just feel crippled by Anthony's command. I don't know what he wants from me. I don't know how to be charming. But then Mrs. O seems to make up her mind, and thankfully, it's to like me. Her face breaks into another grand smile, this time genuine, its full force directed at me. "Hello, dear. I'm Mrs. O. Patricia O'Neill."

"Lola," I say, extending a hand uncertainly over the counter.

Anthony leaves me hanging, retreating a step as Mrs. O takes my hand. He's already too far away to appreciate the helpless glance I throw his way.

"Pleasure to meet you," the old lady tells me, her hand enveloping mine. We don't shake—she just squeezes. Her skin is tough like a workman's glove, but supple. "I'm sorry if I was rude before. But Anthony has never brought *friends* with him here." She lowers her voice, as if no one else will hear. "A girl or two, yes. Friends, no." I get the feeling she's somehow seen through the lie and knows I'm trying to put one over on her for whatever reason, though this is of course impossible, and what difference would it make anyway? Who is this woman? Why does she matter? Why am I supposed to charm her?

"Really?" I ask, unsure of what to say. "I haven't known Anthony very long." Mads is right. Maybe the truth is easiest. "I just met him, but he seems really nice to me." I turn, hoping to rope Anthony back into this conversation, but he's moving farther away from me. He points to the opposite end of the store as he turns his attention to the food, muttering something about helping Ben. I'm too polite to follow him. And he obviously wants me to impress this woman, though I'm not sure why. I know I'm making way too much of this. And Mom would never forgive me for my shyness. *Just make conversation*, she'd tell me. *You're always so mortified. What do you have to be so worried about?* I can feel Mrs. O's eyes on me, black and flat like steel bars. I want to ask about the tarot cards and psychic readings, but I can't, knowing she would insist on giving me one and I would be unable to say no.

"I didn't say he isn't nice," she says, following my eyes to the tarot cards. "I'm not a medium, at least I don't think I am. But I do like to think I'm in tune. Like you, dear. We feel things out, don't we? I'll just say, it's a happy surprise to see Anthony with a person like you, not the usual—Oh, but you're not a couple. Sorry. I got the impression you were."

"I'm with Mads Byrne," I say.

Her expression remains blank. The name means nothing to her.

"An actor," I say. "One of Anthony's friends." Then: "I haven't known him very long, either."

The old woman takes another, closer look at me, like she might have misjudged me, for better or worse, but now is curious who this girl is who wandered into her store with Anthony Marino. "It's none of my business," she says, "is it—"

"You know Anthony well," I say, "don't you?"

Mrs. O is pleased with the observation. She's proud, I think, of the perception that she's close to—as Anthony put it—the lords of the manor. "The Marinos have come up together, as a family, every year for as long as I can remember. It's a wonderful tradition. I don't think they'd see their son at all if it weren't for these trips."

"So you watched Anthony grow up, then?"

Again, Mrs. O is visibly pleased. "Since he was a toddler. Of course, he was always a quiet kid." She considers her next words before speaking them. I get the feeling she wants to impress me with just how well she does know him. "He didn't seem to have any friends except his old camera. Me and Paul, we were more than happy to have him pal around with our Sammy. 'The kid needs a strong hand,' Paul liked to say. 'Sammy can teach him a thing or two.'"

"Sammy?" I ask, encouraging her to continue.

"Sammy, our son, is only a few years older than Anthony," Mrs. O says, tapping her fingers impatiently on the keys of an old telephone. "They could have been brothers, the way they were back then. Well, I have to say, it's good to see Anthony with friends."

I fumble for a response. I don't know why she's chosen me to gossip with, or how far I'm supposed to take this. Thankfully, Anthony returns at the same moment with an armload of seltzer, unloading the bottles on the counter with a clang. Mads appears behind him, dumping two cases of beer next to the pile. Mrs. O forgets about me and our stilted conversation, and starts ringing up the items, both on her ancient register and scrawling the figures, too, on a pad of yellow paper.

Mads hovers next to me for a moment, an arm curling behind my waist, dropping his voice to ask, solicitously, "Did you get everything you need?" When his fingers do finally find the small of my back, his touch is light. I can sense how awkward he feels about the contact, too.

"I think I'm covered," I say, trying to lean into his embrace, as opposed to away from it. It hasn't been that long since Tuck and I broke up. But already I've forgotten how to be with someone. Or perhaps I'm just not ready yet to be with anyone else. I will have to learn not to flinch when Mads reaches for me. All he does is tuck a strand of hair behind my ear, but still, I feel my shoulders tense. Which isn't fair to him. He's just doing his job. I shouldn't make it any harder for him.

Luckily, though, he's distracted by the pile of supplies on the counter. He moves to help Ben bag everything up, and I breathe a small sigh of relief. Mrs. O, I notice, has been examining me, but she turns away when our eyes meet.

"How long will you be staying?" she asks Anthony, once she's finished tallying up the total.

"About three weeks," he tells her. "Maybe a month. We'll see."

Mads gathers most of the bags himself, leaving Ben with the boxes of beer. The two men shuffle out of the shop, calling for Sofia, who apparently has gotten distracted by the bulletin board in the back. As they exit, I can hear her talking excitedly about fresh lobster. I know I should leave with them, but I don't move. I'm curious to see how Mrs. O and Anthony end their conversation. I get the sense that there's more to their relationship than just the casual acquaintance of storekeeper and customer. Maybe I am *in tune*, like Mrs. O said. My mother, I think, would be proud.

"You're in luck," the old woman is telling Anthony, handing him the receipt. "We've got our Sammy back. He'll be happy to get things set up over there at the Mission."

"I heard he'd moved back last year," Anthony says. He looks bored, as though he's going through the motions of a polite conversation. But I don't know if I believe it. I almost think he's rehearsed these lines, though I can't imagine why. "It must be nice to have him around, now that Paul's—" He lets the sentence hang, waiting for Mrs. O to pick it up.

"You know," she says instead, "I can't remember when you two last saw each other."

Anthony flashes his teeth in a smile. "Fifteen years," he says. "Almost to the day." Then he picks up the last bag of groceries, unceremoniously grabs a pack of gum from the display, and adds, "Well, it was good to see you."

I follow him to the front, but I stop to wave goodbye, as though I'm apologizing for who knows what. "It's nice to meet you," I call to her.

"You, too, dearie," she says, but she's already picked up the phone. I wonder who she's calling. Sammy, I figure. But I don't stop to find out. The bell chimes as the door slams shut, and I'm back outside in the bleak mist. I descend the rusted, vibrating stairs, then head toward the van, toward Sofia's muffled laughter, wondering why Anthony wanted me to meet that strange old woman. I know I'm going to have to get used to being whoever Anthony wants me to be, and maybe this was nothing more than a trial run. I can't help but think, though, that Anthony had an ulterior motive, and that Mrs. O's son, Sammy, Anthony's child-hood friend, had something to do with this. And for whatever reason, I feel a little used.

8

Wrestling the steering wheel of the van as we zigzag down a muddy road to the water, Anthony tells us that we'll be taking something he calls "the garbage scow" to the island. "There're too many of us," he says, by way of explanation. But I don't see any boats at all—garbage scow or otherwise—as we approach the haphazard web of docks jutting from the steely bay.

After parking the van behind a mossy boulder, Anthony points us vaguely toward one of the piers, adding that we should focus on unloading our suitcases and groceries first before "the men" come back for the cameras and sound equipment. Sofia and I share a look. She rolls her eyes, but neither one of us speaks up. Still, my fingers quickly lose all sensation as I trudge across the wet gravel lot behind the group with my bag in one hand and a plastic sack in the other, and by the time we reach the crumbling pier, I'm glad I stifled my objection. If Anthony wants to be a martyr, let him.

Despite how winded I am, I keep my breathing shallow. The air is heavy with salt and what smells like rotting flesh. "Pigskin," Anthony tells me, reading my disgusted look correctly. "They use it for bait." As the group skirts the side of a small white building, I stop to catch my breath and examine an old sign pasted to the center of a flimsy door bolted with a padlock. I'm staring down the barrel of a cartoon gun. Underneath it, the sign asserts, NOTHING IN HERE IS WORTH YOUR LIFE. I have to read it twice to understand that it's not telling me there's nothing of value in here, but that if I break in to find out what it does conceal, I'll die trying.

"There you are!" Anthony is beside me again, his cheeks ruddy from the cold. He has taken off his sweater and is now in a thin shirt, like me, but he isn't shivering. "Once it gets dark," he tells me, "the crossing becomes more of a guessing game, if you know what I mean. We'd better keep moving." But he stops to dig for something in a duffel bag anyway, and finally hands me a jacket.

"You're my hero," I tell him, and I mean it. I'm practically swooning with gratitude.

Wrapped in a big yellow jacket that smells like mildew and cologne, I follow Anthony down the gravel slope to the garbage scow. I stand with Sofia at the base of the pier, water already seeping into my shoes, waiting for "the men" to get us ready for the crossing. At the end of a treacherous gangplank, the garbage scow is much smaller than I'd expected. Bouncing back and forth against the wooden pier, tossed by almost invisible waves, it's about the length of a car. Every inch of its white plastic hull is streaked with crud, inside and out, and it hits me that it really is used to cart trash off the island. Ben steps off the gangplank and positions himself in the middle of the boat, rocking easily with the current as he accepts and arranges the seemingly infinite supply of groceries and suitcases and crates from Mads. It's awkward between Sofia and me. Neither one of us seems to know what to say. We're probably just tired, I guess. After all, it's been a long day. But I can't help but feel as if there's some tension between us. Maybe she resents me for being the star—supposedly, at least. Or maybe she's picking up on how I'm the outsider here. She just wants to relax and have a fun vacation with her friends. She doesn't want to have to hold my hand the whole way through.

As though hearing my thoughts, Sofia nudges me with her shoulder and complains about the cold. I breathe a silent sigh of relief. I'm just overthinking this. *Ugh.* Why do I have to be so insecure?

We don't help with the bags. I just watch, shivering in my borrowed jacket, as the day lurches into night. As though from a great distance, I hear Anthony tell the group that the island is a short ride that way, but he's pointing directly into the blanket of mist. It's going to swallow us up, like an airplane climbing into thick clouds. Once we're inside it, no one will be able to see us. No one will know we're there. And we'll lose sight of the rest of the world, too. *I know it's late and the boat is already loaded,* I want to say, *but can you please drive me back to the train station? I changed my mind. I don't want to do this. I don't want to step on that boat and go farther past the point of no return. Please just let me go home.*

Sofia, though, suddenly disengages from me and skips down the pier, then teeters across the gangplank into the scow, where she huddles against Ben for warmth. A few seconds later, I follow her. Mads holds out his hands to guide me into the boat, and Anthony unties the knots that secure us to the rest of the world. I have no choice. I'm committed. And if Sofia can do it, I can do it. I take Mads's hand, grateful for the help. As soon as my foot touches the deck, though, I slip. Mads's grip tightens. "Whoa, girl," he says, like I'm an unruly horse fighting the bit. "Steady?"

"You're a real landlubber, aren't you?" Anthony says, hopping in behind me with the rope still in hand. He's donned his own coat, an elegant green thing whose material I can't identify. It looks like alligator skin, but soft, and the mist is already beading up on it. He steps behind a small wood partition erected in the center of the boat, and starts the motor.

"I suppose so," I say, wobbling again, clutching Mads's arm for balance. This is my first time in anything smaller than a ferry, but I don't offer this out loud. No reason to point out yet another thing that differentiates me from this group.

"Take a seat," Anthony instructs, indicating a spot on a bench in front of him, and I obey, thankful for the instruction. Cold seeps into the backs of my thighs through the fabric of my jeans as soon as I sit down, and I can't stop shivering. The air feels liquid. Salt fills my lungs. Mads joins me, wrapping an arm around my shoulders, and I resist the urge to shake him off. He's just doing his job, I remind myself. He's my boyfriend now. That's what this is, right? Part of the film. In any case, he's warm.

With a deft twist of the wheel, Anthony steers the boat gently away from the dock, straight into the wall of fog. Surprisingly, I don't get seasick. And once we're inside the mist, we're able to see more than I'd expected. The engine is loud and the choppy water slaps the hull. We don't move quickly, and I have no idea how Anthony knows which direction to take us after we lose sight of the dock behind us, but in only a few short minutes, land comes into view. The spruce trees that loom out of the eerie mist seem to be bigger than the island itself, and even from a distance they cast us in their shadow. As we approach them, over the growl of the engine, I can hear the wind whistling through their branches. It's a soft, natural sound, but there's still something ominous about it. I can sense how dense this forest is, which has planted itself and taken over this tiny, rocky island.

"See those three lights?" Anthony says, his voice muffled by the drone of the trees. "That's the Mission. I guess Sammy must have powered up the generator."

"Will he live here full-time?" I ask.

Anthony doesn't reply. At least, not immediately. When we get closer and the trees have loomed up in front of us like a wall and the island seems to have grown into a much larger, wilder place than it had looked to be from a distance, he shuts off the engine and lets us drift perfectly into place by a small pier that I hadn't noticed. "Sammy lives back on the mainland," he tells me finally, as the boat noses into place, "with Mrs. O."

He tosses what looks like a lasso over the nearest pole, then tugs us snugly against the pier. Darkness is starting to descend. And I get the feeling that once it does out here, it's going to be thick. The white fog surrounding us has turned purple. By the time we've unloaded the boat, it will be black. Mads and Ben begin tossing our bags onto the pier. Anthony wraps an arm around my shoulder to help guide me off the boat, and I'm grateful to feel something solid under my feet again. He calls for Sofia, and gathers her, too, to lead us both up the path to the cabin.

There's a main house, Anthony tells us, and a guest cottage. As the house begins to take shape, I don't yet see the cottage, only the triangular peak and square edges of what appears to be a large Victorian. Finally, the lights burning inside begin to lift the structure from the gloom. It reminds me of the summer homes at Lake Tahoe—old creaking buildings that smell like shaved wood and fish bait—though from what I can see, this place has been restored somewhere along the way, and upgraded into something way beyond a cabin in the process. As we approach, I can sneak peeks inside, of its warm, cozy interior. I'm surprised by how elegant the home is, though I'm not sure why I'd expected otherwise. Maybe it's because we're so far out in the middle of nowhere. When we stop walking, silence replaces our footsteps, so heavy it reads like a hum.

Sofia lets out an appreciative sigh. "It's gorgeous," she says, breaking the spell.

"Make yourself at home," Anthony tells us, sweeping the door open. Sofia pushes past me, eager to get out of the darkness, I think. Anthony turns back to me, as though to usher me inside as well, but I've already taken a seat on a padded bench on the porch. I think I need a minute alone, after such a long day being cooped up with everyone. Without a word, he disappears inside. The two of them flick on every single lamp until the house is lit like a beacon in the darkness, and as they do, I can hear the crescendo of the generator hidden somewhere in the darkness, as the electricity strains its motor. I hope it's a well-maintained machine.

When Anthony returns, he's carrying a glass of amber liquid for me. "Cheers," he says, before jogging back down to help Mads and Ben.

The alcohol burns my throat, and I can feel it travel all the way through my body until it rests, alone, in my stomach. I have to stop myself from downing the entire glass. Not because I want to get drunk. That thought actually terrifies me. I just want the alcohol's embrace.

Comforted by the low tones of conversation as the men trudge up the path, I settle back onto the bench and close my eyes. Off the boat, I'm not so cold anymore. I take a breath. Maybe this won't be so bad. Another deep breath. Another sip of my drink. And then something grazes my cheek. It feels like a fingertip. But when I open my eyes, I see it's an insect. I follow it to the ceiling of the porch, and find a cluster of the same bugs gathering around the lamp. I can't identify them. I've never seen this type of creature before. They're enormous, about the size and shape of a chocolate truffle, with big circular wings that turn bright red in the light. They don't fly so much as hover, noisily, buoyed by whatever air currents they can find.

In no time at all, the bags are all piled inside, the groceries put away. The men dip into whatever drink Anthony gave me before, and I force myself to stand up from the warmth I've created for myself in the bench's cotton cushions and follow them inside.

Anthony leads us through the main house. The foyer opens directly into an enormous living room. There's a well-worn L-shaped couch in the center of the room facing a smaller love seat and a fireplace. Anthony gestures to the wet bar in the back, telling us that this was his father's priority. "Cigars and whisky," Anthony says. "For a man like my father, the kitchen is an after-thought." At his command, we peek our heads into the kitchen itself, a tiny rustic space that contains just enough room for a stovetop, a sink, and a fridge.

Anthony beckons for us to follow him through the living room, into a narrow hallway that leads down creaky floors to two bedrooms. There's only one bathroom, he tells us. "There are two doors, though," he says. "One to the hallway and one to the master bedroom. So be sure to knock."

"What about our sleeping arrangements?" Ben asks, not both-ering to stifle a jaw-splitting yawn. "I'm beat."

Anthony points down the hall. "I'm in the master bedroom—that door there, on the left. The second bedroom, on the right, will be my office. For Ben and Sofìa"—with a shallow bow, like he's prepared this gesture, he yanks at a cord hanging from the hallway's ceiling, and a ladder unfolds, seemingly out of no-where, revealing a hole in the paneling—"there's the attic." As if on cue, Mads and Ben crowd up the ladder to take a look.

"Dude," Ben huffs at Mads. "Chill, would you?"

"You tell him, babe," Sofìa says, rolling her eyes at us.

Mads peeks his head through the trapdoor, then gracefully leaps off the ladder. "That's gotta be the best room in the house," he says.

Curious, I follow Sofìa up the ladder. The attic is small, with only a bed in the center, but it has the feeling of a garret, and the windows are enormous. In the daytime, I can imagine there would be an unobstructed view of the water down the path we followed from the dock. The walls are lined with shelves, filled with books whose spines are cracked from reading.

"Mads is right," I tell Sofia. "You lucked out." What I don't mention are the unmade covers on the mattress, or the conspicuous lack of cobwebs, and the smell of sleep. Or the paper plate under the bed, smeared with the residue of a half-eaten meal, not yet altogether dry. It's obvious enough that someone has been living here.

But as it turns out, my discretion is unnecessary. By the time I'm descending the ladder, Ben is already complaining. "Whoever stayed up there last, they didn't fucking change the sheets, man."

"Fresh sheets are down there," Anthony tells him. "Next to the kitchen." If he's nettled by Ben's fussiness, his voice doesn't betray him. Ben pushes past me, like he's been insulted, and Anthony calls out behind him, "I've seen the sheets you sleep on at home, Ben." When Sofia gives him a soft punch, he adds, "Sorry."

Ben fires off a reply, opening and closing cabinets, looking for fresh linen. "At home it's my own spit on the pillowcase."

I figure the spit in question belongs to Sammy. No doubt that's who Mrs. O called, as soon as we left the store, to give him a heads-up. From the look—and smell—of things up in the attic, I'm betting he barely made it out of here before we docked, and I find myself wondering how he transports himself back and forth to the island. I didn't hear another engine on the water. Anthony brushes past me, startling me from my thoughts. He paces down the hallway to peer into his room.

"So what about me?" I ask, aware of how loudly sound carries in this place. Or maybe it's the alcohol amplifying my voice. "And Mads," I add, doing the math against my will.

Anthony pivots toward me slowly. Mads has wandered back down the hallway to the living room, and for the moment we're alone here, just the two of us, gazing at each other after a day spent in everyone's company. He doesn't answer. But he doesn't have to, does he? There aren't any more rooms here in this house. That's obvious enough. There's nowhere else left for us but the guest cottage. Outside, nestled in the forest, in the dark.

"What could be more natural," he asks me, finally, "than sharing a little hideaway with your new lover?"

I'm not sure if he actually expects a response from me. Maybe the question is rhetorical. But I don't give him one. I just turn and walk away, closing myself into the bathroom. I don't know why, but my eyes are suddenly full of hot tears. Too late, I see that Anthony was reaching for me. It would hardly have made any difference anyway. To stop and let him hug me, I mean, if that's what he'd intended. Right now that would probably only make things worse.

9

In the bathroom, I splash my face with water, then gaze for a moment at my reflection in the mirror.

Anthony is waiting for me, to show Mads and me to the cottage, but I have to collect myself first. He's right, after all. This is what I've signed up for. And I should be grateful that I'm not out there in some little cottage by myself. It's so dark outside now, the windows are black. Like slivers of obsidian. I can't see a thing, even with my hands cupped against the glass. The light that streams through the windows doesn't seem to make it more than a few feet. Except for the sound of waves, and the howl of the wind, anchoring us here, this house could be floating in space. I don't have a good sense yet of how large this island is, though it seems clear enough we're alone out here. I feel helpless. Stranded. But I have to get a grip on myself. The last thing I want to do is alienate myself any more than I already have.

My stomach rumbles. I wonder if we're going to sit down for a meal soon. I haven't eaten anything since leaving New York. It's been a long day, and at this point, I'm so tired, I don't think I'm actually feeling physical hunger. I just know that my body requires something—sleep or food. And it doesn't seem like we're going to bed anytime soon. Out in the living room, I can hear the telltale clink of glasses, and Ben's voice keeps rising above the others as he holds forth about the amount of whisky he consumed the last time all of them were together. I take one last look at myself, trying to rid my eyes of the residue of panic I can see in my stare, then dry my face and push through the door to join them. I'm not going to score any points hiding.

Anthony intercepts me before I can make it more than two steps down the hallway. His expression is solicitous, and I assume he wants to apologize before showing me the cottage. I'm about to cut him off and reassure him I'm okay, I'm overreacting, that's all, when he grabs both my hands and holds me still, like he wants my full attention. He's got something else in mind.

"I know you probably want to join the others," he says, keeping his voice low. He glances down the length of the dark hallway to the glow of the light emanating from the living room. The sounds that echo down to us are inviting. Ben is laughing. Sofia is trying to remember the lyrics from one of the songs on Anthony's playlist. Mads is calling himself "the Firestarter," and I can hear the *thunk* of logs being piled onto an iron grate. There's something comforting about the clamor of a party. I do want to be a part of it. "Do you mind, though," Anthony asks me, "if we do something else first? Just the two of us."

When I don't object, he pulls me by my hand and leads me

back into the bathroom. The burst of light from the overhead bulb stings my eyes.

"Stay here," he tells me, closing the door on me. I can hear his footsteps retreat back down the hall.

The bathroom is small, from another era. Quaint, like the kitchen. A counter covered in periwinkle blue tiles runs along the far wall, stretching from door to door. There are a couple of windows facing out the front drive, one cracked open. I can taste our isolation in the earthy, icy breeze that trickles inside, and I shut the window with a decisive bang. The floor is yellowing linoleum, with at least three shaggy bath mats covering the walk from the bathtub to the counter to the toilet. I avoid the mirror this time and just twist around, examining the floor, wondering what Anthony has in mind.

A few seconds later, I hear footsteps again. Then Anthony toes the door open with a socked foot. He places a bag on the counter and drags a chair into the center of the room, then, shutting the door again, instructs me to sit while he prepares the bleach. We're going to dye my hair now. Not tomorrow. Right now. I feel myself deflate even more, like a shriveling balloon. He warned me, I guess. But this feels like a premeditated assault.

I'm just barely hanging on, I want to tell him. *Can't this wait until tomorrow, when I feel more settled?* But that's the point, I guess. He wants me out of my shell. That's what he said earlier, right? I have to break out of the confines of what Betty would do. He's taking *me* away from me. I don't know what's better. To try to resist, or to let him.

Whatever Anthony has in mind for my hair, it's a much more

involved process than I would have thought, with powders and bowls and brushes and intimidating bottles of shampoo. He mixes some sort of powder with water, fills a spray bottle with peroxide, then sets everything out neatly along the counter. Like he's done this before. He doesn't even have to read the instructions on the boxes. This whole pantomime happens in silence, with the solemnity of a performance on a stage. All the while, my stomach clenches and rumbles, half from hunger, the rest nerves. I force myself to stay still, watching his hands as he organizes everything, not quite believing yet that he'll actually put this concoction on my hair. No big deal, I tell myself. I can always dye my hair another color if I don't like this one. My heart leaps into my throat, though, when he reaches into his pocket for a pair of scissors and a comb. It's not an accident that my hair is below my shoulders. I wear it up most of the time, but I can hide behind it if I need to, and I suppose I often do. Hadn't Anthony hired *me* for this part? Since I was a little girl, this hair has always been me.

Sensing my unease, Anthony hesitates. He turns to face me, grabs my shoulders, and fixes me with a stare. "Lola has short hair," he tells me. "She's not a kid. She doesn't cling to the vestiges of her childhood. Remember what I said to you? She's who you want her to be."

Who I want her to be, or who you do? I wonder. But there's no point in resisting him, so I don't speak. I left home. I left Mom. I got in that van. I got in that boat. I'm here. I'm committed to this. I'm Lola now, not Betty. I can take this leap, too.

A shiver runs up my spine. Not just out of fear. Anticipation. I find that underneath my immediate knee-jerk horror at the thought of chopping off all my hair there's another sensation. Another emotion, uncoiling in my stomach, spreading through my chest, my heart. It's the same feeling I had when I boarded that flight out of California. Excitement. *Cut it off. Leave it all behind.*

The fumes from the chemicals gelling on the counter begin to sting my eyes. The smell is caustic. The room fills with the stink. Like someone has tried to strip off a residue of overripened fruit from the counter with a commercial detergent. But I don't mind. *Cut it off. Leave Betty behind.*

"Before we start," Anthony says, "where's your phone?"

I indicate my purse on the floor, without fully understanding why he wants to know. When he asks me to get it for him—"Give it to me," he says bluntly—I finally find my voice, tasting the bleach in the air on my tongue. "What do you want it for?" I'm not able to hide my distrust.

"No big deal," he responds with a shrug. "I'm taking all our phones and stowing them in a drawer. I don't want anything that will distract us from the film. And there's no service out here anyway."

While I consider this, he arranges the scissors and comb on the counter next to the mixture of chemicals. I pull my phone out of my bag, as though holding it will help me make up my mind. It's my lifeline to the outside world. But as Anthony indicated, it isn't picking up a signal. Will it be so terrible to give this up? For $40,000, I can relinquish my phone for a few weeks. Before I can finish my internal deliberation, though, a hand covers mine, and Anthony makes the decision for me. Just like that, my phone is gone. He slides my mom and my whole universe into his pocket.

"You're in this now," he says. "It's time to become Lola, officially."

"Doesn't Lola have a mother?" I ask, but my attempt at humor falls on deaf ears.

He plucks one last object from the bag of hair products: the same camera he used for my audition. "Every minute you stay here is a choice you're making," he tells me. He switches on the camera. "You want to get rid of that jacket." It isn't a question, but another command.

I hadn't even realized I was still wearing the old jacket he'd given me back before we boarded the scow, which feels like ages ago now. I let it slide from my shoulders. Goose bumps immediately climb my arms, but I try to ignore them as I toss the jacket to the floor, on top of my purse. I sit up straight and run both hands through my hair, looking Anthony in the eye as he snaps a couple of pictures. I can do this.

His voice echoes off the tiles when he says, "Now your shirt."

I suck in a breath, but catch myself before I blurt out something sharp, like *Do I have to?* I hold his gaze, but can't for more than a moment, so instead I locate myself in the mirror behind him. My eyes are rimmed red from the bleach fumes. I know there is going to be nudity in this film—he said so—but this is too fast. And it's too intimate. This feels personal, like a violation. There's no camera rolling, no Lola yet, no matter what he says. This body belongs to me, and it isn't for sale. Or is it? Maybe I've already sold it. Maybe that's why this hurts so much. My fingers toy with the edges of my shirt.

He says, louder, "Take off your shirt, Lola."

I close my eyes. What bothers me most is how certain he is. He knows I'm going to give him what he wants. I already know I'm going to say yes, but how is he so convinced? I know there is no going back for me. I have nothing except this film. Everything else is gone. My father killed himself. My condescending mother is waiting on the sidelines for me to fail. I have no money. No real friends. Not even Sofia.

I open my eyes and consider Anthony. He's leaning against the counter, waiting for me to undress. And I almost laugh. He knows I'm going to do it, because this is who I am now. I'm the woman—the *girl*—who runs away from home, with no money, no job, no plans. To him, I must seem reckless. What was it Ben said? I'm just his type. *Tall, thin, lost.*

And I guess I am reckless. Because I'm not nervous anymore. Who cares if he takes my phone? Who cares if he bleaches my hair? Who cares if he changes my name? These are just details, labels. A few strands of hair, a couple of syllables. *Every minute you stay here is a choice*, Anthony said. And it's true.

Chop it off.

Leave Betty behind.

I will become Lola, whoever that may be. I started this journey back in the tiny airport back home. This is only the next step. Even now I have no idea where I'm going, no idea where this path is leading me. No idea where I'll end up.

Nevertheless, it still takes a few beats for me to master myself enough to take off my shirt. It's a boxy white shirt I brought with me to New York from Humboldt. A red turtle swims across the front. I bought it at a gas station the first time I got high. My boyfriend at the time had held the shirt up against my torso and said it was my spirit animal. "It's a turtle," he said seriously, "but a red one." It's my favorite shirt. I close my eyes, and it comes off easily over my head. Anthony takes it from me and folds it onto the counter. It feels like my stomach is floating, somewhere in my chest. Like it can't decide whether it wants to leap into my throat or push through my ribs.

My bra is new, from New York. I had gone with Sofia to a store in SoHo that was covered in glitter. It's a bralette made out of tight pink silk. When I tried it on in the dressing room, Sofia told me life was unfair. "My bras perform a function," she said, lifting a tan bra with large cups. "They strap my boobs to my chest. I can't even imagine what it would be like to buy one like that." I wonder what she would say if she could see me now. Maybe she wouldn't feel the same envy.

My breathing is unsteady. In the mirror, I can see my heart beat in my ribs. I see Anthony see it, too. A prickle of awareness rakes down my spine. His breathing has become just as heavy as mine.

I want to reach for him, but I hold back. Maybe we're getting closer to the truth of why I'm here. Maybe that's what this is really about.

Even so, his next command stuns me: "And the bra."

My fingers shake as I obey, and I can't tell for certain if it's only my fingers or my whole body. I fold the bralette carefully on top of my shirt on the counter. I ache, knowing how far away he is from me. I can't stop an invitation from etching itself into my trembling smile. *Touch me,* I think, tracing his hands with my gaze. *Don't make me sit here alone.*

The camera is in front of his eyes now, between us. The shutter answers my unspoken request. It freezes me in place, eternally removed from my clothes. Then he chuckles. The sound stabs me like so many daggers. "Good," he says, settling the camera across from me on the counter. I stare into its mechanical eye, stunned. "Let's get started." He drapes a towel across my shoulders, pulling it into place. "I knew I was right about you," he says, giving my hair a tug.

I'm about to ask what he means, when he starts hacking away at my hair with the scissors, and then I can barely move, except to watch him through the mirror. In the end, he elaborates, without my having to ask. "This isn't an easy decision for you," he says, cutting a chunk from the side. "Your emotions are right there on your face. The thing is, though, you give the camera what it really wants." The cuttings cascade down my front, sending another shiver through me. In no time at all, he's finished. My hair isn't short, necessarily, but it isn't long. The ends barely reach my jaw, tickling my earlobes. And then he starts applying the burning chemicals to my scalp, methodically explaining in that same slippery voice every step of what he's doing to me. In the sunshine, my hair looked like flowing beer, Tucker had told me. Or honey, as my father had said. I loved my hair.

This is like a dream, one where I have discovered how to fly. The secret is to stop caring. If you get scared, you'll fall from the sky. If you just let go of yourself, everything is possible.

Let go, Betty. Let go.

10

After what feels like hours with his fingers in my hair, Anthony tells me he'll grant me privacy to shower off the tint. It seems like an odd concession, because there isn't much he hasn't seen at this point. And anyway, he's already rinsed my hair so many times that the shower is superfluous, at least for my hair. But that means, I think, we're done. Before I can stand, though, Anthony stops me with a hand on my shoulder.

"Thank you," he says. His gaze drops to my mouth, lingering for a second too long, as though he's memorizing the shape of my lips. I'm not imagining this. I can feel his interest in me. It's acute. I know he's struggling with it, just like I am. He chose me for this part for a reason. But before he allows his impulse to translate into anything irrevocable, he slips out of the room, shutting the door behind him with a quiet click.

I take my time washing up, scrubbing the smell of bleach from my skin. I could itch and scratch my scalp until it bled, and I just barely resist the temptation. Likewise the rest of my body, which feels contaminated by something I can't see. Then, in the shower, without quite knowing when or how it occurs, something happens, even before I see my image in the mirror. When I emerge from the water, I move like Lola. Slower. Languid. Betty's hair was drawn like threads from molten beeswax. Lola's isn't made of anything at all. It's moonlight, and when I finally do see my new reflection, it gives me a small jolt.

The bones around my eyes are sharper, more delicate, against the backdrop of the platinum hair and darker eyebrows. I'm exhausted—I know that—and hungry and woozy from the fumes. But I can't look away from myself. It's like I'm examining a separate being.

My reflection returns my smile. This is what I wanted, isn't it? Freedom. I guess I just didn't expect it to happen so quickly.

When I exit the bathroom, I'm greeted by the gruff cacophony of male laughter, punctuated by clinking glasses, drowning out the steady crackle of a fire. Mads is the first one to notice me as I enter the living room from the dark corridor, and he raises his arms to grab me, but then stops to gawk at me. The gesture is so clumsy that he spills his drink. He's already drunk, I realize. Ben, too, who also fixes me with a surprised stare. Sofia, meanwhile—who never seems to get drunk, no matter how much she drinks—raises her eyebrows histrionically, like she's only miming her shock. She simply can't stand the idea that anything could happen without her being in on it, especially if it involves me. I ignore them, all of them, stepping gingerly around boxes and overflowing bags, making my way to the enormous couch in the center of the room.

"Betty," Mads exclaims, reaching to take hold of my wrist. "What happened to you?"

I stop at his touch. In the bathroom, with Anthony, I had almost entirely forgotten he was here. My fake boyfriend. Are we supposed to keep pretending even now? Without Anthony present, without the camera rolling? And—I feel a pulse of shame at the thought—why is he even here at all? Why am I playing his girlfriend, and not Anthony's? I gently pull my wrist out of his grip and run a hand through my hair. "Don't you like it?" I ask him.

Ben hovers, a bit unsteadily, behind the bar. "You look like Sailor Moon," he announces. "Babe, don't you think she looks like Sailor Moon?" Finally, a reference I get. I even dressed like her a couple of Halloweens in a row. I'm about to correct him that her hair is long, like Betty's, but Sofia beats me to it.

"She has long hair," Sofia says with a laugh. "And it's *yellow*. Not platinum." To me, she says, "I think he's trying to say it looks good." Shaking her head, she crosses the room, mentioning something about finally getting to pee and shower.

Ben looks momentarily lost. Then he shrugs. "I still think it works." He gestures to a bottle of Johnnie Walker. "Can I get you something to drink, Ms. Moon?" He pours the whisky up to the top of the glass. I guess he can see I need it.

"If everyone's having one," I agree, "I won't say no."

Ben slides the glass toward me, then refills his own. As we tap our tumblers in a silent cheer, Anthony enters through the back door, his elegant New York City clothes dusted with dirt. He takes me in first with a wide smile, then turns his attention to Ben. "I need help with the woodpile. Sammy must have nailed the tarp to the ground."

Ben takes a big gulp, then reluctantly sets his glass down and follows Anthony outside. I join Mads on the couch, not too close, and sip at my drink. It blazes down my throat and roils my empty stomach. I know I should be careful. I'm a lightweight. But it feels too good. I close my eyes and listen to the distant clatter outside. I wonder why Anthony needs more wood. There's already a fire going. Aren't we ever going to eat or sleep? Mads interrupts my thoughts with a pat on my thigh, his hand lingering longer than I want it to. He has sidled up next to me, and he's leaning in so close, I can smell the whisky on his breath. But there's concern in his expression, where I'd been afraid I'd find something else.

"Are you okay?" I ask, though I think I might be echoing the question he was about to ask me. I take another sip and feel as though I'm breathing fire.

He lifts a shoulder. Drops it.

"How did you meet Anthony, anyway?" I want to hear Mads Byrne's version of Anthony Marino. There isn't much information to dig up online. There's a lot of speculation—that Anthony and Mads are in love and the movie was a coming-out story, or they're actually brothers, or Mads was a homeless runaway Anthony found. Everyone has a different theory. Mads is notoriously tight-lipped on social media. *I love the guy* is about all he has to say on his relationship with Anthony Marino. Some fans use this party line as evidence of something more than a typical bromance. But watching them together, it's clear that, as complex as their relationship is, there's nothing physical about it.

Mads deflects with a question of his own. "How do *you* know Anthony?"

I tell him about Sofia. How kind she and Ben have been, taking me in and then introducing me. As I tell the story, I find myself marveling at how fast it all happened. "We just got dinner," I say. "And now here I am."

He doesn't look too surprised. "He does that," he says.

"Does what?"

"He finds you." He winces as he swallows another mouthful of whisky. "I moved to New York after high school to become an actor. You know the story. I became a waiter. Shared a tiny apartment with too many people. That whole thing." He grins to himself. "This fucked-up modeling gig led to a part in a show on Off-Broadway. Make that Off-Off-Broadway. I had to eat an eyeball onstage. Well, it wasn't a real eyeball. It was a quail egg, wrapped in fruit leather, but it was still pretty gross. Anthony, he was one of the few people in the world who saw the play. Next thing I knew, I was in *Reverence*."

Not too different from the homeless-runaway theory. My drink sloshes, so I guess I must be sitting up. "So you were in *Reverence*?" I ask, remembering how little I'm supposed to know. Mads nods and reaches for my hand again, this time as though to steady me, so I figure I must be getting drunk now, too, and I tell myself to slow down. I take hold of his fingers and squeeze, as though that'll help sober me up, or maybe it's just a way to keep him off me. "I never saw it," I say. I realize I'm probably overplaying this. But my story has to be consistent, and I might as well get as much out of him as I can. "What was it like to act with him?" I ask. "I've heard he can be pretty intense."

Mads sizes me up. He seems to find whatever he's looking for, because he leans in close, like he's telling me a secret. "At first," he says, "I thought it was more of the same shit I was doing before. You know, violent, off-kilter stuff. Amateur hour. But as soon as we got started, I understood it. What Anthony was doing. Who he is."

"What was he doing?"

"This might sound improbable to you, because most people aren't like this. But I think he needs a camera to function. Until he sees himself on film, he doesn't know he's real."

I feel something deep within me give way. That's exactly what I had felt, watching his movie, though I hadn't yet been able to put it into words. That's exactly what it's about. Finding out who he really is. Not the person everyone else expects him to be, but the person he can see when he takes a step away from himself. Maybe that's what makes Anthony so unique. I can sense just how elemental film is to him. His camera is part of his psyche. I wish I had pressed Anthony a little harder about *Reverence*—or just admitted that I had watched it—so I could have told him that that's what I'm doing here, too. Letting myself go, on film, to find out who I am. But maybe Anthony already knows this. It must be written across my face, as he says. "So how did you fit in?" I ask Mads, aware of the silence growing between us. "I mean, what was your role?"

Mads looks uncomfortable. He cranes his head, to check that we're still alone. The muffled spray of the shower can't quite hide Sofia's soft, mumbled singing. Anthony and Ben seem to have disappeared on their quest to get firewood. "It's hard to describe," he says, settling back down next to me. "It was sort of Dr. Jekyll and Mr. Hyde. *Fight Club.* You know. I played Anthony's second half. And I mean that literally. For a while, whatever he did, I did the same thing, right next to him. It took a lot of choreography. Then I started to, you know, move on my own, separate from him."

"Why?" I ask dutifully. "What happened?"

"He lost control of me," Mads says. He bounces his knees up and down, like even now he's excited by the memory. "It happened slowly, in stages. I started out as part of him, then became my own person. Eventually, when it became clear that this was what I had to do, I killed him." He reflects for a moment, then adds, "In the end, though, I never knew which part of Anthony was finally victorious, the good part or the bad part."

My next words slip out before I can stop myself. "I don't know what this movie is about. At all. No one will tell me anything." I squeeze Mads's hand again, then let him go with a gentle shove. "That's a bit strange, don't you think?" Guilt washes over me, because it sounds like I don't trust Anthony. I do trust him. Don't I?

"I'm sure Anthony has a good reason for that," Mads says, parroting what Ben had also told me. "He knows what he's doing." He polishes off his drink, then pushes himself up, and stumbles back to the wet bar for a refill. "I owe him big," he says, twisting the giant bottle open. "Everything. If it weren't for *Reverence*, I doubt I would have made it into Yale. I got my scholarship because of him. And even though people always think I could have afforded it anyway, because that's the show I put on, I couldn't. My folks don't have that kind of money."

"Mads," I start, but he interrupts me before I can get the question out. Something like *Do you really think you owe him for that performance?* Mads gave so much of himself to that film. Anthony's the one who owes him, not the other way around. Though what I really want to ask is *Why is Anthony hiding things from me?*

"My real name is Madison," Mads blurts out, like he's ready to change the subject. He collapses on the couch beside me, balancing a precariously full drink. He watches me for a reaction, his eyes wide and trusting. When I don't say anything in response—I'm not sure what he expects from me, my approval? my understanding?—his face falls. "If you and I are going to be a couple," he says, fidgeting with his drink, "I think we ought to break the ice a little. Don't you think? So there's some real intimacy here, so we don't have to pretend."

"That sounds good," I say, relieved. In his own way, he's trying to help me. He's giving me something solid to hold on to.

"I'm embarrassed by my name," Mads says. It seems like he has to force himself to look directly at me. "It's really silly, I know. But I was a small kid with a pip-squeak voice and a girl's name and older brothers who treated me like a punching bag. They made fun of my name so much, I hated it." He hesitates. "Anthony was the one who suggested I call myself Mads."

I slouch into the sofa next to him, now closer than I want to be, and we sit there in silence, each of us contemplating our own tragic circumstances. I swallow a generous mouthful of whisky and listen to him repeat, "I owe him everything," as though this is the first time he's realized his debt. "You know what I mean? He's like my brother. Not like my actual brothers. He's what a brother is supposed to be."

I wonder if I should tell him a secret now, too. Maybe I already did before, when I told him I didn't know anything about the movie, but maybe I should tell him something more personal. That I come from a poor, dysfunctional family, too. That I'm even more lost than he is. But he doesn't seem to need anything from me. He settles deeper into his cushions, consumed by his own thoughts.

Part of me wants to laugh, just a little, at Mads's confession. At the idea that his name is such an embarrassment, that his older brothers teasing him for it is his secret pain. Or maybe at how much he seems to believe he's indebted to Anthony, for "saving" him. But that's not really funny, is it? It's not even unique. Anthony is Ben's personal savior, too. I think I've even heard Ben describe him using those exact words.

It hits me, slowly, as I contemplate how unquestionably loyal Ben and Mads are to Anthony, that I can't really judge them. After all, who am I to laugh? I've known him only a few days, but that's who Anthony is to me now. My own personal savior. The epiphany sinks in with a twinge of something I mistake for pain, but that I think is fear. I hardly know him. But already I'd be devastated if he let me go.

11

I'm awoken some time later by an insistent shake of my shoulder. For a moment, I think I'm back in Ben and Sofia's apartment. But the hand gripping my arm doesn't belong to Ben. It's bigger. The fingers dig into my flesh, rattling me like a doll. I raise my eyes. "Hey, Sleeping Beauty," Anthony says. "Wanted to make sure you were still alive."

"She's Sailor Moon," Ben calls from across the room. "Not Sleeping Beauty. Get it right, man."

I hear Sofia tell them they're both wrong, I'm Alice in Wonderland, but none of this really registers. I'm too disoriented. I must have passed out in front of Mads—I can't remember anything else beyond his proclamation of love for Anthony—and what's worse is he let me. I push myself upright on the sofa and the room spins. I must look like a mess. I'm grateful when Anthony sits down next to me, one long arm draped over the cushion above my head. I lean into the inviting space underneath and let him run a hand through my cropped hair. When I look up at him, his expression is serious, but other than that, I can't read it.

"You need to eat something," he tells me. "You're looking green. Ben's made some pasta, if you think you've got the stomach for it."

"What time is it?" I ask. "Isn't anyone else tired?" But no one answers me.

I wait patiently for pasta that doesn't come. Anthony pinches one of my cheeks, smiles, looking almost like he's going to kiss me. I don't blame him when he turns away instead, to talk to Mads about something I can't bring myself to listen to. I think I'm still drunk, not to mention a little hungover already, too. I cross my arms over my chest and try to warm myself up. Despite the heat emanating from the fireplace, I'm shivering. I should have put on Anthony's jacket. I must have left it on the bathroom floor, and that feels miles away.

Summoning my energy, I shove myself off the couch with a lurch and shuffle into the kitchen. I fix myself a plate of spaghetti with way too much Bolognese, battling the feeling that I missed out on something while I slept. It's not like this group doesn't already have a leg up on me. They've known one another for years. I really do need to force myself to interact with them. Standing at the counter, I shovel the food into my mouth and gulp down as much water as my stomach will hold. By the time I wander back into the living room, as heavy as Ben's cooking is, at least I'm feeling somewhat better.

I wait for an opening in the conversation. They look like they're bird-watching and the room is full of birds. Ben points at a corner of the ceiling and the others swivel their heads and say, "Yes, definitely," and then he'll gesture to the mantel above the fireplace and the whole process begins again. "You mind clueing me in on what everyone's doing?" I ask Anthony, after Ben leads Sofia and Mads down the narrow hallway, mumbling something about "angles."

Anthony's first impulse is to smile at me, indulgently, as though it should be obvious, to anyone except a child, that is. But then his expression softens a little, as he looks at me more closely. I flinch a little, because I realize, in the same instant, that he feels sorry for me, and that's about the last thing I want. "Ben's just showing them where we've positioned the cameras," he tells me finally, then turns away from me to point at one himself, above the fireplace. It sits on the mantel next to a few porcelain figurines, and honestly, I don't think I would have ever noticed it if Anthony hadn't directed me to it. "They're all over the house now," he says.

"You don't think this is something I should know about, too?" I ask.

"I don't want you playing to the camera," he says.

"What about Mads? And Sofia? You're not worried they're going to play to the camera?"

He offers me a helpless smile, as though he doesn't know what's bothering me.

"So it's just me?" I take a step toward the sofa, then stop myself. "I'm serious, Anthony. Why are you singling me out?"

Because everyone else here knows what they're doing. Anthony's unspoken reply writes itself in the furrow of his brow, but he doesn't defend himself. Instead, he says, "You're tired, Betty. I think I better get you to bed."

For an instant, my resentment—my insecurity, I guess—bubbles up inside me. Why is he always so condescending? I get a hold on it, though, and take a deep breath. After all, he's right. I am tired. And I am the only one here who has no idea what she's doing. "At least tell me this," I say. "Are they on already?"

He offers me yet another shrug. "For the last hour."

"So you're recording this? I'm on tape now?"

"We're live."

"So this is part of it? *This* is the movie?"

Anthony considers me for a moment, then takes a few steps to close the distance between us, and wraps me in his arms. "You're tired, Betty," he repeats. "Let's get you to bed."

"Shouldn't it be Lola now?"

He grasps my shoulders and leans away from me, far enough to fix me with a stare that seems to pierce through me, all the way down into the hidden depths of what I would probably call my soul. "If you're ready."

I don't answer him. Because I know he's asking me a question, and I know I'm not sure yet.

He reads this on my face, too. Like everything else. Then, giving my shoulders a gentle squeeze, he lets go of me and directs his voice down the hall, toward the back of the house. "Mads?" he calls. "Mads! Get out here, would you? It's time to take"—he hesitates—"your girlfriend," he decides. "It's time to take your girlfriend to bed."

||||||||||||||||||||

Shouldering my overnight bag, Anthony leads Mads and me to the back door. I follow in his wake, turning to Mads with an apologetic shrug. "I didn't realize we had to go together," I tell him.

"No problem," he assures me. His eyes are glazed, and I realize he's tired, too. "It's been a long day."

I call out a quick good night to Ben and Sofia. Sofia's voice is singsong, high-pitched, and full of laughter as she shouts, "Sweet dreams, lovebirds."

As soon as we cross the threshold, my nausea recedes beneath the onslaught of fresh night air, though it's quickly replaced by a sense of dread. That feeling you get when you know something bad is about to happen, but you don't know what and you don't know why. It's cold out here. And dark. And quiet. Leaving the house is like stepping into a void. In the distance, I can just barely make out the rhythmic sounds of the water lapping the shore. I take a tentative step in front of Anthony, and it feels like I'm coming untethered, slipping out of orbit into the emptiness of space. Then, thankfully, with the abruptness of an explosion, the tiny pinpricks of light in the bushes—fireflies, I think—are overwhelmed by a sudden flare, and the pathway to the cottage is illuminated by a series of lamps tucked cleverly behind landscaping stones.

"I'll show you how to turn these on from your cottage," Anthony tells us, joining me on the path. "Or you can leave them on all night if you want, in case you have to come into the main house. We have floodlights, too, but I've kept most of them off so you won't be woken up every time a deer or raccoon wanders past."

"Cool, man," Mads says. His voice seems to be muffled by the weight of the stillness out here.

We follow the winding path through the trees until it feels like we've stepped into another universe entirely, one that has no sound other than our own footsteps, no light but the ones guiding our steps. I don't want to get to the cottage anymore. I would rather just keep walking, down this tunnel carved by the landscape lighting into the black, outside of time. Once we get to the cottage, I will have to share a bed with Mads. He's Mads Byrne, sure, but he's still a total stranger. He's been nice enough, and Sofía seems to love him, but I don't know him. Maybe—hopefully—there will be a couch one of us can sleep on. We're supposed to maintain the ruse of being a couple, but do we have to do this at night, in the privacy of our own room? I had a hard time sleeping next to Tuck, and he was my actual boyfriend. How can I possibly relax around this hulking foreign man?

Soon, though, I can make out a building. The structure, from what I can see, is a small square with a peaked roof, nestled into the vegetation. It's difficult to tell in the dark, but the tiny shack looks almost like a utility shed, older than the main house, or at least not as well maintained. There's a single large window punched out of the wall beside the front door. Anthony pauses at the door to fish around in his pocket for the key, scraping it once or twice against the lock before finding the slot. "This was the original cabin on the island," he tells us. The door gives way with a silent *whoosh* of air. He gestures for me to step inside first. Mads follows, then Anthony.

When Anthony shuts the door behind us, the pathway lights keep the space lit, and I realize the windows aren't covered with curtains. Maybe my concern is written on my face, like all my other emotions, because as he lowers my things to the floor, he says, "Don't worry. There's no need for drapes. It's dark enough to sleep without them. Even in the morning, because of the trees. You'll see when you wake up. The forest is pretty thick on this island. It's practically swallowing us up. I don't know if you noticed on the way out here, the canopy covers the path so tight, you don't even see stars."

I can't suppress a shiver. I'm freezing. There's no sign of a heater in here. But that's not what's giving me this chill, is it? *No stars.* I'm supposed to sleep all the way out here in this small wooden box, in the middle of a forest so thick it's eating us whole, with Mads Byrne in my bed. I feel like I'm underwater, looking up, trying to see through the murk to judge the distance to the surface. I can't help but think of Iceland, where at night the entire universe was visible in the sky like a wash of paint. "There are other reasons for curtains," I say, "than keeping the light out."

"Relax," Anthony says. "You guys are far enough away from the house. No one will see you."

"Is that supposed to make me feel better?" I ask with a nervous laugh.

There's no answer. Instead, there's a click, and we're all bathed in light. The dark windows become mirrors. The cottage is composed of a clean, spare bedroom, nothing more, reminiscent of Ben's attic, and a bathroom. A dresser has been built into the wall separating the room from the bathroom, but there's no nightstand, no unnecessary furniture. No couch. Only a bed and a lamp. There is a large window on each wall. No privacy, except the bathroom, I'd guess. I poke my head into the bathroom, which is equally simple. Another large window there, too, facing out the back. No curtains.

Mads drops his bag by the dresser, kicks his shoes off, and wanders around the cottage, taking in the same details. He gives the bed a rough shake, testing the mattress. "Do you like to sleep on the right," he asks me, "or the left?"

"Whichever," I say, trying to match the casualness of his voice. He seems so unconcerned. But I guess he's had more time to get used to this idea. Anthony touches my shoulder, not like he wants my attention, more like he's keeping me away from him. I hadn't realized how close he was to me. He's slouching against a wall. In this position, we're almost the same height. He isn't the one who moved toward me. I must have gravitated back toward him, without thinking. I turn away, too quickly, and the room races to catch up to my eyesight. I didn't drink that much, did I? But I have never been good at drinking. That's how Tucker used to put it, like it was a fundamental skill I was lacking, like folding sheets or dancing.

I redirect myself to the bed instead. Mads has chosen the right, so I aim for the left, and sit down, wondering whether Anthony is going to wait forever out here, watching us. "I'm tired," I say, lamely.

"Same," Mads says, flashing Anthony a pointed look.

"Well," Anthony says, pushing himself from the door, "here's the key, just in case." He tosses it onto the bed, and I pocket it. If there's only one, I want it. "Sleep well, you two." Still, though, he doesn't leave. "We'll go over the project tomorrow morning," he tells us, "when we're all a little more rested—and sober. Okay?"

Then, finally, when neither of us answers, with a yank on the door, he steps outside. As soon as the door is cracked, the sound of the waves and the trees floods into the small cabin. I didn't realize how quiet it had become in here. Or how much unfamiliar noise emanates from the forest. It's like a living, breathing creature.

The door shuts with a soft thud. I drag myself to it, automatically locking it, though I'm immediately uncertain whether I should. Mads steps past me with a polite *"Excuse me,"* reaching into his bag and pulling out his toiletries. "I'm going to wash up," he tells me. Then, as though he's wrestling with the same thoughts, "This is a private island. You don't have to lock the door. It's just us out here."

"Old habit," I say, embarrassed. Nevertheless, I don't unlock the door. I don't know why. I really don't. I just get the feeling something might be lurking out there. Something menacing.

Shrugging, Mads closes himself into the bathroom. I take a deep, steadying breath, and walk back toward the bed. My steps feel wooden. I don't feel connected to my body. What am I doing here? And then, just as I'm reaching the bed, someone taps at the window above the bed. I throw a hand to my mouth, and freeze in place, my heart pounding an irregular, horrified rhythm in my chest.

I lean toward the window, slowly, steeling myself for the sight of Anthony's face against the glass, at the same time wondering how he could have circled the cabin so quickly. *He wouldn't.* And why would he come to this window, and not the door? But I can't see anything. And then the tapping restarts, erratically, like fingers flickering over a keyboard, and I pinpoint the source of the sound.

It isn't Anthony trying to scare me. It's a flurry of moths pounding themselves relentlessly against the glass, trying to get through to the light.

I release a shaky breath and turn away. I think I'm too tired to clean up in the bathroom like Mads. Too tired even to undress. Dirty linens give you pimples, Mom had told me. But I don't have the energy, and I think I'll lose my nerve if I spend any time preparing myself. Instead, I slide beneath the icy sheets and stiffen my body, waiting for some semblance of warmth to return to my limbs. I clench my eyes shut and wait for my earlier exhaustion to sweep over me.

But it doesn't come. It's too cold, too quiet. I can hear the buzz of Mads's electric toothbrush, and it seems to be counting down the seconds until he reappears. I can hear my own breathing, so loud it sounds like I'm panting. I try to slow down—I don't want Mads to hear me—but I can't stop. Without warning, I feel my throat close over a burst of sobs. I wish I could talk to Dad. I wish I could hear his voice. I had never had trouble sleeping until I left home to live with Tucker. And then, whenever I couldn't sleep, I would sneak into the other room, lie down on the too-small couch, and call my father. He always had the same reaction. *Oh, sweetheart. Can you try to sleep?* And somehow, with those words, my anxiety would lift, and I'd have to speak through yawns. It was like he was giving me permission to let myself go. I would wake the next day, sprawled on the couch, and I'd lie to Tuck, tell him that his snoring had kept me awake.

The sink runs, and I hear Mads gargling. I reach for the light switch and return the room to darkness, before he emerges, so he can't see the tears on my cheeks. I wipe my eyes and curl up into a ball, under the sheets.

After another long moment, the bathroom door opens, letting in a sudden, dazzling wedge of light. "Whoa," Mads says, confronted by the dark room. He turns off the bathroom light and stumbles toward the bed. In a whisper, he asks me, "Are you asleep?"

"Not yet," I whisper back.

He trips over something—probably my purse—and lets out a quiet curse. Finally, he's here. The mattress dips under his weight. The blanket is pulled gently away from me to accommodate his bulky body as he slips under the sheets. Luckily the bed is just large enough so that we're not touching. But I can feel the heat emanating from him. I can hear, all too well, the soft wheeze of his breathing.

He shifts in place, searching for a comfortable position, accidentally kicking my leg. "Sorry," he says. Then, in the silence that follows, he clears his throat. "Don't worry," he tells me. "We'll leave a lot of room for the Holy Spirit."

"What?" My voice barely belongs to me.

"You know," he says, patting the space between us, "the Holy Spirit. I went to Catholic school. At our dances, the nuns would force us to keep at least a foot between our bodies when we were slow dancing. *Leave room for the Holy Spirit* is what they'd say."

No one wanted to slow dance with me in middle school, I think. I was too tall. Mark Jennings told me it was like dancing with his mother. Mark Jennings. I bring the image of a freckled face to mind, teeth laced with braces.

"I'll bet he regrets saying it now," Mads says. At first I think he has read my mind somehow. But then I realize I've spoken out loud after all. I must be falling asleep. Why else would I have said anything?

The mattress wobbles with another shift in Mads's position, and I flinch away, automatically. But I've overreacted, once again. He's only stretching himself out, onto his back. His breathing slows.

"Good night," he says, the last word disappearing in a yawn.

In another minute, I can feel him drift off into sleep, and I'm grateful. It would be terrible to lie here in silence, knowing he was also awake. Or if he didn't want to sleep at all. If he tried to break the ice even more.

I turn away from him and try to get comfortable without jostling him. Maybe I will dream about my father. Since I can't call him. Tonight, I'll have to conjure him. I can still remember his voice. Can't I? I know what he would have told me. *Sleep, Betty. Let go of the day and sleep.* Tonight, that will have to be enough.

I'm nearly there. I'm nearly all the way gone, when something occurs to me. It begins like a small, nearly imperceptible tickle in the back of my mind, before it finally blossoms into words. *Are there cameras set up out here, too?*

And I open my eyes.

12

As much as I resist, I wake with the sunrise. Peach-colored light filters through the cabin, transforming it into a kaleidoscope of shadows and pastels. I must not have moved much during the night, because sleep creases snake up my left arm and coalesce in a tangle on my cheek. They read like a lizard's skin on my fingertips. I check the time on the alarm clock on the floor beside the bed: six a.m.

I squeeze my eyes shut, hoping my sour stomach will settle. I could burrow under the blankets and try to sleep, but I force myself to sit up. I do it carefully, trying not to disturb Mads. This is an opportunity to explore the Mission, on my own, in daylight. Maybe everything will seem less frightening with the sun shining. It's always like this—everything is scarier at night. And I would also like to get out of here before Mads wakes up. Somehow, the light in here doesn't seem to bother him. He's sprawled on his back, an arm thrown over his head, mouth drooping open, chest rising and falling in deep, regular breaths. His old, beat-up jersey has ridden up to his chest, exposing the contours of his stomach, and his sweatpants are twisted uncomfortably around his waist, but at least he's wearing something. I hadn't been able to tell last night. As harmless as it felt to fall asleep together, I don't know if I can handle the intimacy of the morning after. There's something so vulnerable, and yet so comforting, about waking up next to someone. Even though he's a stranger, I can already feel myself warming to him. And while I know that's a good thing for the movie, for our fake relationship, I can't help but resist this. It's too sudden.

And I have to admit, if only to myself, Mads isn't the man I want to wake up next to.

By the time I emerge from the cottage, shutting the door quietly behind me, it's nearly seven. I don't think I did much more than stand in the shower, swaying under the hot water, and dress, clumsily, into another, somewhat cleaner pair of pants and a shirt, but somehow I lost an hour. Last night's chill is already burning away. It's going to be a hot day. I can feel it. I pull on my shoes and step across the pebbles and twigs lining the path to the main house, trying not to wake anyone else with my clatter.

I follow the trail all the way around the house, to the front porch, trying to get a sense of this new place, which will be my home—my whole world—for the next month. Creeping up to one of the living room windows, I peer in to check for signs of life. The coffee table is littered with glasses and a toppled bottle of Johnnie Walker. But the room is dark and empty. From this angle, I can see part of the way down the hallway, far enough to confirm that

Ben and Sofia's ladder is still tucked into the ceiling. Letting go of the sill, I wander around the perimeter of the house, to the windows of Anthony's room. He didn't close his curtains. I'm tempted to spy on him, though I'm not sure why. It feels like stumbling on a dollar lying on the sidewalk and not picking it up. An opportunity lost. But I resist, if for no other reason than I hope no one peeps through my window, either.

I'm turning back around when I'm surprised by a throaty laugh. The sound is distant, carried on the back of an early-morning breeze, but still, it startles me. The voice doesn't belong to any one of us, and I can't imagine where it's coming from. My skin prickles. I thought we were supposed to be alone on this island. I listen for it again, but hear a louder noise. A splash, followed by what sounds like a shout. I pick my way down the short drive to the water's edge. It seemed a long distance last night, but the house practically sits on the beach.

Even before I begin to investigate, I throw a look over my shoulder behind me, suddenly nervous that I'm being watched. I don't know why I should feel guilty. I'm not doing anything wrong. I can't escape the sense, though, that Anthony wouldn't approve, and as if in echo to this apprehension, I feel Anthony's fingers running through my hair again, then possessively gripping my neck. The fear of disobeying him is already ingrained in me, almost enough to make me retreat to the house and wait dutifully for the others to wake up. *Almost.*

The strange noises lead me farther away from the Mission. I step over flat boulders, and dip into the woods, along what looks like a footpath worn into the mossy forest floor, skirting the shore as it curls closer to the mainland. A long, low gust of wind rolls through the treetops like a wave, setting off a musical roar of swaying branches and falling leaves, and I stop, closing my eyes to listen. These are the sounds I remember from last night, from the depths of my sleep. I thought I was hearing the roar of the surf pounding the rocks, but I realize now it was the forest, breathing.

As dense and foreign as these wilds are, they remind me of home somehow. Of my walks with Dad. Toward the end—when he began to need me, I guess, as much as I needed him—he would race home early from work to pick me up so the two of us could wander through the hills out by the water, following the craggy outline of the coast. We didn't talk much. We were quiet, lost in our own thoughts, listening to the faraway crashes of the waves against the cliffs, smiling when we caught each other's eye. We wouldn't walk for very long, but by the end of it, both of our faces would be blazing with color, our eyes bright. When we returned, Mom would be ready to eat, exasperated by how late we were for dinner. I never thought about this before, not until this very minute, but I wonder if it hurt her, that neither Dad nor I ever invited her to join us.

I wait for the pain to come. I slow my steps to prepare for the sudden cold spike of dread that pierces through me every time I think of my father. But something is different today. Maybe I'm too far away from him now. Instead, there's a hollow emptiness, deep in my chest. Another kind of pain. I'm not mourning Dad. I'm longing for Mom. I'm remembering her fluster when we'd return from our walk. The kiss she'd plant on my father's cheek, not to greet him, but to keep him off her. The way she would intone, "I don't know what the two of you have to talk about." Not realizing how nice it was for both of us not to have to talk at all. Because we understood each other without words. The way she never would.

Homesickness washes over me as I walk. But I try to leave it behind. I can't look back. I'm here now. The problem is, I do miss my mom. As much as I want to prove my independence, she could wrap this little illicit foray to this island up into a safe bundle, too, the same way her disapproval somehow managed to sanctify my adventures with Dad. Her judgment has become my validation. The way a priest's reproof also contains the seeds of penance.

This place isn't home, anyway. These trees are not our trees. This landscape, so beautiful on first glance, gets bleaker the longer I stare at it. It reminds me of a forest in a fairy tale. Maybe because of the way the branches are intertwined, like arms and fingers. And the way they sway, creaking like old doors, at the slightest breeze. As Anthony had told me that first night at dinner—which now feels like another lifetime—being out in the wilderness here had made him believe in vampires. With a chill, I wonder if it's because of the darkness that seems to emanate from the mulchy soil. Despite the heat of the sun, I can still feel winter here. The trees are flinching in the sunlight, as though they don't trust its warmth. Or maybe they just don't want it.

The voices and sounds I've been tracking get suddenly closer, and I wonder if I'm going to bump into someone around the next bend. The path I'm following veers sharply to the water, and a few steps later, I'm out of the brush, on a long, rocky promontory that juts toward the mainland. Across the steely water, I can see a sprawling yellow mansion. The house is far away, but close enough for me to make out columns lining a porch. It's out of place here, a manor like something out of a New Orleans travel brochure. The sounds must be coming from there, echoing and amplifying as they travel across the placid water. Even though I'm curious to make sense of the conversation I've been chasing—a man's voice insisting, *I'm not going*—I'm careful not to step beyond the tree line. I don't want to betray my presence. If I lean out a foot farther, I might reveal myself. If I can see paint peeling from the eaves of this house, there's no doubt they could see me, exposed on the rocks.

The garden surrounding the mansion is lush and wild, but cultivated, planted with rosebushes and thick hedges. From here, it looks as perfectly manicured as a dollhouse, despite the telltale signs of rot and decay. The property is grand, but it's old, and it's probably impossible to maintain. I edge a few steps closer, and more of the house and the driveway are revealed just as a door opens and a short, stout woman appears. She's a patchwork of plaid and khaki. It takes a couple of beats, but I realize with a small surprise that it's Mrs. O. She's waving a hand above her head as she shouts a goodbye at someone inside, but she keeps her head down as she marches toward a beat-up Toyota parked askew beside a decrepit detached garage.

A few seconds later, almost before the front door swings shut behind her, someone else bursts through it in a light jog. My first impression of the man is of a blur. Not that he's moving so fast. In fact, I can see him clearly from here. There's just something fluid about him. Liquid. Like a snake. It's hard to fasten him down until he stops, when he seems to materialize out of the air. He's not wearing a shirt, and his torso is knotted and muscular. Maybe he used to be an athlete, this man. But I get the impression that his physique has been hardened by labor. Despite how easily he moves, there's something worn and rigid about him.

"Mama, Mama, Mama," he says, his voice skipping like a stone across the water. "Don't be like that."

This must be her son. Sammy. Who else could it be?

It doesn't feel right, spying on these two, any more than peeping through Anthony's window. But I can't bring myself to look away. I wonder what's happened between the two of them. They're obviously upset. Mrs. O had been running away from the house. And Sammy isn't just trying to placate her. He's both supplicant and forceful, in equal measures. Mrs. O, hands on her hips, head bowed so far forward her chin must be on her chest, refuses to turn around.

When Sammy catches up to her, she raises her head. "These visits," she says, her voice carrying across the water with a metallic clang, "are not for us. They're for your father."

"Us?" Sammy retorts. He's caught up to her now, and I can read his hesitation as he reaches a hand toward her shoulder. He wants to yank her around to face him, but he decides not to. He won't even touch her. He's not much taller than she is, though it takes me a moment to appreciate this, because he seems to hulk over her, as if she's half his size. Nevertheless, he's scared of her. "What are you talking about, *us*?" He sounds frustrated, maybe as much with himself as with his mother, as though he resents this intimidation he feels and it's bubbling up inside him. "Since when was there any *us*? Where was he when I got sick? Where was he when Archie Miller pounded my skull every day on my way home from school? Every day, Mama—"

"He was working his fingers to the bone," Mrs. O says. "That's where he was. Paul was working his ass off to put food on our table."

"He hit me."

Mrs. O hasn't been moving. But these words somehow seem to stop her cold. Her hands gather into fists. She takes a deep breath.

Behind her, Sammy takes a half step backward, as though he's recoiling. But he insists anyway, "He hit *me*."

Now Mrs. O does finally wheel around. Not quickly. And not in anger, at least not uncontrolled. If she's seething with anything, it's more like hatred. "You don't know what you're saying, Sammy," she says, surprisingly calmly.

Sammy takes another small step backward, apparently involuntarily. "Don't," he says, and I find myself wondering exactly what this sinewy, powerful man believes this tiny woman will do to him.

"You tell me something," Mrs. O says, stopping to take another deep breath. "When was the last time you visited him?"

"I was living in another state," Sammy says helplessly.

"How long, Samuel?"

He retreats another step.

"How many years since you've seen your father?" she barks at him.

"Mama" is all I can hear. Then, carried on the wind, "Fifteen."

"He's cooped up there," she says. A chill runs up my spine, so cold I wrap my arms reflexively around myself. Maybe I should have already made this connection, but she's talking about a prison. She must be. "Like an animal," she's saying. "An animal in a cage. The least you could do—"

"That's what he is," Sammy says, but without conviction, as if he simply can't resist blurting this out.

"He's your *father*," she insists.

Sammy nods his head, a few times too many, but otherwise remains silent.

Mrs. O seems to realize how defeated her son is. "If you're not coming with me," she says finally, "you take yourself back inside and put some clothes on. You've got chores to do, and the Marinos are in residence now on the island. You should be over there now, seeing to their needs. We need them, now more than ever." Without waiting for an acknowledgment, she turns back around and lets herself into the car. Sammy taps on the window as if he wants to say more. The window slides open, but the whine of the engine drowns out whatever he says next. I catch her response, though, a tired *I'll be home tonight*, and then, *You take care of the Marinos*, before she pulls out of the driveway.

Sammy watches the car roll away, remaining motionless until it disappears. Alone now, he cracks his neck and twists his torso back and forth, reminding me of a boxer preparing for another round. The early-morning sun shines on the top of his skull—his hair has been buzzed close enough to the scalp for it to not even matter—glinting a little as he walks back to the house. Or not walking. *Prowling* would be a better word. Already, I get the sense he's forgotten his collapse in front of his mother. He's feeling good again. Like the master of his small, dilapidated domain.

As though sensing my presence, right before he reaches the stairs at the end of the path, he sends a sudden, sharp look my way. I can barely stop myself from jumping. I'm hidden in the trees. There's no way he can see me, I tell myself, my heart pounding in my ears. But still, he seems to be staring right at me.

As he strides along the side of the house, bypassing the porch for another path to the back garden, my breathing returns to normal. He's looking past me—maybe at the Mission—not at me. Nevertheless, I remain frozen in place, waiting for him to disappear. When I hear a door slam, I can't repress a shiver. It feels as if he's caught me out somehow. My knees are weak. I have trouble walking, like I can't find my balance. It's not just the coarseness of the conversation I've overheard that's affecting me—it's something else. As I make my way back to the house, I can't help but feel that this man has been the one to spy on me, not the other way around.

I follow the distant rumble of men's voices back to the Mission. As far as I can tell, from little glimpses through the leaves, Anthony and Ben have woken up now and are occupied with something in the garden. I catch sight of Anthony's lean form as he strides alongside the house, a hand gesturing in the direction of the forest.

"There you are," Mads calls out behind me as I cross the back lawn. He steps out of the cottage, his hair flattened to his forehead with sleep. "Anthony wants to talk to you." The light glinting off the window next to him is so bright, it stings, especially in contrast with the shade from the encroaching woods. Mads squints, trying to bring me into focus. "You feeling okay?"

"Don't I look okay?" The words come out with more of a snap than I'd intended.

He shrugs. "We drank a lot, is all."

So he isn't worrying about my state of mind. He's just wondering if I'm hungover, too. He fidgets with his hair, trying to primp the limp locks hanging over his forehead. He looks a bit more like the heartthrob I met yesterday, but still, there's something different about him. And it isn't just how puffy and dazed he is this morning, compared to the carefully coiffed, stylish heartthrob who descended from the train. It's something I can't put my finger on. Maybe he's settling in more, becoming more familiar. Or maybe the difference is something that's occurred in me. Maybe I'm not as smitten with him as I thought, when he first seemed to walk off the screen and climb into the van.

"I could have slept all day," I offer, feeling guilty. "If we actually had curtains. Did the sun wake you up, too?"

"No," Mads says, mournfully, "Anthony did." He throws a hand in the direction of the house. "You'd better grab him. He was looking for you."

Inside the kitchen, Anthony and Ben are conferring by the back door. Anthony has climbed a small ladder, while Ben hands him a small round object from a heavy case. Another camera, I presume.

Mads trails me across the lawn, then gives my shoulder a squeeze. "How about some coffee, dear?"

I send Anthony a quick wave, which he barely acknowledges, then return my attention to Mads. "Are you asking me if I want some, or if I'll make some?"

Mads lets out a dramatic sigh. "Women," he says, sliding past Anthony and Ben to fiddle with the coffeemaker. "I guess I'll make enough for you, too, then," he mutters.

I stop at the base of the ladder, beside Ben, and watch Anthony as he lines up the camera to its anchor. "Mads says you want to talk to me?"

"Give me a second," Anthony says, without looking away from the camera. He's using a screwdriver to fasten it to the wall, just below the ceiling, and the angle makes it difficult to turn the screw.

Sleep still muffling his words, Ben asks me how my night was. I lift an arm to show him the creases from my sheets, but discover they've already faded. When I ask Ben how he slept, he perks up a bit. "Like the dead," he tells me. "Sofia's still asleep. Couldn't wake her."

Pleased with his work, Anthony hops down from the ladder and claps a hand on his friend's back. "You okay to keep going without me for a bit?" he asks Ben. "You should get a move on the outside. I want to capture the lawn and the main paths."

"The guest cottage, too?" Ben asks, inadvertently answering my question from last night.

"Interior and exterior," Anthony tells him.

"Sure, boss," Ben says, eyeing the rest of the box. He pulls out a folded piece of paper from his pocket, unfurling it to show a rough, yet surprisingly detailed, diagram of the main house and the grounds. "I'll have to see how many of these are rated for outdoor use."

"You're covering the whole place," I say, stunned. I had known this wasn't going to be a traditional shoot, but I can't believe how elaborate this plan is. I can't help but notice a couple of dots in the bathroom. Are they filming there, too? Is that even legal?

"Once this is done," Ben tells me, refolding the paper and

shoving it into his pocket, "there's no need to follow anyone around with a camera. The biggest challenge will be sound."

"Will we wear microphones?" I ask. I'm thinking about those necklaces the actors wear on reality TV shows, and the small, lumpy packs strapped to their backs.

"Not if I can help it," Ben tells me, with an obvious note of pride. "It depends on the fidelity I can crank out of these mics. It's like recording a live concert. A good sound mixer can amplify the music without—"

Before he can say anything more, though, Anthony takes me by the elbow and leads me down the hallway. "We'll be in my office," he tells Ben, guiding me into the second bedroom. "If you need me."

This is the first time I've been inside this room, and it doesn't come as a surprise how tidy it is. The sheets on the spare bed have been tucked into hospital corners, and the surplus boxes and bags of clothing from the van have been arranged in neat stacks. My focus, though, is drawn to three large computer screens set up on the desk like a command center. The screens are dark, but it's clear enough that once everything is up and running, Anthony will be able to monitor the entire property from here.

"It's time to talk about the project, I know," Anthony tells me, crossing the room. He ferrets out a bulging black paper sack from one of the stacks. I recognize the brand. I wandered into their store once, in the West Village, daydreaming, took one look at the price tags, mumbled something to the incredibly cool woman wandering toward me, and practically ran out of there. "But first," he says, "Sofia told me you barely brought anything to New York. Is that right?" He doesn't wait for my answer. He already knows. He saw my bag. I'm wearing the same shirt I wore when we first met. "The weather here can be unpredictable. You need some real clothes."

I close my mouth. Swallow. "Any chance I can keep all this stuff afterward?" I ask.

He bristles a little at the question, which I find strange. At dinner, I had gotten the impression he wanted to demonstrate how wealthy he is. That a pricey dinner and $40,000 are nothing to him. But I guess I'm not playing my part correctly. I'm supposed to be grateful, not entitled.

He tosses me the bag, and when I catch it, it's surprisingly light. I take a peek inside and discover only T-shirts. I have enough of those already. I thought he was going to give me sweaters. Something warm. I know the days can get hot, but the nights are cold, practically freezing. What's the point of having me dress in a skimpy outfit? I pull out one of the gauzy short-sleeve shirts from the bag. What is it that he wants me to do? Who does he want this Lola to be?

"I didn't have a lot of time to browse," he tells me. He hands me a pair of shorts, which aren't going to leave much to anyone's imagination. "But it doesn't matter much. The look I had in mind for Lola was simple. Elemental."

"And revealing," I say, holding up a shirt that is so light in my hands, it seems to float in the air. In another bag, I spot a pair of jean shorts. Daisy Dukes. With my newly platinum locks, I'm going to be unrecognizable. These aren't clothes I would have chosen for myself, not even as a teen, and I'm wondering why Anthony has—and how comfortable I'm going to feel wearing them. "Anthony," I say, clearing my throat. I want to sound assertive, but my voice is tentative. "I don't know what you expect from me. At all."

"We'll talk about all that in a minute," he says. "Get yourself changed first. You can use the bathroom if you're feeling shy."

I flash him a look. I want it to be a sophisticated, knowing one, but my hands are shaking. "What's the point?" I ask him, glancing at the screens on his desk. "You'll be sitting in here watching the whole thing anyway, right?" Before he can do anything more than blink, I grab the bottom of my old shirt and yank it over my head.

||||||||||||||||

Goose bumps prick my exposed arms and legs. Anthony swears that it will warm up today—"Believe me," he tells me, "you're going to bake in this sun"—but inside his office, the air is chilly, and I can't suppress a shiver. The mattress beneath me might as well be a slab of ice. Anthony swivels in his desk chair to face me, his chin resting on his hand. He eyes me critically, and suddenly it feels like I'm back in school again, and I've failed yet another math test, and my strict, exhausted teacher doesn't know how to explain the simple logic of geometry to me in a way I'll understand. All he needs is a pair of crooked glasses, and he could be Mr. Kowalski.

When there's a tap at the door, I'm grateful for the interruption. Mads's disembodied voice announces that there's fresh coffee in the kitchen, if we want any.

"In a minute," Anthony calls out, just as I'm opening my mouth to say, *Thank God.* I'm not as hungover as Mads, but this is going to be another long day. I can feel it. I will need whatever help I can get. Anthony wheels the chair toward me, close enough to take one of my hands in both of his. Clearing his throat, he asks me, "How well do you remember *Cape Fear?*"

"We only watched it three days ago," I say. "Right?"

"Remember Robert Mitchum? The criminal?" He waits for me to show him that yes, I do remember. Then: "Like I said before, we aren't remaking the movie. But it is our inspiration. A sort of framework for what we're doing here. Something for you to hold on to. If you take the basic story idea—man terrorizes family— that's essentially what we're going for. Does this make sense?"

"Not really," I say, automatically. But it finally registers, what he's saying. "Wait—man terrorizes family? Who's terrorizing us?"

Anthony takes a deep breath. "There's a sixth person in this film," he tells me. And then he waits, as though I'm going to immediately figure it out.

"Who?" I ask, though I already know what he's going to say next. It should have been obvious to me, after I'd spied on him this morning.

"Sammy," Anthony says, echoing the voice in my head. "Mrs. O's son."

"Does Sammy know about this?" Again, the answer is obvious.

Anthony tightens his grip around my fingers, as though he's suddenly afraid I'm about to slip away and he's going to lose me. Then, with a shake of his head, he says, "I told you. This is going to be real." Raising his voice, as though I'm about to start objecting, when in reality all I can do is stare at him, he tells me, "Trust me, Betty. Okay?" This, I realize, has become a refrain for him. I start to resist, and he reassures me, not with answers but with the simple appeal for me to ignore my gut and trust him. "There's a narrative I'm going for. But it's got to be natural. Once we co-opt him and push a few of his buttons, Sammy will propel the story forward. You'll see. He's a"—he searches for the right words—"force of nature. I know him. You put him in a certain situation, he'll react in a certain way. A compelling way. Understand?"

I pull my hand out of his. I want to tell him I understand. I *wish* I could understand. But I don't. I have no idea what's going on here. "Isn't this unethical?" I ask. "Illegal?" I don't really care about these concerns, not really. They're easier to voice, though, than my real question. I've caught a glimpse of Sammy, and something tells me he's not going to like this. No one would like this. No matter what Anthony's plans are, this will be humiliating for him, once the movie comes out. At the very least, it's a violation of his privacy. Does he really deserve that?

And just what are Anthony's plans? What kind of situation are we putting him into, to make him react in a certain way? To terrorize us, like Anthony said. And why didn't he tell me this before? But I guess I already know the answer to that question. It wouldn't have mattered then, just as it doesn't matter now. I would still have said yes. I'm surprised, that's all. This feels malicious. Wrong.

As if reading my thoughts, Anthony tells me, his voice low, "I know how this sounds. But it's not that complicated, Betty. We aren't doing anything more than inviting him over here, then interacting with him. We have three weeks. More, if we need it. You have time to relax, get your bearings, find your rhythm. I'm here to steer the ship a little—but only a little. I'll let you know what I want as things unfold. But everything depends on the chemistry of the group. Understand?"

"I think so," I say.

"Sammy's coming over in about an hour anyway. Actually," Anthony says, with the barest hint of satisfaction in his voice, "he was the one who called me, just this morning. He has some things he wants to bring us. Supplies. So that'll be the first formal bit of the movie. Everyone meeting him. All I want is for you to talk to him. We'll see where we go from there. Are you comfortable with that?"

The room goes so silent. I think I can hear my own heartbeat. There's more he isn't telling me. I know there is. What is Anthony hoping will happen? This whole production can't be this flexible. This simple. *Cape Fear* was a thriller. What was it Anthony told me, back in his apartment? *I want to make a movie that scares people, in the way that movie scared me.* "He's the Robert Mitchum character," I say, but my words feel inadequate. More than that. I don't know what I'm asking, or how to ask it. "Terrorizing a group of friends. That's what you said. So how is he terrorizing us if he's *invited* over here?" Then, realization dawning: "I'm the daughter character. The helpless girl." I tug at my new T-shirt. "Dressed in tissue paper. What do you think he'll do? I'm not in any danger here, am I?"

Anthony shakes his head. He tries to lighten the mood. "Have you seen Mads? The guy is a tank." But it doesn't work. There's nothing funny about any of this. Not to me. I feel like bait. And

I've already caught a glimpse of the animal I'm supposed to catch. "Look," he says, both hands molding themselves around my knees, "you just have to trust me." I have to admit, I'm getting tired of these words. "All you're doing today is meeting the guy. Getting a sense for how the two of you talk to each other. How the rest of the movie goes depends on you." He gives his next words a little consideration. "You're overthinking this, I promise. You're in charge. You have control over how far this goes. I'm only here to give you a nudge now and then. Okay?"

I nod my head.

He releases my legs. "Go get some coffee," he tells me. "Take a shower. Go for a walk. Just be back here in about an hour. Sammy will come over soon. You'll hear his boat."

"Okay," I say.

"You still seem unsure," he says.

I shrug. He's right. I'm not convinced about any of this. But he's also right that I should be able to handle a simple conversation with Sammy. I push myself up from the bed, but he grabs my hands again and doesn't let me go.

"Say it so I believe you," he says, then adds, "Lola."

The name makes me flinch. But there's something liberating about it after all. Betty would never dress like this. I don't like to put myself on display. But maybe Lola would. Maybe Lola does. I smile at Anthony. That's it, though. I'm not going to bark whenever he tells me to. Who does he think he is? Who does he think I am?

He reads me, then finally lets go of my hands. "Okay," he says.

As I make my way to the door, I can't help but feel that I've been handled. That's how Dad used to put it, when he and Mom argued. *You're handling me,* he'd warn her. *Like I'm a goddamn child.*

I'm at the door when Anthony stops me, with a quiet "Oh, and, Lola?" He waits for me to turn around and face him, before he speaks. "Don't forget. You're here with Mads. Not with me."

14

I don't know where else to go while I wait for Sammy to arrive, except the cottage. Mads has left for a run around the island—though this probably means more of a hike, since the trails are pretty primitive, as I discovered myself this morning—so luckily I'll have some privacy. Even with some breakfast and coffee, my stomach feels hollow. And my nerves are on edge. In the quick glimpse I got of Sammy this morning, I saw just how rough he is. I'm not sure how I'll feel about him, face-to-face. Or how wise it is to try to incite him. His father's in prison, right? Anthony doesn't know about people like this. *I* don't, either. Anthony wants this to feel real. But this isn't a film we're shooting. We're recording a reality we have no ability to control. I'm afraid Sammy might give us more than Anthony anticipates.

I know it's not there, but once I'm inside, I kneel beside the bed, searching reflexively in my bag for my phone, compelled by a sudden urge to hear my mother's voice. It's such a sweet, familiar voice. Like she can only say fragrant words like "strawberries" and "heather." The desire sharpens into an ache. I want to hear that voice more than anything, even though she'll be furious I abandoned her in the city after she made such an effort to come find me. But as my hand claws the sandy bottom of the bag I begin to wonder what I'm doing. Do I think that I can will my phone to reappear?

I dig through my clothes one more time, searching in vain for an errant Kleenex to wipe the tears away before they streak down my cheeks. It catches me by surprise when I let out a small sob, remembering the look on my mother's face when I said goodbye to her in New York. She'd walked with me through SoHo as I dropped off the puppies, then had even ridden the subway with me out to Brooklyn. There hadn't been an argument, only disbelief. She'd told me she would call me the next day to arrange a lunch date. Outside Ben and Sofìa's apartment, I'd hugged her, and told her again that I loved her, but that I was going. I wouldn't be here for another lunch. She didn't respond. And I'm having a hard time recalling what she said as her goodbye. What I remember is how she had insisted on standing on that corner and seeing me safely inside the building before she left. As if to protect me. As if that would be enough. As if the things threatening me were right there on the sidewalk, and she could put her body in front of them. It's not Anthony, though, that I need protection from. Or his film. It's me.

I'm the one hurting myself. I'm the one making reckless decisions. Why can't I just stop? But it's not that simple. Leaving home was the best thing I could have done for myself, for my sanity. If I had stayed, who knows what would have happened? My relationship with Tucker had fractured the minute my father stopped breathing. Suddenly Tucker was just a stranger who either couldn't understand or couldn't handle the depth of my grief. And I hated him, immediately and irrevocably.

I run my thumb along the bumpy scar on my index finger. Following that pale white line, I skip down to my ring finger. My pinkie. The holes where the stitches thread themselves through my skin haven't quite healed yet. If I focus, I can discern each individual mark. This must be what Tucker's scar looks like, too.

I remember the look of horror on his face, the alarm etched into his forehead, when he'd seen the blood. He had been so understanding after Dad's death. You would have thought he was a therapist, not the assistant manager of a sporting goods store. He kept saying, "Take all the time you need." No matter what I screamed at him, he just said, "Take all the time you need."

I still don't know what I did. Not exactly. I remember him telling me that it was okay to be angry with my father—that's how he thought I felt, angry at my father—because suicide is a selfish act, and then I remember the satisfying explosion of glass against the wall. I remember Tucker saying, "My lamp!" I remember the blood on my hand, tracing crimson lines down my forearm, and the realization, even at the time, that I was grateful somehow for the pain. And then taking aim at his face with a swipe of my hand, and the sensation of my nails snagging on his cheek. After that, Tucker's benevolent concern seemed to dissolve into the ether, replaced by a much more comprehensible raw fury. As he drove us to the hospital, he kept muttering, *Fucking bitch.* It took him forty-eight hours before he finally said it again. "Take all the time you need." At that point, though, I got the feeling he was talking to himself.

No, I had needed to leave. Mom will watch this film and see who I am now. Maybe it will help her to finally understand me. But it's also going to devastate her when she sees how ineffectual she's been at keeping all the demons at bay. Still, maybe that's why I'm here. Maybe that's what I'm learning to do. All by myself.

When Mads returns from his run, he's a sweaty mess. His hair is laced with tiny leaves from the forest, and his calves are caked in mud. His Nikes, which were pristine, are smeared with the green of moss from the trails and carry the pungent stink of brine from the rocky shore. I collect myself to hurry out of his way before he notices how somber my mood is, but not before he peels off his shirt. I can't help myself. I steal a quick look. He really is huge. He's not just muscular—his arms and chest and even his stomach ripple. I wonder how he has time for anything but the gym. He catches my eye, but neither of us smiles. The door slams with a rattle behind me.

Inside the main house, there's still no sign of Sofia, which I have to admit doesn't bother me. Ben is in the kitchen preparing a light meal, while Anthony worries over the arrangement of the furniture in the living room. I sit down in a chair to watch, but he stops me with a wave of his hand. "You mind sitting here instead?"

He indicates the love seat by the fireplace. "I want to test something."

I comply, and he crosses the room to the wet bar. For a second it looks like he's reaching for a particularly high bottle of green liquor, but then his hand stops just short of the bottle, and I catch sight of another one of those small cameras. He tinkers with it for a moment, then performs the same maneuver in the opposite corner of the room, with a camera I'm only now noticing hiding in the shadows. I'm not sure how many cameras are hidden in this room, but I'm guessing a number of them.

"Like this," he says to me, "in postproduction we can change angles, zoom in for close-ups, even splice together different bits from different takes. It's all digital."

I watch him, silently. I don't know what it is about him, but I've never been attracted to someone like this before. I have no interest in Mads's muscles, beyond simple curiosity. With Anthony, though, I'm drawn to him like a magnet. I think he must feel the same pull, toward me. This kind of spark, it comes from two people, doesn't it? It can't just be my imagination.

"Want to see what I mean?" he asks, settling beside me on the love seat with his laptop.

I reply with a shrug, but I'm sure he can read my eagerness.

He props the computer up on the coffee table and clicks through what looks like a million different programs until he finally finds the one he's looking for. The screen splits into ten distinct squares, like a security monitor at the mall. "It's like a kaleidoscope," I observe, leaning in to get a better look. It takes a brief second for my many reflections to follow the movement. And through the computer's tinny speakers, my voice echoes, *It's like a kaleidoscope.*

Anthony laughs at my expression. "You like?"

Actually, I'm not sure how I feel about it. "It's crazy," I say, as Anthony's voice filters through the computer's speakers.

There's a sharp rap on the front door, and I jump, even before it registers. Anthony and I have time to exchange a look, then there's a second, more insistent knock. My heart is in my throat. The thought of meeting Sammy fills me with dread. I'm either going to let Anthony down, or I'm going to figure out how to goad this stranger into becoming a monster.

Anthony closes the laptop, then touches my knee. "Are you ready for this?" he asks me.

"I think so," I tell him.

He looks every bit as nervous as I feel. "Okay, then, Lola," he says. "Answer the door." In the kitchen, the water stops running, and Ben goes silent. He's watching me, too.

"Isn't anyone going to answer that?" Sofia asks, appearing at the end of the hallway, her face streaked with sleep creases, her hair in a tangle.

Anthony swivels toward her, a finger to his lips. "Over here," he tells her, pointing to the sofa. Then, to me, "Go on. You've got this." And when I'm finally up and walking toward the door, "Keep it natural. You don't know anything about him."

The silhouette on the glass, obscured by the nearly translucent gauze curtains, is angular and stout, shorter even than me. I watch the shadow of a hand float upward, then coalesce into a fist. When it raps again, I stop moving, frozen in place for a couple of beats even as I try to force myself to move forward. When the man outside grows impatient and presses his face close to the glass, the curtain turns him into a specter. His eyes appear far apart, the sockets hollow beneath thick eyebrows. I take a deep breath, then reach for the knob.

"Hi," Sammy says, the instant the door is cracked. His voice surrounds me viscously, like syrup. He oozes confidence. It's evident in every aspect of his bearing, even his eyes. "Sorry to bother you." He gestures vaguely behind him, as though he hasn't quite seen me yet. "But I brought over some goodies for you guys, courtesy of Mrs. O, and well, I figured I'd check in, to see if you need anything else." When he turns back toward me, to face me squarely, he does an obvious double take, which he makes no effort to conceal. For a split second, I can read confusion in his bulbous eyes. I get the impression he thinks he knows me. Like he's seen me somewhere before and wants to give me a more familiar greeting, before he realizes he hasn't.

Up close, I see this is an unpolished man. Weather-beaten, like he spends his days outside. His hands are blistered, the fingers thick, with nails that remind me of a parrot's beak, and his nose appears to have been broken. He isn't quite bald, but his hair barely covers a spot on top, though he's camouflaged this with a pair of reflective aviators digging into his scalp. Exactly as he had this morning, he reminds me of a snake. Not a dry rattler or a poisonous cobra, though. A huge, muscular, oily python. And it's not just how the different parts of him don't seem to quite match or fit together. It's not only physical. My first impression of him is that there's something primal about him. He has hardly opened his mouth, but I can already feel it, maybe in the way he's looking at me. He's not assessing me. He's not even ogling me. He's sizing me up, like prey.

Still, there's something slick about him, too, and I can't quite put my finger on this. As coarse as he seems, the pose he strikes reminds me of the men I'd see—insurance salesmen and accountants and lawyers—hanging around the bar at the country club where I'd found my first summer job when I was sixteen, babysitting rich kids while their parents played tennis and golf. He knows how to mask his brutishness with the veneer of conventional behavior. The same costume a lot of men wear, I've noticed, for a multitude of reasons. He waits for me to speak, lines bunching up around his eyes as he offers me an artificial smile, which he nevertheless manages to infuse somehow with genuine charm.

"You must be Lola," he surmises.

"Sorry," I echo, with a guilty grimace, feeling rude. I have been scrutinizing him unabashedly, too. "You must be Sammy?" I barely resist the urge to throw Anthony a look over my shoulder.

"Yes," he says. "Sammy O'Neill. From across the way."

I make a show of looking beyond him to the mainland, then give him a warm smile. He raises his eyebrows, and the sunglasses shift backward. "Nice to meet you," I say, keeping my hand hanging loosely at my side. As friendly as I think Lola should be, I'm not quite ready to touch him. "So—what did you bring us?"

He takes a half step back and gestures to the edge of the porch, where there's a wooden crate overflowing with sweet potatoes and blackberries. I spot a well-worn novel resting on top—the same piece of pulp Mrs. O had been reading in the store.

"Your first time up here?" he asks me. Through the baggy shirt and jeans, I can see the thick muscles I remember from this morning. Not muscles chiseled by weights in a gym, like Mads's physique, but a body thickened by hard work. It takes me a few beats longer to realize he's barefoot, and for some reason, when I do, it gives me a small shiver. He knows this place well. He's comfortable here, the way a person is inside their own house.

"Yeah," I answer. "It's gorgeous. But cold." Then, when all he does is nod, slowly, in agreement, I offer, "It must be nice living here?"

He peers into my eyes, and I can't help but return the stare. His eyes themselves fascinate me. There's something reptilian about them, and though I hate to say it, this isn't purely unattractive. The pupils are enlarged, rimmed with the golden orange color of his irises. "It's home," he says, with no inflection, no invitation for me to understand whether he loves it here, or that he is dying to escape. It just is.

I know what my instructions are. I'm supposed to develop a rapport with this man. But I'm suddenly feeling too uncomfortable to keep this up, and I twist around and find Anthony, who hasn't even stood up yet to join me. *You want to come help me out here?* I nearly blurt out, and he must see my distress because he does finally push himself up and begin to saunter over.

"Is that Sammy?" he asks.

"He's brought us some supplies," I tell him, then take a step backward, to watch the two men meet.

"What a pleasure," Anthony says, as he takes my place in the doorway.

Sammy's eyes narrow as he looks up at Anthony. He makes no effort to summon the same false sincerity, but instead greets Anthony with a frown and a quick nod of his head. I can see on his face the moment when he decides not to retreat, even a step. As much animosity as I can sense in his posture, it strikes me, too, that there's something else buried underneath. Fear, maybe. I saw the same layers of response in the dogs I was walking in New York, as I led them into confrontations with other, more dominant dogs. I recall Mrs. O's parting words to him, this morning: *You take care of the Marinos now.* Sammy and his mother depend on the money they receive from serving the Marinos. And suddenly, in spite of my revulsion, I realize I'm actually feeling sorry for Sammy. For whatever reason, he doesn't like Anthony. Fundamentally. And the feeling is noticeably mutual. But Sammy has forced himself to be here anyway, to serve Anthony.

"How've you been keeping yourself, Sammy?" Anthony asks him. "It's been a long time."

Sammy can't mask his surprise at the question, but I can read the instant he decides not to answer. It's conscious, his choice not to submit to Anthony, not in the least bit. No matter what his mother may tell him. I wonder what has transpired between them to account for all this mutual animosity. Whatever happened, it was significant.

"Like I told your charming friend Lola here," Sammy says, sweeping a hand in my direction, "all I'm doing is dropping off some goodies from Mrs. O. This isn't a social visit." He peers around Anthony to speak directly to me, lowering his voice. "I'm the help. The Marinos don't want to mix with any of that."

Anthony steps out onto the porch to join Sammy, fidgeting with his watch while he walks, unclipping it and refastening it around his wrist—like a baseball player tightening his batting gloves. I have already become so accustomed to Anthony's wealth that I hardly notice it anymore. The crazy-expensive jeans, the long-sleeved T-shirts designed to look simple and casual, tailored to fit him perfectly. Next to him, Sammy seems to be dressed in practically a potato sack. Anthony glances at the wooden crate. "How's your dad, Sammy?"

Sammy shrugs. "Locked up," he says. And then, again to me, in a hushed voice. "Ten to fifteen years for manslaughter. Conviction came down last year. If young Master Anthony hasn't already told you."

I shake my head and try my best not to look too distressed. I already knew about the prison, of course, but manslaughter? Does Anthony really want to play around with this man? "No," I manage. "I didn't know."

"He'll get to it," Sammy tells me. "Don't you fret." Then, in what sounds like a practiced speech: "I can walk you all through the house, if you like. It doesn't seem like it, on a nice day like today, but we get a lot of squalls out here. It'll knock out the power, and the electrical box can be a little tricky to find in the dark. And it gets dark here."

"I know the house," Anthony says.

Sammy points at me. "They don't," he says, indicating Ben, too, who has sidled up next to me. "Hi there," Sammy says to him, summoning a smile that reminds me of a chimpanzee's grimace. "Sammy O'Neill. I'm the caretaker here."

Ben pushes himself past me, extending a hand. "I'm Ben," he says. "Nice to meet you, man. I'm Anthony's partner here."

For a moment, Sammy's face registers confusion. "Business partner, I assume?" he asks.

"He works for me," Anthony snaps back.

"Sound mixing," Ben says lamely. "On his last film." He steps away from the group, and leans himself against the railing of the porch, as though to watch. He's been dismissed, but he's curious to see what happens.

Sammy nods, taking this in. He turns to Anthony. "Mrs. O says you're up here having a party. Is that right?"

"You could say that," Anthony says. "We'll be here for two or three weeks, I guess."

"It must be nice," Sammy says.

"For you, too, then," I hear myself say. "Right? I mean, you're here all the time."

Sammy forces a smile. "Working," he says. "Not too much partying."

"Which reminds me," Anthony says. "We're going to need more firewood. And some help with the laundry. You know, the usual things."

Sammy doesn't acknowledge the order. Instead, he offers me a doleful stare, which, despite myself, I find disarming. He might be rough, but he's also sincere in a raw sort of way. Next to him, Anthony's charm suddenly appears a bit contrived. Sammy isn't pretending, at least not as far as I can tell. He isn't conscious of himself enough to pretend. "Don't let him push you around," he warns me. "I don't know how long the two of you have been together, but it's important to let him know right from the start. You ain't going to be his bitch." The last he says with a bit of a twang, to let me know he's kidding. The words, though, still give me a chill. He's not talking about me. He's talking about himself.

"Oh," I say, stunned, "we're not together."

"No?" Sammy is genuinely surprised. "You're not with this one, are you?" he asks, glancing at Ben. There's enough of a hesitation between "this" and "one" for me to appreciate that "one" wasn't the first word to pop into his head.

"No way," I hear Sofia say, behind me. She steps out of the doorway and offers Sammy a sheepish grin. "He's mine."

As if on cue, Mads appears, too, not from inside the house, but from across the lawn. His hair is wet, and so is his shirt. It looks like he leapt out of the shower and raced over here, which he probably did. He gives me a wink.

"That's my man," I say, wondering at the same time where those words have come from. *That's my man*? When have I ever said that before?

"I'm Mads," Mads says, jogging up the steps and extending his hand toward Sammy. "Nice to meet you."

"Mads Byrne," Sammy says. "I know." He takes a moment to size Mads up, again without camouflaging it, then, in a burst of movement, he clutches Mads's hand in one of his own.

Mads looks flattered, as though Sammy recognizing him is a great compliment in itself. He drops an arm around my shoulders, physically roping me back into the conversation. "You liked the movie, did you?"

Sammy considers this, while Anthony seems to be fighting off some strong emotion. His jaw is working, but his eyes are veiled. I don't think it ever occurred to him that Sammy might watch *Reverence*. I can't tell if he's pleased—flattered, like Mads—or disappointed. No matter what he says, scripted or not, *Reverence* was a deeply personal film. He took everything from his own life. Like a diary entry, almost. If a stranger read it, it doesn't matter. But if it's someone you dislike, who dislikes you, it's different. Humiliating.

In the end, all Sammy does is shrug. To Anthony, he asks, "So no one's here for you?"

Anthony dismisses him with a smirk. "You know how it goes," he says.

This makes Sammy laugh. It's a dry, bitter sound. "Sure I do," he says with a nod. Then, straightening himself up, he leans into Mads. "You better keep an eye on your girl," he tells him. "He doesn't like to stay single for too long."

"What's that?" Mads asks. The movie star smile falls away in the blink of an eye. I can never get used to this. How ready some men are—I mean, usually, at least—to launch themselves into a fight. If Sammy's bulk gives Mads any pause, he doesn't show it.

Sammy shakes his head. He flashes me another unreadable, doleful look.

"Well," Anthony says, clearing his throat, "thanks for stopping by." He wanders in the direction of the stairs, like he wants to lead Sammy out of here.

Sammy, though, doesn't move. He's pinned me with his bulbous eyes. "Mrs. O told me you were a brunette. How'd she get that wrong?"

I don't know what to say, so I don't respond. I feel my teeth dig into my lip. Anthony's gaze is like a physical weight on me, but I don't want to look at him and give him away.

"He cut your hair, too," Sammy says, "didn't he?"

"What?" I ask, genuinely startled by the question. Mads tightens his hold on my shoulders, but it's too late to hide my reaction. How could he guess that? And what does Anthony expect me to say?

"It looks good," Sammy tells me, ignoring my surprise. "Really good." He nods toward the box by Ben. "There's a book there, too. Mama said it was for the cute brunette. In case she gets bored."

"Maybe she meant Sofìa," I say, floundering.

Sammy's eyes don't leave my face. "She meant you," he says, then swivels and starts, slowly, down the stairs, past Anthony without even a glance.

Ben picks the book up from the box. "I didn't know anyone read these," he says with a laugh. He offers the chunky book to me, but I reject it with a shake of my head. Not right now. As strange and disarming as Sammy is, I don't want to pile on to the hostility. With a shrug, Ben tosses the book back into the box and hoists it into his arms. "Let's get this shit inside," he says, loud enough for Sammy to hear as he retreats across the lawn, making me flinch. Sofìa follows Ben into the house, and I can just barely catch her frenzied whisper: *Oh, my God, babe, that's the guy? Why didn't you tell me he was that creepy?*

Before Sammy disappears into the woods, he stops again, to take off his shirt. I'm so stunned, I hardly notice the scowl that distorts Anthony's face. And then, without another word, he's gone, weaving into the web of knit branches with the ease of a buck.

I pull myself out of Mads's grip and peer after Sammy, but can't track him, not even his footsteps. A moment later, there's the unmistakable sound of water breaking. I can't see it, but I know what's happened. He has dived into the channel, expertly, barely making a splash. This is followed by the rhythmic chop of his stroke. "Is he *swimming*?" I ask, unable to repress a shiver. How can he swim in this frigid water? The sun is hot today, sure, but the breeze coming off the water alone gives me the chills.

"His *mama* must have ferried him over in their boat," Anthony says. He joins me at the porch rail, leaning a hip against it, his back to the woods. "He was captain of the varsity wrestling team in high school. That's his claim to fame. People around here still remember. He can do no wrong, because he brought them back a state championship in his senior year. But he was on the swim team, too. The guy's an athlete. He's a machine."

"He's going to swim home? That's insane." After the word is out of my mouth, I realize I've spoken it literally. And not just about what he's doing. About Sammy. The man. I wonder if Anthony really knows what he's getting us into. I turn to see if Mads agrees, but he's gone. I think I can hear him inside, talking to Sofia, but I can't make out what they're saying. Sofia's excited, that much I can tell. Meeting Sammy was a thrill for her. She's in the movie, of course, but she might as well be watching us on a screen, for all her involvement. She doesn't have his eyes on her. She doesn't have to get close to him. To measure her chemistry with him, for some mysterious purpose.

I'm brought back to reality when Anthony wraps his arms around me. I don't hesitate. I don't stop to question this moment.

I just let my eyes close. I want to savor this embrace. It's so different from Mads's unfamiliar, heavy touch. But I can't escape the feeling that I'm about to incur Anthony-the-director's wrath. After all, the revulsion I felt for Sammy was pretty obvious. I can't fathom how I'll be able to pull this off. Talking to Sammy, I mean. Getting him to trust me, if that's what Anthony is asking me to do. Instinctively, I don't want to be anywhere near him. I'm half expecting Anthony to twist me around and reprimand me. Instead, though, he pulls me in tighter, and his lips touch my ear. "You did good," he whispers. "This is going to be tough. For both of us. But you did good."

16

Beneath the afternoon sun, steam rises in slow waves from the water, like gauzy sheets of silk. On the porch, Sofia is sprawled in a lounge chair, a book splayed in one hand. She looks up when I settle into the lounge chair opposite her, as though it takes her a moment to remember where she is. She's reading something she brought with her, *Wuthering Heights*—which isn't unusual for her. She was always the smart one. That's how I remember her, in school, back home, just about wherever I saw her, with her nose buried in a book, and almost always an old one I wouldn't have ever thought to pick up myself.

Sofia lets the book drop to her lap. "How are you doing?" she asks me, giving me a critical once-over. "It's hard to get used to this"—she gestures to my hair—"whole thing." Then, with a gasp: "You look like your mom."

I make a face at her.

She slaps a hand over her mouth, histrionically. "Same expression, too," she tells me. She cranes her neck around, and says, to the house and its many cameras, "Sorry, Anthony." She gives me a guilty grin, like we're back in school and the teacher just caught her passing notes. I wonder if the cameras can pick up what we're saying. If Anthony's hidden microphones are actually that powerful. "Maybe we're not supposed to be childhood friends anymore. Has he said anything to you?"

"No," I say. "You're probably right, though. I don't think it's a good idea." And it really isn't. Not just because it will make it harder for her to think of me as Lola and not Betty, but also because the fact that she grew up three streets away from me is another tether tying me down to Betty. I don't want to think about home. The whole point of changing my hair, my wardrobe, my story, is so I can forget about these things. About Betty. And that's already hard enough to do with Sofia just being here. To her, that's who I am. Who I'll always be. Betty Roux, the gangly girl who was her best friend for sophomore and junior year of high school. I dye my hair and nothing changes, except now to her I look more like my mom. There's no space to breathe, to exist as Lola, with her around.

She loses interest in me, quick. She still asks me what I'm going to do today, but her voice is distant, and her eyes are back on her book.

I'm rescued from having to lie about what I was going to do next—pretending like I had actually thought about it when I hadn't—by Anthony. He slips out the front door, catches my attention, and beckons me over to him.

When I reach him, he pulls me inside to give us some privacy, but still pitches his voice low. "Sammy's chopping our firewood," he tells me, and it strikes me as he speaks that I've been hearing the steady beat of the ax for some time now, without identifying it. The metallic thud reverberates over the water with a hollow echo before the thick overgrowth of trees surrounding us swallows it. "I'd like you to talk to him. Alone. Are you up for that?"

I take a deep breath, trying not to let my anxiety show. *You ain't going to be his bitch.* I haven't been able to get Sammy's warning out of my mind. It wasn't so much what he'd said that bothered me. It was how he'd said it. The simmering resentment he couldn't conceal, for the domination Anthony exerted over him. I can't escape the feeling that there's something specific that happened between them that has kept them separate for however many years. I'm walking blind into a hornet's nest. That's what Anthony's asking me to do. "What excuse do I give," I ask him, my unease threading itself through my voice, "for joining him?"

Anthony holds up a chilled bottle of water, which I take from him. "Not," he adds, "that you need a pretext. He'll just be happy to see you."

He leads me through the house, into the kitchen, to the back door. The chopping gets louder, and I expect to find Sammy just outside, but when the door swings open, there's nothing but the grass swaying gently in the breeze. Anthony doesn't cross the threshold with me.

"Follow the noise," he instructs me. Then, when I stop, too: "Don't worry. I'll be watching the whole time." He points down the hall, toward his office.

Despite his good intentions, this isn't exactly comforting. All it means is Anthony will be eavesdropping, judging me. I will be hyperaware of his gaze on me, on us. And it's not like I'm in any danger here, right? After all, I'm just saying hi. I'm getting to know the man. What is it Anthony thinks he has to protect me from?

I step into a wave of heat. The buzz of flies competes with the loud, echoing chops of Sammy's ax, which I'm supposed to follow. Into the woods, it seems. Into that forbidding jungle.

"Break a leg," Anthony says.

"Thanks," I mutter. And then I step into the glare and trail the vicious, determined clank of the ax like I've been told to, searching for Sammy.

|||||||||||||||||||||

It turns out, I don't have to walk far to find him. The path to my cottage has a fork in it that I hadn't noticed before, and I follow the muddy line along the edge of a thicket to a small mossy clearing. There are an old bench and worktable, some rusted tools whose purpose I could never even begin to fathom, and in the center of this open space—that still manages to feel claustrophobic, like the trees are slowly but surely closing in on us—is Sammy, wielding an ax with a big rusted blade. It sounds like he's taking huge savage swings. In fact, though, his stroke is truncated. Economical. He's not making a show of this. He has a job to do, and he knows how to get it done. His violence is controlled.

He's winding up for another blow, when he stops, frozen. I don't think I've made too much noise, but he seems to have felt my presence, nevertheless. He lets the ax drop into one hand as he pivots around, finding my eyes as if he knew somehow exactly where to place me. For a moment, he looks confused. Dazed, almost. Like he's walked down the staircase in the dark and he's forgotten a step. And then he finds himself. "Lola," he says. I wait for him to say more, but that's it. Just *Lola*.

"Hi," I say, shooing a mosquito away from my face. "I'm sorry if I scared you."

He looks at me, puzzled.

I hold up the water bottle. The condensation drips through my fingers. "It's hot out here." As if to emphasize the point, my cheeks burn. *You ain't going to be his bitch.* I feel foolish. It would have been enough just to follow the sound here. I'm the one who should determine who Lola is, not Anthony. I shouldn't feel compelled to do everything he tells me to. Sammy is just another person. Another man. All I have to do is get to know him.

Sammy says, "Thank you," but he doesn't move. He isn't going to be the one to close the distance between us. I'm going to have to put the bottle in his hand. I know I'm overanalyzing this. But it feels as if he's testing me. He wants me to prove my interest in him, and he's ready to use it to subdue me and establish his dominance. *You ain't going to be his bitch. You're gonna be mine.*

I try to shake off my nerves. I can do this. I force my feet to walk, and I place the slippery plastic bottle into his waiting hand. His palms, I notice, are blazing red, from the friction of the handle. He isn't wearing gloves. But the skin is callused, and it isn't torn. He's used to this. Up close, I can smell his sweat. More than that, I'm suffocating in it. The hot stink of sulfur practically chokes me. He isn't wearing a shirt, and the skin on his shoulders and arms and torso is thick, too, like his hands, tanned into a strange combination of gold and pink. He accepts the water, drops the ax to the side, and drinks it down in practically one large gulp.

I take a discreet step back, to escape the smell. But no more than that. His gaze fixes me in place. The doleful expression is gone. These eyes are sharper. Curious. Awake.

"I'm sorry," I tell him, though I don't know what I'm apologizing for.

He raises his eyebrows.

"For interrupting you," I finish, limply.

"It's my pleasure," he tells me. And I can feel how much he means it, just like I can feel the heat emanating from his body. The air seems to vibrate with his energy.

I resist the urge to search the trees surrounding us. Has Anthony really had time to install cameras out here? Where are they? Can he actually hear us? Does it even matter? I have to resist the urge, too, to offer Sammy another apology—*Sorry I'm being so awkward, I just don't know what we're supposed to talk about*—and then I hear myself say, "That's a nasty scar." I'm pointing to his temple. A broken, disjointed line cuts from the top of his cheekbone over his ear, stretching toward the back of his head. The hair, shorn so close to his skull, is divided in two along this mark. The sweat rolling down his forehead to his cheeks and clinging to his chin sickens me somehow. I don't know why. Or maybe I do. Maybe it's because there's something intimate about it. And maybe I'm not sickened by it so much as my own reaction to it.

Because I'm not only repulsed. I almost want to touch it. Wipe the pendulous droplets off his jaw.

He runs a hand over his scalp, compulsively. "You can thank Archie Miller for that," he tells me. "I don't think of it as nasty, though."

"What happened?" I ask.

"Have you ever been bullied?" he asks me, in answer.

"Not really," I say, though I'm not sure if I'm telling him the truth. It feels like a lie. I didn't escape being tormented in school. It's just that nobody thought of me long enough to consider bullying me. That truth, though, belongs to Betty. Not to Lola.

"Things are different now," he continues. "There's online bullying, all that invisible stuff. That didn't exist back when I was a kid. Back then it was physical. Personal. Archie Miller hated me. You know what I mean? He had it out for me. Decided to make my life hell. This"—he runs his hand over his scalp again—"happened when I finally fought back. This was after years of him waiting for me, teasing me, hounding me, grabbing me. Hitting me. Bullying me. Archie Miller and his friends. Buddy Rhodes. Jason Smith. The whole gang of them. Then one day I didn't want to be hit no more. Simple as that."

"Oh, my God" is all I can say. I have a hard time picturing this hulking man as a small child. He's got too much presence, too much confidence, for me to imagine him as a helpless, desperate kid.

"I tried to kill him," Sammy says. "He tried to kill me."

"I'm so sorry," I tell him, and it finally sounds sincere.

His hand rests on his head, forgotten. "That was the end of it," he says. He smiles at me. Satisfied. Even after all these years, whatever he did to Archie Miller, it still nourishes him.

The scars on my fingers, on Tucker's face, suddenly seem inadequate—pathetic, compared to the wound on Sammy's skull. Yet I can still remember the look on Tucker's face, when I threw that lamp, when I reached for him. And I feel a sudden connection— a real connection—to this man, because I still experience some sort of animal pleasure at the memory, regardless of my shame.

"You know," Sammy says, crumpling the empty plastic bottle and tossing it onto the workbench, "you look really familiar, Lola."

Underneath that watchful gaze, I become aware that I've wrapped my arms around myself, like I'm cold, rather than boiling under the sun, and I force my hands to relax their grip and shake myself loose. "Oh?" I ask.

"Like Darla," he tells me, simply, like I should know who Darla is. I can't remember the last time he's blinked.

"Darla?" I ask, when it's clear he's not going to say more unless I prod him.

"Darla," he repeats, again like it should be enough. And then, finally: "My first girlfriend." He makes an odd swirling gesture over his head. "She had hair like that. She cut it herself. Dyed it." For a minute, he looks confused, genuinely, and I find myself wondering if there might not be something wrong with him. Something slightly off. Maybe when he got that scar, he got more than just a cut. "Do you know Darla?" he asks me.

"No." My tone is patronizing, like I'm speaking to a child. "I don't."

"Really?" And there's something about the question that touches me, even as I'm realizing that this is no accident, that this is why Anthony has dyed my hair, to set me up, like a piece of bait. The man in front of me is floundering. The question he really wants to ask isn't if I know this Darla. It's if I *am* her. His eyes search my face, but it seems to take him a long time to find me. When he does, it reminds me of a boxer after a particularly brutal fight, in the moment when he embraces his opponent. Now that the bout is over, they recognize each other, not in spite of their stupor but because of it. There's a bond between them, and a distance that separates them from the rest of the world.

"That's too bad," Sammy says. "She was sweet," he tells me. "Sweet like you."

17

When I return to the main house, no one knows where Anthony is. Still curled up on the lounge chair on the front porch, Sofia's been lost in another world, she tells me, waiting for Heathcliff to find his way across the bay to the Mission. Ben tells me he's been adjusting the cameras around the estate. He's just returned to the main house, and no, he doesn't have any idea of where Anthony would be. Mads, meanwhile, has been working out on the beach—I guess a run in the morning isn't enough to maintain that physique—and he swears he hasn't seen him.

No one questions why I'm searching for him. They already know. I can see it in their faces. Anthony has told them about my one-on-one with Sammy. I bet he's even told them about Darla. About the dyed hair, and how I look like her. I try to suppress my paranoia, because that's what this is—insecurity, paranoia—but I can't. They *have* to know, because that's what this film is about. Luring Sammy over to this island. To attack us, right? Like a bull with a red cape. And look at them all, carrying on as if nothing is up. Letting me put myself in front of Sammy without so much as a warning. I feel tears burning at the corners of my eyes. Anthony never saw anything special in me. He chose me because I look like Darla. I'm such an idiot. He doesn't care about Betty coming out of her shell. He cares only about Sammy. About inciting Sammy, with the ghost of his first girlfriend.

What hurts the most, though, is Sofia. Her silence. She's allowed all of this to unfold without a single word. She let me embarrass myself. What must she think, of all that talk from Anthony? *You're perfect for this.* It's humiliating. She must be laughing at me. At the burst of hope she had seen blossoming in me. I can only imagine what she and Ben are saying about me.

I push through the front door into the house and let it swing shut behind me, then drop onto the couch in the living room. Ben can't get out of the house fast enough. Through the large windows that face the water, I watch him cozy up to Sofia on her lounge chair. Mads, emerging from the kitchen, has prepared himself yet another meal. He gives me a hopeful look, like he thinks with the power of his good humor he can break me out of my bad mood.

"I'd like to be alone," I say, digging my fingers into the flesh of my forearm to stop myself from apologizing or backing down.

Mads swerves away from me and heads to the front door, only stopping to catch my eye on the threshold. "Everything okay?" he asks. His concern sounds genuine. But the way I see it, it's too little too late. He could have told me what was coming. At least what he knows. After all, we spent a night together in the same bed. In the same isolated cottage. Just the two of us against the world.

"I'm fine," I tell him.

I watch his back, tensed now from my mood, as he maneuvers his overflowing plate to the table outside. He tucks into his food immediately. I hear Ben call over to him, but I don't pay attention to their conversation. Instead, I stand up and cross the room, then follow the dark hallway to Anthony's office. It's the first place I checked, and I know he isn't there, but still, as I throw open the door, I steel myself to find Anthony.

The room is empty, of course. I hesitate. Then, taking a tentative step inside, I close the door behind me, my heartbeat pounding in my ears, and ease myself into his desk chair. As soon as I touch the mouse, the three screens come to life. It shocks me, not only how many small separate windows there are into the various parts of the island—like a disorganized mosaic composed of green leaves, empty rooms, and the rough wood of the two buildings— but how trusting Anthony is, leaving the computer accessible like this, unprotected. But I should be grateful. Because I don't have to search long for him. The small windows are mostly still. The only movement is the breeze pulling at the grass and branches, except in a few cells, where the three people lounge on the porch, where Sammy continues his work in the clearing, now stacking the wood he has chopped into a neat pile. And one, in the corner, where Anthony's face, up close, practically obscures the window as he installs another camera.

I can't immediately figure out where he is. When he leans

back, to grab another screwdriver, the only clues I can discern in the background are more trees. More shadows. More moss.

Then, his fingers, giant from this perspective, slip, and the camera falls abruptly down to the side, revealing what can only be my cottage. He's behind the structure—high up in a tree, it looks like. I don't stop to think. I'm out of the house, my footsteps crunching on the gravel path, before I realize I have no idea what I intend to say to him when I reach him.

Around the back of the cottage, the moss is thicker. My shoes sink into the green like it's a wet sponge, slowing me down as I approach. I find him, finally, half hidden by the long, swaying branches of the tree, on a ladder, about twenty feet into the woods.

"Anthony." The intensity of my own voice startles me. His name echoes like the crack of a whip.

On the ladder, he tosses a look at me over his shoulder, almost like he's been expecting me but still can't believe what he's seeing. "You mind handing me that screwdriver?" he asks, nodding toward a toolbox at the base of the ladder.

I have to take a breath before I can speak. "Get down," I say. I know it's inadequate, but it's all I can manage. It feels like my heart is about to burst through my chest. How long has he been here? Wasn't he supposed to be watching me talk to Sammy? Wasn't he supposed to be *protecting* me? "I need to talk to you."

"In a second," he says, focused on his work.

"Now," I insist.

Still nothing.

With a burst of frustration, I say: "Darla?" My voice is louder than I'd intended.

His eyes glint when he twists to look at me. He's not thrilled. At last, though, he releases the camera and descends the ladder. "Keep your voice down," he tells me, and when he glances into the woods, I realize how clearly I can hear the *clunk* of wood as Sammy continues to stack the split logs.

"You have to tell me what's going on," I counter. "Now. Or I'm leaving." The threat slips out of me, unbidden. Truthfully, though, it comes as a surprise to me. I haven't even thought of leaving, at least not consciously. But I can't take it back, and why should I? Everyone here has lied to me. Anthony has asked me to trust him, every step of the way, chopping off my hair, bleaching it, forcing me to share a bed with a complete stranger who's supposed to be my *lover*, using me as a pawn in some sort of long-standing feud with a man who hates him, who clearly has something off with him. To *trust* him. That has been his refrain. But he hasn't trusted me. Not with the truth. Not with the same information he's shared with everyone else. All he's done so far is use me. All he's shown me is his disregard. His selfishness. His arrogance.

"Let's go inside," he says with a sigh. When he takes my hand, I bristle. I'm ready to resist. I can't, though. I hate to admit this, but his touch still jolts me like an electric shock, and by the time it reaches my chest, it's a warm, vibrant feeling that calms me, despite my anger, despite his betrayal. He leads me to the cottage with a hand on my shoulder, like a leash. Once the door is closed behind us, he asks me, "What's wrong?"

"Weren't you watching?" I ask, trying to recover some of my fury.

"Yeah," he says slowly. Now he's the one speaking to me like

I'm a child, the same tone of voice I employed with Sammy. "You did great. That camera out there, though, the one I was working on, is supposed to face the clearing. Not the cottage. It's an important angle. Ben screwed it up. I had to fix it."

"He told me about Darla," I say, determined not to let him sidetrack me. "He said I look just like her. Is that why I'm here? Because I look like her?" I don't want to cry. Voicing my thoughts aloud, though, makes this all sound so real. And the truth is pretty stark, isn't it? I wait for him to laugh at me. To ask, *What did you think I hired you for? Your talent?*

But Anthony doesn't laugh. He just wanders toward the bed and folds himself onto it. Mads didn't make it, after he got up, and I haven't bothered to, either. Anthony is sitting on the bare sheets, and for some reason, this feels too familiar, especially for this kind of serious discussion. He pats the mattress beside him. When I don't move, he releases another long sigh. "Betty," he says, "I'm going to tell you everything. But I'm not going to fight with you. Please sit down."

"What happened to Lola?" I ask.

He just waits. And I feel myself relent. I want to hear what he has to say for himself.

"Can you explain," he starts, patiently, "what's got you so upset? Everything went perfectly, between you and Sammy." He reaches for my hand. I let him take it. "Absolutely perfect," he repeats, squeezing my hand.

"I don't know what you're doing here," I say, trying to keep my voice level. "I don't know what's going on. You've made me into this"—I gesture to my hair, my clothes—"into Darla. To get to

Sammy. Why her?" Then, before he can speak: "Actually, no. Why *Sammy*? Why are you doing this to him?" I think of that scar zigzagging along his skull, the sick smile he gave me. *That was the end of it.* "It feels like we're—I don't know—we're bullying him. Humiliating him." If we're really modeling this movie off of *Cape Fear*, it seems like we're the antagonists. Not Sammy. We're the ones seeking revenge. But for what?

"We aren't bullying him," Anthony says. Suddenly, there's some venom in his voice. He practically spits the words at me. "Yeah, I heard what he told you about Archie Miller. Poor little Sammy. I heard it, and I've heard all about it before. Don't let him fool you. He sent Archie Miller to the hospital." He shakes his head, his eyes closed. "Sammy took care of himself just fine."

"But this—," I start. Then: "Now, what we're doing. It feels cruel."

"Believe me," Anthony says, color rising in his cheeks. "What we're doing is nothing compared to what he's done. You think he's some angel?"

The look on Anthony's face shakes me. I'm used to his control. To his usual, easy, sophisticated disdain. But he's unguarded now. Genuinely wounded. Defensive. "What did he do to you?" I hear myself ask.

Anthony scrubs at his face with both hands, like he wants to erase the vulnerability from his expression. And when he raises his head, the emotion is gone. Somehow, he has managed to recover himself. He looks fine, once again almost bored by the conversation. "I spent a lot of time with Sammy," he tells me.

"Growing up. His father—the one who's in prison now for killing a man named Ryan Lane in a bar fight—took care of a lot of the construction work for the Mission, and he brought Sammy with him. My parents liked to spend some time alone, so they'd ask Sammy to let me tag along with him. He's only four years older than me, but those were critical years. I'm pretty sure my parents paid him to watch over me. I think he hated me from the start. It got worse when he was in high school. The local hero. Destined for bigger things. The last thing he wanted was to babysit some spoiled rich kid, even if he was taking my parents' money. But neither of us had much of a choice, so we just"—Anthony searches for the right word—"tolerated each other."

"What happened?"

"He humiliated me," Anthony says, simply. "When I was fourteen."

"How?" I ask, when Anthony doesn't offer more.

He shrugs.

"Physically?" I ask.

"Psychologically," Anthony responds quickly. "And yeah, physically."

"How?" I ask again.

"I don't have a clear memory of it. I remember the lead-up to it, you know, and the start. I remember the fear. The pain in my ribs. He took me down. He was a wrestler, see? I was a kid. A scrawny little kid. I don't remember exactly what happened next. It's been wiped clean." He looks at me, reads the horror in my face, and almost cracks an unbidden, incongruous smile. "I didn't tell you before, because I'm embarrassed. Something happened. When I was a kid. I should get over it. I don't know, Betty. Maybe this is my way of doing that. By putting it on film."

This last bit finally gets me. It's like what Mads told me. Anthony has to see himself on film to know himself. "Okay," I say, and repeat the word a few more times. There isn't a lot of room to challenge Anthony's story. I don't think I can press him more than I have already. *He humiliated me.* How? What does that look like, for a fourteen-year-old Anthony Marino? Instead, I ask, "How does Darla come into this?"

"Darla is his weak spot," he says. "She was his first love." He slides over to me, closing the gap between our bodies, then lifts my chin with one of his long, sculpted fingers. Another shock pulses through me and finds its way into my chest. "Do you still want to leave?"

"I'm not an idiot," I tell him. "I know what you're doing." *You're trying to distract me. And it's working.*

"I never said you were."

Still, though, something is nagging at me. "What happened to her?" I ask. "What happened to Darla?"

"She broke his heart."

"Anthony," I start, "I don't think—" I take a deep breath. "Are you sure you know what you're doing? Reopening all of these old wounds?"

Anthony's eyes flatten. Just enough for me to read him—the same way, I guess, that he's been able to read me. I'm still his actress. As personal as this is suddenly, he's still the director. This is still his film. It doesn't matter what I'm feeling, except as my emotions figure into the drama he's constructing. Even now. Because, I realize, the cameras are on. We're on film. Even now. By the time he chooses to answer me, I already know what he's going to say. The same old refrain. I'm just going to have to get used to it, I guess.

"You'll just have to trust me," he says. Then he repeats it, in a whisper, and folds me in his arms. "You're just going to have to trust me, Betty."

And the saddest thing is, as trite as these words have become, I do.

18

The days pass, almost in a blur, and the semblance of a routine begins to emerge. I find myself forgetting, for hours at a time, about the cameras. I've never been much of a morning person, but these days, I wake before Mads, before anyone else, and I look forward to my time alone. It's peaceful in the main house, watching the lobster boats careen through the channel, throwing down traps, listening to the coffeemaker bubble and spit. Most days, Anthony is right behind me, stumbling out of his room with his long hair golden and wild like a lion's mane, vulnerable and quiet. We drink coffee in silence. Then he disappears into his office.

Mads's days are occupied with his body. He has to run, to work out, and to eat, in three-hour intervals. Some afternoons, Sofia and I gravitate to the porch to watch him lunging down the beach. Sofia will wolf-whistle when he bends over, which I think bothers Ben, even though it's an obvious joke. Otherwise, Sofia reads, or she trails after Ben while he checks up on the various cameras and other sound equipment, and sometimes they'll disappear for hours, returning with leaves in their hair, mud caked into their shoes, secret smiles passed between each other.

Once the sun tips toward evening, everyone gathers on the porch, for a toast, before Ben gets to work on cooking dinner for all of us. I've never had this much to drink before, consistently. But it takes the edge off the rest of the night, when I have to return in the darkness, to sleep in bed with Mads.

Even though we're supposedly lovers, we don't touch more than we have to. I've woken, in the middle of the night, to his arms wrapped around me. And I don't push him away. He's dropped a kiss on my lips a few times, but only when Sammy is somewhere near, doing chores. Because it's become obvious that that's what this production is about, entirely: Sammy. Mads and I aren't a couple unless Sammy's around. We don't perform little skits that Anthony has devised for us except to entertain Sammy. I'm not even Lola ninety percent of the time. No one else uses the name unless he's there to hear it.

I've noticed, though, that I'm never alone with him. Not since that first day, when I brought him water while he chopped wood. Anthony hasn't asked me again to pull him aside, and I get the feeling that he's deliberately keeping us apart. In fact, except for my mornings, I'm never alone. If Ben and Sofia have left on one of their "secret" liaisons, Mads or Anthony will drop what they're doing—casually, trying not to make a big deal of it—and join me. I've caught glimpses of Mads and Sammy speaking, but they're quick conversations. Mads pressing. Sammy rebuffing him, in that silent way of his. He opens up more to Ben, which seems to please Anthony. I've managed to overhear him, a couple of times, telling Ben as much. *You're doing great, buddy. But we need more. Prod him about his mother. They're really close, but they fight a lot. You can hear it sometimes at night, across the channel. Find a way to get him talking.*

I've felt Sammy's gaze on me. I know he's coming here more often than he necessarily has to. There is a lot to do around here, but not *that* much. So far, he hasn't approached me—or he hasn't had the opportunity, I guess—and I'm not exactly impatient to be alone with him. *He humiliated me.* Anthony's words, that brief flash of pain in his eyes, before he could master himself, the hatred pulsing out of him at the mention of Sammy, haunt me.

I could almost believe that we're actually on vacation. I could almost believe that Anthony's plans have changed. That they no longer involve me. Or that I have served my purpose, in luring Sammy in to spend more time on the island, to be prodded by the others and eventually to open up. To spill his guts in front of the cameras. But it's not that simple. I can feel something coming. Something Anthony's been waiting for. I just don't know what it is.

||||||||||||||||||||

One afternoon, while we're soaking up some sun, listening to tinny pop music on an old radio Ben found hidden in a closet, Sofia tells me this will be her last night here. "I have to get back to the real world," she says, peering out across the channel, to the mainland, as if we're marooned in an actual alternate universe, like Neverland. Like the small expanse of water Anthony calls "the sound" represents more than a physical separation. It hasn't been that long since we've been here, but already I've lost track of time. "Will you miss me?"

"Of course," I say, but it's only an automatic response. My voice sounds different, disembodied. It was comforting to have Sofia here, in the beginning. I'm not sure I would have been able to get in that van, in Greenpoint, without her there. I don't doubt that Anthony was counting on her friendship with me to guide me through whatever jitters or reservations I had in trusting three strange men. At this point, though, she's served her purpose. That's true. For Anthony. And maybe for me, too. If I'm being honest, I won't be sorry to see her go. In fact, I'm relieved at the thought. I tell myself that the fault lies with her. There's something about her—her steadiness, her sarcasm—that's so heavy, it's like a weight on me. The truth is, though, I'm the one to blame.

She knows me too well. Sofia knows me in a way no one else here does. She knows my mom. She knows Tucker. She knows the girl who didn't know how to make friends, the girl who ate her lunches alone outside while the other girls whispered and giggled and shared their food around tables in the cafeteria. She knows the girl whose father committed suicide. She knows me as Betty. And with her here watching me, I haven't found the courage yet to shed my past.

"Well," Sofia says, like she knows exactly what I'm thinking, "you'll find ways to have fun without me."

Before I can think of an appropriate response, Ben bursts through the front door, a can of beer in each hand. "Fun?" he re-peats, divining the substance of our conversation. "Babe, we'll go crazy without you here." He drops down onto the chair beside her, places the beers on the low table between our chairs, and wraps his arms around her, shaking her until she relents and smiles at him. To me, he says, "The goodbye party starts now." He picks up one of the beers and cracks it open, then takes an uncomfortable gulp. He's the only one, I think, who will really miss Sofia.

Ben stifles a burp, then calls out to Mads, who has taken to running, strangely, in place in the sand. "Mads! Time for a beer, dude!"

The muscular man doesn't answer. Instead, he just raises his knees that much higher. A robot couldn't perform the exercise any better.

llllllllllllllllll

On the porch, Ben plugs Anthony's cell phone into an amplifier he's dragged outside, and the music pumps out in a steady, vibrating beat that echoes dully as it skids across the water. Mads brings out a handful of glasses, a bottle of whisky tucked under his arm. Anthony pours, while Mads distributes our drinks. Ben puts on his usual cheer—"Fill'er up to the tippy top," he tells Anthony— all smiles, but it's a strain. I can see how painful Sofia's departure will be for him, and there's something genuinely touching about it. He's like an athlete gamely playing through an injury. Once we all have our drinks, we raise our glasses.

"To Sofia," Anthony says.

"To the movie," she counters. Then she stops herself with an embarrassed grimace. "Sorry," she says. "To me!"

I clink my glass into the fray and mouth the words along to

whatever song is playing as I sip my whisky. We drift into our various seats on the porch. Ben and Sofia settle onto one of the lounge chairs, huddling together like two lovebirds sharing the same perch. Mads sits on a pillow on the floor, leaning back on the rail. Anthony sits stiffly on one end of the overstuffed outdoor couch. I lower myself onto the cushions next to him, silently, without asking permission, while Mads and Ben resume some conversation they've been having about some guy they both know.

Anthony picks up his phone, gives it a few quick taps, and the music stops. A few seconds later, the opening notes of a familiar song vibrate through the dark, humid air. They hit me like an assault, but I feel myself let go, anyway. It's the same song Anthony played on repeat in the van, the twisty rap intercut with a woman's throaty, almost syrupy voice. I lean over, nudging Anthony with my shoulder. *This is our song.* The words hover on my lips, but I don't dare speak them.

He seems to understand, regardless, because he gives me a quick, almost invisible wink, and wraps his arm over my shoulders. Warmth courses through my chest, and I can feel, suddenly, my heart squeeze in a sharp crush, as it hits me: I'm really enjoying this. Being here, I mean. Every second. Who cares if Anthony hired me because I look like Darla? Who cares if Sofia didn't tell me? I'm here. That's all that matters. I've come a long way since leaving California.

And then, in the blink of an eye, I suffer a small relapse, which threatens to drown me. A moment of panic, when I think about calling Dad to tell him about all this so he can share my happiness with me. I'm no longer on an island off the coast of Maine. I'm standing with him, in Iceland, watching the sun set, sending streaks of purple and gold across the sky. I haven't let myself think about that evening, not since we arrived here. The memory is too painful. The threads of the Northern Lights were so delicate. It had looked like they were casting themselves against an invisible barrier. As we watched them trace that imperceptible boundary, the world got smaller. The atmosphere shrank into a bubble, and the night sky became a cup. And he said to me, *I'm so glad we saw this together, sweetheart. It's like sharing a secret. How magical the world is. It's something no one else knows back home.* And while those words echo through my mind, it feels like I'm drinking in each of those luminous threads again, a second time, as they turned the sky into an enchanted ball of electric cotton candy, lighting a path from my tongue down to the very center of my being.

In another instant, though—thankfully—Anthony's arm yanks me back to this other Neverland. And I will myself to flip the switch, to extinguish these visions. I swallow the last remnants of my father's ghost, and feel him burn away, metabolizing into the strength I'll need to move forward without him. The world has become magical again, here, on this island. Here, with Anthony. When I never thought it would.

This is where I'm meant to be, I tell myself. I repeat the words, again and again. Until they feel natural. Until they feel true. This is where I'm meant to be.

And this is who I'm meant to be, too, as long as I'm here.

19

When the night fades into black, like the end of an old film, we drag the party inside, escaping the mosquitoes and the chilly air. Beneath an inky, threatening sky, the house throbs with music. No doubt the sounds of our extended party are audible as far away as the O'Neill house. But I force myself to ignore the disturbance we're causing, and by the time I'm finishing my third whisky, the windows are darkened to slate and nothing else exists beyond the confines of the Mission's walls.

"Move your body," Sofia instructs Ben, pulling his limp, rounded frame off the love seat. She shimmies her hips into his, and after a few seconds when it looks like he wants nothing but to be left alone, he abruptly responds. Mads, Anthony, and I find ourselves laughing as Ben transforms from a couch potato into a club dancer, grinding in beat with Sofia. It's so unlikely, yet at the same time it does make sense, too, because he's as moldable as a lump of clay. Unable to stop giggling, Anthony tightens his grip around my shoulders and buries his face in my hair, sending a current down my spine.

Sofia beckons to the rest of us to join them, but I can't bring myself to move out of Anthony's embrace. Mads holds up his hands and shakes his head. I think he's had more to drink than any of us. Anthony's long fingers sweep stray hair out of my eyes, tucking it ineffectually behind my ear. He's so close I can't read his expression, and I find myself first focusing on his mouth, then memorizing the shape of his eyes.

"Want to dance?" He breathes the words against my cheeks. We are almost kissing. I wait for him to lean just one inch closer. His pupils are so dilated, they obscure the blue of his irises.

He must take my dazed silence as a yes, because he pries the glass out of my hand and places it on the coffee table. Staggering as he stands, he leaves me alone on the cushions, cold without his body heat, then offers me a helping hand. As his fingers clamp over mine, I don't simply quell my usual inhibitions. It's bigger than that. I don't stand up to join him. Someone else does. He ropes her in closer and together they sway. Not to the music, like Sofia and Ben, but to their own slow and hypnotic beat.

||||||||||||||||||

I'm dizzy. Anthony is spinning me in circles, knocking our shins into the coffee table and veering too close to the fireplace. When he launches me into the sofa, I drop onto the cushions. And there I stay, not because I don't want to get back up, but because it feels like I've been drugged. The room is whirling, and it's all I can do not to throw up. I peel open my eyes and focus on my breathing, following the shadows of the dancers as they separate and conjoin on the ceiling. Sinking farther into the sofa, I begin to drift away. As darkness envelops me, I find myself thinking again, *This is where I'm meant to be.* Everything is going to be okay. I'm doing what I want. And I'm happier than I've ever been.

||||||||||||||||||||

When I open my eyes again, Sofia has climbed onto Ben's lap on the love seat, straddling him with her back toward me.

"Get a room," I tell them, my voice cracking. I'm not sure if I'm joking. Probably not.

Sofia flips me off in answer. I search for Anthony and Mads, but they're nowhere to be found. "Where—," I start to ask, but I know these two aren't listening. The music must have died somewhere along the way, because I can hear crickets outside. I force myself to sit upright on the couch, but slowly, to keep myself from retching. Ben murmurs something that sounds like "Upstairs" into Sofia's curls, but she ignores him.

I lurch off the couch, desperate suddenly to get away from these two before they take their clothes off. I already witnessed more than I care to remember while I bunked on the sofa in their cramped apartment. The kitchen is empty, and entirely too bright, but I stop and down a glass of water in one vicious gulp. It helps a little, even though my stomach clenches, and then I drift through the living room, following the sound of voices down the dark hallway. Away from Sofia's obscene moans, I can discern Anthony's slow and steady drawl, muffled through a door. Then a staccato laugh from Mads. At the end of the hallway, both doors are shut. Blue light leaks out of the office, outlining the door in neon, reminiscent of an old sci-fi movie about alien invasions. I'm wrapping my hand around the knob, when I hear Sammy's name.

Look at him, Anthony says. *Be honest. Can you really take him?*

Mads's answer is immediate. Almost exasperated, like they've had this conversation many times. *Dude, I'm twice his size.*

He was the wrestling champion in high school, Anthony says. *All four years.*

Yeah, he's jacked. But I've got at least fifty pounds on him. Don't worry.

I let go of the doorknob like it's given me a shock. I turn away, instinctively, but have to stop myself. I realize that I've never truly felt the room spin before. I've heard the phrase. I've even used it a few times myself. But I realize now I had experienced something much more mild. Because right now everything is actually spinning. I have to keep refixing my gaze on the floor. If I leave my eyes too still, it slides away.

Look how effortlessly he chops the wood, Anthony says. *He's a machine.*

His knees, Mads says. *You see how he flinches a little each time he lifts the ax? He's in pain. It's his knees, man. I've seen it before.*

Moving as silently as my numb body will let me, I close myself in the bathroom. Mads is preparing to fight Sammy. Is *that* what this is leading up to—a cage match of some kind? A bullfight? I'm the red cape. Sammy's going to, what, attack me? And Mads is here to pummel him, in retaliation? My stomach clenches even tighter. Shaking, I straighten myself up, lean on the counter. Try to calm myself down. When the fluorescent light flickers on, I'm startled by my reflection in the mirror. My eyes are bright, but they're surrounded by purple rings, and my eyelids are puffy. My cheeks are burning. My forehead is splotchy. In slow, hesitant movements, I splash some water on my face, then slick back my hair.

My mother dragged Dad and me to a zoo once when I was a kid, lingering with me by the big cats, telling me to watch their shoulders. "They slide," she whispered into my ear, pressing her cheek into mine and pointing at a tiger's retreating back. "Up and down and side to side. See?" She was entranced by its shoulders. But when we reached the water exhibits—polar bears and seals— she lost her enthusiasm and announced it was time to leave. My father hoisted me into his arms even though I was much too old and heavy to want to be carried. "The seals' eyes," he told me. "They scare your mom. She's afraid of them for some reason." Then he lifted me over his head and dropped me down onto his shoulders, and as we trundled past the cage, I swiveled to take one last look at the seals, my hands clamped on his forehead, my shoulders hunched in an imitation of the tiger's. I hadn't been able to figure out what scared her. The seals' eyes were black and glossy and extraterrestrial, but they weren't hostile. It wasn't their fault they had such luminous eyes.

But now I think I understand. They're like Sammy's eyes. Fathomless. Uncomprehending. I run the water again, splashing away the tears suddenly spilling down my cheeks.

I stare at the door for a long moment. I'm suddenly exhausted. I want nothing more now than to return to the cottage and collapse into bed, even if it means Mads will follow me down the path and climb into bed beside me. Before I can understand what I'm doing, though, I twist the latch and bolt the door to the hallway. Then, moving in what becomes a blur, before I can change my mind, I slip through the connecting door into Anthony's bedroom.

The phone is an outdated, enormous plastic box, like the one we used to have in the kitchen back home. The receiver cradles the side of my head. I sink heavily onto the side of Anthony's mattress, and listen to the dial tone.

I punch the numbers for home, then clench my eyes tightly shut. A trickle of sweat, or maybe it's the water dripping off my hair, slides down my back, describing the notches of my spine. *Mom, Mom, Mom.* At last, on the fifth ring, she picks up.

"Hello?" Her voice is flinty from sleep. It must be late here for her to be asleep on the West Coast. Then, more sharply, *"Hello?"*

"Mama," I whisper, tangling my fingers into the cord and pulling it into my stomach as though I've been winded.

"Elizabeth?" She's too tired to be angry, I guess. All I hear is relief. And an undertone of panic. "Where are you? What's wrong?"

"Oh, Mama." Just repeating those syllables wrings my heart. *Mama.* I can hear her sitting up in bed, fumbling as she pulls the sleeping mask off her eyes. Her silk pajamas, ancient and elegant enough to have been issued to a passenger on the *Titanic*, will pool around her, catching in the sheets and clinging with static to her long limbs. I can almost see them in the rustling that crackles over the tinny speaker.

"Where are you?" she asks, more insistently. "What's going on? Elizabeth, talk to me."

"I don't know." I'm speaking the truth—I don't know exactly where we are, and I don't really know what's going on, either—but I realize how dramatic this sounds. "I'm staying in Anthony Marino's summer house in Maine," I add quickly, to explain. My universe has narrowed down to this house, this island. Looking around the room now, though, I can barely recognize it. The colors are duller, the space smaller than I remember. Mads's words flood through me—*I've got fifty pounds on him*—drenching me like cold water. "On an island," I continue, speaking over my mother, who's trying to ask me another question. "It's off the coast, right by a little town they call the Strip." I wince as I speak, because I sound so young and vulnerable, even to myself, when all I want is finally to be an adult. But I don't even know the name of this place.

"Who's Anthony Marino?" she asks, sighing. The life suddenly bleeds from her voice. She's not concerned anymore. She's exasperated.

"He's the director. Remember? We've been up here filming at his family's cabin ever since your visit." The phone line skips like a blank record while I wait for her to speak. "I'm sorry," I say, when the silence starts to make the room spin again.

When she does speak—"Are you in trouble?"—my reaction catches me by surprise. I find myself bubbling over with the same age-old resentments she always evokes, in exactly the same way I infuriate her, too. We can never find common ground. Not even on zoo animals. I try to conjure the feeling of well-being I'd experienced earlier in the night, but it doesn't come. I tell Mom I'm shooting a film, and she doesn't ask what it's about or what part I'm playing. She only hears that I'm calling for help. And it embarrasses me that she thinks my apology is an admission. I'm not a kid anymore. I realize too late that I've said some of this out loud. She interrupts me with a sharp *Elizabeth*.

"I can't do this," she says, her voice so distant she must have turned her head away from the receiver. Louder, she says, "You're just like him. You know that?"

"Like who?" I ask. But I know who.

"Sometimes it's so similar it's frightening. You can't help someone who can't even see the problem themselves. It's the middle of the night, and I've been worried sick. I don't think I'll ever *not* be worried sick. I've spent the past twenty-odd years of my life worrying myself sick. I can't do this." I can hear the precise moment the tears start. I can see the unconscious flick of her finger as she brushes them away.

"Don't say that," I beg, careful to keep my voice down. "You—" I stop, unable to find the words. Inside, I'm reeling. She means well, I know. But it strikes me, too, how much of her venom is actually intended for my father. All I want is for her to see me. *Me*, as I am. Not me, my father's daughter. Or worse, her little girl. Is that too much to ask?

"Selfish," she croaks. "That's what you are. Selfish. Every bit as much as he was, to the very end."

It was a mistake to call her.

"Who is this Anthony?" she asks, sniffling.

I should feel grateful she wants to know, but there's an inflection in her voice when she speaks his name, like she's already decided he's terrible. Someone she wouldn't approve of, or even like. "I'm in love with him, I think," I hear myself say, but the words fall flat, and I regret, instantly, having spoken them. They reduce an ocean of feeling into one pathetic drop of water.

She chuckles, so drily it sounds like a mixture between a sob and a gasp. "Of course you are. Well, I'm happy for you. I really am. I'm glad you've moved on so quickly."

"Mama." It's the only word that will come out.

"I have my own life, too. Here, in this house. Has it ever occurred to you that I have to use the bathroom, the *tub*—" There's a thump on the line, as though she's covered the receiver with her hand. She comes back in the middle of a sentence. "—just like it didn't occur to your father."

She has always gone directly for the jugular. When I was little, we used to scream at each other in the car, our voices bouncing off the windshield, Mom veering wildly through traffic until I was begging her to pull over and let me out. I feel the same way now, even though she hasn't raised her voice.

"You don't know what you're saying," I tell her, staring at the phone's cradle like I had stared at the handle of our car door. But I can't hang up, just as I could never leap out of that car.

"I love you, Elizabeth," she says, sniffling. "But you left. You're the one—I hope you're okay. Really. But I can't do this right now. You moved on. Let me do the same."

A second later, the line goes abruptly dead.

⁙⁙⁙⁙⁙⁙⁙⁙⁙⁙⁙

I rush to the bathroom, making it to the toilet just in time to retch. The sound of a fist pounding the door penetrates through my heaving, but I can't stop to think, let alone to unlock the bolt, or even to say something inane like *I'm fine*. Eventually the knocks and my vomiting subside, and I prop myself up beside the toilet. I close my eyes against the harsh light.

At the unexpected touch of a damp towel on my cheek, I jump, accidentally bumping the back of my head against the wall. When I crack open my swollen eyes, I find Anthony hovering above me, his expression surprisingly tender. "Hey," he says, kneeling down closer and sliding an arm over my shoulders. "You okay?" He peers into my eyes. "That was a lot of moonshine you swallowed tonight, huh?"

I don't speak as he gathers me into his arms and, pulling me backward with him, finds us a comfortable position on the hard floor. I listen to his steady, insistent heartbeat, and follow the gentle glide of his fingertips on my spine, the rest of the way to oblivion.

In the moments before I let go, I hear his voice, gentle, so very far away, asking, "What did she say? Your mom. Betty, what did she say?"

|||||||||||||||||||

I don't know what time it is when I open my eyes, but the room is so dark, it must be the middle of the night. My heart pounds in my ears. Sweat drips slowly down my cheek. Something is wrong. The sheets are tangled around my limbs. If I could just get one leg out from the covers, to cool myself, maybe I could fall back asleep. But as soon as I try, I discover I'm paralyzed. My body won't respond. I struggle for a few beats before I realize that I can move after all, but that there's something on top of me, pinning me in place, preventing me from escaping.

The room is quiet. I manage to turn my head, just an inch, to check to see if Mads has woken up, too. But his side of the bed is empty. I think I can remember seeing him passed out on the couch in the main house's living room, and I guess he still isn't back from the party. He hasn't splayed himself out on the mattress.

He isn't the one holding me in place. It's fear.

Because I know, instinctively, that I am not alone in this impossibly dark room. There's an intruder, somewhere close. Watching me sleep. And it isn't Mads.

I feel a scream deep in my throat, but I know I won't be able to voice it. I've had this dream before. Not very often. Only when I was so exhausted it felt as if I'd forgotten how to sleep. And not since I got to New York. At Tuck's, after my father's death, for a while I had this dream every other night, at least. I began to wonder if my father was visiting me. Standing in the dark corner of the room, waiting for me to bridge the impossible distance between us. Wanting to say something I couldn't hear, because I couldn't reach him. And he couldn't move closer to me, because he was dead. I understood that it was up to me to join him. He was calling to me, and I had to push myself up, to drag myself across the room, to walk to him. But I couldn't.

Tears gather at the edges of my eyes. Because here he is again, after so many weeks without him. I try to force a single simple syllable from my mouth. *Dad?*

The shadow in the corner remains still. But for just one second, I think I can see its head tilt to the side. As though to say, *Yes.*

My pounding heartbeat slows. I force my eyes shut. These strange dreams—I don't think I can call them nightmares—had lost their power over me. Dad had begun to let me go, appearing only in conscious, warped memories. Until now. And then it hits me, and I almost laugh. It makes so much sense.

When I moved to New York, Dad didn't know where I had gone. He had to catch up to me, all the way out here. I feel my body slowly, gently relax. Sleep drifts over me once again. Dad has found me again. He has come back to look over me. To tell me everything will be okay.

And maybe sometime soon, I'll be able to reach out to him, and to give him the rest he needs, too.

Everything will be okay.

I wake the next morning, on the edge of the bed, my body a series of throbbing pains. My mouth is dry. My eyes sting. Sometime in the night, I wrapped the sheets around me like a cocoon. When I peel myself free, I discover I'm still in the clothes I wore yesterday. I check for Mads and am surprised to see his side of the bed empty. So he really didn't come back last night. I consider closing my eyes again and waiting for the hangover to finish punishing me. But it feels like there isn't enough air in here. I push myself up from the bed, splash water on my face and brush my teeth, then, squinting in the sunlight, wander down the path toward the house.

Can you really take him? That's what Anthony asked Mads. *I've got fifty pounds on him,* Mads said. Whatever Anthony is planning, I have to tell him I won't do it. I won't be a part of this. Maybe I'll leave with Sofia. I don't want to go. But I also don't want to be part of this vanity project. Because that's what it is. An elaborate, staged vendetta. They're sandbagging Sammy. No matter what he may have done, whether he deserved it or not, it's not just heartless. It's cruel. And it's dangerous.

After the noise of last night's party, the silence makes me feel as if I've gone deaf. No doubt I'm the first to wake up. I let myself into the messy kitchen. Smudged glasses litter the counters. Dirty plates clog the sink. Pots and pans, too. Ben is usually a neat chef. It looks like he let loose last night, but I don't remember him cooking. In the living room, Mads is still sprawled on the sofa, one foot down on the floor, his head covered by a pillow. He looks like a sleeping giant, from an old cartoon I can't remember the name of, disguised as a mountain. The peak rises and falls with every inhale and exhale.

The hatch leading to Ben and Sofia's attic is open, the ladder unfurled. Probably they left it down so they could find their way to the bathroom, drunkenly, in the dark. Anthony's bedroom door, however, is shut. The house is quiet. It's filled with the stench of whisky breath and puke. Probably mine. Last night comes slowly into focus. My mother's voice crackling over the phone. Did I actually call her? It feels like a horrible dream. But no, I did, and it went badly, too, so bad it makes me flinch. I let my mind return instead to the reassuring grip of Anthony's hands, hoisting me upward and carrying me out of the bathroom. *You're okay. Don't worry. I've got you.*

I pause in front of Anthony's door. My first instinct is to retreat. To get some coffee and wait for him to emerge on his own, when he's ready. But my anxiety gets the better of me. I have to know what he's planning. Now. Before Sofia leaves. Taking a deep breath, I don't even knock. I twist the knob and open the door.

The room is dark. It's early still, and the shades are pulled shut. Anthony is just a shadow on the bed, curled into a loose ball. Light spills across the floor from the doorway, landing on his chest. He murmurs, shifts, then blinks. His eyes immediately find mine. "What time is it?" he asks me, his voice croaking.

I check the clock beside his bed. "Ten," I tell him, shocked. It's later than I thought.

With a groan, he sits up. "What's going on?"

"I need to talk to you," I tell him. "And I want the truth. All of it."

IIIIIIIIIIIIIIIII

It takes him a while to rouse himself. Long enough for me to get us both a cup of coffee. I meet him in his office. He doesn't look happy, but I don't get the feeling my urgency comes as a surprise, either. "You heard us last night," he says, dropping into the chair and indicating for me to sit, once again, on the bed. "Me and Mads," he clarifies.

"Yes," I say. "You're trying to provoke Sammy."

Anthony shrugs. "Something like that."

"You're using me, to give Mads a reason to beat him up."

"Not exactly," Anthony says.

"His knees are injured," I say. "That's what Mads said. He's going to go after his hurt knees."

"You make it sound more clinical than it is," Anthony objects.

I look away from him. A thousand mortified thoughts crowd my mind, but I don't know how to articulate them. My tongue feels like it's covered in hair. The coffee is too thick. I should have stopped to get some water, before confronting him. Frustration wells in my chest. It occurs to me how little voice I seem to have with Anthony. It's been that way right from the start.

"Sammy humiliated me," he says, simply. Quietly, like he wants to figure out a way to tell me the truth—*his* truth—so that I'll understand.

"So you're getting your revenge," I say, "by asking a man twice his size to rough him up?"

Anthony squints at me. "I can't say this isn't about revenge," he admits. "At least on some level."

"Why would you even pretend to have a movie, then?" I ask, my voice rising. Why can't he just answer my questions? Why does he make everything so complicated? "Why not just take your camera and film Mads beating him up?"

"I'm not pretending to make a movie," he tells me. "I am making one. *We* are. It's about my relationship with him."

"Why?" I ask. "What did he do to you that was so awful?"

"You're furious," Anthony says. "You're angry with me." He doesn't look at me directly. His eyes are on his bare feet. He shakes his head. "I can't talk to you about it when you're like this."

"I'm—," I stutter. I don't know what to say. Of course I'm upset. Everyone else knows what this is about. They've all been lying to me, essentially nonstop. Just when I get my bearings, when I decide to enjoy this, as it is, it flips on me again. I'm trying to decide for myself what I want to do. Is that so wrong? "I'm not *angry*," I correct him. "But you have to know how I'm feeling. This is so—" I bite my lip to keep myself from finishing that sentence. *This is so unfair.* The complaint will only make me sound like a child.

But Anthony seems to hear it, regardless. I catch the suggestion of a faint smile on his lips. When he looks up, though, his expression is sincere. "I know," he says with a sigh. "You feel like you're left out."

"You want to hurt him," I say.

"You're not hearing me. He *humiliated* me."

"You want Mads to hurt him," I insist.

"If it comes to that, I want Mads to be ready, in case he has to." He watches me, reading me. But there's something else. He's trying to ask me a question, without voicing it. I catch my reflection on one of the dark screens behind him. My fluorescent hair. The streaks of forgotten mascara under my eyes. I don't look like myself.

"This isn't necessarily physical," I say.

"Exactly," he says.

"So you want *me* to hurt him," I say, quietly. "Mads is just here as backup. To protect me. I'm the one who has to take him down."

Anthony blinks a few times, then lowers his head. I get the feeling that the truth unsettles him. He hadn't appreciated how much he was asking from me.

"You're going to have to tell me why." My voice is surprisingly firm, and I realize how resolute I am. This is an ultimatum.

Anthony drops his head into his hands. He takes in a few deep breaths, like he's pulling them into the depths of his torso. I can't tell if he's weighing his options, or if he's acting for the cameras, or if he's just simply trying to steady himself. When he speaks, it's to his lap. "I told you I don't remember what happened all those years ago," he says. He waits, as though for me to confirm. I put a hand, lightly, on his knee. He doesn't take it in his own. But he doesn't push it away, either. "I was lying, Betty. I don't need to *remember*. I *know* what happened." Another breath, as deep as the others, sucking the air from the room.

"What?" The admission stuns me, and I rear away from him. "How?"

But he doesn't speak. He doesn't even seem to hear me. This is suddenly real for him now, too—as a person, as Anthony Marino, not as a director. He's experiencing something on his own, distant from me. Something I can't fathom, or touch. I wait for him to return to the present, trying to keep myself steady, too. This is it. This is what I've been asking for, since the first moment he mentioned the movie. The truth. The simple, unadorned, unsophisticated, raw, painful truth. When Anthony finally does look up at me, his expression shocks me. The color has drained from his face.

"I was a strange kid," he tells me. "I don't know. Maybe I was autistic. Maybe I am. I had a camera. I had a few of them. I was obsessed with them. I haven't changed much." This brings a smile to his face, but it's lifeless. "Sammy used to come over to babysit me, right? Neither of us wanted it. But I don't know, I was—I was little. I'd never met someone like him before. And he put on a good enough show of being okay with me. I followed him around because I had to. And because, you know, I was curious. In that way that kids are fascinated with what frightens them. His father was a brute. A real brute. He looked like he'd walked right off the set of *Deliverance*. You know that film? And his son was this huge wrestling star with a gorgeous girlfriend. I was drawn to them. For whatever reason. So I—whatever. I recorded them."

With another shake of his head, he turns away from me. He brings the computers back to life and taps some keys, digging through the hard drive. "Darla was beautiful," he continues. "Like you. I fell in love with her. I took her picture. I gave her some of the pictures. She loved that. Sammy never seemed to notice, or if he did, he acted like he thought it was funny. 'Puppy love' is what he called it." He finds whatever he's been searching for and clicks on a video file. The image on-screen is out of focus, just a brown blur. I can only make out shadows and lines. It looks like a floor. "And then," he says, "this happened."

When he presses PLAY, the frame swings wildly around a room. I catch a glimpse of a window—long enough to place it, with a spike of adrenaline, as the window in my cottage—before it's replaced by a kid's face. The video is choppy, practically pixelated, but the teenager on-screen is undoubtedly Anthony. I recognize his eyes. His mouth. He's so young he still has the remnants of baby fat in his cheeks. His nose is too big for his face, in the way that all boys' noses seem to pop out around age fifteen. His blond hair is pale, cropped short. The camera settles, like he's put it down on a flat surface, and Anthony steps away.

"Fourteen," Anthony says, as if I've asked him a question.

On-screen, the interior of the cottage comes into focus. It's rougher than it is now. Unfinished. The wall separating the bedroom from the bathroom is little more than plywood. The bed in the middle of the room is a single, not the queen that's since replaced it. The camera must be sitting on a nightstand.

There's a knock on the door, but before Anthony can answer it, Sammy walks in. He's younger, too, but already hardened, and no less imposing.

"What—," the young Anthony says. His voice is high-pitched. Unsteady. "What are you doing here?"

I feel Anthony shift beside me. "I was expecting Darla," he tells me. "Instead . . ." He trails off, gesturing to the screen.

Sammy doesn't answer. He doesn't even seem to hear Anthony. He walks into the room, taking his time. His hair is fuller, but you can already see some hint of it thinning. He moves like an athlete. All bounce and glide. Unconscious grace. "Get down on the floor," he says, finally. The command gives me a shock. Not just the instruction itself, but his voice. It lacks the drawl he's developed since. The words come out quick, spring-loaded in his throat like ammunition. "On your hands and knees." There's no room for disobedience.

"Why?" Anthony squeaks, unable to mask his fear. Despite the age difference, they're the same height. But Anthony's limbs are long and delicate, his chest practically concave. In comparison, Sammy looks like a bull.

"Get down on the floor," Sammy repeats. "Hands and knees."

"What are you going to do?" Anthony manages to say.

"Teach you a lesson, that's what." Sammy closes the door behind him. Anthony has no way to escape. "Hands and knees," he says, louder this time. Angry that he has to repeat himself yet one more time. "Get on your hands and knees, hear me?"

"When my father gets back—"

Sammy laughs. "This isn't about your daddy." He places a hand on Anthony's shoulder. "Down. Now."

Anthony hesitates. His eyes widen. I can barely look. His terror is so real I can feel it, all these years later. Finally, he obeys. But clumsily, as if his arms and legs have locked up and he can barely comply.

"Okay," Sammy says, crouching down beside him. "This is the easiest breakdown. I put my arm here"—he loops one arm around Anthony's middle and wraps the other around the shoulder closest to him, like a snake coiling around its prey—"and here. And—" With a tilt of his weight, the two collapse to the floor. Anthony's breath leaves him in one quick exhale of pain. "Is that all you've got? You're supposed to fight back. Resist me."

"What are you doing?" Anthony asks him, pleading.

"What do you think I'm doing?"

Anthony is panting. I can only imagine what he's thinking. He's not too young to know what this man might do to him, with no one to help him out here on this island, just the two of them.

"What do you *think* I'm doing?" Sammy asks again, as if the implication is an insult.

"I don't know," Anthony whines.

"Get up," Sammy orders him. "On your knees."

"Why?"

"On your knees," Sammy repeats, grabbing him by an arm that

looks like it will come loose in Sammy's hand. He pulls him back up, and Anthony complies, assuming the position of a wrestler on the floor, too scared to try to escape. "Now resist," Sammy tells him, but when he gives him a light shove, Anthony nearly topples. His arms shake. "Resist," Sammy says, trying him again with another shove. Satisfied, he lowers himself onto him again, then tightens his grip. "Ready?"

Anthony's voice crackles over the speakers, but it's too muffled for me to make any sense of it.

"Speak up," Sammy says. He shifts his weight onto him, digging his chin into Anthony's back.

"Let me go," Anthony says.

"On three," Sammy says. "One. Two. *Three.*" This time, Anthony puts up a struggle. But it doesn't last long. Sammy overpowers him, once again crushing him to the floor. And this time, he doesn't let up after Anthony is down. He moves on top of him with surprising speed and even more surprising grace, locking his arms around him and squeezing until Anthony's face turns beet red. Anthony manages to free an arm. He links his hand around the one choking him, but it's useless. The arm won't budge. What horrifies me, more than anything else, is the silence. Anthony doesn't have the time, or the energy, to make a sound. He barely even breathes. He's working with all his might to get loose. But Sammy simply shifts his weight again, and Anthony's face disappears underneath him.

Finally, Anthony gives in. "Please," he says.

"What's that?" Sammy asks.

"Please," Anthony shouts.

"'Please, sir,'" Sammy corrects him. "Show your opponent some respect."

But Anthony won't say it. Sammy digs into the boy's spine, but he won't beg.

Anthony's quiet voice next to me rockets me back into the present. "This is where I blacked out," he tells me. "Everything goes fuzzy." His eyes are fixed on the screen. But when I reach out and grab his hand, he pulls himself free. I understand. The last thing he wants right now is to be held. Not even by me.

Looking at Anthony, the adult Anthony, I feel sick. I don't want to watch any more of this. This is brutal. He's just a kid. But then the door on-screen opens, and I'm drawn back into the video. A girl steps inside, a blur of dyed blond hair and loose, gauzy clothes, and gasps. I can't help but gasp, too, just as sharply. It's Darla. And yes, she does look like me.

"Sam!" she exclaims, staring down at Sammy and Anthony on the floor. "What are you doing?" She has seen Sammy wrestle before. She knows how strong he is. And how vicious. Underneath Sammy, the boy emits a choking sound. "Let him go, Sam," she pleads. "You're going to kill him."

"I saw the pictures," Sammy tells her. In the light pouring in from the open doorway, I can make out a sheen of sweat on his forehead. The exertion is finally getting to him. His mouth twists as he tightens his grip. "That's right," he tells Anthony. "I saw your fucking pictures. You owe Darla an apology."

Anthony pants. When he finally decides to speak, his voice comes out in grunts. "I'm sorry."

"You heard him," Darla says. "Now let him up."

"He's not finished," Sammy says. "He still owes me an apology, too." Again, his grip tightens. "Say 'Sorry, sir.' Say it." Anthony doesn't speak. "Say it." Sammy switches his hold, digging an elbow into his spine, slipping an arm around Anthony's throat. Next to me on the bed now, Anthony has stopped breathing.

"Sorry, sir." I feel myself wince.

"Say 'Sorry, sir, for being such a freak.'"

Darla takes a step closer, as though she can't hold herself back. But something prevents her from intervening. She's afraid of Sammy, too, I realize. Every bit as much as Anthony is. "Let him up," she says again. "He's just a little boy. Come on, Sam."

"He knows the words," Sammy says. "It's up to him. All he's got to do is speak them."

The video pauses. Anthony's hand drifts away from the keyboard, leaving the three of them frozen in place. I come back to the room slowly, in stages. I realize I've wrapped a hand around my mouth.

In a low voice, Anthony asks me, "Enough?" He's close, so close I can feel his breath on my skin. He's shaking. I can see it in his fingers, which tremble as if he's shivering.

Without thinking, I lean forward and gently rest my forehead against his. There's nothing to say. I can almost not think. I keep hearing Sammy's taunt, *Say "Sorry, sir."* And then the story of Archie Miller. The scar dividing his skull into two. *I tried to kill him. He tried to kill me.* Why would he do this to Anthony? No matter what Anthony had done—no matter what pictures he had taken and shown to Darla, if that's what this was actually about—

he didn't deserve this beating. He is right. Sammy humiliated him. In fact, that's an understatement. I can't wrap my arms around the cruelty. But does it really make sense to try to exact revenge upon him? Will it really make any difference to Anthony to film Mads doing the same thing to Sammy that Sammy did to him? And what does this mean for me? Is that what this is about, then— reconstructing this scene, with me playing the part of Darla?

Anthony leans away from me. He looks steadier. Now that the secret is out, he can move back onto more familiar ground. "I'm not antagonizing him," he tells me. "Even if it feels like it. I want him to feel the way I did, all those years ago. You saw what he did to me. I didn't know what was going to happen. So when I heard he moved back here, after all this time, I realized—" He shakes his head. "But there is a story here, Betty. A structure. The movie is about me. Do you understand? It's about me, not him. About this—" He waves to the screen. "About getting over this. The only way I know how."

"And you need me to"—I hesitate—"to give Sammy something to fight for?"

"He's been watching you, Betty. As I knew he would. You've confused him. The thing is, though, it's not enough." He takes a deep breath. Lets it out slowly. "It isn't enough that he's curious about you. You need to flirt with him. What he needs is a little encouragement."

I'm on my feet before I know I'm going to stand. I check myself, but I take a step away from Anthony anyway, away from the overly bright screens. My headache has come back with a vengeance. My heart beats in my temple. "What do you mean, *flirt with him?*"

Anthony follows me with his eyes. "No matter what happens," he says, "just remember, Mads will be right there."

"That's what you're counting on," I say. "That is your whole plan. You want him to make a move on me, the same way you made a move on Darla. So Mads can teach him a lesson."

Anthony shrugs.

"No," I hear myself say. I think of Sammy's eyes. The twist of his grin. The way his body curled around Anthony. The way he choked him, made him beg. He repulses me. I don't think I could let him near enough to me to flirt with him. And at the same time, I don't think I can bear to watch Mads hurt him, either. "I can't do that. I *won't*. That's— No, Anthony. I'd rather go back with Sofia. Don't make me—"

"Sofia left this morning," Anthony cuts in, shaking his head. "She and Ben left early, to catch her train."

This announcement winds me. I'm alone. That's it, then. Sofia has gone. And she didn't even say goodbye. I guess I could have said something last night. I had known she was leaving. Why didn't I say anything? She's my best friend. Or something like that. She hasn't exactly been acting like it since we got here. Still, though, I could have told her thank you, at least. Thank you for taking me in. For introducing me to Anthony. No matter what her motivations have been—and I doubt she has been thinking of *me*—she has helped me. Maybe that's why things have been so strange between us. She's been waiting for me to bridge that gap, and I have been avoiding her because of this debt I can never repay. And because—if I'm being honest—I don't think I should have to. She didn't warn me about Sammy, or my role in luring him into Anthony's web. I'm glad she's gone. Grateful, in fact. She's been a distraction since we got here. A reminder of home. Of how awkward and friendless I am. That's right, Betty. You're better off without her.

But, a small voice whispers back, as easy as it was to begrudge Sofia when she was here, at least she was another woman. Now I'm the only woman among this group of angry, resentful men.

I take a halting step toward the door. I don't know where I'm going, I just know that I have to get out. *Out.* Into the open air. I have to run. I have to breathe.

As though in answer to these thoughts, Anthony pushes himself up and corners me before I can reach the door. His hands frame my face, stopping me in place. "This is a lot to take in," he says. "I know." He leans in close, so close I can see only the blue of his eyes. "But please don't go. Don't leave me."

"You're—," I start, not even sure what I'm going to say next. "It's not that I want to go." *I have to.*

"Then don't," he says simply. "We can talk about what you're comfortable doing. But please, don't leave me here alone with him."

It's an agonizing second before his lips finally touch mine. And then the room starts to spin, and I'm lost.

One of Anthony's hands migrates from my face to my lower back. This isn't the clumsy, drunken kiss we shared in Ben and Sofia's lobby. This time, there's no reluctance. No hesitation. We can't seem to get close enough to each other. The warmth of his body—its solidness—envelops me like water. I'm drowning in him, in the smell of his skin, in the scrapes from the rough edges of his stubble, in the caress of his hands on my waist. I can't get enough air. But I don't need it. All I need is him. From the way he's breathing, I know he feels the same.

Blindly, clutching me close, he takes a step forward, and I retreat. Another. And another. Until I can feel the corner of the spare bed knock into the backs of my legs. As I crumple onto the mattress, I realize how lost I am. I've forgotten everything. Everything except him. I know only the movements of his body, and the beat of my heart, pounding in my chest.

I reach for him, to pull him down to join me, but he resists. It takes me a moment to realize he's listening to something outside the room. I make sense of the sputtering rumble of a boat motor echoing over the water.

"That's Ben," he tells me. "Back from the mainland." He links his fingers with mine and gently tugs me up to sitting. "I have to talk to him about the cameras." He drops a chaste kiss on my forehead, but despite the gesture, my cheeks burn with embarrassment. I feel exposed. I wouldn't have been able to stop, at least not so easily. "And I don't want him walking in on us."

I try to shake myself out of my daze. "What's up with the cameras?" I finally ask, attempting to match his businesslike tone.

"Some of them have moved," he says with a shrug. "We have to make sure they're secured properly when we position them."

I watch him straighten his shirt and comb his fingers through his hair.

"Anyway," Anthony says, reading my disappointment, "you need time to think. We'll talk tonight. Okay?"

I consider telling him that I've already reached my decision. That as soon as he showed me that clip, as soon as he told me the truth, as soon as he kissed me, I knew I was going to help him. That I don't want to say no to him. That I don't want to lose him. But I think he already knows this. And to say it all out loud, this fast, would be a mistake. So instead I nod my head, and mentally let him go.

Anthony holds my gaze for a moment, until he's satisfied that I've read his thoughts, too, and then he's out the door. From the living room, I can hear Mads's pained groans as he slowly regains

237

consciousness. He mumbles for everyone to keep their voices down, then barks when the front door slams behind Anthony.

On my own in the office, I sit down at the desk and return to the computer monitors. Anthony left the video up, on-screen. The three figures are pixelated blurs. Darla, a stick figure in white. Sammy and Anthony, a conjoined heap on the floor.

Left alone, I feel myself settle back down into reality. Anthony wants me to find a way to instigate a confrontation between Sammy and Mads. That's what he's asking me to do. That's my direction. To create a situation where Sammy expresses an inappropriate interest in me and Mads can intervene and teach him a lesson. The same lesson in humility that Sammy taught young Anthony. So that's why I have to understand, in detail, the confrontation between Sammy and Anthony, in front of Darla. I hit PLAY on the video, and the scene comes back to life.

"Stop it, Sam," Darla says. Her arms reach for Sammy, but she stops, about a foot away from his body, like he's protected by a force field. *You're killing him.*

"He knows the words," Sammy repeats.

Anthony's face is a tapestry of purples and reds. His eyes are squeezed shut so tight it looks like he's trying to will himself out of this room. Finally, something inside him breaks. I think I can see the exact moment it happens. His body slackens. All the fight has been squeezed out of him. He looks older suddenly. He says the words as best he can. "I'm sorry, sir, for being such a f-freak."

For a moment, the room is still. Darla looks like she wants to be relieved, but she knows Sammy too well for that. She's still scared for Anthony. In the space of that instant, though, I see something else course through her as well. Her disappointment, in this young boy, that he capitulated. That he couldn't find the impossible strength to fight his way out of the older man's hold. As much as she's concerned for him, she's also embarrassed for him. I can imagine what Anthony feels when he watches this. What he must have felt when he first watched it back, his body still bruised and throbbing, still in the invisible clench of Sammy's arms. Watching Darla's deflation. Listening to her say, *He's just a little boy.*

And then, so suddenly it makes me jump, Sammy laughs. I stop the video. Sammy's mouth is frozen wide open, teeth flashing in the light, eyes scrunched up to nothing.

I try to picture the man I saw my first morning here, chasing after his mother, cowed in front of her. Pleading with her to understand why he didn't want to visit his father in prison. *He hit me.* Or the man who told me about Archie Miller. But I can't recall him any longer. All I can see is this man laughing in triumph. Cutting off Anthony's air. Reveling in his surrender.

On one of the other monitors, Anthony and Ben cross the lawn toward the woods in real time. In another frame, I can see that Mads has returned to the cottage to shower. Despite my newfound resolve, I feel myself shiver. I wrap my arms around myself. I tell myself I know what I'm doing. I tell myself how good I'll feel, once I figure out a way to rope Sammy in and help Anthony wrestle him to the ground. I hope I'm right.

||||||||||||||||||||

After a late, hazy dinner filled with more alcohol and Ben's over-the-top stories about meeting Sofia's parents—I never knew she'd taken him home to Humboldt—I tell Mads that I won't walk back to the cottage with him, the way we usually do. "I need to talk to Anthony," I say.

"I'll leave a light on for you," he says.

"Don't," I say, too quickly. Then: "It might be a while."

I watch the understanding wash over him. "No problem," he says, with a shrug, adding that he needs to sleep anyway, because he hasn't had a hangover this bad since rush week. He winks at me before wandering out the back door, into the night. Ben is already in the bathroom, getting ready for bed. He seems lost without Sofia. Every conversation leads back to her. Anthony has already disappeared into his room.

I follow the light down the hall, to his open doorway. "I've thought about what you said," I tell him, hesitating on the threshold, speaking just a touch too loudly, for Ben's benefit. "About the movie."

Anthony is at the window, leaning back on the sill. Almost like he's been waiting for me. "What do you think?"

The room smells of oregano, the leftover fumes from Ben's cooking, laced with the tendrils of the fresh, mulchy air seeping inside through the cracked window. It feels like I'm in a dream, suddenly. Or as if I've stepped into another life. Another person's life. Someone who is confident. Who has handsome, charismatic men waiting for her. And when this man in front of me sees this other, more secure woman, he comes to life. I feel giddy. Light. My body practically vibrates with this feeling. Like I could do anything, because it's not really me who's standing here. It's not really me who's about to go to him. It's this other girl. The one Anthony promised me. The person I've always wanted to be.

I pull the door shut behind me.

"I've reached a decision," I say.

He waits for me.

I stop a few paces in front of him. "I'll do it."

He folds his arms across his chest. He tries not to react, but still, the relief is evident in his face. His mouth loosens from its frown.

"You shouldn't have lied to me," I tell him. I want to approach him—to cross the distance between us and pick up where we left off this morning—but this new girl stands her ground. This is a turning point for us. We both need to understand just how momentous this is.

He considers my reproach. "I didn't lie," he says, finally. "I told you what you needed to know."

"You have to trust me," I tell him. "The same way I trust you."

He holds my gaze for a long moment. I can't tell what he's thinking. But he seems to come to a decision. When he speaks, his voice is low. "I didn't hire you just because you look like Darla," he says. As though he's listened to my every horrible thought. "The resemblance is uncanny," he continues. "But I wasn't lying, back in my apartment. There's just something about you." He pushes himself away from the windowsill. But whatever he's about to say next is interrupted by Ben's shout from the hallway. "All yours." The bathroom door rattles shut in his wake.

Anthony straightens his posture, as if we've been caught doing something illicit. As Ben's ladder retracts into the ceiling, Anthony runs a hand through his hair. He eyes me for a moment. Deciding something. "I'm going to take a shower," he tells me. And then he's brushing past me, closing himself in the bathroom. The faucet almost immediately squeals on, and the room is blanketed in the soft white-noise spray of the shower. It occurs to me he hasn't asked me to stay here. But he knows already that I will.

When the bathroom door opens again, I'm on the bed, and the lights are low. My heart is racing. But Anthony, clothed only in a towel, doesn't show any sign of surprise. He simply closes the door behind him and switches the last light off. "You're on my side."

I don't move.

In the darkness, I can barely see him drop the towel. Seemingly unconcerned by his nudity, he goes to the windows first, to pull the curtains closed. Then he joins me on the bed. The mattress utters a quiet squeak beneath his weight.

He lifts the blankets, and I slide underneath, grateful for the cold sheets because I'm suddenly so flushed, I'm practically sweating. The covers rustle as he settles in beside me, close but not quite touching. After that, the only sound in the room I'm aware of is the steady rhythm of his breathing.

His voice is soft. "Come here."

My eyes have adjusted enough that I can make out his profile. He's lying on his back, staring at the ceiling. I prop myself up on an elbow next to him, stretching a leg alongside his, then reach an uncertain hand out to touch his cheek, gently nudging him to face me. I remember that first night I met him, at the restaurant, when I placed my hand on this very same cheek. How automatically he rejected me. This time, he's quiet, and I'm not sure if I imagine him leaning into my hand. "I . . . ," I start, but trail off. I don't know what I want to say, anyway. My hand travels down his jaw, lightly tracing the contours of his neck, his collarbone. Begging him, in so many ways, to be the brave one and kiss me first. But I don't think he will. He's making it clear, I think, that this choice belongs to me.

I don't let myself hesitate. I lean forward. I brush my lips against his. It comes as a surprise to discover that he's trembling. My hand follows the line of his ribs to his stomach, down to his hips.

"You don't have to," he says, but he closes his hand around mine, pressing it flat on his stomach for a moment, then leading it farther down.

I don't speak. I simply wrap my leg around his hips, then slide on top of him. Time seems to stand still, or maybe it's leaping forward, I don't know, because I don't remember taking off my shirt, or being rolled onto my back. All I register is his weight, heavy, pressing me into the mattress, and his breath, hot, against my neck. At first I think he's saying my name. But in the darkness, almost lost in the rasp of our breathing, I hear him calling instead for Lola.

I was the one who found my father.

That is the question people are really asking when they find the courage to whisper, "How are you doing now?" *Who found the body? Was it you?* If I tell them, they get bolder. Usually, the next question is "How did he do it?" Most of the time, I don't answer, because the thought of all that blood still makes me dizzy. If I do respond, though—"He slit his wrists"—this generally shuts them up. But I know what they are wondering, even if they already know that people who slit their wrists do it in the bathtub ninety-nine percent of the time. *Where did he do it?* I've never been brave enough to ask them in turn what they picture. Do they see the tub in our house? Or did he, in their minds, do it in some seedy motel?

For whatever reason, they don't seem to have any trouble asking me whether he left a note, even though this is the most personal aspect of the suicide, his final words to his wife and daughter. And this, almost always, is the last question they ask. As though this finally satisfies their curiosity, which is something they feel entitled to demand of me.

Dad closed himself in my childhood bathroom—the only one in our small house, the one with the geometric midcentury wallpaper he'd pretended to hate—drew himself a bath, tested to see if the temperature was right, disrobed and climbed in, then opened up his veins with deep, certain cuts, and died alone. Everything about the ritual was deliberate. He knew he was going to be found, and he went to pains not to make a mess. There was no blood on the floor, and almost no splatters above the water line. He had been thoughtful to that extent: Whoever found him, my mother or me, wouldn't have to mop up any blood. All we'd have to do was pull the plug and flush the stain down into the sewer. Nevertheless, the water was as red as wine. And I was the one who saw it first.

What no one ever asks is why. I'm grateful for that at least, because I don't yet have an answer, and I don't know if I ever will. But I think *why* is the wrong question, anyway. The right one is: "Did he know *you* were going to find him?" I have reached the only conclusion I can live with: No, he didn't know I would be the one to open the door. He loved me too much for that. I think he put the possibility out of his mind, because that's the nature of this act, and there was no real way to eliminate this risk.

He hadn't been in there long. We had seen each other in the morning, when he drove me to the diner on Main Street, where I was scheduled to work the brunch rush. It was a short commute, about fifteen minutes, and I spent most of the time complaining to him about Tuck. Tuck and I had been fighting, in fits and bursts, about everything, and I was ready to break up with him. Dad listened to it all and gave me the same advice he usually doled out. *Don't let him walk all over you, speak up.* But then he cleared his throat and said something about how I wasn't just who I was to him. I was an amalgam of all the Bettys whose hands he'd held over the years, since I was born. *You used to be so tiny,* he said. *You insisted on being carried everywhere. I held you on my shoulders for so long walking around the house, I'd almost forget you were there. I still think of you that way.* I laughed, but didn't say much in response, because we had already reached the diner. He didn't lean over to hug me. But when I opened the passenger door to get out, he grabbed my arm and held me there, to take another look at me. I stared back at him, confused. Then I climbed out. "Thanks for the ride," I said, and slammed the door. I didn't look back to wave.

In the end, my shift got cut short. I was still upset about my fight with Tuck, so I didn't want to go back to the small room I shared with him in a house we rented with another couple. I went home, to Dad.

There was no note. Only a photograph, on the floor next to the tub, its edges curled and wilting from the steam, of my mother and me. The picture is old, out of focus, so that my mother is a blur of blue eyes, white teeth, and shimmering hair. She's clutching my infant body tight to her chest as though my father is trying to take me away from her. There's a splotch in the corner of the frame that could be a clumsy thumb over the lens. Or maybe Dad actually had been reaching for me.

I called my mother's office from the side of the tub. Her first words, when I finally made myself clear enough to be understood through the tears and coughs—the smell was thick enough to stick to my clothes, my hair, and I couldn't get the taste of blood out of the back of my throat—were "He's awful." No questions, only that. And then: "He hates me."

She was the one who notified the authorities. I sat with him in our bathroom, in total silence, until I heard my mother arrive outside, with the police. I kissed his cheek goodbye, like I had every day growing up when he dropped me off at school, and then I walked away. When my mother declared that we wouldn't be having a funeral, I wanted to ask her why, but I didn't, because I knew she wouldn't tell me. I'm sure she had her reasons. She was angry with Dad, for killing himself, or she was ashamed, as if his suicide was somehow a reflection on her. She just wouldn't tell me, because all I was to her was her daughter. Still, I was relieved, because I didn't want to see his casket or his gravestone. I wanted to believe my father was out there somewhere. Maybe he was back in Iceland, eating sharks from the ground and climbing glaciers, waiting for me to join him.

I wonder if I should tell Anthony this. To tell him that I understand. Certain wounds can never heal. Sammy, his arms cinched around his neck, screaming at him to say *Sorry, sir,* and still not relenting, Darla's impotent pleas, witnessing his humiliation. These ghosts haunt him, the same way I sleep with mine.

I was the last person to see Dad alive before he drove himself back home, calmly, maintaining the speed limit, before he shut himself in the family bathroom, before he disrobed, before he filled the tub and climbed into the water, before he emptied the blood from his body. And I was the first person to see him dead. I can never speak to him again. I can never tell him how sorry I am. How much I miss him. I can't heal. I will just keep living, without him.

This is the past I'm running from. This is the present I'm locked into. This is the future that awaits me. There's no escaping my ghost. Nor do I want to. There's only learning to live with it. Exactly as Anthony is seeking to come to terms with his.

23

I follow Anthony onto the porch. It's early, but it's hot already, humid and stifling. The sun hides behind a thick layer of haze, but I can still feel its scorching radiation as soon as I step outside. The wood is hot enough to sear my bare feet.

"Look at those clouds," Anthony tells me, indicating the sky with a tilt of his head. I can see only a puffy white ridge over the tree line, barely distinguishable from the steamy haze. "That's a squall coming our way." He sniffs the air, and I become aware of the earthy perfume of rain laced with the briny stink of the seawater evaporating on the rocky beach. "I think I'll grab Ben and head over to the mainland, to the supermarket before that thing hits. Mads has eaten everything except the plates." When Ben wanders out behind us—drawn by the sound of his name, I think—he's yawning so wide, it splits his face in two.

"I'll come with you," I say.

Anthony shakes his head. "Better not to leave anyone here alone," he says. "We should buddy up." He draws me into an encompassing hug. When he next speaks, it's into my hair. "We'll be back in a couple hours. Probably before Mads even wakes up."

I tighten my grip around his waist, then let him go, so I can follow him down the front lawn, grass and mud tickling my feet. Ben trails behind in our wake, silently. I'm not sure how much he knows about Anthony and me. Most mornings, I'm in the main house already, before he's woken up. Today might have been no different. But there's a new tension between Anthony and me. A new understanding. Maybe Ben can sense it, the way Anthony can smell the storm coming. He gives us space as we trace the path to the pier, then looks away, pretending to busy himself with the mooring, while Anthony leans down to give me a last kiss.

I watch as the two men settle onto the garbage scow. Ben had ferried Sofia over to the mainland just fine by himself, to get her to the train station. He grew up fishing in the Great Lakes, he'd told me, which had surprised me, because of his Brooklyn hipster demeanor. Nevertheless, Anthony takes the wheel as they putter away from the pier. Ben raises his hand in a salute, while Anthony twists around, finds me, and holds my gaze. It's only for a moment, long enough to send a small jolt up my spine. This is real. What's happening between us is *real*. It's not just me, and it's not just physical. By the time I can sort these thoughts out, Anthony has turned away again, and Ben is settling into a seat. The boat roars into life, sending a smooth curl of waves behind it, as they arc toward the mainland. I watch them, until the boat shrinks and finally slips from view.

The island feels suddenly empty. Small, without Anthony here. I turn in place, defeated—pathetic. Come on, Betty. Don't be such a sap—resigning myself to the prospect of spending a couple hours alone, when something I can't identify enters my field of vision. It happens so abruptly, I can't assimilate it at first, and my first reaction is to gasp and raise a hand to my mouth.

The blur resolves itself into a person. Sammy materializing from the air, almost like a ghost. Not three feet from me. Hands on his hips. Watching me. How he slipped up behind me without my hearing him, I have no idea.

His face is serious, stiff, but then the skin stretches into a sly grin. "I didn't scare you," he says, "did I?"

"How long have you been there?" I ask him. I have to remind myself to slow down. There's no reason to be afraid. At least, not yet.

"You don't think your boyfriend is going to be upset with you," Sammy drawls, "do you?"

It takes me a few beats to realize he's talking about Mads. Not Anthony. And then another to appreciate what he's really saying. He's answering my own question: He's been here long enough to have seen Anthony and me kiss. My mind whirls, before I finally settle upon a tack. "Mads? I never said he was my boyfriend, did I? I only met him a few weeks ago. He invited me up here with him, that's all."

Sammy looks disappointed. I can read his reaction. I'm familiar with it. Men who don't immediately tie themselves down are given a pass. We say they have a fear of commitment, like it's a bit of a joke. Women who aren't strictly faithful—even before a relationship is exclusive—cheapen themselves.

"No strings," I say. "Not yet."

Sammy's expression solidifies as he considers me. Again, I can read his thoughts. At least, I think I can. He's realizing I'm available. If I don't belong to Mads, maybe he can make a play for me as well. And maybe Anthony's interest in me makes me that much more attractive to him. At the same time, though, he's wondering whether he's interested in me after all. Because I'm loose. I'm no angel, not any longer. To him, I'm a slut. Like the other girls he's known. Maybe even like Darla.

"How did you get here?" I ask him, trying to distract him from these thoughts.

He shrugs.

"Did you swim here?" I ask, infusing my voice with a little more energy. I realize, too late, that his clothes are dry.

"Not this time," he tells me, shaking his head. It occurs to me then to wonder just how long he's been over here on the island. Because I don't remember hearing the sound of an approaching motor. Maybe he reads these thoughts, too, because he explains: "There are other places to tie up a boat. Not just the pier."

"I can't imagine swimming this channel," I say, figuring a little flattery can't hurt. "Isn't it dangerous?"

He stares into my eyes for a moment too long. Just taking me in. Unlike Anthony's shared gazes, this one isn't trying to transmit anything, or seeking to understand anything in me. Or if he is trying to connect, it's in some kind of alien language. I'm suddenly back in that zoo, on my father's shoulders, staring into the seals' eyes, and I understand my mother's visceral reaction to them. It makes you feel bottomless, when you realize the creature staring at you is thinking something you can't decipher. He holds me in place for another instant, and then he blinks, and the moment is over. "I've been doing it my whole life," he tells me. Matter-of-fact. "It takes a strong swimmer to get through those currents. You have to be fast, because the water's so cold. If you hesitate. If you stop. You're gone. Swept out into the ocean."

I have to suppress a shiver, despite the heat. I resist the urge to search for the watching eye of a hidden camera. As if our being observed would somehow offer me some protection. And from what? As unexpected as Sammy's presence is here in this moment, this conversation is exactly what Anthony has been wanting. This is my opportunity, finally, to develop my relationship with Sammy. Now is not the time to shrink from this challenge. Anthony believes in me. He's seen something in me. Something special, which no one else has ever seen before. I want to prove him right, and not just for his benefit, but for me, too.

And it strikes me in the same moment, I don't even need to flirt with Sammy. I don't need to draw him in. He's already here. He's interested in me, sincerely. I can feel it. I can feel how much he wants to get to know me. To figure me out. To draw me to *him*. All I need to do is talk to him. All I need to do is open myself up a little.

Sammy seems perfectly content to gaze at me, in silence. He has even clasped his hands behind his back, assuming the guise of a passive spectator. But he's not judging me. He's waiting for me. I'm in charge of this situation. Without my help, he's too submissive to know how to approach me. At least now. At least initially.

"You haven't come around much," I tell him. "I was kind of expecting to see more of you."

His eyes narrow. He's smarter than I want to believe. He knows what I'm up to, and he doesn't like it. "I don't figure you were too broken up about it," he says.

I take a step toward him, deciding the best approach is to be honest. "Actually," I say, "I've been hoping to continue our conversation." Not because I want to. Because I'm supposed to.

"I took a couple of days off," he tells me, bristling. A thought passes over his face like a cloud, and then he releases the grip on his hands and brings one of them from behind his back and raises it toward me. "I had to let this heal a bit," he says matter-of-factly. "Couldn't hold anything for a day." My stomach lurches. The knuckles of his index and middle finger are a muddy combination of yellow and purple, dappled with fresh scabs.

"What happened?" It looks as if he put his fist through a window.

Finally, a genuine smile. He likes my reaction. He stretches the injured fingers, then tightens them into the head of a hammer. He wants me to see the injury. He wants me to know he's capable of violence. I remember the flash of disappointment on Darla's face, after Anthony surrendered to him. She was scared of Sammy, because she had a reason to be. But she was drawn to him, too. Whereas I'm suddenly nervous again. This game Anthony wants us to play is dangerous. It's as real as these cuts on Sammy's hand.

"Guys around here," Sammy says, cryptically, "they can get themselves all worked up over me being wrestling champ. Varsity. Even though that was years ago, and I don't fight no more."

I let the words sit for a moment. From the look of his knuckles, he must have hit the other man pretty damned hard. The next thing I do is without any reflection. I raise my own hand up and, trying to keep my fingers from shaking, offer it to him for his examination, flexing it into a fist to show him the jagged white lines on my skin. Between my knuckles. "When I had to get these stitched up," I tell him, "the nurse warned me that the numbing shots would hurt more than the cuts. She said, 'This is going to be the worst part of your day.'"

He leans forward and reaches for my wrist, loosely hooking his callused fingers around the joint to revolve my hand from side to side. "What did you do to yourself," he asks, dragging his gaze up my arm to my eyes, "to give yourself these?" He's impressed with me, I can tell.

I don't immediately answer, because of the way he's phrased the question. There's no doubt in his mind that I gave myself these cuts, on purpose. He assumes I took a razor to my skin. He assumes I'm like my father. Self-destructive. And, I realize, there's some benefit to letting him believe this. To being whoever he seems to want me to be. He isn't too far off, anyway. "Let's just say I got them in a fight, too," I say at last.

"I don't think so," he says, shaking his head. He still hasn't let go of my wrist. He's examining my fingers, as if he can divine the source of these cuts forensically.

"What do you think, then?" I ask him.

It takes him a moment to formulate his response. "I think you're every bit as complicated as you look," he says. His grip on my wrist becomes a clasp. Like we're holding hands. I have to resist the urge to rip myself away from him.

"Is that a good thing," I ask, "or a bad thing?"

Rather than reply, he assesses me. His eyes travel slowly up and down my body, from my toes to my shoulders, and I realize that there's nothing I can do to hide the blush that's creeping up my chest, my neck, my cheeks, under this bald stare.

"What would you think," he asks me, "about coming over to me sometime?" There's something almost charming about the invitation. Or disarming, at least. Almost. It sounds like he's inviting me over to his house for a playdate. But the man in front of me is still gripping my wrist, tighter than I'd like. And he isn't blinking. "I could show you the town. We have some of the best lobster you'll ever eat in your life. That's what everyone says."

I dip my head down a little, the way I would if I were pleased with the invitation. "Yeah," I say. "Why not? That'd be really fun, Sammy."

"How about now?" he asks. He's still using that same slow drawl, but there's an urgency in his voice. Like he can't believe his luck, and he doesn't want me to change my mind.

My heart is suddenly pounding in my chest. I'm trapped. That's how it feels, like I've been cornered. What would Anthony have me do? Refusing him will risk destroying this connection we've made. But there's no way I'm going anywhere with this man. And even if I did go, there are no cameras off the island, so what would be the point?

As it happens, Mads rescues me. The front door swings open, and he bursts out onto the porch. "Lola?" he shouts, loud enough for his voice to rumble across the lawn separating us and echo on the water. "Are you okay out there?" Then: "What's up? Where is everyone?"

Sammy jolts a little. I can't read whether he's scared at being caught like this with me, or just surprised. There's certainly no ambivalence in Mads's voice. His intention is clear. Not only to dominate, but to intimidate. At the moment, I'm nothing but relieved. Finally, Sammy releases my wrist. I can feel his reluctance as my hand slips through his fingers.

"Lola?" Mads repeats. He's closer now. Ready to step in.

Nevertheless, Sammy's eyes remain fixed on me. "Later, then," he says. He doesn't move yet, though. He's waiting for me to respond.

"Later," I say, quietly. Mads's footsteps approach me from behind.

"What's going on?" he asks me. I can feel the heat pouring off him. "You okay?"

"I was just leaving," Sammy says, at last acknowledging him with a glance.

"Yeah," I say at the same time. "Everything's fine."

"Don't you worry about that," Sammy tells Mads. "Your girlfriend here can take care of herself."

Mads joins me, with a heavy arm wrapped around my shoulders. Never in my life have I felt more grateful for someone to stake a claim on me.

Sammy's gaze darts to my face one last time before he turns around. It takes me a second to decipher the expression on his face. He's wounded. Not by Mads. But by me. He wants to say more. He wants to ask me if I'll still join him. I can feel it. He wants my reassurance. "I'll see you around then, I guess" is all, though, that he can manage.

"Later," I say again, realizing as I speak the word that the emotion I hear in my voice is genuine. Maybe I feel sorry for him. I don't know. Maybe I'm still desperate to prove Anthony right. Whatever the case, though, I've given Sammy what he wants. What he needs from me.

Sammy whistles as he wanders down the path, back into the woods to find his boat. Still, though, Mads doesn't let me go until we're inside. And then he's bouncing up and down on his toes, shaking his shoulders, working out his restless energy.

"We're almost there," he tells me. "I can feel it coming."

I'm in the bathroom splashing my face with water before I realize with yet another shiver that I recognize the tune Sammy was whistling. He disappeared into the forest serenading me with our song. Mine and Anthony's.

24 While we wait for Anthony and Ben to return, Mads and I sit in the living room and watch a thick layer of mist slowly suffocate the remains of the sun, drawing the color from the sky. As the living room windows turn gray, it feels to me as if we're being submerged in a bath of tepid, soapy water, and I push myself up from my comfortable position on the sofa to switch on the lights, even though it's way too early for this and they hardly do anything against the gloom. Mads has hardly left my side since his confrontation with Sammy. When we first returned inside, he performed a series of pull-ups, using the lintel above the entrance into the hallway as a bar, as if he needed to burn off an excess of hormones still churning through his system. Since then, every half hour or so, he stretches himself out—keeping himself ready, I think, in case Sammy comes back.

When he emerges from the bathroom, cheeks flushed and hair

dripping from the shower, he crosses the room to the windows. "What time is it?" he asks me.

"One," I answer, joining him at the window.

Neither of us speaks. But we're both thinking the same thing: They should have been back by now. They left nearly five hours ago. It hasn't started to rain just yet. But the wind is already whipping through the trees, howling and whistling in the eaves. This is going to be a fierce storm. The island feels unprotected, and the channel is treacherous enough on a calm day. Maybe they're having a difficult time getting back.

Mads clears his throat. "Should we call them?" But it sounds like he's speaking more to himself than me.

"Do they have their phones with them?" I've spent so long without mine, it seems strange to imagine Anthony and Ben carrying them.

Mads strides out of the living room. I follow him down the hallway, into Anthony's room. He goes straight for the bedside table, opening the bottom drawer, without hesitation, and revealing three cell phones. He obviously knew where the phones went. When Anthony had taken my phone, our first night here, he told me he was stashing them away in a drawer. He hadn't specified which. I'm not so surprised, but I make a mental note of the slight. This is yet another reminder how much of an outsider I am here. Still.

Mads nods in satisfaction. "Looks like one phone is missing. Probably Anthony's." He reaches for the landline, dialing immediately. It strikes me that he knows Anthony's number by heart. The two of them are closer than they let on. He presses the phone to his ear, waits a beat, then, frowning, depresses the switch hook, as though to hang up the call. He does this once, tentatively, then again, clicking the buttons a few times, more forcefully.

"*Damn,*" he exclaims. His eyes are on me, nervous. Urgent. "I think the phone line's down."

I'm staring at the phone, like I can will it to work. Then, without thinking, I pick up the receiver and hold it up to my ear. But Mads is telling the truth. There's no dial tone. No sound like a skipping record. It's just a flimsy piece of plastic in my hand. "Must be the storm," I say, though I'm thinking it's not windy enough yet to knock out a phone line.

"What do we do?" he asks me.

"If the phone line is down," I say, finally replacing the receiver in its cradle, "the electricity is probably next. We need flashlights. And a fire."

Mads's relief is palpable. I'm going to take charge of this crisis. He'll do whatever I ask him to do, but he's not making any decisions. He tells me he thinks he saw a flashlight in the closet by the kitchen. "I'll start the fire," he says, heading back to the living room.

The utility closet smells of old leather and bug spray. While Mads kneels in front of the hearth, I manage to dig out a few large flashlights, and toss them in a pile on the sofa. He's finally getting the fire going when I hear the mechanical whirr of an approaching boat. "Thank God," I say, making for the front door. The wind grabs it from my hands as I push it open, and I'm barely able to catch it before it slams backward into the wall. I wrestle it back into the frame until I hear the latch click.

Mads is already off the porch. I have to practically jog to keep up with him. By the time I reach the shore, he's on the pier. My legs slow as I sidle up next to him. The wind is so briny, it stings my eyes, and my vision is blurred. Maybe that accounts for my confusion, as I make sense of what I'm seeing. The boat pulling up to our dock is not the garbage scow. It's another, smaller dinghy, and it's manned by Sammy. Sitting in the front, bundled up in thick blankets, are Anthony and Ben. The garbage scow trails behind Sammy's boat, listing helplessly in the wind, its nose bouncing dully in the increasingly choppy waves.

Sammy doesn't throw Mads the rope. Instead, he leaps onto the dock himself and lashes his boat to the pier, clutching the knot tight before signaling for the two men to disembark. Mads grabs Ben's hands to assist him, even though he seems unhurt, just a little shaken. His cheeks are drained of color, and he holds his body stiff, like he's on the verge of shivering.

"What happened to you?" I ask Anthony, looking over at the garbage scow, which is weighted down with a ballast of overflowing plastic grocery bags.

Anthony shakes his head. He doesn't look ready to speak yet.

Ben claps Mads on the shoulder, then gestures to the garbage scow, which is still drifting, knocking against the pier. "The engine just *died* on us, dude."

"Lucky I spotted you," Sammy says, grunting as he corrals the scow and lashes it expertly to the dock. I watch as the oily rope rips the scabs from his injured fingers. He doesn't even wince. He catches my stare and locks his gaze on mine. "When I caught up to them," he tells me, "they were practically out to sea."

"Are you okay?" I ask Anthony, who doesn't seem to hear me.

"I should have warned you all when I got here," Sammy continues, leaning over to begin unloading the groceries. "That engine doesn't have a lot of horsepower. You shouldn't have been out there. This current here will take you out to sea so fast even the Coasties won't be able to find you." He brushes past Mads, bags rustling and hanging from his arms, and starts up toward the house, shaking his head. The scow knocks into the side of the pier with a deep, reverberating sound, but it looks stable enough.

Anthony clears his throat, then directs Ben and Mads to grab the rest of the bags. To me, he says, "I'm fine, really."

And then together, as a group, we follow Sammy up the path, to the porch, where he's deposited all our food. He's skipping down the stairs when we reach him.

"Thank you, Sammy," Anthony says, stopping short in front of the shorter man. "I don't know what we would have done without you."

Sammy nods. Once.

"Stay for lunch," Anthony suggests. From the tone of his voice, it's clear he isn't grateful at all, and he doesn't actually want to make this invitation. He's seizing an opportunity for the film. That's all.

Sammy pushes past him, like he's going to ignore the offer, but then stops, pulling himself up next to me at the rear of the group. "Actually," he says, "I was hoping to ask Lola here to join me." He's responding to Anthony, but he looks at me instead. "If she still wants to come over with me to the mainland for a bite of lobster."

Anthony looks confused, but not unduly. He glances up at the sky. "With this squall approaching?" he objects. "Why don't you just stay here, Sammy? We've got enough to feed an army."

Mads doesn't appear to register Anthony's objection. Instead, he approaches Sammy and me, moving in close like an enormous shadow. He's still keyed up from this morning's confrontation. "What did you say?" he barks. "You didn't just say that, did you, bro?"

Sammy stares for a moment at the ground in front of his feet, as if he's considering the question. Then, finally, he raises his bulbous eyes to Mads. When he speaks, though, he speaks to me. "We have plans. Don't we, Lola?" His voice is soft. Still, there's absolutely no mistaking the challenge. I glance at Anthony, uncertain what I should do. I can feel this escalating. I know that's what Anthony wants. I recognize that this is exactly the moment he's been prodding us toward, and I can almost taste his excitement. He nods at me, nearly imperceptibly. Urging me forward. Willing me to help Mads instigate this confrontation. But it's happening so quickly. It's upon us so unexpectedly, despite the buildup. I'm not ready for this yet. And I don't know how to react.

"What are you talking about?" Mads asks, looming over me, as he sizes Sammy up. "She's not going anywhere with you."

Sammy's eyes don't blink. They lock themselves onto Mads's face. But not on his eyes. On his mouth, I think. On his chin. His own lips curl into the suggestion of a smile. "Why don't you let her decide?" His voice is sweet. Patronizing. "She was eager earlier."

The next thing I know, Mads's anger is directed at me, rather than Sammy. Two massive hands drop onto my shoulders without any warning, heavy enough to crush me. He isn't violent, though.

If anything, he's incongruously gentle. But before I can catch my breath, I'm being twisted around in place. The hands slide down to my biceps, his fingers digging into my flesh. I don't recognize this version of Mads. I've seen him intimidate Sammy. I've never seen him angry, though, not like this. It turns his beautiful features ugly. He's a gargoyle of himself.

"Tell me this is bullshit," he says. Like I disgust him. "You didn't tell this moron you were going to eat *lobster* with him, did you?"

"Yes," I stutter, too confused by the dramatic transformation to speak anything but the truth. Then, out of reflex: "Let me go."

I feel the air shift behind me. I can sense Sammy moving. He's probably taken a step closer, on those quiet feet of his.

But Mads isn't paying attention to him. His eyes are boring into mine. "What the hell are you doing, Lola?" he asks me. "Do you have any idea how many girls I could have asked up here? What the fuck—" He gives me a shake, tightening his grip.

I know what he's doing. But his anger feels genuine. I feel trapped, and I can't help but react in kind. "You're hurting me," I tell him, trying to escape his hold. It's impossible, though, to free myself. As gentle as he is, I'm caught in a vice.

Sammy materializes beside us. Arms loose, like he's relaxed, except that his muscles are bulging. "I'd take your hands off her," he tells Mads, matter-of-factly, "if I was you."

Mads ignores him, but I can feel the tension in his fingers as he readies himself for this next escalation. It looks like he's holding me. He's prepared, though, to grapple with Sammy. I can hear it in his breathing, just how eager he is to destroy him. "You make me sick," he tells me. "Sick."

"I said," Sammy says, stepping in closer, so he's practically on top of Mads, "I'd take your hands off of her."

Finally, Mads shifts his attention to Sammy. He gazes at him, breathing through his nose, then releases me, pushing me backward, out of the way. "What are you going to do?" he asks Sammy, puffing up his chest. "You gonna make me?" He looms over the shorter man. But Sammy doesn't flinch. Instead, he seems to lean his weight forward, tilting his head up, to meet Mads's eyes. Mads is breathing hard, like he's suddenly out of breath, and I think it must be the adrenaline coursing through him. The contrast with Sammy is stark. He looks focused. Like he isn't even breathing. And it occurs to me, he doesn't realize yet what's about to hit him. After all, he has no way of knowing that he's being set up.

I take a step backward, instinctively getting out of their way. I don't risk another glance back at Anthony. I know he's there, just on the edge of my field of vision. Waiting. Tense and ready. I can almost smell the bloodlust in the air. My stomach clenches, and saliva gathers in the back of my throat, like I'm about to vomit. This is abhorrent. Mads is twice this man's size. Nearly half his age. He's been preparing for this moment. Ready to aim for Sammy's injured knees—and, I remember, with another twist of my stomach, Sammy's voice as he showed me his torn hand. *Couldn't hold anything for a day.* Mads is going to break him. I know I shouldn't feel this way. I know what Sammy did to Anthony. But I feel sorry for him. I don't know if I can watch the same thing happen again, this time in reverse, to yet another unsuspecting, helpless victim.

Sammy's voice yanks me back, horribly, into the moment. "Lola," he says, eyes fixed on Mads's chin. "Let's go." He doesn't understand yet that the fight has already started. He still believes that this confrontation is about me. That my fidelity is still the issue, and still up for grabs.

"Are you kidding me?" Mads says. "She's not going anywhere with you. Now get the fuck out of here."

"Not," Sammy says, savoring each syllable, "without Lola."

Before he can finish uttering my name, Mads's hands are on him. Shoving him, savagely. Sammy lurches backward, caught off guard, hands flying out as he tries to regain his balance. But Mads is way too strong, and his legs can't move fast enough to catch himself, and he buckles to the ground in a clumsy heap, one of his knees taking his full weight on the gravel path. He winces. Mads was right about his knees. There's no doubt. I can read the pain on his face as he stands back up. And once again, I feel sorry for him as he squares his shoulders and gears himself up to attack. He's like a bull, too thickheaded to know anything else but to charge. Mads, though, is not like a toreador. He has no intention of getting out of this smaller man's path. He raises himself up to his full, intimidating height, preparing to knock Sammy into unconsciousness.

My own voice shocks me. "No!" I shout, suddenly desperate. "Please, Mads. Don't hurt him." Sammy is momentarily unsteady on his feet. His knee doesn't want to straighten fully. I can feel a hand on my shoulder holding me back. Anthony. He doesn't want me to intervene. This is his big moment. Finally, his big revenge. Mads is going to pummel Sammy until he capitulates. Until he's humiliated. And the whole thing is going to be caught on tape. I'm certain Anthony has already told Mads how he wants this moment to play out. The scene won't be complete until Mads has Sammy pinned to the ground and he has extracted an apology from him.

As he steadies himself, Sammy's gaze is on the ground, head jutting forward. At last, he takes a deliberate step forward, toward Mads. Then another. He doesn't look up, like he's concentrating on something on the ground in front of him. Another step. Bent over like this, his head is barely higher than Mads's chest. He's walking right into the bigger man's punch, I think, wrapping a hand around my mouth. Preparing myself for the inevitable crunch of bone splintering bone. Sammy stops, a few paces away still, head down. I think he's scared. For a split second, I wonder if this is over. Maybe he's come to his senses. But then, in the space between two heartbeats, he launches himself forward, so fast he becomes a blur. It's like he's moving through a strobe light. Everything has sped up and slowed down, in equal measures. I see Sammy disappear into Mads's middle. I expect Mads to crush him. But the next thing I know Mads has been hoisted up off the ground, his mouth open in shock. And then there's a loud, sickening crash as his huge body lands on the gravel, his back flat. I don't have time to take in a breath to scream.

Sammy's on top of him, wrapped around him expertly, shoving the man's face back with a forearm, the other hand pinning Mads's arms into a painful tangle. Mads is struggling, with all his might. But Sammy holds him still. His arms bulge, but he isn't straining. He tightens his grip, then leans his head back to take a good look at Mads's pink, winded face. "Apologize," he says, his voice betraying the effort he must be making.

Mads's only response is a painful wheeze.

"You can do better than that," Sammy tells him, digging his forearm harder into the soft flesh under Mads's chin. "Apologize."

"S—," Mads starts, mouth wide open, his normally full lips swollen like he's been kissed. He takes a short, rattling breath. Then: "So—"

Sammy drops a hand to Mads's leg, which he yanks backward, forcing Mads's face farther into the ground, all the way from this impossible angle, like a lever. "I don't have all day, boy," he tells Mads.

Mads gasps, overcome by the pain. This has happened so fast and it's so unexpected, that not one of us—Ben, me, or Anthony— has figured out how to react. We're stunned. Frozen in place. "Sorry," Mads grunts. There are tears in his eyes.

The hand lifts from my shoulder. Finally, Anthony is moving. He pushes past me, his face white. He's reaching for Sammy's back, as if to pull Sammy off his friend, when Sammy releases Mads, twisting around to face this new aggressor so quickly it stops Anthony in his tracks. But not before he gets one last dig in, into Mads. I don't see what he's done at first. I *hear* it. There's a horrible popping noise that I can feel in the pit of my stomach, and then Mads howls in pain. The sound travels up my spine, clos- ing in a fist at the top of my neck. The large man curls into a ball, reaching for his leg, his whole body shaking. And I realize belatedly what has happened. Mads had gone for Sammy's weakness. Sammy had decided to turn it into his.

"My knee," Mads cries, the words barely more than a rasp. Ben rushes to his side, his face white. Mads whispers, "He broke my—"

Sammy's already on his feet again, yanking himself out of Anthony's grip. "Don't touch me, Anthony," he tells him, pointing a finger in his face.

No matter what his intention may have been, Anthony flinches away from him.

Sammy has to swallow a laugh. "You coming, Lola?" he says, still facing Anthony. And it strikes me. For him, this really is about me. Anthony had wanted a fight. This man wanted *me*. My blood runs cold. Sammy actually expects me to leave with him, even after this violent display. He expects me to get on a boat with him and sail away, with Mads's hoarse screams following us. I shake my head, realizing only as I do how much this will hurt him.

Sammy waits, finally turning toward me, eyeing me as if he can't understand my hesitation.

I find my voice. "No," I tell him. More softly: "No."

For a moment, his face drops. But then he recovers himself, quickly. As if by rote, like this is something he's had to do before. His eyebrows gather together in a concentrated frown. For a few beats, I think his mood is going to shift and he's going to attack me. At last, though, he just turns away from me and jogs back to the pier. As his footsteps fade, Mads's wretched crying grows louder and louder, as if Sammy is delivering him to us as he retreats. I watch Sammy leap onto the boat. Already, his own knee seems to have healed.

Anthony seems to shake himself out of his stupor. "Wait," he says. And then, louder, in a shout: *"Wait, Sammy."* He sets out across the lawn at a run. I stand there, frozen in place, until I understand what Anthony has seen. The scow is still attached to Sammy's boat. And it doesn't look as if he has any intention to untie it.

I race after Anthony, catching up to him at the pier.

"That's our boat," Anthony says, but Sammy has already pushed away from the pier. It's too far to jump.

"I'll fix it," Sammy tells him, already pulling away. "The engine's shot, anyway."

Anthony's face turns red. I can't tell if he's angry or scared. "You can't take—"

The boat's motor roars to life as Sammy guns the throttle, kicking water out in its wake, drowning out Anthony's objections. I have to strain to hear Sammy's next words, shouted over the spray: "Don't worry," he promises us. "I'll be back."

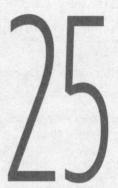

25

It takes both Ben and Anthony to pull Mads
back up to his feet. He can barely do it.
When he tries putting weight on his injured
leg, he nearly collapses to the ground. Between them, the two men
manage to keep him upright. "My knee," Mads gasps. His whole
body convulses, and his pain vibrates in his voice. "I can't—"

"Focus, Mads," Anthony tells him, his voice strained, too, as
he practically carries him up the porch stairs. Ben grunts as Mads
lurches into him.

"I can't," Mads says, shaking his head. The color drains from
his face so quickly, it looks like he's going to faint. He needs med-
ical care. A hospital.

Anthony tightens his grip around his waist as he maneuvers
him inside. "Don't black out," he says. "Just a few more steps."
Then, once he deposits him on the couch: "What does the pain
feel like?"

Mads practically wails as he lifts the injured leg onto the pillows. "It *hurts*," he says.

"We'll get you some ice," Ben tells him, trying to sound soothing, but he's out of breath from the exertion, and his voice comes out irritated.

Mads sweats like he's run a marathon. Veins bulge in his forehead. Purple splotches color his face. His eyes roll, reminding me of a wounded horse. When he finally examines the injury, he lets out another howl. The wounded joint doesn't look like a knee. It's an angry, throbbing, swollen sac of flesh dividing his calf from his thigh. "We have to—," he starts. Then: "Doctor." He directs those rolling eyes at Anthony. "I need a doctor, man." And then at me, when Anthony doesn't respond: "Tell him, Betty. I need a doctor. He's got to get me to a hospital."

Ben returns from the kitchen with a couple packs of frozen peas. "Here," he says, shoving them into Mads's hands. When he starts to rearrange the pillows under Mads's knee, Mads doesn't just flinch. He bucks, then grabs Ben by the collar and gives him a shove.

"Bro," Ben whines. "I'm just trying to help."

"These aren't even frozen," Mads barks, tossing the peas back at Ben. "And don't touch me. This is bad, Ben." He's hyperventilating, but he manages to slow himself down. "Real bad. I'm fucked."

I've lost track of Anthony. I can't do anything except stare at Mads. There's blood trickling down his neck, from a small wound above his ear. Probably from a sharp piece of gravel when Sammy brought him crashing to the ground. Tears stain his cheeks. He's trembling with the pain. But I don't think he's in a state of shock. To me, he looks scared. I don't think he will be able to walk out of here. That is, if and when we do manage to leave. Sammy stranded us here, on this island, deliberately, with no boat. Our phone line is down, our cell phones don't work. Mads isn't alone. I'm scared, too.

I walk down the hallway to Anthony's room. I grab the phone, hold it up to my ear, praying for a dial tone. I feel as though I could will the device back to life. But there's only silence, and the faint echo of Mads's heavy breathing down the hall. I crumple onto the mattress, cradling my head in my hands. *Don't worry,* Sammy had said. *I'll be back.* A shiver climbs my spine. He's not finished with us yet.

Outside, the storm has settled all around us. Rain finally begins to fall, plunking down in thick, rhythmic drops on the roof at first, then lashing the sides of the house in bursts of wind that rattle the windows and even the shingles, before crashing down on us in a torrent. The thick wall of trees surrounding the house reverberates with different tones that sound almost like notes blown from the pipes of an old cathedral organ. I lie back on Anthony's bed and close my eyes. I'm not tired, but sleep begins to overtake me anyway. It's another means of escape, I guess. And that's all I want right now, to find a way off this island.

"Don't!" Ben's voice pierces through the house, like a lightning bolt, jolting me awake. There's a flurry of rustling, of pained gasps and venomous whispers. Something crashes to the floor and Ben shouts: "Anthony!"

Footsteps thunder down the hall, punctuated by an odd clattering *thunk* for every second step. Ben's voice gets closer. "Don't, Mads. You'll—"

"Get out of my way," Mads tells him. They're right outside the door. "I need to talk to Anthony."

My head is still reeling from the surprise. I take a deep, shuddering breath and push myself up. In the hallway, I find Mads, leaning heavily on an upturned broom, which he's using as a makeshift crutch, one hand steadying himself on the wall, face red from exertion. Ben is behind him, practically in tears. He can see how much pain Mads is in. He knows he shouldn't be on his feet. But he's helpless. Even in this, there's nothing he can do.

By the time Anthony emerges from the office, the color is draining from Mads's face again. "You need to lie back down," Anthony tells him.

"What I *need*," Mads says, "is to get off this island. Now, Anthony. What I need is to see a doctor."

The lights flicker as the wind roars overhead. Behind Mads, Ben glances up at the ceiling, like he's worried it will fall down on him. Anthony, though, only sighs. "What do you want me to do about it?" he asks Mads. "We can't get out of here until the storm has passed. We don't have any way to call the mainland, and even if we could, we wouldn't be able to make it across the channel." His voice is so calm, I know he's faking it, and I feel goose bumps prick my arms and tickle the back of my neck.

It hadn't yet occurred to me: He's scared, too. *Anthony Marino* is scared. There's something magical about him. So long as Anthony Marino was here, so long as I was stranded here with this larger-than-life director, it's felt to me as if nothing bad could

275

happen. Not to me. Not to any of us. Nothing fatal, at least. He had everything under control. But it turns out he's not larger-than-life after all. He's in over his head, too, like the rest of us. Scared to death of this situation he's created. This beast he's poked, who's now out there somewhere, circling, figuring out how to attack us.

Mads sticks a finger in Anthony's face. "You get me off this island," he says. "I swear to God, Anthony, you get me out of here. Now. That psycho broke my goddamned leg."

Anthony splays his hands. "Mads, I—"

"No," Mads says. "He *wrecked* my knee." The anger leaks from his voice. "Don't you understand what that means? I can't help you. I can't do anything. I can't protect Betty if he decides he doesn't need to ask her *permission* to take her off this island. I can't even walk without this goddamn broom." He shifts his weight off it, then swings it against the wall with a *thwack* that makes Anthony wince. "The movie is over, Anthony. Done."

Ben nods his head solemnly. "He's right, Anthony."

"I want off this island," Mads continues.

Ben's voice chimes in again, softer. "He's right."

"Before he comes back. Do you hear me?"

"He's not going to—," Anthony starts, but it doesn't seem like he can convince even himself. He runs both hands through his hair. "It's not my fault," he says. Then, so quietly I can barely hear him: "You knew what you were signing up for."

"You can't be serious," Mads continues. "You're not that clueless, right? Don't you see what's happening here? This guy is fucked-up. He wants to hurt you."

"He sabotaged the boat," Ben says. Mads tries to turn around, to catch Ben's eye, but the pain won't let him. His knee isn't the only injury he sustained in that fight. He landed straight on his spine, on a bed of gravel. I saw the bruises. He's having trouble breathing, like his ribs might be broken. I don't know how he can still stand.

"What makes you say that?" Mads asks. "Ben? What are you saying, man?"

"Isn't it obvious?" Ben retorts. To Anthony: "There was no problem with the motor on the way over to the mainland."

My own voice surprises me. "He probably cut the phone line, too."

"You're being paranoid," Anthony says. But his eyes are on mine, too wide. Wounded. Like I've turned against him, and he never, ever imagined I would. "You're giving him too much credit."

"No," I say, shaking my head slowly. "I'm not. This is what you wanted, Anthony. To rile him up. To turn him into a monster. And now—" A wave of dizziness washes over me. This is too much to bear. I can't shake the image of Sammy's grim smile. That promise. *Don't worry. I'll be back.* How he so effortlessly destroyed Mads. Those bulbous eyes on me. The genuine pain he felt when I rejected him. What is he going to do when he comes back? Mads is wrong about one thing. It's me he's after. Not Anthony. I can feel it.

"We can't turn on each other," Anthony says, trying to regain some control over the group. "Mads, you *have* to lie down. He didn't break your leg. He twisted your knee. Right now there's nothing we can do, except the obvious, which is what a doctor would probably tell you anyway. Ice and elevate. So that's what we'll do." To Ben: "We can't fall apart here. We're going to hunker down. Wait out the storm. Everything will feel better tomorrow, when the sun is out." Then, finally, to me: "It'll be okay." It looks like the energy has drained out of him, all at once, like a leaky balloon.

"Jesus," Mads says. He's angry. He's been angry. But there's something else in this exclamation that demands our attention, and all three of us raise our eyes to look at him. He's had an epiphany, and it's winded him.

"What?" Anthony finally prods him.

"You're still thinking about the movie," Mads says, gawking at him. His face is as white as a sheet. I don't want to believe him at first, because the accusation is too ugly. But then I catch Anthony's reaction—his own cheeks color, and if only for an instant, his gaze flickers to the floor—and I realize Mads is right. *This* is precisely what Anthony wanted. The cameras are still rolling. This chaos, this uncertainty, this moment of crisis when no one knows what will happen next or whether we will even survive another night—*this*—is the film Anthony plotted. This is *Fear*.

"Don't be crazy," Ben says, putting a hand on Mads's shoulder.

"Panicking isn't going to help," Anthony tells him.

"Isn't that what you want?" Mads counters. He's looking at Anthony like he's never seen him before. "For us to panic?"

"We have to keep our heads," Anthony says. "Work together."

Mads shakes his head. "You're insane," he says finally. Like he means it, literally. "You know that? You know what you've done, Anthony? You've ruined my career. You've hurt me, okay? This is over. It's bullshit. I don't want anything more to do with it."

Ben puts a hand on his shoulder again, and then, when Mads lets him, he grabs his side. "Let's go, dude," he says, pulling him away. He shoots Anthony an unreadable glance, but then he has to concentrate on shepherding the large man down the hallway.

When we're alone, in the dark hallway, listening to Ben's reassuring murmurs, Anthony turns to me. "Betty," he begins, like he's pleading with me. "It isn't like—"

"Don't," I tell him, interrupting him. I step away from him before he can reach for me. "I have to think."

Suddenly, he looks like the fourteen-year-old I saw on film. Vulnerable. Out of his depth.

I have to turn away. This is the first time he has needed me more than I need him. But right now I can't deal with this. I'm overwhelmed. I can't just fall into his arms and pretend like nothing has happened today. Or that nothing will happen later, whenever Sammy decides to exact his revenge. Because that is what is actually going on here. As much as I want to believe this is about Anthony, the real star of this movie is Sammy. And he's coming back. I need space. I need to think. To clear my head. I need to remind myself exactly who I am in all this.

"Wait," Anthony says, stopping me in place. I'm already halfway down the hall. "Where are you going?"

"I'll be back," I say automatically, and my blood runs cold. I speak quickly, as if to erase my own echo of Sammy's words from the air. "I'm going to shower in my cottage. And then we can talk." Before he can respond, I hurry down the hallway, then through the living room, ignoring Ben and Mads, who are huddled on the couch like two kids on time-out, into the kitchen, to the back door. When my hand connects with the doorknob, I hesitate. It feels for an instant as if I must be dreaming, as if the ocean will flood into the house the second I crack the door. The storm howls. There's so much water on the window I can't see outside. I'm the type of person who runs away. I ran away from home. I ran away from Mom, all the way out here. And now the only place I can run to here is the cottage. Upon this threshold, in between the safety and comfort of the main house and the maelstrom outside, between Anthony and my own fears, I wonder, briefly, what it would be like if I were different. If I were braver. If I could just turn around and go to Anthony and help him. The way he wants me to. The way *I* want to. But the moment passes, and I twist the knob, and dash into the rush of wind and rain and hail and freedom.

||||||||||||||||

When I finally reach the cottage, I'm soaked to the bone. The trees above and around me rattle and sway, as fluid as marionettes dancing on their loose joints. I yank the door open and step inside, letting a blast of water and cold air into the small cabin. I'm charging toward the bathroom, to get out of my wet clothes. I can't wait to be under the warm spray in the shower. But I come to an abrupt halt in the middle of the room. Rainwater drips to the floor beneath me, pooling like drops of blood in the shadows. I don't know what has stopped me. Maybe it's the smell in here, which I don't immediately recognize. Like seaweed and brine. Maybe it's the trail of dark footprints on the wooden floor, which don't belong to me. My heart pounds in my chest so hard, it feels as if I'm going to faint. Blood pulses through my ears with the steady roar of a freight train. Out of the corner of my eye, without turning my head, I begin to make sense of the bundle of shapes in the corner.

It's exactly like my dream. And for a second, I wonder if I really am asleep. If I am back in Anthony's bed, curled in his arms, unaware of this particular nightmare now waiting for me. If this were a dream, though, I would know what to do. I would cleave my tongue from the roof of my mouth, wet my lips, and say, softly, "Dad?"

But this isn't a dream. Because in my dreams, the silhouette beside me cannot approach me. And I'm paralyzed. The single thing I am able to do is reconstruct this silhouette. Not into a ghost this time. But a man. Despite how dim the light is, I'm able to discern his features. I know this face so well now. I wish I didn't. But I do. The eyes especially. Those sad, all-seeing, unblinking, reptilian eyes. Those desperate, those hungry eyes.

"Sammy," I say, in barely more than a whisper. *Sammy.*

26

"Don't scream," Sammy tells me, holding his hands up as though he could physically ward off my fear. "I don't mean to scare you."

I can't breathe. Maybe he mistakes this for acquiescence, because he takes a step closer to me. He switches on the lamp next to my bed. The light lifts his face out of the dark and casts a thick shadow behind him. He wipes a hand over his balding head, and it comes away damp. "I really don't want to scare you," he says again, stretching his mouth in what is supposed to be a reassuring smile. "I'm here to help you."

Help me? What else do I have to be afraid of, except him?

"You're making a mistake with Anthony," he says, as if in response to my unspoken question. "I want to show you who he really is, before it's too late for you."

"I'm here with Mads," I protest lamely. "Not Anthony." But my words sound hollow, even to me.

When he shrugs in response, it strikes me, this man knows more than he's letting on. Since the moment we arrived, he's been watching us, the entire time when we thought we were watching him.

My heart beats a truncated, painful rhythm in my chest. The door is at my back. I could make a break for it, try to escape. But Sammy is fast. I've seen how quickly he can move. What would happen if he caught me? Would he be upset? Maybe it's better if he thinks I trust him. Besides, he isn't doing anything more than standing there, staring at me, with that same doleful, sincere expression on his face. He believes what he's telling me. He believes he's trying to help. To save me. And I have to admit, too, there's a part of me that wants to hear him out. I've heard Anthony's side of the story. What does Sammy have to say? What is it he thinks I have to know about Anthony? Sammy's eyes glisten in the light as he watches me. It would be easy enough for him to take a step into the room and cut off my retreat, but he doesn't. He waits for me, patiently. Like I'm holding his life in the balance, not the other way around, and he's prepared to trust me with it.

It feels like I'm suffocating. Panic rises in my chest. Not because of the threat he poses, because I know the decision I'm going to make. To stay. To listen.

Finally, as if he's been able to read all this, too, he shifts closer to me. "I don't bite, Lola," he intones.

"What do you want, Sammy?" I ask, before he can take another step toward me.

He manages to look offended. "To talk," he says, waving his bruised, swollen hand over the mattress, inviting me to take a seat.

When I still don't move, he adds, "You're going to want to see what I have to show you."

And this manages to convince me. I take a tentative step toward the bed. Actually, it's more like a shuffle. I couldn't run away, anyway. Not into the storm. Not when he knows the woods so much better than I do. Not when he can pick up a man twice his size and pin him down flat on his back. I shudder at the thought of what he could do to me, if he wanted to. If he wanted it, it would have already happened, right? Besides, for every step I take, he retreats back, away from me. Like he's trying to show me he won't touch me. I don't think he would hurt me. Would he? He reacted so strongly when Mads grabbed me, out of concern for me. But I never expected him to be so violent. I perch carefully on the edge of the bed, keeping my eyes on him, waiting for his next move.

He pulls something out of his pocket. Examines it for a long moment. Then tosses it onto the blanket beside me. I recognize it immediately, but don't pick it up. My driver's license. "Is Lola a nickname for Elizabeth?" he asks me. I flinch, but it's not an accusation, I don't think. It's a real question.

"How did you get that?" I counter.

If this is possible, he looks embarrassed. He remains where he is for a moment, hands hanging loosely at his sides, and then, dropping his gaze politely, he joins me on the bed, close enough for me to smell the sweat and the forest on his skin. He puts a hand out toward me, stopping just short of touching me, as though to hold me in place. "I'm going at this the wrong way," he begins. Softly, like he's chastising himself. "But I can't figure out, you know, the right way to say this. Anthony, he has this way of"—he cracks his neck from side to side as he contemplates his next words—"bending the truth around him. I had this plan, these words I thought about speaking to you, Elizabeth—Lola—but now that I'm here, I'm getting confused again." His face wrinkles in thought. I know he's reflecting on the situation, but he reminds me of a dog contemplating its master, waiting for a clear instruction. That's the nature of his introspection. I don't get the sense that it's articulated, even to himself. "Did he tell you about him and me and Darla?" he asks at last.

I shake my head.

"Now I have to admit," Sammy says, "I find that a bit surprising."

My cheeks burn with the lie. I find myself wondering again how much Sammy knows. He could have eavesdropped on every conversation Anthony and I have had, for all I know.

He reaches into his back pocket once more and this time pulls out what appears to be an old snapshot. He gazes at it, longingly, like he's getting lost in the frame, then tosses it onto the bed next to my driver's license. When I reach to pick it up, my fingers shake. It's a close-up of a girl, that much I can see. But the old dyes are so saturated that it takes me a moment to realize that she's topless.

"Darla," Sammy says. And then he adds, "As photographed by young Anthony Marino." He reads my reaction with his seal eyes. "I thought you might want to see that."

"Anthony took this?" I blurt out. What I really want to ask is *How?* And *When?* And *How, Sammy, how did you get it?*

He reaches over and snatches it back from me, out of my hands, then stares at it some more himself. "You know," he tells me, "it's true what they say about the first cut. It truly is the deepest."

"She was your first love," I say.

Sammy nods, then tucks the photograph back into his pocket. "That's true," he confirms. "But I was talking about Anthony."

As innocuous as the comment is, it sends a shock through my body. It was my impression that this entire conflict had revolved around Sammy and Anthony. That Darla didn't matter, not in the details. She was just something to fight over, a prize to be won or lost. But maybe that's too simplistic. Maybe there's more to this than I understand.

"You might think," Sammy says, "that all this happened a long time ago. And it did. And you might say I should let it go. That's what they say, isn't it? The past is the past? But as far as I'm concerned, it didn't just happen yesterday. It's still happening now. Anthony is still taking things away from me with his camera. You see what I mean?"

I take a deep breath. I force myself to hold it, then release it gradually, but this does nothing to slow the pounding of my heart.

"See, the thing of it is," he continues, "the essential thing, is that Anthony likes to take pictures. That's who he is. He takes pictures. A hell of a lot of them. He's taking them now. Of you. I've seen it. And he took them then, of Darla. Understand?"

I don't answer.

"Sammy's asking you a question," he says, and this—the way he refers to himself in the third person—sends another shiver through my body. Like there's more than one of him sitting on the bed next to me. A patient one, and maybe another one, who's becoming frustrated with me. "Lola? Sammy's asking you if you understand what he's saying."

"Yes," I hear myself say. "I think so."

"You see," he says, settling himself in more comfortably, resting his weight on one thick arm, "the way Anthony tells it, I'm some kind of animal. A brute. Isn't that the word he uses?" Something in me gives way. He knows about the movie. That's what he's getting at, isn't it? He knows what Anthony is doing here. He knows what Anthony wants from him. He knows the role he's supposed to play. He's been one step ahead of us, right from the start.

"I humiliated him," Sammy says. "That's what he told you, right? I *humiliated* him. Well, you want to know the truth?"

"Yes," I say, and I mean it. I really do want to hear what Sammy has to say.

"The truth," he begins, then buries his face in his hands, pressing his palms into his bulbous eyes until I'm sure he can see stars. "I thought it was cute at first. Kid stuff. Puppy love. He followed her around like the tail of a kite. Darla ate it all up, of course. She liked to tease him. I didn't think much of it. But you have to remember, Lola, who Anthony Marino is. That camera. I found these pictures"—he pats his back pocket to demonstrate—"in her bag. He spied on her. He spied on her getting out of the shower. He spied on her getting dressed. He spied on her getting herself ready for me. He spied on her when she was sleeping. Snap, snap, snap." He shakes his head, lifts it out of his hands, blinks like he's coming to. "And then he gave them to her." He pounds a hand on the mattress so hard, it makes me jump. "So I did what my own father would have done. I showed him what's what."

Just as abruptly as he exploded, Sammy seems to retreat. He drops his chin to his chest, as if he's been yanked into another dimension. Lost, I understand, in the memory. I wonder what he wants from me. Maybe to take Anthony Marino away from me. To convince me that he's the wronged hero here, not Anthony. But I don't care that a fourteen-year-old Anthony spied on Darla. So he was curious. At the same age, I meticulously kept a diary full of elaborate dreams. I can remember, with perfect clarity, a particular fantasy. I wanted my crush, Jake Thomas, to pull me aside at recess, tell me he loved me, take off his shirt, and kiss me. At the bottom of the entry, I wrote, *Burn this after he kisses you.* Like a backward, optimistic spell. Of course Anthony at fourteen would take pictures of Darla. Besides, he already told me he'd given her some of the pictures. Hadn't he said she loved them?

"I found the photographs," Sammy continues, focusing on me again. "This one in my pocket here among them. I don't know how many there were. A few. Quite a few. Snap, snap, snap." He stretches his neck, rolls his shoulders. "At first, I just thought . . ." His voice trails off. He doesn't share his first impression of the stash of photographs. Instead, his face hardens. "Darla told me—" He wipes a hand over his mouth, back and forth. It scares me, how worked up he is suddenly. I watch him as he struggles to bring himself back under control, waiting for him to complete his thought. "She was naked," he stammers at last, practically stuttering. "Naked. Understand? This was my Darla."

He seems to be waiting for a response. I don't know what to

say. All I can manage is "I can understand how angry you must have been."

"I taught him a lesson," Sammy says. "At least, I thought I did." He shakes his head. "I meant well, see? I thought I could give him some guidance. But all these years later, look at him now. Look at him. Look at what he's doing with that camera of his. Ain't that right, Darla? All these years later. Who's the brute? Huh? Who, Darla? Him or me?"

I feel my breath catch in my throat. I have to force myself to breathe. "My name is Lola," I mutter. I know I have to say this firmly, but my voice fails me. I barely manage a whisper.

He stares at me, uncomprehending. He doesn't blink. His face shows no sign of recognizing the mistake he's made. It crosses my mind to wonder what it is he's seeing right now. Is he here in this room with me? Or is he here with Darla? And then he says, "The thing is, I don't care anymore."

When his fingers touch mine, my heart leaps into my throat. The contact sickens me. The touch of his skin repulses me. At the same time, though, I'm frozen. Too scared to move. When his fingers begin to intertwine with mine, I don't take my hand away. I don't even object.

"Do you know why that is?" he asks me.

Yes. But I'm too petrified to answer. I simply can't.

"Sammy's asking you a question," he says. "He wants an answer."

Finally, I manage to shake my head. *Don't,* I'm thinking. *Please don't.* My eyes close, as if I can will him to disappear.

"Because this isn't about Anthony anymore. It's about you now. About you and me."

The fingers tighten around mine as I feel him shift his weight forward, toward me, on the bed. I don't open my eyes yet, but he's close enough to me now that I can feel his breath on my forehead.

"At first," he says, his voice hushed, reverent, "I figured he was doing something to get to me. I thought this was just going to be the same old fight. Anthony overstepping his bounds, me teaching him another lesson. But the more I watched you, the more I found—" He takes a breath. "I can't look away from you. I'm unable. Unable."

His other hand wraps itself around the back of my skull. The contact terrifies me. But still I can't open my eyes. My body stiffens. I can't pull myself away from him. Even though I know what's about to happen, I can't resist.

Then, with the softest whisper of a sigh, Sammy brings his lips to mine.

With a jolt of adrenaline, at last, I feel life return to my body. I bring my hands up against his chest to push him away. But he doesn't budge. He's too strong. I can feel the thick gristle of the muscle in his chest, palpitating under my fingers. I apply more force, beginning to panic. Still, I can't budge him. My hands tighten into fists. I pound his chest, once, twice. And then, miraculously, I'm free. When I open my eyes, he's staring back at me with a dreamy, confused look on his face. And I realize I haven't extricated myself. He's let me go. Because he thinks he's in love with me, and I'm just being feisty. I'm just being difficult. In his mind, I want him, too, every bit as much as he wants me.

Our eyes connect, and what he reads there seems to wound him. He looks suddenly like a deer, struck in the heart by an arrow, still on its feet but aware that it's about to fall. And I, I realize, I am the one standing in front of him, holding an empty bow. I watch his face as he takes this in. I watch his eyes as he gathers himself and his confusion and hurt begin to transform themselves and sharpen into something else. Into anger. I try to steel myself. I try to prepare myself for what, inevitably, will come next, when he finally collects himself again.

Before he can recover, though, before I can catch a breath to tell him to please, *please* get out of here, Sammy, please leave me alone, please don't do this, please don't make this worse, the door crashes open. The burst of movement sends my heart into my throat. I'm too stunned to react. I have no idea what's happening. The man beside me, though, leaps to his feet. Instinctively. Like an animal. Ready to fight. Swiveling to face the doorway, where Anthony appears, chest heaving, soaked, his feet bare and covered in mud, eyes wild. Behind him, the forest churns and the air is black with freezing rain. Wind gusts into the cabin, slapping our faces and scattering leaves on the floor.

"Get off her!" he shouts. "Get your fucking hands off her!"

Sammy takes a restless, agitated step toward Anthony, tightening and untightening his fists. For a few beats, I imagine he's going to take a swing at him. I think Anthony feels the same, because he hangs back a bit, unconsciously keeping distance between himself and this man while he assesses the situation. His eyes lock onto mine for a moment, then dart back to the threat in front of him once he satisfies himself I haven't been hurt. It crosses my mind that he must have seen Sammy here on my bed on the monitors in his office—that's what has brought him out here in such a panic—and I wonder how much he had to see before he finally decided to brave the storm to help me.

The cabin feels too small to contain the three of us. I want to push past Anthony and flee, or at the very least to join him and take refuge in his arms, but the thought of provoking Sammy any more holds me back. Next to me, Sammy's breathing like a bellows. The mere sight of Anthony inflames him. I can feel his fury boiling up inside him. In the end, though, he seems to master it, and instead of lashing out, only loosens a fist, then extends his hand to the taller man, holding it open as if to indicate he wants to shake. Anthony examines the hand but doesn't take it. Maybe he reads it like I do: a handshake offered before a match.

"Come on," Sammy says, keeping his hand in place. "Didn't your daddy teach you your manners?"

Anthony peers over the man's head, finding my eyes again. "Are you okay?" he asks me.

The question is so inadequate, I almost laugh. But I don't want Anthony's attention focused on me. Not when Sammy is there in front of him. Wounded. Barely able to contain his rage. He moved so fast. When he'd attacked Mads, Mads hadn't even seen him coming. And Mads is *Mads*. There's no imagining what he would do to Anthony, especially driven by such hatred. So I lie. "I'm fine," I say.

"What did you think I was gonna do to her?" Sammy asks Anthony, stepping closer to him, still with his hand raised. He moves differently, I notice. His steps are still loose, but they're measured, and once again I'm reminded of his takedown of Mads.

"The cameras," Anthony says, and Sammy freezes in place. "You moved them." To me, he says, almost desperately, "I didn't see him walk up here. He cleared a path."

A smile creeps up Sammy's cheeks. "Take my hand," he insists. "It's a question of manners."

Anthony hesitates. He doesn't want to look cowed, even though that's precisely how he looks when he grasps the other man's hand. "Bygones," he says, giving Sammy's hand a gentlemanly squeeze. When he's ready to take his hand back, though, Sammy won't let him. He holds on to it easily, like a prize.

"*Bygones,*" Sammy echoes, but not sincerely. Facetiously. "All is well," he says. "Is that what you think?"

Anthony gives his hand a tentative tug, but Sammy doesn't release him. There's nothing I can do if this becomes physical, but I take a half step toward the two men, reflexively. Again, I'm reminded how small this room is. I'm so close to them now, I can smell them. Sammy's salty, oily, masculine stink. Anthony's familiar, almost flowery fresh scent. The wind whips through the open door, and raindrops spatter across the floor. The light flickers. Sammy doesn't let go of Anthony's hand.

He registers my proximity, but only for an instant. His eyes remain locked on Anthony's face. Not on his eyes. But on a point somewhat lower. As with Mads, perhaps on his mouth or his chin. "You got three rounds in each match," he tells Anthony, as if they're in the midst of a conversation and Anthony knows what he's talking about. "Round one, we call that the neutral round. We start out on our feet. Round two, we go to the ground. I'm on top. You're on your knees. Round three, it's the reverse. Understand?"

Anthony gives his hand another futile tug. His cheeks are reddening. His eyes avoid mine. "I don't want to fight you, Sammy," he says, managing to keep his voice firm.

Nevertheless, his protestation brings a smile to Sammy's face. "Too late for that now," he says. "Don't you think? We started this particular match years ago, son. Didn't we?" He pulls the taller man a little closer into his body, until his hulking shoulder grazes

Anthony's ribs. It's becoming apparent that he has no intention of letting his hand go. "The way I see it, you've scored some points and so have I." He flashes me a quick, vicious grin. "We've gone two rounds. The only question now is, who's gonna take round three?"

Anthony's eyes narrow. For an instant, they dart past me, to the far corner of the room—to the location of one of the hidden cameras, it occurs to me with a small shiver. But this isn't about his film, I don't think. Or at least not about *Fear*, or about its appeal as a movie. There's something in his expression that arrests me. A certain calculation, perhaps. As if he's peering into a mirror and reassuring himself—that kind of look. And it strikes me that he isn't afraid anymore. Whatever he sees in that camera, whatever comfort he takes in existing in its lens, it's enough to make him square his shoulders. And I think Sammy recognizes this change in him, too, because when Anthony locks eyes with him again, Sammy's face falls. He has a sudden premonition, perhaps, that he might be the one who isn't prepared for whatever might happen next, not Anthony. At the same time, however, his rage only increases that much more. Anytime he wants to, he can take this taller man down. That's what he's thinking. No matter how subtle this contest is, that's what it comes down to. A physical fight that he can win. All this transpires in the course of a few seconds, in the permutations of a few expressions. In the whipped silence of the storm.

Anthony gives his hand a more deliberate tug, then leans into Sammy, close. "Let me go," he says. "You think it proves anything, holding on to my hand?"

Sammy snorts. "Bygones," he says. "Right?" Then, pressing his lips together, he begins to squeeze. I don't see his exertion in his arm. I see it in Anthony's face.

"Let me go, Sammy," Anthony repeats.

And just like that, the tables have turned again. It's Anthony who's desperate once more, Sammy whose face is as smooth as polished wood.

"Goddamn it," Anthony says. But Sammy's grip only gets tighter. "Let me go." Anthony starts to struggle.

At last, without conscious thought, I take another step forward and grab Sammy by the wrist. "Let him go," I say. Then, when he turns to face me: "You're hurting him."

For a moment, Sammy can only stare at me. It's as if he'd forgotten I was here. Then, his expression softening, he releases Anthony.

Anthony looks down at his hand, then—in a display of wanton pride that unnerves me—gives Sammy an unnecessary, reckless shove backward.

Sammy's mouth constricts. Still, though, he holds himself in check, arms raised. "Is that really what you want to do?" he asks.

Anthony throws another glance toward the camera hidden in the corner of the room, then seems to reach some sort of decision. As if retreating into himself, he focuses on his hand—which Sammy has clearly bruised. He stretches it a few times, then kneads it with his other hand, before finally looking up at Sammy again. "I never did hear exactly," he says, "what Darla told you."

Sammy stops breathing. His face turns into a mask devoid of any expression. Then he lets out a lungful of air and shakes his head.

"You always thought," Anthony continues, "that I caught her coming out of the shower. Isn't that right? That's how I caught her naked, that's how I took those pictures. Spying on her, right?"

I can see Sammy begin to connect the dots. He blinks a couple of times. But he's otherwise still. Frozen.

"You were eighteen," Anthony says, drawing this out. "Captain of the varsity wrestling team. Darla was sixteen. A sophomore cheerleader. You stole a ring from your mother's jewelry box and gave it to her. That's what she told me. Is that right, Sammy? You gave her one of your mama's rings? You wanted to marry her—"

Sammy pulls himself up. But he doesn't even seem to breathe. He's entranced, waiting to hear what comes next.

"She was afraid of you," Anthony says.

Sammy takes a halting step toward him. Just one. Like he's not aware of what he's doing.

Out of reflex, Anthony retreats. Another half step, and his back will be against the wall. But he doesn't look worried. Sammy's fighting one battle. He's fighting another. Psychologically, he's the predator again, zeroed in on his prey. "She wasn't coming out of the shower, Sammy," he says. "I wasn't spying on her. She was the one who wanted to take her clothes off. She posed for those pictures, Sammy. She *posed* for them."

After Anthony stops speaking, nothing moves. *Nothing.* It's like we're caught between heartbeats suddenly. Even the wind stops blowing. The howl of the forest doesn't just recede—it's gone. The room is entirely still. And then, before I can figure out what's happening, in a burst of movement, Anthony's body careens backward into the wall. It happens so fast, I don't have time to reach for him. And when I do try to help him, we lose our balance and tumble onto the wooden floor in a heap. Anthony's shoulder slams into my chest, knocking the air out of me, and I roll away from him, gasping. My head is spinning, buzzing. Anthony, though, has already pushed himself up, onto his feet. Someone is shouting, I think, but I could be imagining it. I roll onto my hands and knees, and then, abruptly, I'm outside. The world is a blur. Wind whistles through my ears. Rain and sleet pepper my face. I move out of instinct, down the path, following the sound of their voices. Then, ten or twenty feet away from me, fading in and out of the mist, drenched in rain, I see two figures circling each other on the rocky shore.

I take a shaky step toward them, then another, a little faster, and another, until I'm sprinting toward them. "Anthony!" I cry. I'm scared for him. Terrified. "Sammy!" I shout. "Please, Sammy. Don't!"

When I reach them, though, they don't react. Neither one of them. They're locked so intently on each other that they don't even see me. "You get the hell out of here, Sammy," Anthony tells him. "Now."

"What are you gonna do, son?" Sammy taunts him. "You gonna call my mama? You gonna call the police?"

Anthony closes the gap between them and gives him a shove.

"Don't!" I shout. I lurch toward him and grab both his arms. My presence here is the only thing that's stopped Sammy from lashing out at him—and Anthony must know this, too. Sammy is angry enough to kill. I can see it in his eyes, how empty they've become. He's not seeing Anthony anymore. He's somewhere else now, back in time, operating on a different level.

"Those little cameras of yours can't protect you," he tells Anthony, too calmly. "Not from me." He takes a step forward, brushing his chest up against Anthony's, dislodging my hold on him. When he speaks, his voice is so low, I can barely hear it over the rush of the wind. "You can't go running to my father anymore. You knew he was going to beat the shit out of me. You knew. You knew he wasn't just going to take my allowance away." He raises his hands to Anthony's chest. Not to push him away, but to clutch his shirt in his fists and pull him toward him. He tilts his head to the side and brings his mouth up toward Anthony's. "It's just you and me now."

When Anthony's head jolts backward, it happens so suddenly, I can only figure out what's happened in retrospect, as blood begins to tear with the rainwater beneath one of his eyes: Sammy has headbutted him, hard, in the forehead. I tell myself to close the distance and help him. Close the distance and stop this. Move, Betty. Sammy will kill Anthony, right here, in front of you, if you don't do something. But my feet have rooted themselves into the ground. I'm frozen where I am, in terror. All I can do is watch as Anthony's body goes momentarily limp in Sammy's hands. "Please, Sammy," I manage, whining, pleading with him, just like Darla had. "Please. Let him go."

My voice comes out in a whimper. Nevertheless, he seems to hear it. Because he turns toward me, as if to measure my reaction to this punishment he's meting out. And in this same instant,

Anthony seems to shake himself back to life. His body uncoils, and he gathers a hand into a fist and lands a punch on Sammy's chin, holding nothing back, so hard that Sammy releases him and Anthony falls backward to the ground.

Sammy stumbles to the side, reeling, one hand clamped over his jaw. Recovering his balance, he stops in place, gingerly testing the bone of his jaw with his fingers while Anthony picks himself back up onto his feet. For a second, I imagine—I pray—this will end it. But then Sammy lunges toward Anthony and grabs him again, this time by the throat, squeezing until he can't breathe, then, with both hands in Anthony's face, shoves him backward.

Anthony's feet slip in the mud, and he tumbles again, hard, onto the rocky beach, where he lands in a heap. I rush to him, but he pushes me off, and, clambering to his feet, moves toward Sammy, not charging him, but slowly, deliberately. I see his hand tighten into another white-knuckle fist, but Sammy doesn't. Sammy has time to glance at me and taunt his opponent with a sneer. Then Anthony slams his fist into his stomach, and Sammy folds in two. Anthony doesn't wait for him to recover. He swings again, aiming for his head. Sammy, though, is too quick. Before he has even straightened up, his arm is already hooked around Anthony's shoulders, and with a twist of his torso, he brings the two of them crashing down onto the rocks.

I stagger backward, turning in the direction of the main house, and hear myself scream. "Mads!" I shout. "Ben! Mads!" Through the heavy mist, I think I can see movement in the windows. The door opens. Ben, barely more than a silhouette, rushes out, hatched into a blur by the rain, leaving Mads struggling to walk on the porch. I don't stop screaming, though. I can't. For someone, anyone, to help Anthony.

At my feet, the two men are fighting and writhing, lashed by the waves that are riding into the shore on the back of the storm. I can barely make sense of it all. All I can see is that Sammy has Anthony in a headlock and that, as much as he's struggling, Anthony can't get himself free. He's choking, barely able to breathe. His skin is blue. His eyes are bulging. Water crashes over him, momentarily swallowing him, and when he reappears, he's coughing, choking. Suffocating. A hand grabs my arm. It's Ben. But I don't stop howling.

"Mads!" I'm screaming. "Mads!" And then to Ben: "Do something. Do something, Ben. He's killing him. Don't you see? Help him."

But Ben doesn't do anything. He doesn't move. Like me, he's frozen to the spot. Too terrified to take another step. Anthony's eyes bulge and bulge, and then start to close into lazy slits. It looks almost as if he's going to sleep. It looks peaceful. Like he's not being choked and the rocks underneath him aren't gouging into his back and his spine isn't being twisted and the sea isn't drowning him and the man on top of him isn't killing him, right in front of our eyes. It's over. That's what I'm thinking. Mads, our savior, limps across the lawn, still too far away to see, let alone to help. Ben is too weak even to try. I'm still shouting. The cameras are still rolling. And Anthony's dying. Anthony Marino is lying on the beach at my feet, already dead.

And then, all of a sudden, with a sickening thud, everything changes. For what feels like an eternity, I can't figure out how. I don't know what's happened. Then I watch Anthony's red, spidery hand pull away from the side of Sammy's head. It confuses me for a moment, that his fingers would be so widely spread in a fist, but as the outstretched hand trembles in the air, I make sense of what I'm seeing. There's a rock, about the size of a tennis ball, clasped in Anthony's hand. Someone cries, *Oh, my God, oh, my God, oh, my God*, so loud I can't hear anything else. I wish they would stop— then I realize it's me.

The rock falls from Anthony's hand onto the ground, and Sammy follows it, in slow motion. Another wave crashes over them, and for a moment the two men disappear completely. But as it recedes, Anthony picks himself up and stumbles away from Sammy.

I'm the one who tries to help the unconscious man. "Sammy?" I drop to my knees onto the sharp rocks next to him and give his limp body a shake. "Sammy!" I look up at Anthony, and then at Ben. And Mads shuffling toward us. "Help me." I hear my voice as a shout, but I don't think it has emerged as anything more than a whisper, inaudible above the rain. "Help," I mouth. "Help me, please."

I lean over Sammy's unmoving body. Rain and tears cascade down my face as I run my fingers over that monstrously strong torso, rolling him onto his side. Blood drips from his ear. He's covered in it, to the point where I can't tell where it's coming from. I wonder if he's dead, when his eyes suddenly clench shut, giving me a jolt. A spasm of choked breathing dislodges my hands from his chest.

"Sammy," I mutter, and his eyes open, finding mine as though he'd felt me looking at him. I register a series of emotions in his face—gratitude, love, confusion, rage—before he abruptly muscles me to the side and staggers to his feet. "Wait," I tell him, standing up, trying to stop him, but reeling. It feels like I'm going to vomit. Throwing a look over his shoulder at Anthony and Ben and Mads, Sammy takes a few uncertain strides toward the trees, and I follow, speaking through my nausea. My hands are quivering. My legs can barely carry me.

Without looking at me, he says, "I have to get back to Ma. She'll know what to do about this." He touches a couple of fingers to his ear, then draws them away, scarlet with blood. He stares at the gore, momentarily transfixed, then shoves his fingers into his mouth, to suck them clean.

I haven't heard anyone approach. A pair of hands, though, wrap themselves possessively around my shoulders, stopping me from following him any farther. I struggle to free myself, but without conviction. Then I stop and collapse into Anthony's arms.

"He's too hurt," I manage, in a gasp. "He can't—"

Already, though, Sammy has lurched away from us, disappearing into the trees, determined to find his way back to his mother.

Anthony's arms tighten around me. "Ben," he calls out. "Get over here. Take her inside." He doesn't let me go until Ben joins us and grabs my elbow. Then, with a grim set to his mouth, he starts after Sammy himself. "I'll make sure he's okay," he tells us through the rain.

I want to go with him. But Ben obediently drags me back to

the house, and I'm too disoriented now to resist. Mads catches up to us, hobbling on his makeshift crutch. "Just get yourself inside, Betty," he says. "Anthony can take care of himself." I throw one last look over my shoulder, but Anthony, too, has disappeared into the woods. The wind gusts, and the storm rages. There are footsteps on wet leaves, then nothing at all but the torrent of rain.

I'm standing in the bathroom, shaking. I'm covered in blood. The rain didn't wash it off me. It's everywhere. In my hair. On my shirt. Dripping from my fingers, landing in small precise circles around me. Sammy's blood. Mud clings to my thighs. Its slow slide down my bare legs gives me a shiver. I'm frozen to the bone. It feels like I'll never be warm again.

Reaching into the shower, I twist the knobs with numb fingers. I drag my drenched pants down my legs, yank the T-shirt over my shoulders, and step inside the hot spray, watching my pale skin blossom, carnation pink. My father once told me that, however much of a cliché this might be, flowers were the secret to romance. "Everyone thinks they know this, but they don't," he said, waving a dismissive hand over the steering wheel. It was Valentine's Day, and we were driving to the florist. "The key is to find the right color. This is what they don't know. It has to match the woman. Blue hydrangeas for your mother's eyes. For you, pink carnations to complement your blush." Against the porcelain tub, Sammy's blood looks like it would demand a red dahlia. It's too vibrantly crimson for roses.

I'm startled out of my reverie by the sound of the bathroom door opening. Ben's brusque voice pierces the white noise of the shower. "Not looking. Just grabbing your clothes."

"Why?"

There's no answer. I duck my head around the curtain to see if he's still there. "I'm going to wash them," he says, already halfway out the door. His voice cracks. "Just in case."

He doesn't elaborate, but he doesn't need to. I think I understand what he's doing. What *I'm* doing, in this shower. Scrubbing away the evidence. Because we don't know what's going to happen next. Silently, I retreat behind the curtain and attack my body with the soap.

||||||||||||||||||

Wrapping myself in a towel, I step into Anthony's room. I haven't heard anyone since my shower. It feels like I'm the only one in the house. Fingers still stiff from the cold, I drop my towel to the floor and rummage through Anthony's drawers for clothes. When I'm dressed—or at least covered up—I cross the room to the window and crank it open. Outside, the storm sounds like it might finally be letting up.

I drape myself against the window frame, breathing in the chilled, wet air. I'm so tired. But I can't bring myself to close my eyes, let alone lie down. Anthony is still out there. I would've heard him come back inside.

The sky bursts open with a blinding flash of lightning. It's so bright that, for a split second, it punches the entire world from the black like a snapshot. I freeze when I catch a glimpse of Ben on the far side of the house coming up from the pier and, a few feet behind him, someone else. Anthony. I listen for their voices. It sounds as if Anthony wants to go somewhere, and Ben is talking him out of it.

I lean farther out the window, ignoring the sharp bite of the sill cutting into my stomach, to get a better view.

Ben seems to be marshaling Anthony back to the house. Through the storm I can hear that his voice is charged with un-characteristic anger, but I can't decipher exactly what he's saying, just a few stray words.

Once they're inside, though, it isn't Ben who is yelling. It's Mads, from his position on the sofa. "What was that, man? What the fuck happened?" Silence. Then: "Tell me he's okay, at least."

I open Anthony's door and step cautiously into the living room. When Anthony shakes his head, water drips from his long hair. He's shivering. He's so pale, he doesn't look human. His skin could be parchment. His eyes find mine, but his gaze wavers and he lets me go before he can read my reaction.

Mads, observing this shift in Anthony, shuts his mouth. He looks to Ben for help, but Ben is too focused on his pale friend. "What did you do, Anthony?" Ben asks him. "I trust you, man. But you've gotta tell me what happened."

"What do you think happened?" Anthony asks, his voice low.

Ben falters. He can't say it out loud.

"I went to help him," Anthony says flatly. Ben shuts his eyes. I must make a sound, because Anthony glances my way again. He knows we're all shocked, looking for signs, waiting for his explanation. "I was just defending myself," he tells us. He opens his mouth to say more, but the words don't come. His voice breaks when he finally finds it again. "When I realized how hard I hit him, I went after him, to make sure he got home."

"So did he?" I hear myself ask.

Anthony doesn't answer.

"Jesus," Mads breathes.

Anthony takes a couple of indecisive steps toward the hallway. "He's okay. I followed him for a bit. Really, he'll be fine. Me, I—" He peers at his body and then lets out a laugh that's actually a sob in disguise. "My clothes." He tries to smile, unsuccessfully. A bruise is deepening around one eye, already swelling. Abruptly, he faces Ben again, tugging his shirt up and over his head, the way a toddler would. I gasp and hear the same sharp intake of breath from Ben. There are bruises spiraling around his ribs, onto his hips. A shallow set of gash marks snakes up his back, as though he was mauled by a big cat.

"You're a real prince, Ben," Anthony murmurs, handing him his wet shirt. "You'll wash everything. Right?" Ben nods, too cowed to answer any other way, let alone look at him. Next, as though he's alone in the room, Anthony strips off his waterlogged jeans and underwear, leaving the clothes in a pile on the floor by his feet. His legs are trembling, his white skin rippling with goose bumps. "Betty," he says, approaching me before I can react, because my eyes are fastened on his mutilated body. "Do you mind?" He gestures toward the hallway, which apparently I'm blocking.

I move out of his way.

As Anthony disappears into the bathroom, Ben gathers his abandoned clothing. The shower whines.

"What happened?" Mads asks us, his voice low, urgent. "Seriously, guys, what just happened?"

Ben shakes his head. "I found him on the dock," he admits. "He wanted to wait there, to watch Sammy's boat cross the channel. But he was"—he gestures weakly to the bathroom—"like this. Dazed, you know. You saw. Shivering."

"Jesus," Mads groans. *"Jesus."*

In the silence that follows, I find my voice. "Sammy was going to kill him," I tell the two men.

Ben wraps his arms around himself. "When we were on the porch," he tells us, "I looked back. There was so much mist, I could barely see anything. But I saw his boat, I'm pretty sure, out on the water." He takes a deep breath and lets it out in a rush. "We just have to find a way off the island, before he has a chance to come back."

I don't want to hear the rest of the conversation, so I simply shut myself back inside Anthony's room, slip under the blankets, and wait.

||||||||||||||||||||

We don't speak. Sleep doesn't come for hours. We wrap ourselves around each other, shivering and searching for warmth. I don't know what time it is, only that hours have passed, and we're still intertwined. I'm aware that he's awake, because the tension hasn't left his body yet. But I'm pretty sure he thinks I'm already asleep when he whispers into my ear, as softly as if he's telling me a secret.

I'm sorry, he tells me. My heart skips a beat, but I don't move a muscle to give myself away. And a few minutes later, I feel myself let go. I'm drifting, actually falling asleep, when he murmurs, so quietly I wonder if I've only dreamed the words, *I love you, Betty. I love you so much.* Then, when the darkest hours of the night surround me so heavily that I can barely breathe, *Don't leave. Please don't leave me.*

As sleep finally takes me, I wonder how much of any of this will be real in the morning.

29

The morning bursts inside in a blaze of sunshine. I'm the first to wake. I peel Anthony's arms from my torso and stumble out of
his bed. I don't know what to do with myself. With a mug of coffee
in hand, I plant myself in a chair on the front porch and try to
make sense of what's happened. The ground outside is still muddy,
but already the puddles dotting the gravel path down to the shore
are shrinking under the heat of the sun. Butterflies flicker across
the porch, birds float on airstreams, and mosquitoes swarm my
bruised legs. It suddenly seems impossible to me, the nightmare
that unfolded after Sammy revealed himself to me in the cabin.
The image of Anthony striking him in the skull with that rock feels
as nebulous as a dream.

Gradually, the house comes to life. First, I hear Ben's ladder
drop from the ceiling onto the floor, followed by the sound of a
door opening and a stifled yawn. Mads, propped up on the couch,

wakes with a muffled groan and calls for some food. Then, minutes later, the rhythmic rattles and bangs of someone pulling dishes and mugs out of the cabinets reverberate through the silence.

The screen door swings open, and Ben joins me on the porch. He hunches over his food, slapping at stray mosquitoes. I wait for Anthony, but he doesn't appear. He must still be asleep.

"What do we do now?" Ben asks me, his voice croaking.

"I don't—," I begin, but stop, cutting myself off. There's something in the water. I push myself up to get a better look as Ben says, "Oh, Christ." Then he's disappeared inside, calling for Anthony. I can't move. My heart pounds in my chest. Sammy's dinghy is carving a straight line through the channel, toward our dock. It's like seeing a ghost, reliving yesterday's horror. Once again, the scow trails the dinghy in an odd, listless wake.

Sammy is back. Sammy is here. Coming toward us. It's not possible.

After a final moment of hesitation, I push myself up. On shaky legs, I force myself to walk. It feels like an eternity crossing the porch, descending the stairs, following the path.

Behind me, before I'm even halfway to the water, a door opens and slams, and footsteps patter on the gravel. Then Anthony brushes past me, barefoot, still in his pajamas.

"Mrs. O," he says, coming to a sudden, breathless stop as he reaches the dock.

I stand beside him and watch as Mrs. O lashes Sammy's dinghy to the pier. Ben hustles up behind us, and the three of us wait there, uselessly, while she secures the scow to the dock as well.

Mrs. O is wearing the same outfit she had on when I met her, but she looks entirely different. Her shoulders, so square before, curl forward. Her jovial, animated face has shrunk into a mask of deep lines. "Anthony," she says, eyeing all of us but choosing to address him alone. "I'm sorry to show up like this unannounced—," she starts, as if she might have rehearsed what she wanted to say, but then she pauses and instead examines us, one at a time, a cloud slowly gathering in her expression. "What's going on here?" she finally asks.

Anthony takes a step toward her, trying to force a natural smile. He must realize how we look to her, gawking at her as if we're seeing a ghost. "The storm knocked out our power," he tells her, as if to explain. "We had a rough night. The phone went out and Sammy took the scow from us, so we felt stranded. I guess we're a bit freaked out."

"Where *is* Sammy?" Mrs. O asks.

"Sammy?" Anthony echoes. His voice sounds hollow. His confusion is an obvious lie. But Mrs. O, worried for her son, thankfully doesn't seem to notice.

"He didn't come home last night. I didn't think much of it, until the Coasties found his boat this morning, drifting out to sea. Towed it back to me."

"I'm sure he's fine," Anthony says. "He's an experienced sailor and a strong swimmer. I can't imagine—" He shakes his head, unable to articulate the rest of his thought.

Mrs. O's eyes narrow. "You haven't seen him?" I feel myself flinch when her gaze passes over me.

Again, Anthony shakes his head. "Like I said, the last time we saw him was just before the storm hit. He found Ben and me crossing the channel with engine trouble, and towed us back in to the dock." He turns to Ben, asking for his confirmation, which Ben provides with an unconvincing nod. "After that," Anthony continues, "he took the scow back across to the mainland. He said he'd fix it and bring it back."

"I don't know anything about that," Mrs. O says, clearly growing more worried. "All I know is he left the house yesterday afternoon, said he was coming over here to check on you all, make sure you were surviving the storm."

Anthony splays his hands. "Like I said, we haven't seen him since."

Mrs. O's face wrinkles into a ball. She bites her lip, trying to hold back tears as she takes this information in. It's clear enough she had imagined—she had hoped—she'd find Sammy here, holed up with us for the night. He had come over to help us, and his boat had somehow gotten away from him. The storm had pulled it from its mooring and carried it out to sea. He hadn't called, because the phone line was down. She had been coming over to collect him. End of story. Now, though, her worst fears are crashing down upon her in a heap. She can't sort them all out. But one thing is clear. Her son has gone missing.

"It's just not like him," Mrs. O says, on the edge of breaking down. "I mean, I know accidents can happen, but he wouldn't—" She wrings her hands. "Well, he just wouldn't—"

"We'll take a look around the island," Anthony tells her. "Now that the weather's cleared."

"Would you?" Mrs. O says, but her voice sounds distracted.

She stares down at the dinghy, lost in thought. There's water sloshing up and down the floor, and streaks of mud covering almost every inch of the boat, but it looks largely unharmed. Her eyes stray to the scow, which seems pristine in comparison. "You said—" She falters. "Sammy must have fixed the scow, then," she says finally. "If that's what he told you. I started the engine myself this morning, and it's fine."

"Thank you," Anthony says, frozen to the spot. I can practically hear him swallow.

"Just help me with it," she tells him, with an exasperated smile. "I need to untie it from the dinghy."

It takes Anthony another moment to react, but he finally joins her at the boat.

"You all right?" Mrs. O asks him. "Your face," she says. "Looks like you got into it."

"We just—" Anthony hesitates. "We got caught up in the storm."

"Really?" Mrs. O asks. "It looks to me like you've been in a fight."

Anthony shakes his head. "My friend," he says. "Mads. We—" He shrugs.

Finally, she turns the key in the ignition and starts the dinghy's engine. "If you would," she says, indicating the edge of the boat. Anthony unties the mooring and tosses the rope into the boat, then shoves the boat away from the dock. Without another word, Mrs. O twists the wheel, forcing the boat around in a long, jerky arc, then, without so much as a glance back at us, throttles the engine. As the boat disappears beyond its own foamy wake, my shoulders slump.

When I turn back to the men, I expect to see the same relief mirrored in their expressions. Instead, however, I'm met with something else altogether. Rather than commiserating, it looks as if Anthony and Ben are fighting.

"What the hell?" Ben asks, barely able to restrain himself, his voice threatening to break into a shout. "Oh, my God, Anthony. I mean—" He splays his arms, lost for words. "Why did you lie like that? So what if we saw him? I mean, isn't that what he's going to say anyway? That he came over here? Christ, you hit him with a rock. His skull was cracked wide open. How are we going to hide from that?" Then, with a wide-eyed look: "He's probably dead now, man. You fucking killed him."

Anthony reacts as if Ben had shoved him. "You saw what happened yourself," he says, the words coming out like a whip. "You saw it, Ben. You were there. I hit him. In self-defense. But he got up. He was *fine*."

"He must not have been so fine," Ben says. "He's gone. He didn't make it home. And now you've lied about it."

"What am I supposed to say?" Anthony demands. "That I hit him in the head with a rock and we let him wander off in the storm, but it's not our fault he didn't make it home?"

"What if he's still here?" Ben protests. "His boat could have just drifted out—in that storm. He could still be here."

"Jesus," Anthony breathes.

"This is crazy," Ben says. "Either he's dead and you killed him, or there's a maniac on the loose. This is too much, Anthony." He stares at him, hard, daring him to challenge him. "I'm out of here, man. Out of here."

"What about—," Anthony starts, but Ben cuts him off.

"Fuck the film," Ben says. "Mads needs a doctor, man. We have to leave."

Anthony's face crumples under the weight of his own thoughts.

Ben's voice softens. "Look," he says, "Mads and me, we're not going to let you down. We'll stand by your story. Sammy is a scary fucking dude. You did"—he shakes his head—"what you had to do. But we can't stay here any longer. And neither should you."

Anthony turns to me, asking for help. My voice is hoarse. It doesn't sound like it belongs to me. "Just let them go," I say. "It's over, Anthony. We don't need them anymore. Just let them go."

Ferrying Ben and Mads off the island feels more mechanical than emotional. It takes a while to pack up Mads's things in our cottage. To help him out of the house and into the boat. The swelling in his knee hasn't gone down overnight. If anything, the joint looks worse. It's bruised now, and the skin at the back of his leg is turning yellow. But Mads doesn't complain much, once he realizes he's been given a reprieve. He just hobbles down the path on his makeshift crutch to the pier and waits for us. We shove off a little after two, with the sun still scorching overhead, and we motor across the channel in silence, passing small fishing boats bustling with shirtless men tossing wide nets and clunky metal cages into the water. After the storm, life goes on as if nothing at all has happened. Even without Sammy. No one mourns.

The van waits for us in the parking lot. The salt in the air has plastered itself onto the windows like a chemical residue, and the seats inside are frozen, despite the day's heat, but the engine turns over without complaint. I feel myself go numb as soon as we start moving. I'm willing time to pass now, waiting for the moment when Anthony and I will be free. As we turn off the gravel road, onto the paved highway that leads us through town, I crane my neck to get a look at the general store and catch a glimpse of a dark door before we've whizzed by.

Once we get to the other side of the village, we're joined by a little traffic along the narrow road. Only a few cars zip past us, overtaking us on the occasional straightaway, but it feels crowded. I find myself shrinking into my seat, glancing up at Anthony as we rocket down the asphalt—into the real world again, if only temporarily. His face is tanned, and it hits me just how striking he is. The squint of his eyes, the shape of his features, the slight tilt of his head above his shoulders, which are wider than the seat— every single detail of his appearance has been impressed into my memory. But I have forgotten how these different dimensions all fit together into this magnetic man sitting next to me. He gazes back at me, and for a moment I think he's going to tease me for staring at him. But I'm rewarded instead with a blush, which blooms like a rash on his cheekbones. His eyes dart back to the road, and I follow his gaze, discovering with a start that we're already approaching our destination.

Pulling into the train station lot, Anthony parks on the far side and fishes his cell phone out of his pocket. "Your tickets are under your names," he tells Mads and Ben, finding them in the rearview mirror. "You can print them out at the kiosk. The train should be here in about half an hour." Shifting in his seat, he digs into his jeans and yanks out his wallet, then unfolds ten pristine bills, separating the pile and handing the notes to the men, who accept the gift without comment. "I'll cut your checks as soon as I'm back in the city."

Ben helps Mads out of the van, then reaches back inside for his makeshift crutch.

"Are you going to be okay?" I ask Mads, eyeing the thin line of the broomstick, which bows slightly beneath his weight.

"I don't think so," he tells me, honestly. "At least for a while."

"I've got your bag, dude," Ben offers.

Mads flashes me the shadow of that old movie star grin. "That's not what I meant," he says.

Anthony gestures for us to join him in a huddle. "We don't have a lot of time to talk this out," he begins, searching each of our gazes in turn, ending on mine. His expression arrests me. He looks sad, like he's close to tears. This isn't the domineering Anthony Marino I'd expected. He's one hundred percent sincere. Vulnerable, even. "I know how insane this got. But I—"

"You don't have to explain," Ben says, and I realize he's suddenly pretty close to tears, too. "We're in this together." He looks to Mads for confirmation. "Right?"

It takes Mads longer to answer. When he does, he looks grim. "All of us."

"It was my fault," Anthony insists, "for pushing him so far." I feel a shiver run through his body. He inches away from me, leaving a cold spot where his shoulder had pressed into mine. "I knew he was going to lose it. But I didn't know it was going to go off the rails like that. . . ." His voice trails off, and he shakes his head in disbelief. Still, the reality of what has happened hasn't sunk in. "But I didn't kill him. I can't have you leaving, thinking that I would *ever*—that I—" He stops, midsentence. His eyes are haunted, and I feel my heart breaking. My hands squeeze into fists. Finally, he resumes. "It might have been naive, but everything I did was for the film. Not to hurt anyone." Ben releases a shaky breath. Mads drops his gaze to the ground. Neither of them looks particularly convinced. "Anyway, that's it. I owe you my gratitude. I know how much I owe each of you."

"Once the check clears—," Ben says, holding up his hands. "I love you, but." It's a full sentence. *I love you, but.* This feels like a final, irrevocable goodbye. His eyes are desolate. This is harder for him than he ever thought. The end is suddenly here at last, and he can't find the will to stave it off.

With a smile so incongruously sad I know it's genuine, Anthony tells him, "It's okay, Ben, really." The sharp angles of his face soften. "Put this behind you. You're a real talent. You don't need me."

Ben nods, and they hug, Ben still limp and noncommittal as Anthony's long limbs encircle his stouter frame. When they disengage, Ben is looking directly at me. "Goodbye, Sailor Moon," he says, extending a hand to shake mine. "Good luck, you know, with saving the universe or whatever the hell she was doing."

"Bye, Ben," I say, giving his sweaty hand a squeeze, in the same moment realizing that I'm saying goodbye to Sofia now, too. He won't want to see me again, either. Neither of them will.

Without warning, he pulls me in for a hug. While Mads and Anthony speak—I can hear them saying their goodbyes, exchanging stilted words about indie directors—Ben whispers in my ear, "I just want to forget."

I don't say anything in reply, because there's nothing for me to say. Instead, I pull myself out of his grip and turn to Mads. "This is goodbye for us, too," I tell him.

He stares at me for a moment, face blank, then dips his head, as if to say, *Yes, it is.* "I'm glad it was you," he tells me. "In the movie, I mean. I'm glad he picked you." And then his voice cracks a little, and he seems to lose the brittle layer of his reserve. "You sure you don't want to come with us?"

I feel Anthony's gaze on me, hot, like a beam of light. Ben looks like he'd rather be anywhere else but here. "No," I say. "I'm staying with Anthony."

Anthony wraps his arms around Mads's shoulders, and he allows him to. "Take care of yourself, Mads," he says. "Don't be afraid to get in touch. You know, if the mood strikes you. Otherwise, you'll see your money soon. Thank you, thank you, thank you."

We hug one last time, then let go. With every touch, it's like we're trying to erase our recollections, not impress them deeper. It reminds me of my last days of school. Trading yearbooks with people I had known since first grade and embracing them with tears, like I wouldn't see them at the grocery store later that week. Ben is the first one to disengage. He hugs each of us in turn— even Mads, despite the fact that they're leaving together—then he hoists their bags on his shoulders and steps away, waiting. When I hug Mads for the last time, my throat constricts with unshed tears. But I don't want to cry, so I just touch a hand to his cheek, and then, in the blink of an eye, he's gone, too, leaving behind only a couple of parting words, which linger in the air until I finally hear them.

"Watch yourself," he had whispered into my ear.

And then time skips forward, and just like that, Anthony and I are alone, at last.

31

I release a breath I hadn't known I was holding, and Anthony actually laughs. It takes us a few beats to find the courage to look at each other. But when we do, we both conceal smiles. Then he takes my hand and guides me back to the van. We don't say anything, not a single word. We simply race away from the train station, from Mads and Ben, from the real world, back to our hideaway. I feel time slow down once more. We're alone. Truly alone. Anthony turns up the music, playing our song, and I roll down the window to let in the fresh, warm air. If I could wish for anything right now, it would be to stay in this van forever. Sunlight filters in through the windshield, not bright enough to blind but enough to illuminate the freckles dotting Anthony's cheeks. My own cheeks, I realize, are aching, and it hits me: I can't stop smiling.

I'm happy. I never thought I would feel this way again. Happy. Free. I can hardly describe it, even to myself. It has everything to do with Anthony, and yet nothing at all to do with him, at the same time. I'm so light, I'm dizzy. Anthony reaches for me, intertwines his fingers with mine, and I know he feels it, too. The landscape passes in a blur. *May this last forever, please, please, please, let us never reach a place where this will stop.*

As we approach the end of the Strip, though, Anthony's fingers slip from mine, and he pulls his hand away to switch off the stereo. He slows the van to point at Mrs. O's store across the way. I try desperately to hold on to my sense of bliss, but the mood has already shifted. Then I see what Anthony is showing me: a white square fixed to the front door of the shop. Scrawled across the poster board is one word, the ink already fading in the sun: CLOSED.

It isn't until we're on the boat that Anthony breaks the silence. "He's actually dead," he says, like he can't quite fathom it.

I don't know what to say. Anthony clubbed Sammy with a rock. He can't get the feeling out of his fingers, his arm, his body, just as I can't get the image out of my mind. It's tormenting him. But he was defending himself, like he said. He was defending us. If he hadn't hit him, Sammy would have killed him. And the fact is, no one knows any of this except the four of us. This is something we'll have to get comfortable with on our own. We are all responsible for what has happened here. I don't worry if Ben or Mads will say anything, because they would have to explain their role in this, too. They could lie, I guess, but they won't. Because they know, fundamentally, that they, too, are guilty. And they aren't the kinds of people to sacrifice their lives to justice. That's not who Anthony would ask to help him with this movie, and he picked his crew carefully.

I covertly wipe my sweaty hand on my shorts and reach for Anthony's arm. I tug at his elbow, beseeching him to release one hand from the wheel. It takes him a moment, and he sighs almost imperceptibly before he obeys. His grip tightens on my hand. I watch the scars on my fingers turn a fluorescent white against my skin.

"It's real," he stresses, as he cuts the throttle. We drift toward the dock. As he ties off the rope, he adds, "Not just what happened with Sammy. All of this." He guides me off the boat and peers down at me, his blue eyes almost disappearing in the sunlight.

"Are you okay?" I ask, even though it's an empty question. Of course he isn't okay. But I want him to keep talking. I want to know what he's thinking.

He looks at me, as though he's confused by the question. Confused that I'm even speaking. "Are you?" he asks me.

I can't find my voice, so I pull him toward me, lacing my fingers in his hair. Distantly, I hear the lapping of the waves on the shore, the whistles of the birds, and the roar of fishing boats, but underneath it all is my own beating heart, pounding out a rhythm I can't quite keep up with, because it's tangling with Anthony's. When we break apart, he whispers his next words into my skin.

"Betty," he says. "Betty Roux."

It takes a minute, and then it hits me: I'm not just Lola to him anymore.

We spend the day closing up the house. By the time we're finished, the sun is setting over the mainland. Pink ribbons streak the sky, and the house is awash in blue. I join Anthony on the couch, take a sip from his glass of wine—evidently, he's saved the good stuff for us—then gently shut his computer and pull it off his lap.

"What's up?" he asks me.

I take a deep breath. Count to five. Then let it out. "I have to tell you something," I say.

"Betty, I already know—"

"No," I say. "I have to do this. I have to tell someone."

He looks like he wants to say more, but doesn't. If I had let him, I wonder what he would have said. What he had thought I was about to confess.

"I knew my father was going to kill himself," I say. Until the words are out of my mouth, I had expected tears. I had expected my voice to quaver and fail me. But it's easy to say this, once I start. "I knew it for a long time. We talked about it once, when I was fourteen. I'd heard him say it before, when I was younger, that he was going to commit suicide one day." In fact, this was something he'd told me more than once. I don't remember the first time. But it was something he'd told me he'd do when he was older. I never knew how old he'd meant, but he said he knew there would be a day when it felt right. "It was always there," I tell Anthony, "like a noose around his neck." I glance up at him, wondering if this is something he's capable of hearing. His expression, though, doesn't betray his thoughts. "He didn't tell me how he would do it, just that he was going to, and I should be ready. He didn't tell me why, either, and I didn't ask. I didn't want to know." It was something that was going to happen, I understood, because it had to. I guess I figured it was because he didn't want to let anyone or anything else kill him. But I didn't think about it. I cried. I tried to explain how much it hurt me to even *think* about it. He said he understood—really, he did—but that it was his life and I had to remember that. When I kept crying, he started to laugh a little, like I was being foolish. He told me that I shouldn't be unhappy, because he wasn't unhappy. He wasn't scared. It wasn't that he thought about killing himself every single day. But he knew there would come a day when he would wake up, and he would.

Anthony runs his hand through my hair, tangling his fingers into a knot at the back of my head. Maybe to give me strength. Maybe to stop me from saying more. I don't know.

"For a long time after that, I watched him," I say. "Especially over breakfast. I'd convinced myself that I would be able to see the change in him—that resolve—in the way he ate his cereal. But somewhere along the way, I—" I close my eyes, remembering the morning ritual Dad and I shared, every day growing up, eating cereal from the same yellow bowls. "I stopped believing him."

Anthony considers this. "He made it feel like you were responsible. But you weren't. You aren't."

Anthony is right, of course. But that doesn't make it any easier. I'll never escape the feeling that I could have stopped him.

"When we were in Iceland," I continue. "This was only a few months ago—" My voice breaks. The burning begins at the back of my throat, and the fire spreads quickly through my sinuses, into my eyes. "He told me he was thinking about it again." I press the heels of my palms into the hollows of my eye sockets, pressing just hard enough to blot out Anthony's watchful gaze and replace it, instead, with the image of my father standing in that dark field, his breath coming out in puffs of steam that swirled like the Northern Lights did, just above us. We had considered joining a tour group, one designed to drive us out into the darkness, so that we could have an unobstructed view of the lights. But he told me that was ridiculous. Too impersonal. So we drove ourselves, not talking, laughing occasionally, taking whatever roads we could, until we were thoroughly lost in some field, out on the edge of the earth, where we stood together, craning our necks, watching as the heavens split open above our heads. So close it felt as if we could touch it. At last, the sobs I'd been expecting swallow my voice. I'm gasping for air. But I can't stop now. "He told me he was scared. He was so sorry, he said. He knew he was being selfish.

But he wanted me to know." I can hear Anthony's breathing, the rush of nonsense words meant to comfort me, which don't. "I couldn't—I was—" I can't find the right way to tell Anthony that I was dismissive when he first told me. "I asked him not to talk about it. Because I'd heard it all before, and it hurt too much." My ribs burrow into themselves and my whole body shakes. "He promised he was okay." I can't get out more, not without sobbing. After that, we finished the trip as if he hadn't said anything. And then we got home. I didn't say anything to Mom. I don't know, even now, why I didn't. Maybe I hadn't believed he would actually do it. Maybe I had pushed the thought out of my mind, again, because it was too overwhelming. Maybe—and I think this might be the truth—I had understood that to tell my mother would be a betrayal of my father's trust. My father loved me. I was his daughter, but I was also his closest friend. Maybe his only friend. If he wanted Mom to know, he would have told her. He wanted me to know because he knew I wouldn't. And then two days later, after we got home, without another word to me about it, he went through with it. Alone. When I next speak, I don't recognize my own voice. "He's gone. And now I can never—"

At this, Anthony gathers me into his arms and I collapse into the embrace. I don't know how long we remain locked together like that, or how long it takes me to stop shaking. I try to remember a world outside of the bathroom where I found Dad, back in California, with its blue tile and peeling wallpaper, but I can't. I can't see Anthony sitting right here beside me. I can't see anything else but my father's open, lifeless eyes staring back at me in accusation.

I wipe my face with my sleeves and wait for my sobs to fade, then turn in Anthony's arms to get a better look at his face. His eyes are red, and his mouth is working, though nothing comes out. "I never told anyone this," I say. I think sometimes that Mom knows. She can read it on my face. And what I sense is—what I *know*—is that she blames me, too. Anthony shakes his head, starts to speak, but I don't let him. "I don't think you can understand this. But I kept it a secret from Mom, what Dad told me." I don't know how to explain. She doesn't know what I'm hiding, she just knows I'm hiding something. And it's this secret that's come between us. It's the secret that's killing me, not what Dad did. But I can't undo what's been done. It's too late. There's no going back now, and nothing will ever be the same again. "I should have just told her," I say. "I never should have let it come between us."

Anthony reaches for me again, but I lean backward, away from him. He starts to try to comfort me, but I don't allow him. There will be time for that later. First, there's a confession I have to complete.

"Which is why," I say, my voice a hollow rasp, "I want to know"—I search for the best words—"if you know." I look at him, waiting. "Anthony? Do you?" I wait some more. "Do you know? What I did, I mean."

Anthony doesn't speak. He doesn't even seem to be breathing. Finally, though, slowly, he nods. He opens his computer on the coffee table and presses PLAY on a video file, and gradually, inexorably, I start to understand. The frame is a bit off, but I recognize the exterior of the house. The camera is set at an awkward angle, so the tree line in the background is sloped, leading downward to the edge of the water. In the top corner of the screen, the sky is dark, undulating with the inky clouds of the storm. I lean forward, despite myself, to get a better view through the raindrops dotting the screen. In the foreground, there are four figures, one doubled over, two conferring, one standing farther away. I watch as Anthony steps into the trees, following Sammy into the darkness, as Ben drags me away, out of frame, with Mads not far behind. A fresh wave of rain spatters the screen.

"Watch," Anthony tells me.

I don't need the instruction. Even though the screen is empty, and we're just staring at the trees now, I can't look away. Time lapses. How much, I don't know. And then a white figure climbs from a window and emerges from the house, into the storm, then slinks across the screen, retracing Anthony's path, following Sammy and Anthony into the woods. Before the figure disappears into the shadows, it throws a look over its shoulder, as though checking to make sure no one else has seen. And through the blur of rain, I stare, briefly, into my own eyes.

The rain had battered the glass as I unfastened the clasp. I pushed the bathroom window open, then climbed outside. Into the dark, into the cold. A gust of wind nearly tore the window from my hand, but I managed to close it quietly behind me, without giving myself away. I stopped for a moment to make sure. Inside the living room, framed by the large picture windows, Ben was pacing, back and forth, panicking, trying to calm himself down after the fight, trying to figure out what to do while I supposedly cleaned myself up. I watched him until I was certain he hadn't heard anything, then started forward again. The rain pummeled my face and my shoulders, freezing my skin. Wind howled in my ears. Icy water soaked my shoes, swallowing my footsteps on the sharp gravel. I wasn't shivering anymore, though. My heart was racing. My blood was pumping.

I already knew which way Sammy would walk, so I followed

the same path, quickly. It didn't take long to catch up to them. Not long after I entered the thickest part of the forest, I caught sight of Anthony's fuzzy form ahead of me as he chased Sammy toward the cove where he'd hidden his dinghy. In the dark, he lost dimension, like a shadow slipping between trees. It was nearly impossible to see. My own hand, shielding my eyes, was no more than a series of shapes. I stumbled over roots, tore my skin against branches, lost my footing as my feet sank into muddy puddles. Pushing myself harder, I struggled to keep up. The forest was deeper than I remembered, and I was making a racket. Thankfully, the storm provided cover, and after a few minutes, I had closed the gap and Anthony was only about twenty feet in front of me.

In a flash of lightning, I caught a clear glimpse of Sammy, like a snapshot, maybe two paces ahead of him. He was doubled over, in the middle of a small clearing, his hands braced on his knees. In between claps of thunder, I thought I could hear him heaving. He wasn't simply hurting. He was disoriented, nauseous. The blow Anthony had given him to the head had almost killed him, and he was having trouble finding his way back to the boat.

I slowed, taking cover off the path behind a tangle of bushes. Anthony, too, hesitated. Then he made up his mind and pressed forward, raising his voice over the storm, "Sammy!" He caught up to the injured man, reaching him before Sammy realized he was coming. In the far distance, tiny dots of light poked through the trees. The mainland. I slipped back onto the path, edging forward, then slid back into the brush, out of sight again, but now almost within earshot. Whatever Anthony said to Sammy got lost in the wind. I could hear Sammy's rough response, though: "Don't touch me, son." Another flash of lightning bathed him in its phosphorescent silvery light. Blood leaked from the wound. More lightning struck, like a strobe. Ooze stained his forehead and blackened his ear, sliding like oil down his neck and seeping into his shirt. In the black again, these images remained with me like a series of photographs. I crept a little closer.

"You're hurt, Sammy," Anthony said, taking stock of the other man's injuries for the first time, too. His voice reached me like a whimper. He grabbed Sammy again, wrapping a hand around his upper arm, but Sammy jerked away, overcompensating and collapsing, landing heavily on one knee. Even from this distance, I could hear his labored breath. *He's dying,* I thought, and a chill ran through me as I gazed at Anthony. His expression was blank, his eyes almost unfocused. I couldn't see him any better than I could see Sammy, but I knew him so well by then. I knew this expression. He was considering something. Making up his mind. Whether to help Sammy, perhaps as he had set out to do, or just to let him die. The moment passed, though, when Sammy's other knee buckled, and he pitched forward into the mud, nearly sprawling before catching himself by planting his hands in front of him. Anthony's face crumpled. He looked like a little boy, ready to cry—not in sympathy, but to protest his innocence. I knew this, too, without having to delineate his features through the rain. "Sammy? Come on, man. You're really hurt. Let me help you."

"You did this," Sammy said through gritted teeth. Then, clenching his jaw, again rebuffing Anthony, he pushed himself back up, onto his feet. "Just wait." He shook his head, slowly, as though to clear it, but stumbled again. "Just you wait," he said as he began to fall.

Anthony clutched him reflexively, looping an arm around his waist to hold him upright. "Sammy, please." His voice had grown desperate. "Come back to the house with me. We'll clean you up, get you warm."

I edged forward, transfixed, sinking even lower to the ground, shielding myself in the thick, sopping moss. I hate to admit it, but as I'd followed him into the woods, I had begun to believe that Anthony intended to stop Sammy from getting home. Now, though, I wasn't so sure. Maybe he did actually mean to help him.

I was close enough now to get a better look at Sammy's eyes. They were wide, shadowed. Incredulous. "Come back with you?" he echoed, in disbelief. He rolled his shoulders, trying to loosen Anthony's grip from his torso. "This is it for you. Don't you understand that? This is round three, and Sammy never loses the final round."

Anthony let go of him, turning away from him a little. I could read his indecision, and I felt myself shiver. He had reached his crossroads, and he knew it.

Without Anthony's arm around him, Sammy started to sway. The adrenaline from the struggle was wearing off, and he was fading. The fight was draining from him. Once again, instinctively—because this was his basic impulse, despite what had happened between them years before—Anthony reached out to steady him. Sammy, though, slapped the hand away. "I don't need your help, son," he shouted. Then, gathering himself, more quietly, enunciating each syllable through his teeth: "You tried to kill me. You think I'm some kind of fool? That's what this goddamn thing has been about. Setting Sammy up for a kill."

The shadows hid Anthony's face, but I knew he still wasn't panicking, even as his world was falling into a shambles all around him. Why was he always so calm? Didn't he realize what was about to happen to him? Sammy would go to the police. This wasn't some innocent scuffle. Anthony had planned this whole thing. It was premeditated. He could be charged with attempted murder. His life would be ruined. I had started to shiver again, crouching there in the mud, watching. Listening. Waiting. The rain had let up momentarily, into a drizzle, but I was already drenched, and the wind whipped through my clothes as if I wasn't wearing anything at all. I became aware of the water creeping down my back. My fingers and toes ached. Finally, Anthony seemed to reach a decision. "You do what you have to do," he said, his voice flat. "My conscience is clear."

I could barely hear Sammy through the wind, over the rush of waves on the shore, somewhere behind the curtain of those trees. "Don't kid yourself," he said. "You don't have no conscience. You never did."

Anthony's mouth twisted, but he didn't try to defend himself. He peered through the forest. Then he nodded. "Will you make it home okay?" His voice was despondent. He had given up so easily.

Sammy pointed a finger in his face. "You don't have to worry about Sammy," he said. "You just worry about yourself."

Anthony opened his mouth to speak, then shut it again. After another tortured few seconds, he repeated what he'd already said.

"You do what you have to do." Then, with a jerky shrug, he started back down the path, directly toward me, retracing his way to the house. *You do what you have to do.* My limbs were frozen. My breath was caught in my throat. I couldn't have called out for him even if I had wanted to. And then he was gone.

As his footsteps faded into the drips of rain off leaves behind me, Sammy squared his shoulders, straightening himself back up. Then, with a remnant of his athletic grace, he managed to swivel around and continue down the path. He had to catch his balance on tree branches, but he was moving more steadily now. I heard him mutter, *Son of a fucking bitch,* to himself as he slipped and righted himself clumsily.

Before I knew what I intended, I followed him, racing as fast as my icy, numb legs could carry me, sliding on leaves. But he was fast, even injured, even dying. Faster than me. I only caught up to him at the rocky beach, after we cleared the trees, where the moss gave way to sand. The sound of the surf overwhelmed me. He was already at his boat, leaning into it. Not dragging it into the water or trying to board it, but removing something from it. I couldn't see what it was. I figured, though, it was his phone, stowed in the waterproof hold.

"Sammy!" I shouted. My voice was hoarse. "Wait!"

He snapped upright, then turned to face me, his expression registering his surprise.

I took advantage of his hesitation, and closed the distance between us. "Please," I begged him. "Please don't do this."

He didn't speak, but just stared at me. Blankly. As if I no longer mattered to him. As if he couldn't see me anymore.

I persevered. "You can't turn Anthony in," I told him. "Please. Don't call the police." As I spoke the words aloud, another shiver passed through me. I couldn't bear what was about to happen to Anthony. To all of us. Because we were all involved. Me, too. We would lose everything. *I* would lose everything. My life would be ruined, too, just now, when it's finally beginning to start. "Please," I repeated. "Don't call the police." *Don't do this to me.*

Sammy shook his head, slowly. "Don't worry," he told me. He was so close to me, but he sounded so far away. "I'm not going to call the police."

My relief was physical. I could feel my spine give way, and if it weren't for my frozen muscles, I might have fallen to my knees. All I could do was drop my head into the palm of my hand, staring blindly down at the shore. Everything was going to be okay.

"I'm not going to call the police," Sammy said again. Then he lifted a hand, as if to show me why.

It took me a long moment to understand what I was seeing. The object in his hand, which he had been retrieving from the hold, wasn't a phone, but something else. It seemed to absorb light, like a heavy chunk of coal. Of course I knew instantly what it was, but I still had difficulty articulating it. I had never seen one in person before, not so close. Not held by someone other than a policeman. It sucked the air out of my lungs. And then, as comprehension dawned, I understood what Sammy was saying. He wasn't going to call the police, because he was going to take care of Anthony himself. With a gun.

And then it happened, almost too fast for me to assimilate. I had seen a branch, waterlogged, dragged by the surf onto the rocky beach by my feet. I had nearly tripped on its long, thick, craggy fingers as I'd chased Sammy to his boat. And now, though I don't know how, this branch—this heavy, sopping, leaden branch—was in my hands. I wasn't holding it. I wasn't considering it as a weapon. It was just there in my hands, and I was watching as it swung through the air in a blur toward this man's wretched, ugly, evil face. I watched it as it connected with his skull. I felt the reverberation vibrate through my arms, my skeleton. I saw him reel, then stumble, then fall backward, into the side of the boat, then farther down, into the water. I let go of the branch and followed him. He rolled, gasping for air, while I clawed at his shirt to get a better grip. I felt his gaze on me as the struggle left his body, as he finally understood.

It was surprisingly gentle in the end. He had already lost a lot of blood, and the blow from the branch had done the rest. I simply gave him one massive heave, like I was launching a small ship—as I would do only a moment later, to his boat—and watched as he floated away. He had been so strong, even injured. He could have killed Anthony easily. And he would have. Me, too. All of us. I was only doing what had to be done. Defending Anthony. Defending myself. And Mads and Ben, as well. That's what I told myself, as I fed the gun and the branch into the water, as I stood back and watched the current draw the body away. He would have been impossible to stop, otherwise.

Maybe it was just the movement of the surf, because the waves were violent in the wake of the storm and the surface of the water was churning, but the body seemed to writhe and buck at first. Its limbs reached into the air, searching for purchase. There was a moment when I even thought it might start swimming. But then it began at last to surrender, and I could see the very instant when it lost its will, just a few seconds before it started to sink, drawn out to sea in the unrelenting current.

And then Sammy was gone. Nevertheless, I waited. I knew it was over, but I didn't believe it yet. I counted to thirty. My hands were numb. I had no more feeling, not anywhere in my body. Nowhere except in my eyes, which were burning. Nothing happened. I took a breath, and the air surged down my throat with the searing heat of a flame.

He was dead. We were safe.

34

Back in the living room, the setting sun sends rays of light through the windows, casting a halo around Anthony's hair and streaking the floor with long, impressionistic golden shadows. I wish I could take his picture. I wish I could capture this moment in time, when anything is possible. Before he speaks, before all this becomes real, one way or the other. I wish I could immortalize him, right now, as he is. Beautiful, unmoving, like a statue. But I can't. All I can do is try to memorize this feeling.

As the silence lengthens, though, and the sunlight weakens into shadows, I feel myself losing my grasp on this peace. I can't figure out what he's thinking. I want to ask him what he felt when he first watched that tape. I want to ask if it scared him, when he realized what I had done. I want to ask him if *I* scare him.

Betty, he had said, on the pier. *Betty Roux*. Had he known then?

But there is nothing left for me to say. I have said it all. Instead, I draw Anthony's hand into my own, and I wait. Inside our picture frame. Inside this moment, on the threshold of what's to come. I wonder if he expects me to apologize. I hope he understands that I can't. I won't. I did what needed to be done. And now I've spoken the truth, too. I've confessed. There are no secrets between us. Nothing left that can tear us apart.

When he does speak, his voice is firm. Certain. "I saw it," he says. Despite his resolve, though, I can hear the barest hint of a question in his voice. "It was self-defense."

Sammy was the one who had gone for the gun, I want to protest. Even though he wasn't pointing it at me, he might as well have been. The words, though, die in my throat. After all, Anthony has already spoken them.

His eyes finally find mine. Even bruised and hooded and bloody from his fight, even after everything that's happened, their gaze still sends an electric jolt through my body, lighting me up from the inside out. But there's something different in his expression. He isn't reading me, I realize. He isn't trying to scour my face. He's just—looking at me. Expectantly. Waiting for me. To do what? I find myself wishing, again, that I had a camera. To give to him, maybe. To ask him to take my picture now, to show me what he's seeing.

And then, with a flash of horror so violent it feels like my heart has clenched into a fist, I understand. "The cameras," I say.

Anthony's gaze remains steady. This is what he's been waiting for. *The cameras.* The film. Everything we did—everything *I* did— it's all on tape.

Somehow, in the physical, ecstatic rush of my confession, I forgot what had brought us here in the first place. *Fear.* This is what he came to film. This is what he wanted. And he has it now, all of it, stored inside his computer.

"We can't—," I begin. Then, correcting myself: "You can't—" I can't bring myself to finish the thought. *You can't make this film. You can't show this to anyone.*

Anthony's eyes drift from my face. He pushes himself off the couch with a wince of pain. Before I can say anything more, he pulls me up beside him, then leads me down the hallway, to his office. The computer monitors are alive with the sunset, a kaleidoscope of pinks and purples and greens, and in the corner, they follow us as we cross the house into the room of mirrors. Anthony stands at the desk and stares, riveted, at the screen.

"What are you going to do?" I ask, my voice hushed. "Anthony? What are you going to do?"

Anthony doesn't answer. Instead, he fastens me with a look I can't decipher. I search his expression, his eyes, for the truth. For the vulnerabilities I've come to know. For the deeper truths he's allowed me to comprehend. I want to tell him that the movie has already served its purpose. He's witnessed enough of a reflection of himself to move forward, past the pain of his childhood, too. But I don't think I have to say anything. Because all I can see is the blue of his eyes, and his bruised skin, and, somewhere just beneath the surface, the tiniest glimmer of something that might be grief. Nothing else. Nothing else at all.

And yet, rising up inside me, I feel an emotion that begins to lift me. Picking me up as if it's hoisting me in its arms. Something irrepressible. Something I can't yet fathom. It takes me a moment to recognize it, because this new sense of freedom is something I've never experienced before. It's a euphoria, this feeling. An epiphany. I don't know what's coming, but whatever it is, I'm ready for it. Wherever I'm going, I won't be running, and I won't be leaving myself behind.

"Delete it," I tell him. "All of it."

After, I reach for him. He thinks I'm going to kiss him, but I don't. I simply wrap my arms around him and breathe.

ACKNOWLEDGMENTS

First and foremost, I want to thank my agent, Jamie Carr. Thank you, Jamie, for your understanding, your brilliance, and your friendship. No one has ever had a better partner.

I must also thank my editor, Danielle Perez, as well as Jenn Snyder and the entire team at Berkley for helping to make my dream a reality. Thank you, Danielle, for your insight, your belief, and your time. Thank you for seeing the story so clearly, and for pushing me to get it right. This has been a conversation from the start, and I appreciate how rare that is.

Thank you to my global and multimedia champions: Caitlin Mahoney and Flora Hackett at WME, and Jenny Meyer, on behalf of The Book Group.

I owe Norton Island and the Norton Island Residency for Writers and Artists my eternal gratitude. To the Damn Few, those who kept me alive in Maine: I adore and miss you all. Stephen and Rosemary Dunn, Alane Spinney, Ryan Matthews, Carol

Goodman, Morris Collins, Jackie Clark, Sherri Byrand, Jennifer Hand, Emily Tuszynska, Christine Stroud, Andrew Blossom, Xavier Atkins, and Dan Poppick. Thank you, each and every one of you, for your originality and your company. I'll see you all at the main house for happy hour.

I likewise owe tremendous thanks to my teachers at Columbia: Lara Vapnyar, Julie Orringer, Alexandra Kleeman, Rivka Galchen, Lauren Grodstein, Rebecca Godfrey, Joshua Furst, Lee Siegel, and Binnie Kirshenbaum. Thank you, Lara, for your help from the very beginning. I carry each of your lessons with me like precious gems. Thank you, Julie, Alexandra, Rivka, Binnie, and all of my workshop classmates for reading so many drafts of the first hundred pages. Thank you to my professors at NYU: Stacy Pies, June Foley, Barbara Jones, and Linn Cary Mehta.

I want to thank Michael Mejias, Celia Taylor-Mobley, and the Writers House Internship Program. Thank you, Michael, for your mentorship, your sharp advice, and your support. From the first moment we met (a phone interview in which you asked what I liked to read, and I panicked and answered *Ulysses*), I have been in awe of you. I hope to see you again soon.

To my friends, for their patience, their support, and their tenderness: Thank you. Thank you, Kristen Head, for everything. Thank you, Mina Hamedi, for Iceland and for changing the course of my life. Tayma Kessler, Mo Faramawy, Ramzi de Coster, Zeynep Özakat, Annie Kronenberg, and Kiran Subramaniam.

To my family, each and every one of you: Thank you. Thank you, Mom, for always being there, for the lessons in poetry, and for your laughter. There is nothing else like it, and there is no one else like you. To my brother, Ray, the other half of my soul: Thank you. Thank you, Sophie, Brody, and Jeff, for the love. Thank you to my grandparents, for your stories and your support. I was somehow lucky enough to be born into a family of artists and mythical heroes.

Finally, I want to thank my father, for being my teacher, my inspiration, and my best friend. I try every day to live up to your image.

SHUTTER

Melissa Larsen

QUESTIONS FOR DISCUSSION

1. If you were in Betty's position, would you have said yes to Anthony's offer? Would you have stayed on the island and acted in the movie? Why or why not?

2. Do you think Sofia knew what she was getting her friend into when she introduced Betty to Anthony? How does that make you feel about Sofia?

3. Over the course of the novel, we see that Betty's relationship with her mother is strained. Who is more to blame for the way their relationship has deteriorated—Betty or her mother?

4. Was Anthony abusing his power as a celebrity and as the film's director in his relationship with Betty?

5. Is Betty a willing participant in the film, or has she been taken advantage of? Has she chosen what she wants?

6. Is *Fear* really Anthony's way of working through past trauma? Or is he being vengeful?

7. Discuss Betty's relationship with her father. Why do you think he told Betty he was planning to commit suicide? Do you think he was being manipulative in any way?

8. Was Sammy's death really a matter of self-defense? Who is complicit in his death, and why?

9. What does the future hold for Betty and Anthony? One of the major themes in the novel is the meaning of intimacy and the role secrets play in relationships. Do you think Betty and Anthony will be able to find happiness given the secret they now share?

Photo © Emily Hlaváč Green

MELISSA LARSEN has an MFA from Columbia University and a BA from NYU's Gallatin School of Individualized Study. She has interned and worked extensively in publishing. She lives in San Francisco, and *Shutter* is her first novel.

CONNECT ONLINE

Melissa-Larsen.com

🅞 LissaLarsen

Ready to find
your next great read?

Let us help.

Visit prh.com/nextread